A BRIEF SYNOPSIS OF ATTACKED

Every city on Earth with a population of fifty thousand or more is attacked by aliens who exterminate the political, industrial, economic, and military leadership of the world. Over seven billion people are disintegrated in two hours. Eleven people discover the general area where the alien command post on Earth is, and set out to attack it. They don't know its exact location, or have a plan of attack, and no idea of how to get into the command post if they locate it. And they have a weakness within their group. But they acquire two allies who know something about the aliens and join them. They have nine days to get into the command post and stop a fleet of alien ships from reaching Earth and conquering Earth, and the aliens are prepared for them.

ATTACKED

R. CHAUNCEY

Ordering Information:

For orders and inquiries, please contact:
1-888-375-9818
www.toplinkpublishing.com
bookorder@toplinkpublishing.com

Printed in the United States of America

CHAPTER 1

Day 1, May 3, 2032, Monday

Commander Rush was sitting in his command chair in the control room on a two foot high eight by eight foot wide dais, to show his commanding position, looking at Dram one of the twenty-five warriors under his command preparing his computer for an attack on Earth which would render any surviving governments on Earth helpless to defend themselves against the fleet of alien space ships coming to Earth. He looked at the clock on his desk and noted the time was 8:15 p.m. mountain time in the American state where his command post was hidden. He didn't think about his job because there was no need to do that. He knew what his responsibilities were and he had every intention of carrying them out. The cost in human life meant nothing to him.

Theia, an attractive muscular woman with short black hair, working on the main computer paused to glanced in Rush's direction and knew he was waiting for Dram to tell him everything was ready for them to begin the first phase of the Tabor conquest of Earth.

Rush noticed her glancing at him and asked, "Are you ready?"

"Yes, Commander," she said in a feminine voice. "As soon as the other systems are on line I will be ready to activate the satellites."

"All the targets are locked into the computer?" he asked in a deep bass voice.

"Yes, they are, sir," she said.

He could have complimented her but why? Theia, like all the other twenty-four Tabors, had been trained for ten years to do their jobs. And like all Tabor Warriors, the warriors considered themselves to be the only intelligent class to have ever lived on the planet Tabor, everything would go as planned. No one on Earth knew they were on Earth, or that Earth had been selected for conquest and domination by the Tabor Warrior Class. But those few that survived soon would once Theia activated the satellites by pushing a button on the control panel in front of her. And then Dram would activate the disintegrator rays within the satellites. Some of the people on Earth would know something was wrong but only for about a few seconds as they saw those about them die.

Once the disintegrator rays in the twelve satellites revolving around Earth were activated the satellites would fire at every target on Earth they had been programmed to fire upon. And would continue firing until every target had been swept by the death rays.

Within two hours every major political, military, industrial, technological, and scientific center on Earth would be swept by the rays. And every person in those centers would cease to exist a second after the death rays had passed over the cities or installations. Every industrial and scientific leader on Earth in those cities or installations would die in a second along with billions of other people in those cities and installations. Every type of aircraft on Earth the death rays had passed over would either fall from the sky or continue flying on its automatic pilot until it ran out of fuel and crashed, or the automatic pilot landed the plane. Afterwards Earth would be ripe for conquest by the half million Tabor Warriors on the one hundred warships that were in deep space approaching Earth.

"Have any of the Earthlings moved from the targeted areas?" he asked Theia.

"Yes, sir, people are constantly coming and going from all of the places targeted, but none of the high ranking political and military officers who possess control of their nuclear weapons," she said. "They are all at their posts, because this is the beginning of their work week on this side of Earth, or a day later on the other side."

Nuclear weapon Rush thought in a scornful manner. *Only the fools of this planet would be foolish enough to think such primitive weapons could stop us.* "What about the general population?"

"What about them, sir?" she asked.

"How many of those peace loving idiots will be alive two hours after we've launched our attack?"

"Out of a population of over eight billion, sir, analysis indicates that maybe a billion will still be alive. But with few political or industrial or technological leaders to organize them, sir," she said. "Most of them will be dead of disease and hunger within a month, sir. Many of the intelligent ones will begin to organize the survivors to reduce death by disease and hungry, but they will not be in a position to stop our conquest of this planet when our fleet arrives."

"But they will make an effort to resist us as soon as they realize what has happened to their world. And many of them will know that within a few hours after we have attacked them," he said as he looked at the large one hundred foot long forty foot high screen above the twelve foot long desk the four computers and control panel were on. Behind the screen protected by unbreakable glass was the main computer that controlled everything within the Tabor command compound. He saw a picture of Earth spread out across the screen and two hundred thousand targets marked in green on the screen. "A few of those peace loving equality loving fools will survive to make attempts at resistance. But their attempts will fail."

"We are ready, sir," said Dram as he looked at the key on the keyboard in front of him he'd have to push to activate the disintegrator rays. He was a young man dressed in the blue and yellow uniform of a Tabor warrior and like all Tabor Warriors he was anxious to prove his loyalty to the Warrior Class and the Overlord.

"All right," Rush said. "Now is the time to begin our first attack on the primary targets of this planet of peace loving fools."

Dram, Theia, and Rush were the only warriors out of the twenty-six in the main control room. Twelve were on guard patrol outside the compound ready to repel any Earthlings foolish enough to attempt to attack their compound. The other eleven were in the compound preforming their duties as they had been trained to do so.

"I want an operations check run on every place on this planet we've targeted," he said. "Begin now."

Without a word Theia moved to one of the computers and she and Dram began to check the targets on their computers.

"Every city on the American continents with a population larger than fifty thousand has been targeted," Dram said sitting in front of his computer. "So has every city on the European continent of similar population size has been targeted, sir, as well as every city of similar size on the other continents."

"As well as all the cities of Australia, New Zealand and the other Pacific Islands have been targeted, sir," replied Theia.

"What about the installations on the north and south poles on this planet?" Rush asked in a loud voice.

"They are small scientific stations of no military importance," Theia said. "If you wish, sir, we can target them after we've exterminated life in the primary targets."

"That is acceptable, Lieutenant Theia," Rush said.

"All the warships on Earth at sea or in a harbor have been targeted, sir, and the major industrial areas. The leaders in those areas should be in them." Dram said.

"Does that include their submarines on active duty?" Commander Rush asked.

"Yes, sir," Dram said. "Down to a depth of five thousand feet and there are none on this planet that can go that deep, except their small scientific submarines and they are no threat to us."

"We can located and destroy them later along with the polar scientific stations," Commander Rush said.

"Yes, sir," Dram said and began to program the disintegrator rays to strike the secondary targets. A minute passed before he said, "I've targeted the secondary targets, sir."

"All of our satellites are in position, sir, and ready for a firing order," Theia said.

"What about the educational areas," Rush asked.

"All of them have been targeted, sir," Dram said. "All but a few of them are located next to cities that have been targeted, sir."

"And those that have not?" Commander Rush asked him.

"They contain intelligent educated people, Commander, but without the resources of the major areas they will be helpless," Dram answered.

Rush looked at the targets on the screen. It didn't bother him that the cities targeted were filled with billions of people who were either sleep or going about their work. "Let the killing begin."

"Activating the twelve satellites, sir," Theia said as she moved to the control panel and pushed a button on the plastic sheet in front of her activating the satellites.

The twelve Tabor satellites forty thousand miles above the Earth and invisible to every radar system on the Earth because of their electronic cloaking devices had been placed in positions where most of the targets would all be hit with the first firing. They would then automatically move to positions within seconds to hit the rest of the targets. They all turned toward the continents they were over as the metallic shields covering their glass disintegrating screens moved high above the satellites screens. From the moment that happen their cloaking devices shut down and all became visible to every radar screen on Earth.

Generals, admirals, and astronomers all over the Earth no matter where they happen to be were immediately notified by the radar operators or early warning systems of the sudden appearance of the satellites. And all asked the same questions.

"Who do they belong to? And why haven't we seen them before?"

They all got the same answers.

"We don't know who they belong to, and we don't know why we haven't been able to see them. But they are forty thousand miles about the Earth."

The next question the military leaders asked was, "What are they doing?"

The two men and two women on the International Space Station didn't have a chance to contact their governments because they were all disintegrated within a second when one of the satellites fired upon the International Space Station.

Early warning systems all over the world in every military installation that still existed instantly went into operation and began notifying political leaders and scientists and technicians around the world. It was all a waste of time.

Men and women and civilians on all those military bases around the world cease to exist as the disintegrating rays sweep over them first. People in cities in their homes began to disintegrate as the invisible rays sweep over the cities. There was nothing on Earth that could stop the disintegrating rays. Everywhere oxygen went the rays of death went. The only people to survive the rays were those that were in areas the rays didn't sweep over or simply brushed against causing a few disintegrations. The rays shut down communication systems but didn't destroy them. And the rays kept sweeping over areas that had been targeted.

For two hours as the Earth rotated on its axis the disintegration rays from the twelve satellites sweep over the primary targeted areas of Earth. After the people in them were disintegrated, the satellites turned on the secondary targets, and disintegrated everyone in them within seconds. The population of the Earth was back where it had been two hundred years ago. Only the technology of Earth had survived the disintegrating rays.

When all the green lights on the one hundred foot wide by forty foot high screen hanging on the wall were red two hours and ten minutes later, Commander Rush asked, "Have the disintegrator rays done their jobs?"

Theia looked up at the screen and said a moment later, "Yes, sir. Every Earthling in the areas swept by the rays are gone, sir."

"There are no military forces on this world that can threaten us?" Rush asked.

"Small military unit playing their war games have probably survived, Commander," Theia said. "But the weapons they possess are inferior to our weapons and no threat to this command post."

"Cease the sweep. The Earth is ours."

Theia touched a lighted square on the sheet of plastic in front of her and said, "The sweep has ceased, Commander Rush."

"Have the computer use the satellites to check all targets to make sure they have been swept," Rush ordered.

"Yes, Commander," Dram said and ran a check to make sure all the targets had been hit. A minute later he said, "All targets were swept and there are no Earthlings alive in any of them."

Rush smiled and said, "The Overlord will be proud of what we've done, Warriors."

"Yes, he will," Dram said. "We've proven the warriors of Tabor are world conquerors." There was the sound of pride in his voice.

"I will recommend you two and the rest of my command for badges of honor and an advance in rank," Commander Rush.

Those outside heard what he had said over their helmet earphones and felt proud they were a part of Commander Rush's command.

Theia turned around in her chair and looked at him with a smile on her face. "And you, Commander will be promoted to the rank of a Fleet Commander."

"I do hope so," Rush said in a cool voice. "All right you two are on your own for the next twenty-four hours, except for those I have put on patrol. You may go to your quarters or walk around outside if you wish and enjoy this world that is now ours."

"Thank you, sir," said Theia and Dram at the same time.

"Make sure the computer is in protection mode," he said. "Though, I doubt if there is a reason for it now."

Theia turned to the keyboard in front of her and typed, 'protection mode' on the keyboard.

'Protection mode instituted,' appeared on the large screen and on the three smaller screens on the desk in front of her. Any Earthling still alive who was aware of what had happened, and was using a computer trying to locate who controlled the death rays would have their search interrupted by an electrical spike.

"The computer is on protection mode, Commander," Theia said.

"No Earthlings still alive will be able to locate this command post?" Rush asked her.

"All they will detect is the spike, but not where this command post is," she told him.

"I shall be in my quarters. Notify me if anything unusual occurs," Rush said as he stood up.

All the warriors except those on patrol outside the compound went about their business happy that they had served the Overlord.

Rush walked to the elevator and pushed the call button. When the elevator came he entered it and said, "To level three."

The elevator began to move.

A minute later when he was in his quarters he used his communicator and sent a simple message to the Overlord.

"Mission accomplished."

He waited half an hour before he received a reply to his message.

"Well, done, Commander. We shall achieve Earth orbit in nine of Earth's days, Overlord."

"I and my command shall await your arrival, Overlord," he said and pushed the transmit button on the communicator.

Rush stood up and decided to take a walk outside the compound and enjoy the nighttime beauty of Earth.

It was a beautiful world. Rich in animal and plant life which wasn't harmful to the Tabors, breathable oxygen and drinkable water with gravity identical to that of Tabor with vast amounts of minerals, and now after only two hours and ten minutes seven billion Earthlings had ceased to exist. After the Overlord arrived with the fleet the surviving Earthlings would be rounded up and used as slaves to clean up the mess left by the dead seven billion. Then they would be used by the Tabors as slaves.

Rush, like all Tabor commanders, didn't show the pride on his face he felt for having done an excellent job in service of the Overlord. But he felt it.

May 4, Tuesday

Commander Rush had accomplished his mission of killing everyone in Earth's defensive systems, political structure, and industrial and scientific centers. But there were still nearly a billion people on Earth alive who lived outside the major cities and military and scientific areas and other areas swept by the disintegrator rays. And many of them were intelligent and educated.

Les Cartwright was a retired teacher who enjoyed staying up late and sleeping late every day of the week, because he didn't have a reason for getting up early. But he did occasionally enjoy getting up early to watch the morning sun come up in the eastern sky even on a cold winter day. What woke him up at seven in the morning today was the odd feeling while he slept that something was wrong and he couldn't shake that feeling even though he was asleep. But he followed his usual routine. He got up, brushed his teeth, shaved, showered, and went down to the kitchen in his home to make breakfast for himself.

When he had retired from teaching five years ago, he'd enjoyed getting up early and making breakfast for himself because he so seldom had breakfast when he was teaching. But after three weeks of getting up at six in the morning and making breakfast, he was divorced and living alone, he grew tired of it and decided breakfast at nine or ten or eleven in the morning or two in the afternoon was just as good and important as breakfast at six thirty in the morning.

Instead of starting coffee as he usually did he walked into the living room and turned on the TV expecting to see the usual morning talk shows where everything discussed was supposed to be very important, but seldom amounted to more than idle talk, by beautiful women and handsome men in their forties or fifties trying to pretend they were in their thirties and still sexy and young. The women were sexy even if they weren't young the men were just that to him - men. But what he got was nothing.

There weren't even reruns from last year or the past winter. He went through every one of the ninety channels he got on cable and found the same thing, nothing but blank channels. He shrugged his shoulders, made the assumption the cable was down, and decided to open the drapes in his living room to let in the spring sun.

The spring sun came through the white curtains as it always did, but this time he saw numerous columns of black smoke off in the distance. He decided to go out on his front porch and see if there was something wrong. The smoke could have been some fool burning leaves not picked up by the village pickups during the fall. He walked to his front door, opened it, pushed open the steel storm door, and walked out on the dark brown brick steps and looked northeast at the enormous and numerous columns of smoke in the distance. He looked southeast and saw a smaller number of columns of smoke. As he stared at the black smoke he had the strange feeling something was wrong. Then he realized what it was. Everything was quiet and there were no birds in the air.

It's always quiet on this street. I live two blocks from a major street. But where is that smoke coming from? He walked back into his house and locked the front door and went to the kitchen to make breakfast. Then the phone in the kitchen rang and he answered it.

"Something is wrong, Les," a male voice said with the sound of fear in it.

"Who is this?" he asked.

"Me, Chester," the man on the other end said.

"Fuck off," he said and hung up.

Chester lived at the other end of the block and always saw or heard things that weren't there, and had probably never been there. The man was a nuisance who had a desire to be the neighborhood leader, and Les had learned to avoid speaking to him a week after he moved into the neighborhood. Every neighbor considered him to be a busybody, and disliked him because of it. But he was right. Something was wrong.

Les walked to the refrigerator opened it and looked inside wondering if he should make bacon and eggs for breakfast, or just have a donut and coffee. He had bought six from Donkin Donuts two days ago. He had managed to lose ten pounds after retiring five years ago and was determined not to regain an ounce of it and so far he hadn't.

There was a knock on his front door and he closed the refrigerator door and walked toward the door thinking if it was Chester he was going to risk being arrested and punch that nuisance in the face. The man complained to the police about everything. He looked through the six by six inch two way glass window in the door and saw the attractive redhead who lived across the street. She had a worried expression on her face.

He opened the door and asked, "Yes?"

"Have you seen the smoke around the neighborhood?" she asked him. She was wearing a green housecoat button up to her neck as if she was trying to hide herself.

"Yeah, but it's not in the neighborhood. It's off in the distance to the northeast and southeast," he told her.

"There's smoke coming from the west and east, too, and there's no news about what's causing it on the TV," she said.

"The TV isn't working," he told her

"Do you have cable?" she asked him.

"Yeah, I've cable," he answered.

"Are any of the channels working?" she asked him.

"No, none of them are."

"Don't you find that unusual?" she asked him.

"Yeah it is a bit odd," he told her. "There's always something on cable."

"I called the police a few minutes ago and was told to remain in my house and keep my drapes drawn and the door locked. I'm afraid, Mr. Cartwright."

"Did they tell you why you should do that?" he asked her.

"No, but I called a friend of mine whose husband is a police officer and she said the police can't contact anyone in Chicago," she said.

"Come on in, Miss," he said as he stepped back to open the door wider. He had been interested in meeting her for some time. He knew she lived alone. So far all he'd done was wave to her and speak to her as they passed each on the street.

She opened the storm door and walked into the foyer.

"I was going to make coffee," he said. "Would you like some?"

"Yes, if you don't mind," she said.

"The kitchen's in the back," he said as he closed and locked the door. "What do you mean there's smoke coming from the east and west?"

"There are huge columns of black smoke in the sky like a lot of planes have crashed, or someone is burning something," she told him as she walked back to his kitchen. "O'Hare is northeast of the village and Midway is southeast."

"If a lot of planes had crashed that would certainly be in the news," he said as he followed her.

"But there is no news at all on TV or the radio, even the computer has no news on it," she said as she walked into the kitchen.

"My ex-wife and son and daughter were flying to Arizona on a vacation," he said, following her into the kitchen. There was the sound of worry in his voice.

She turned to face him and said, "Maybe what's affecting the TV and radio is limited to the Chicago area."

"No," he said, shaking his head. "Cable transmissions are bounced off satellites. We should be able to find out what's happening in this area from reports outside Cook County." He walked to the refrigerator and opened it. "Please sit down, Miss."

"My name is Alice Simpson," she said as she sat down.

"I'm Les Cartwright. Sorry I haven't introduced myself earlier," he told her as he took the coffee jar out of the refrigerator and closed the refrigerator door and walked to the counter the coffee maker was on. "Have you talked to anyone other than the police?"

"No, I haven't," she said. "Your place is the first place I've gone to."

He started making coffee as he said, "Look, I'll start the coffee and then call the police."

She nodded and said nothing.

Ten minutes later Les was on the phone to the police.

"Listen to me, sir," the officer on the phone said. The man's voice held the sound of fear. "I don't know what's happened, and we can't contact our police in the cars and we can't contact the Chicago Police Department or the FBI office in Chicago."

"How many officers are in the police station?" he asked.

"Just me," the man said. "I can't tell you anymore than to remain in your house, and if you have a weapon get it."

"You sound as if something terrible has happened," he said.

"Mister, something terrible has happened, but I don't know what. And I can't contact anyone by phone, radio, or computer to find out," the man said.

"Like there's no one out there listening," Les added.

"Correct," he said and hung up.

Les looked at the receiver in his right hand for a few seconds before he hung it on the cradle and reached into the cell phone pouch on his belt and took out his cell phone. He had an expression of fear on his face.

"Something bad has happened, hasn't it?" Alice asked noticing the expression on his face. She got up and walked to the counter.

"I don't know," he said as he dialed his ex-wife's cell number. He let the phone ring a dozen times before he ended the call and dialed his daughter's cell phone number. It rang a dozen times before he ended the call and called his son's cell phone number. It ran a dozen times before he ended the call and walked to a chair at the table and sat down. Les was trembling with fear that something terrible had happened to his family.

"Who did you call?" she asked him as she opened two cabinet doors before she found the one that held the cups and took out two.

"My family," he said as he looked up at her with an expression on his face that said he'd lost everything important to him. Then he remembered his ex-wife had left her Highland Terrier with him at four in the morning before she and his son and daughter had gone to O'Hare to fly to Arizona where she'd recently bought a house just south of Phoenix. He got up and walked to the kitchen door looking down at the small door in the kitchen door the dog used to go into the backyard when it wanted to relieve itself. He opened the kitchen door and looked at the small door in the storm door before he opened the storm door and looked into the backyard. All he saw in the backyard on the green grass was the black collar the dog wore around its neck. He walked out the storm door to the collar and picked it up and saw it was still buttoned up.

"What's wrong?" Alice said as she came out the door and stopped next to him.

"Who would leave the collar and take the dog?" he asked as he looked around on the ground.

"Dog thieves sometimes do that," she told him.

"But why put the collar back together?" He saw a small object reflecting the light of the sun at his feet where he'd found the collar and leaned over and picked it up and looked at it. "My God, it's that tracking device my ex-wife had put in the dog in case it ran out of her backyard."

"They cut it out of the dog?" Alice asked in a surprised voice.

"No, there's no blood on it," Les said as he looked around. He was beginning to think beyond his fear. "It hasn't rained in over a week and last night wasn't humid. If this was cut out of the dog there should be a lot of blood on the ground."

"So what happened to your dog?"

"Let's go inside and have coffee while I think about this," he said. He was beginning to accept something he didn't want to accept, even though it was too frightening to even think about.

Five minutes later they were sitting at his kitchen table with the tracking chip and dog collar on the table between them and two half-finished cups of coffee.

"So what should we do?" Alice asked him. "Just go home and wait for the police to tell us what's happened?"

"The officer I talked to on the phone said he couldn't get in contact with the officers in the cars," he said. "If something serious has happened, and it apparently has, those officers in the cars would be the first to know because they're out patrolling the streets. And they would have called in whatever they saw or heard."

"I'm afraid," Alice said in a frightened voice.

"Ann nor either of my children would ever have refused to answer a call from me," he said then added in a voice filled with fear for his family. "If they were still capable of answering their phones."

"I think we should go to the police station and demand some answers," she said in a strong voice.

Les looked up at her and said, "Go home, get dressed, and if you have a gun in your house get it along with all the ammunition you've got." He stopped and thought for a few seconds. "And don't wear something for a garden party or luncheon. Wear shoes or boots for long distance walking and comfortable jeans."

"Why?" she asked. Her face was a mask of fear.

"Look, Alice, I don't know. Just please do as I say. Then come back here and we'll drive to the police station in my car and find out what we can."

"All right," she said as she stood up and headed for the front door.

Les stood up and started to clean up, but decided cleaning up their coffee cups and the coffee maker weren't important. What was important was finding out what had happened, and why his family wasn't answering their phones. He went upstairs to his bedroom and kicked off his slippers and put on socks and the boots he wore for shoving snow in the winter, and got his 9 millimeter Glock and the three magazines he bought when he bought the semiautomatic three years ago. At the time he'd considered it to be a foolish waste of money, because he couldn't think of a reason for buying a gun. But he bought it anyway. It took him a year to get permission from the village to buy the Glock.

Congress had freed itself of being owned by the National Rifle Association over fifteen years ago and repealed all the stupid laws that allowed people to buy any sort of weapon they wanted. They'd passed those foolish laws during the administration of the three biggest fools ever elected to the presidency. Reagan, Bush one, and that damn fool Bush two. Even the states had repealed such stupid laws.

He loaded the magazines from the two boxes of fifty rounds of ammunition and put one in the butt of the Glock, but didn't put a round in the chamber. There was no sense in being foolish. He made sure the safety was on. Les hoped there was an intelligent explanation for what was going on and that his family was safe somewhere in Arizona, but his intuition was telling him his hope was a waste of time. Then he got a leather jacket from his closet his son had bought him four years ago and put it on and put the Glock in the right inside pocket. He put the two extra magazines in the left inside pocket and went downstairs. When he reached the first floor he stopped and looked up the stairs.

God only knows what happened. And I may need more than a gun and a lot of ammo. He went back up the stairs and went up the stairs to the attic where he got an old backpack his son had used when he went backpacking twenty years ago. He left the attic and went to his bathroom where he took a medical kit out of the vanity under the face bowl and put it into the backpack and went downstairs to the kitchen where he got two quart bottles of water out of the refrigerator and put them in the backpack. He started to leave the kitchen when he decided extra water wouldn't hurt, and he got a twenty ounce metal water bottle from a cabinet under the sink, washed it out with cold water, and filled it with water.

The front doorbell rang.

Les walked to the front door thinking if it was Chester he just might take the Glock of his jacket pocket and shoot that annoying ass. He looked through the glass square in the door and saw it was Alice.

He opened the door and looked her over.

She was dressed in desert boots that looked as if they were a designer's idea of what desert boots should looked like and loose fitting jeans that hide her wide hips and a blouse and matching spring jacket that didn't manage to hide her large breasts.

"Are you ready?" she asked him.

"Come on in, my car is in the garage out back," he said as he stepped back and pushed the storm door open for her and opened the inside door wider for her to enter.

She walked into his house asking, "Tell me, Les, what do you think has really happened?"

"I don't know, Alice, but if I were you I'd prepare myself for the worst, because it's the only explanation I can come up with for what's happened." He locked the door. "Do you have a gun?"

"Yes, I do it's in my coat pocket," she told him.

"Don't tell anyone you have it," he advised her.

"Maybe the police can tell us what's happened," she said.

"Maybe," he said, hoping with all his might they could, and hoping that what had happened amounted to no more than a massive communications failure.

It took them five minutes to get into his car and drive to the police station.

CHAPTER 3

Les had expected the parking lot outside the village hall where the police station was to be crowded with people demanding an explanation of what was going on. Instead there were only five cars parked in the lot and two police cars. He parked in a parking space close to the village hall.

The police station was downstairs under the offices of the village.

He and Alice walked into the waiting area expecting to see dozens of people in the waiting area yelling at the police for explanations. There were ten people in the waiting area and one was Chester. As soon as he saw Les he rushed over to him.

"Something terrible has happened, Les," he blurted out.

"Oh, go away, Chester," Les told him as he walked to the glass partition where there was usually a police officer sitting and answering the questions of frightened people.

"He's right," a booming voice to the right said.

Les ignored the voice and walked to the partition and looked through it for an officer.

"There's only one officer in there," another voice said in a calm manner. "And he's still trying to find out what's going on."

"What's going on is a disaster," the booming voice said.

A man at least six four or taller with a muscular built and thick black hair combed straight back walked up to Les and stuck out his right hand.

Les looked at the man's hard pale face and then at his right hand. It was larger than any hand he'd ever seen with long nails filed to a point and they needed cleaning. Les ignored the offered hand and asked, "What do you mean a disaster?"

The man dropped his right hand and said in a booming voice, "I've called some of my important friends in the FBI in the Hoover Building in Washington and gotten no answers to my calls. When the FBI don't answer a call from me, it means something bad has happened."

"I've suggested we don't become alarmed and wait till the officer inside comes out to explain what's going on," the calmer voice said.

Les looked in the direction of the calmer voice and saw it belonged to a white man sitting on one of the plastic chairs with a worried look on his face and decided to walk over to the man and ask him what he knew. "Excuse me," Les said and walked around the big muscular man.

Alice followed him as the muscular man returned to his position next to the door.

"What's going on?" Les said as he stopped a few feet in front of the man.

"I don't know, but whatever is going on hasn't affected the communication systems," he said as he leaned back in his chair and looked up at Les. He had a short military style hair cut with permanently tanned skin and set with his feet spread apart as if he was ready to spring to his feet in self-defense.

"You said systems," Les asked him. "Which ones have you tried?"

"Radio, telephone, and computer," he said.

"I tried using my cell phone and got no answers," he said. He didn't tell the man he'd tried calling his family.

"If those are still working, then someone must be around to keep them working," Alice said.

"Not necessarily," Les said.

"The radio, telephone, and computers have to have someone operating them if they still worked," Alice said.

"No," another man to Les' right said.

"They're all automated and don't need people to operate them to keep them operating," Les said turning to his right.

The man was black and of medium height with a short haircut and a waist line that said he liked eating.

"But if no one is answering any of them that means no one's around to answer them, and they'll start to shut down as soon as their source of power runs out," the man said.

"How the hell do you know?" the booming voice asked.

"Common sense," the man replied. "We may live in an automated world with computers running everything, but without people to make sure they have a source of energy and to repair them they'll eventually shut down."

"So we need to find out what's happened before they begin to shut down," a woman sitting in another chair said.

"What we need to do is kick some ass if we want our questions answered," the muscular man said and then turned to his right and started banging on the door with his right fist. "Open up, damn you! We want some answers!"

"There's only one officer in there and he's doing the best he can," another woman said.

"He ain't doing shit, but eating donuts and having coffee like all these lazy cops do," the muscular man said as he continued banging on the door.

Les looked around the waiting room and saw three women and four other men not counting the muscular man and Chester who was standing behind the muscular man with a smile on his face as if he were happy to be close to him.

"There's not much we can do, but wait," Les told Alice. "Do you want to go home and wait or stay here?"

"We all stay here!" the muscular man said as he continued banging on the door.

"Who put you in charge of us?" asked a beautiful brunette Les had seen jogging around the block he lived on.

"Me, sweetheart, because I know teamwork because I use to be the greatest football player pro ball ever had," he answered as he grinned at her.

"I'm not your sweetheart," the brunette replied.

"Like hell you ain't," the muscular man grinned at her.

"Aw fuck you!" the brunette yelled at him.

The door opened and a pale faced white officer in a blue policeman's uniform with the village patch on his right armed stepped out of the door. The expression on his face made him looked as if his world had suddenly come to an end.

CHAPTER 4

Booming voice stepped in front of the pale, exhausted looking officer and said, "My name is Sam Rawlings, and I want to know what's going on now."

"I wish to hell I knew," the officer said.

"That's not an answer I will accept," Rawlings said, looking at the officer with a stern face as if he was a boss demanding answers from an employee.

"Tell us what you do know, Officer," the brunette said in a calmer voice.

"I'll handle this if you don't mind, girlie," Rawlings said as he looked at her.

"My name isn't girlie, and I do mind your asshole attitude," she replied.

"Now look you -," Rawlings started to say in an angry voice.

"What I know is all the officers who were on patrol last night no longer exist, and that includes the Chief," the officer said with the sound of confusion in his voice.

"What do you mean no longer exist?" the man with the military haircut asked.

"This morning when I couldn't contact anyone by radio I got in my patrol car and drove to where their cars were," he said.

"How do you know where the other policemen's cars were?" Rawlings asked him.

"Global Positioning System," Les said. "All police cars have them in case the officers in them get in trouble and can't call for help. And all police cars have computers in them that can detect the position of other patrol cars."

"Yes, yes, I know about them," Rawlings said.

"Everybody be quiet and let the officer speak," Alice said, standing next to Les.

Silence fell over the waiting area.

"When I got to the cars, all seven of them, I found the uniforms of the officers assigned to the cars in them," the officer said.

"So they're running around naked," Rawlings said.

"No!" the officer screamed at Rawlings. "Their uniforms were in the patrol cars, but not them."

Even Rawlings didn't have a statement for that.

"Like they just disappeared from inside their uniforms," the plump black man said.

"Yes," the officer answered.

"Their pistol belts, weapons, shoes socks, and clothing were still in those cars like the officers were wearing them just disappeared," Les said.

The officer nodded.

"Can you contact anyone?" someone asked.

"Two other officers are driving around the nearby suburbs checking the police stations and they've got the same problem we've got here," he said.

"Have you talked to any police from Chicago?" Les asked him.

"No one, only the police in suburbs farther west of us," he said.

"And what did they say?" asked the man with the military haircut.

"I suggest we all get into our cars and drive around looking for someone who can give us a better explanation of what's going on," Rawlings said.

"Yes, yes, I agree with Mr. Rawlings," Chester said.

"Pardon me," a black man said standing up. "But do your computers still work, Officer?"

"Yes, they do," the Officer said looking at the man.

"And they can be used to contact other computers, police or private?" the black man asked him.

"Yes, they can," the Officer said. "And I've been using them and gotten what I've told all of you."

"Then we don't need to drive around looking for someone," the man said. "All we have to do is get on one of the police computers and access the traffic cameras. All police computers have that ability. If there is someone wandering around we'll be able to see them."

"These officers in the suburbs west of us you said you contacted what do they say?" Les asked.

"They can't contact anyone beyond other police forces in the small towns," the Officer said. "All they get from Chicago, Springfield, and Washington is silence even on their computers, just like me."

Les nodded with a thoughtful expression on his face.

"What are you thinking?" the man with the military haircut asked him.

"If this was a disaster people from Chicago would coming into this suburb and the other suburbs next to Chicago," he said. "But I saw no one on the streets as I drove here."

"They're all hiding," Rawlings said.

"No, not that many," Les disagreed.

"So where are the people of Chicago?" a woman standing behind him asked.

Les turned around and said, "Apparently they've all disappeared, too."

"Aw, that's fucking stupid," Rawlings bellowed.

"I know a little about computers," the black man standing up said. "Can I use one of your computers to see what I can find, Officer?"

The Officer nodded and stepped back toward the open door. "Come on, maybe you can learn something I haven't been able to learn."

Five minutes later they were all gathered about the man sitting at a desk in front of a computer.

"How are you going to find out something this cop couldn't find out?" Rawlings said standing behind a woman dressed in a country dress.

"My name is Alex Drain and I use to work for the C. I. A. in their information section," Alex said as he typed on the keyboard. "I'm what you'd call an advance computer operator."

"A government hacker," the brunette said.

Alex smiled and said, "I've been called that."

"What are you doing?" the Officer standing next to him asked.

"Accessing every traffic camera in Chicago and the surrounding suburbs," he said. "And I'm in them."

"There's a general code to do that?" Les asked him.

"Yes, there is," the man with the military haircut answered.

"How do you know?" Alice asked him

"I use to work at the U. S. Strategic Command until two years ago when I retired," he said. "And we could access every public computer in America that was on the Internet in case of an emergency."

"Or when you wanted to spy on Americans," Chester said.

"No, we couldn't do that without a direct order from the President, and only in case of a nuclear war or an emergency," he said. "Anyone working at the Mountain who tried to do that faced a court-martial and twenty years in prison. All we ever did was run tests on the system to make sure it worked, and then only on military bases."

"Look," said the brunette as she looked over Alex' shoulder at the computer screen.

They silently all looked at the screen and saw thousands of cars standing in the middle of the streets of Chicago as if their owners had left them. Thousands of others had collided with other cars or buildings. Some were burning. Buses that stood empty in the middle of the streets or next to bus stops. A few had even run into other buses or buildings. There were hundreds of small fires. There was no one on the streets. Except thousands of clothes, shoes, and cell phones that looked as if the wearers and owners had just ceased to exist.

"The Commies have attacked us," Rawlings said with an expression of certainty on his face standing behind everyone.

"That's wrong," the military man said.

"How the fuck do you know?" Rawlings growled at him.

"Because we're still alive," Les told him.

"What the fuck does that mean?" Rawlings snapped at Les.

"That profanity isn't going to answer any of our questions," the brunette said.

"If the Russians had attacked us with nuclear weapons, the destruction would be apparent and would cover over twenty miles," Les said. "And the EMP would have shut down every piece of equipment with a microchip in it for five hundred miles, and that includes this computer and our cell phones."

"Maybe they're shielded against Electro Magnetic Plus," the other brunette said.

"No, they're not," the silent man spoke up. "Not cost effective."

"What does that mean?" Chester asked.

"No, company in this world is going to spend billions making their microchips safe from EMP, because it would double the cost of their microchips," he said. "And why do it anyway? The only threat to the world since the collapse of the Soviet Union and the Warsaw Pact has been terrorists. And the Russians and former Warsaw Pact members as opposed to them as every nation in the world."

"Mr. Drain, can you access the security cameras in the towers at O'Hare and Midway?" the military man asked him.

Alex got to work and within a minute he'd accessed the security cameras in O'Hare's flight control tower. He scanned the area around the tower showing six planes had crashed landing or taking off and were burning, and four others had run into other planes taxing to a runway. A dozen planes were sitting on the taxi strips waiting to take off with their engines still running. A dozen other planes were sitting at the loading gates, three had been hit by fuel trucks and the trucks had exploded. Trucks pulling baggage carts sat next to some of the planes.

"Are there cameras inside the control towers?" Les asked.

"There should be," Alex said as he started typing on the keyboard.

"Go to the air traffic controllers' part of the tower," Les told him.

Alex did exactly that and the sight that greeted them was shocking.

Every radar screen had clothing in the seat and shoes underneath them with socks in the shoes or the radar sets had no one sitting at them.

"Where the hell did they go?" Chester whined.

"They disappeared," Alice said.

"Aw, that's crazy," Rawlings said.

"No, it's not," Les said as he stared at the screen and wished what he saw wasn't real.

"Who the hell are you?" Rawlings asked him.

"A retired high school history teacher," he answered.

"And we're supposed to listen to someone who couldn't do so he became a teacher?" Rawlings replied.

"My name's Thomas Level. I use to be a Colonel in the Army assigned to what used to be known as Cheyanne Mountain," the man with the military bearing said. "What do you think, Mister?"

"Les Cartwright and I think we've been attacked by someone with a weapon that can cause a body to disintegrate," he said. "But it effects only living tissue."

"That's impossible!" Rawlings said.

Les turned to him and asked, "What's your name?"

"I said I use to be the greatest football player in the world," he said.

"I've never had any interest in sports," Les replied.

"What are you a Commie?" Rawlings asked him.

"No, intelligent, and sports have always been popular in Eastern European and well as Western European countries," he said. "Now what's your name?"

"Sam Rawlings," he snapped at Les.

"Well, Mr. Rawlings I suggest you stop referring to the women here as girlies and it is possible to disintegrate an object by destroying the magnetic force that holds an atom together. And whatever did this affects only animals because all the plants are still alive, but there are no dogs and cats or birds running or flying around."

"And it's been tried a dozen times by various scientists around the world except it has never worked, because we don't have that sort of technology on this planet," Level said.

"Are you suggesting Aliens?" the other redhead standing next to Level asked.

Level turned to his right and looked at her. "If you were an alien and wanted to conquer the Earth without doing a lot of damage to the planet, the best way would be to disintegrate everyone living in a major city or on a military base. That way you'd get rid of all the political and military leaders and most of the industrialists and technicians. The few people that remained alive would be helpless to prevent you from taking over the world."

"But we're still alive," Chester said.

"Apparently the power of whatever weapon was used only brushed against the village and the few suburbs around it," Les said. He turned around and looked at everyone. "Where were all you people last night?"

"I was at home in bed," the older redhead said.

"Me, too," Alex said.

"And I," Level said.

"I was in my basement looking at old films of my best plays," Rawlings said with a grin on his face as if he'd made an important announcement.

"I'm Nancy Cobbs," the brunette said. "I was at home asleep, too."

"I was in my husband's study writing my husband and sons letters," the woman with brown hair said. She had a look of fear on her face. "I'm Janis Taylor. My whole family is in the military."

"I was asleep," Alice said.

"I was in my basement playing video games," the Hispanic man said, giving Rawlings a nasty look. "My name is Pedro Armando. I operate computers for the telephone company."

"I'm a banker. I work in International Loans for the Chase bank. My name is William Wright," the distinguished looking man said. "I was working in my basement on my computer. I was finishing up some work on some banking business."

"I was asleep. I'm Chester Brown," Chester said. "I didn't go to bed until ten because I was outside with my flashlight checking on possible car thieves in the alley behind my house. You know they're always coming in from Chicago looking for cars to steal."

"Stanley Hass and I was on duty here at midnight," the Officer said. "And you're wrong about car thieves coming from Chicago, Mr. Brown. Most come from the western suburbs, because they know people like you will suspect they come from Chicago."

"Good boy, Chester," Rawlings said as he patted him on the back. "Best to keep our eyes open."

"None of this answers the question of why are we still alive, and nearly everybody else is dead," Nancy said.

Level sighed and said, "If what Les, you don't mind me calling you Les, do you?"

"Not in the least bit considering what we think has happened," Les said.

"If what you say about some ray brushing up against the village then the ray wasn't strong enough to penetrate the roofs of the houses we were in, so there should be a lot of other people alive in the village."

"I didn't see a lot of people on the streets," Nancy said. "So maybe this ray just brushed over our houses and didn't affect us but killed everyone else."

"I know a lot about our country's satellites and if we were attacked by aliens there'll be some evidence of their presence in orbit about Earth," Level said as he looked around the room and saw a computer on a desk on the opposite wall. "If Officer Hass doesn't mind, I'd like to use that computer over there."

"Go right ahead if it's going to answer some of the questions we have," Hass said.

Level walked over to the computer and sat down in the chair at the desk and turned on the computer.

"What are you going to do?" Les asked him as he walked over to him.

"Try and get into the computers at US Strategic Command," he said.

"How? By now all the codes you knew have been changed."

"I'm on what's called special standby," he said as he started typing on the keyboard. "That means I've still got access to certain codes that will let me access the various satellites in orbit."

"Won't you be violating federal law?" Pedro asked him.

"Yes, but if what we suspect is true there's no one around to file charges against me for what I'm doing," he said.

"You've got a point," Pedro said as he turned to his right and saw another computer. He started walking toward it. "I've got codes that'll allow me to access the satellites the phone companies use. If I can get into them we can look around this planet and find out what's really happening."

"If aliens have done this to us we find out where they are and go kick some alien butt," Rawlings announced.

"If we can find them," Pedro said.

"If aliens are behind this mess, they may have used Earth's satellites to position whatever weapon they've got to attack us," Les said.

"And if they did, that means they had to use the same frequency our satellites use," Pedro said.

"Can you locate where they are?" Nancy asked him.

"Maybe, but no promises," he said.

"They would be centuries ahead of us in technology," Les told him.

"That's right," Pedro said.

"So we wait and see what you and Level can get?" William said.

"That's all we can do," Alice said.

Les looked up at the ceiling with a thoughtful expression on his face.

"Ain't no answers on the ceiling, Mr. School Teacher," Rawlings told him.

"Whatever ray the aliens used against us, if we were attacked by aliens, doesn't affect plants," he said as he looked at the ceiling. "And most of the houses in the village have wooden roofs. So the intensity of the ray may have been powerful enough to kill people in houses with wooden roofs in the major cities. But it wasn't powerful enough to penetrate the roofs of most of the houses outside the major cities, because they weren't the targets the aliens were interested in. The ray just brushed against the village. Killing only those who were outside in cars, and maybe a few other people."

"They hit Earth right where they could do the most important damage," Alice added.

CHAPTER 5

For half an hour the others silently watched Level, Alex, and Pedro work on the computers they were sitting at.

"My God," Level said breaking the silence in the room as he stared at the display on the computer screen. "They've taken out every military command post on Earth."

"What about the capital cities?" Judith asked him.

"As lifeless as Chicago," he said. "The only towns and cities on this planet still operating are those of no major military, political, or technological importance."

"Scientifically we're back in the dark ages," Les said.

"We will be," Pedro said.

"Ah, that's bullshit," Rawlings growled.

Pedro turned around toward him and said, "Listen carefully to me, Mr. Rawlings. If these aliens are not stopped within the next four weeks, the various power plants on this planet are going to start shutting down, especially the nuclear power plant because they need direct supervision by humans. A week later nothing electrical on this planet will work. And we will be back in the dark ages."

"I don't think Pedro mean the dark ages Europe went through from the sixth century to the twelfth century," Les said. "What he means is we'll be back where our ancestors were three thousand years before the birth of Jesus, lighting the darkness with torches or candles."

"They wouldn't have done this to us just for the hell of it," Level said. "It's obvious why they've knocked out all the major cities and military installations. They plan to occupy Earth and make it their own planet."

"Why would they want to do that?" Janis asked.

"Maybe they come from a dying world and need Earth to keep their species alive," Alex said.

"Or maybe they're just a bunch of planet conquerors," Les said.

"That's crazy," Rawlings said.

Les turned to him and said, "The history of Earth is a history of people conquering other people just to expand the territory they've already got. If it has happened here, you can be assured, Mr. Rawlings, it has happened on other worlds. And whoever has done this to Earth are space traveling conquerors."

"Eh, Level," Pedro said. "Did you detect a power spike coming from northern Nevada?"

"Yeah, a momentary one, but I can't locate it now," Level told him.

"Neither can I," he said.

"Like our scan was being blocked," Level told him.

"We were detected," Pedro said.

"Yes," Alex agreed from the computer he was working on. "I picked up a weak power source in that same general area, and then it suddenly stopped."

Les turned around to face Alex and asked, "What sort of power spike?"

"A regular electrical power spike," he said.

"Like the kind that comes from electrical power plants?" he asked Alex.

"No," Level said as he was working on his computer. "A power spike like the one I detected didn't just jump up and then decline back to a source that could be detected."

"Five years ago I was working with the scientific branch of AT&T on a project to detect signals coming from space. And not energy signals designed to block a scan like this one was. But a signal produced by an intelligent species attempting to contact other intelligent species." Alex said.

"Can you three scan that area of northern Nevada it came from," William asked them.

"Yeah," Level said as he looked at the screen of the computer he was working on and saw a picture of northern Nevada. "But there's nothing there now."

"You probably ain't looking at the same place," Rawlings said.

"There's a weather satellite passing over the western part of America, and I'm in it and there's nothing there now," he said.

"These computers record what they pick up don't they, Officer?" Alice asked.

"Push F3 on the keyboard that's the playback key on our computers," Hass said.

All three men pushed the F3 button at the top of their keyboards and an immediate replay of the energy spike appeared on their computer screens.

A circle of electrical energy rose rapidly from the northern part of Nevada and disappeared. They all saw the circle of energy.

"That's a spike alright," Alex said.

"Is that normal?" Nancy asked.

"I've never seen anything like that," Pedro said. "Have you, Alex?"

"Yes," Alex said. "It's called a cloaking spike, and it's designed to hide electrical activity in a certain area."

Level turned to his right and said to Alex, "Like a special ops team on the ground moving into a certain area."

Alex turned to his left and looked at Level. "As you probably know most cell phones that have a GPS on them can pick up communications more than five hundred miles away from them. Spikes like the one we've seen are used to blind the enemy to the whereabouts of a special ops team by blocking out its GPS."

"So whoever or whatever attacked Earth now knows there are still some of us alive capable of trying to find out what's happened to the major cities on Earth," Les said. "And they probably know where we are."

"I'd say so," Level said. "And since there's no military left to defend Earth, they could be on their way here now to find out what's going on."

"So what do we do?" Judith asked.

"Get ready for them alien sum bitches," Rawlings said in as mean a voice as he could summon.

Les walked to chair next to a desk and sat down.

"Oh, use some intelligence will you?" Nancy yelled at Rawlings. "If they can destroy the military and political leadership of Earth they can certainly come here and wipe us out in a matter of seconds."

"When it's your third down and the ball is deep in your territory, you do what you've got to do to make that touchdown and win the game," Rawlings told her.

"That maybe right at a football game," William said. "Unfortunately we're not playing football, Mr. Rawlings."

"So what do we do?" Judith repeated. "Sit here and wait for them to come and get us."

"They've already got the Earth," Pedro said. "Getting us isn't going to be much of a problem for them."

"We can fight back," Level said.

The others looked at him and waited for him to explain what he meant.

He looked at them and shook his head as he said, "I know I sound crazy, but what else can we do? Just give up. They've destroyed the top military and political leadership of Earth, but there's still enough left for the survivors to build on. And we know there are other survivors out there beyond the major cities. Probably hundreds of millions who knows maybe billions, and they are worth fighting for."

"But there are just twelve of us," Chester said. "We need an army."

"Well, we don't have an army and we're not about to get one in the next few weeks, because the military doesn't exist," Level said. "So what do we do? Go home and sit on our asses and wait for whoever these aliens are to wipe out the rest of the human race so they can take over our planet?"

"I think we should fight back even if we don't have much of chance of winning," Nancy said. She looked at the faces of the others. "I know I'm nothing but a model, but I'd like to die years from now knowing the Earth still belongs to the human race."

"My husband once said that when a people give up they've already been conquered," Janis said. "I know my family is dead and I'm all alone in the world, but I'd still like to fight back even if we are defeated."

"At least we'll let the aliens know what type of people we are," Alex said.

No one else said anything.

Alice turned around and looked at Les sitting in the chair. "What do you think, Les?"

"I know my family is dead or they would have called me even if only one of them was alive," he mumbled as he looked at the floor.

"I'm for fighting back," William said. "Because like most of you I know I've lost my family."

"I'm for fighting back," Judith said in a frightened voice as she looked at the others.

"I spent thirty years teaching my students that we all have a responsibility to each other no matter where we live or what our politics or religion is," Les said as he looked at the floor. "Now I have no family, and I dearly loved my children, and ex-wife, too. I've a will that includes all of them. But now it's just worthless paper."

"I say let's get some guns and go kick alien ass," Rawlings yelled.

"It's going to take some planning," Les said. "We don't even know where the attack came from." He looked up at them. "I would like nothing better than to just go home and spend the rest of my life mourning the loss of my family. But there are others out there with families who may need my help to keep their love ones alive. And I owe them the right to be free even if I don't know any of them"

"We're all in the same boat," Level said. "And like Les has said there are other people on this world who may need our help."

"Yeah," Pedro said in a mean voice. "If they hit Mexico City, my family is gone, and I want some payback."

"My family is at home," Hass said. "I called them last night when I knew something was wrong and told them to stay indoors with the doors locked."

Les looked at him with envious eyes and said, "You should go to your family, Officer Hass, now that you know what the problem is. Get as much food and water and medicine as you can carry in your patrol car, and turn your home into a fortress."

"Contact some of your neighbors if they are still alive and tell them what's happened," Level said. "Call the cops in every town and suburb you can contact and tell them what's happened. Only by uniting and standing together can people hope to survive what's happened to Earth and rebuilt."

"So who's going to attack them damn aliens?" Rawlings said, looking as tough as he could look.

"Only those who've lost family," Les said. "We don't need anyone with us who's going to be worried about their family or friends."

"I'll go," Alice said. "I'm like Janis. My children are in the military on military bases, and if they've been hit my children are dead. My husband died of cancer years ago."

"I've no one," Alex said. "My ex-wife and children live in Washington."

"I'll go along," Pedro said.

"Me, too," Janis said.

"Include me," Nancy said. "My family lives in a small town in Vermont. So I guess they're alright, but I want to go along anyway."

"This ain't going to be no shopping tour," Rawlings said looking at her with admiring eyes.

"I am well aware of that, Mr. Rawlings," she told him.

Level smiled as he said, "I come from a military family. For two hundred years members of my family have been in the military, and I think I'm the last of them. Because my daughter is a pilot on a carrier and my son is a junior officer in an attack sub. And the aliens wouldn't have left ships like that alone."

"What about your wife?" Janis asked him.

"She lives in Florida right outside the Pensacola Naval base."

"My ex-wife and five children live in Chicago," William said. "So I'm in." He paused then added. "I would have liked to give them a funeral, but burying clothes is a waste of time."

"I'll come along, too," Chester said with a smile on his face.

"This isn't going to be some damn fun trip, Chester," Les told him as he looked at Chester's smiling face. "That energy spike says the aliens know there are some of us alive who might be able to fight them."

"And if they're military, and they probably are, they're going to be waiting for someone to show up," Level said.

"And whatever weapons they've got they're going to be light years ahead of what we've got," Pedro said.

"So let's get this show on the road," Rawlings boomed.

"Didn't you hear what I just told Chester?" Les asked him.

"Yeah, and I'm ready for a good fight," he answered.

"Don't you have family or relatives?" Nancy asked him.

"No, never had much use for them," he told her with a tough guy expression on his face.

"There are eleven of us and we're going to need weapons, food, medical supplies, and transportation," Pedro said.

"We can get a big truck and guns and get going within an hour," Rawlings said.

"No," Les said. "We get two large vehicles and leave tonight around seven thirty when the sun's setting. And we need to decide exactly what we're going to do if we find this spot in Nevada where these aliens might be hiding."

"Inform everyone on the world about them," Alex said. "The people of the world have a right to know who did this to their world."

"I agree with that," Les said. "But we should also realize the aliens know we've detected their spike, and are prepared to repel anyone who gets close to them."

"We're burning daylight," Rawlings said. "We should leave now."

"I don't give a damn," Les said, standing up. "I'd like a few hours alone to mourn the loss of my family."

"He's right," Level said with a sad look on his face. "I'll make out a list of what we need."

"We've rifles and shotguns and handguns here," Hass said. "I can contact the police in a suburb west of here that has a military supply store that carries various types of military equipment."

"We should meet back here around seven," Alex said.

Les turned toward the door and started walking. "Seven it is then."

Alice followed him.

CHAPTER  6

Theia stopped outside the door of Commander Rush's private quarters and knocked on the doorsill of the open door.

"Who is it and what do you want?" Rush said as he lay on his bed.

"Lieutenant Theia, Commander," she said. "We have been scanned by an Earth satellite, sir."

"Do not be alarmed, Theia, it's only one of the Earth's primitive satellites passing overhead," Rush told her.

"They have been passing overhead since we've been on this planet, sir, and they've done nothing but look over the terrain," she told him. "The one that passed overhead a few minutes ago was electrically probing the area we're in."

Rush sat up and said, "Come in, Theia."

Theia walked into his private quarters and stopped and stood at attention.

"Explain to me what happened," he told her.

"The Earth satellite that scanned us was a weather satellite with the ability to electrically scan an area for electrical objects such as we have, sir. And it detected the presence of our equipment."

"Why would they have a weather satellite with such an electrical ability?" he asked her as he sat on his bed looking up at her.

"As you know, sir, this planet has competing states, and a good way to spy on another state would be with a weather satellite," she said.

"Obviously it was looking for an explanation for what has happened to their planet," Rush said thoughtfully.

"That is my opinion, sir," she agreed.

Rush thought for a few seconds before he said, "Someone with a military background has survived our disintegrating ray."

"Someone who is aware that this planet has been attacked by an intelligent form of life these Earthlings call an alien."

"How did our computers handle the scan?"

"By sending an electrical impulse that prevented the satellite from getting an exact location on where we are," Theia told him.

"If this scan was done by an intelligent Earthling, they have a general area to look at now," Rush said.

"That is my opinion, sir," she agreed.

"But the question is will some of the Earthlings that have survived come looking for us," he said.

"The Earthlings that are still alive, sir, know that what's killed billions of their people wasn't a weapon created by them because they don't have such technology," she said. "I'm of the opinion, sir, we are going to be visited by Earthlings looking for what caused billions of their people to disappear."

Rush stood up and walked toward the door saying, "All we have to do is keep whatever Earthlings who come looking for us at bay until the fleet arrives. Then we can destroy all resistance left on this planet."

She turned to her right and looked at him as he walked out the door of his room in the direction of an elevator.

"Come with me, Theia," he said.

She followed him.

"I will order Lieutenant Zack to deploy ten warriors in groups of two in an area of ten miles beyond our position," he said as he walked to an elevator and pushed the call button. "Any Earthlings coming here will be spotted by them and killed before they can do us any harm before the fleet arrives."

"Yes, sir," she said.

He entered the elevator when it arrived and waited for Theia to enter before he pushed the button for the control room. He took out his communicator and said, "Lieutenant Zack, send two groups of warriors out to a distance of ten miles around the area we occupy. Two warriors in each armored car, and have them look for any Earthlings approaching the area. Have them take the heavier armored cars."

A moment later a male voice replied, "Yes, sir, right away."

"Remember, Zack, they must not be seen," Rush warned him. "Whatever Earthlings they may encounter will probably be armed with their primitive projectile firing weapons. And should they encounter any Earthlings your warriors must be aware the Earthlings they encounter will be interested only in revenge against us."

"I will do as you say, Commander Rush," Zack replied.

"They should report in every hour, sir," Theia said.

"Have them report in every hour," Rush said.

"Yes, sir."

He put his communicator back in the pouch on his belt and turned and looked at Theia. "Have the computers scan for any Earthlings approaching this area every hour."

"Yes, sir," she said. "But while these Earthlings' have primitive equipment compared to ours, they may be able to detect our scans."

"Make it a low level scan," he told her. "Even their equipment won't be able to pick that up."

"Yes, sir," Theia replied. When they reached the top level of the compound they went to the control room. Within a minute she'd put out a low level scan that scanned ten miles in all directions up as well as ground level.

"Notify me immediately if you pick up anything," he said as he walked toward the door. "I'll be in my quarters sleeping."

"You should know, sir, that our satellites have detected a military unit of over a thousand of their soldiers not more than forty miles from here," Theia said.

"Do you think they know about the compound?" he asked her.

"There is no indication they do, sir," she replied.

Rush looked at her for a few seconds before he took out his communicator and said, "Zack there is a group of over a thousand

Earth soldiers forty miles from here. Join with a group and attack them."

"Yes, sir," Zack replied.

Rush stared ahead for a few seconds before he said, "If it is possible capture some of them, and bring them here to the compound. We must learn more about these Earthlings so we can destroy what resistance they put up when the fleet arrives."

"I will, Commander," he replied.

Rush turned to Theia and said, "If you detect any more Earthlings close to us, let me know immediately."

"I will, Commander," she replied.

CHAPTER 7

Les went into his house and to his bedroom where he lay on the bed and cried for an hour before he drifted off to sleep.

Alice was shaking his right shoulder.

Les opened his eyes and stared at her wondering who she was and why she was in his bedroom. Within ten seconds everything came rushing back to him like a terrible nightmare he wished wasn't true and he could get away from.

"It's six thirty, Les," she said. "You left your front door unlocked."

He sat up and said, "Mother of Christ, I was hoping everything that has happened was a terrible dream."

"I know how you feel," she said noticing the tear streaks on his face. "I prayed for an hour that everything that's happened was just a horrible joke someone was playing on us."

He put his legs over the left side of the bed and said, "I don't know about you, Alice, but I want whoever did this to my world to pay in blood and suffering. I want them to die horribly for killing my family."

"Go wash your face, and let's go," she said with the sound of determination in her voice.

He got up and walked into the bathroom and washed his face with hot water and soap and walked back into his bedroom drying his face with a towel saying, "I wonder when the hot water will stop."

"Probably when the gas that your hot water heater uses to heats the water stops flowing," she answered.

"Within a few weeks at the very most, and we'll be back to getting water from rivers, streams, and wells," he said. "Even locked doors will be a thing of the past."

"Then in places where there are a lot of people disease will start and the death rate will increase," Alice said.

Les walked to his closet, opened it, and took out a small traveling bag and packed extra underwear, socks, two shirts, and two pairs of jeans he'd taken from the dresser in the bedroom. *In a few days we'll all be back in the dark ages and death from diseases will begin to claim millions who haven't already been destroyed.*

"You know, Les, I've been thinking if we can find these aliens who've done this to us we might be able to convince them to leave us alone so we can avoid having a shutdown of all the power plants on Earth," Alice said. "We can't undo what they've done, but we might be able to avoid worse things from happening."

Les walked into the bathroom thinking as he got two toothbrushes, toothpaste, soap, face towels, and bath towels and walked back into the bedroom and forced them into the traveling bag.

"Don't you agree?" she asked him.

"No, I don't," he said in a voice that had the sound of little hope.

"Why not we may be able to reason with them," she said in a hopeful voice.

He looked at her and said, "Did you pack extra clothing, soap, towels, and toothbrushes?"

"Yes, I did, and you sound as if there is no hope for the human race," she told him in a voice that had the touch of anger in it.

Les looked at her with a hard cold look on his face and said, "Face facts, Alice. If these aliens, if we've been attacked by aliens, were the type of people who could be reasoned with they would not have done to the Earth what they've done." He closed the bag, picked it up, and started walking to the door. "We are dealing with monsters who care nothing for the people of Earth, or they wouldn't have done what they've done."

"You sound as if these aliens are godless monsters," Alice complained.

"We're expendable. I don't know why these aliens who've attacked us want Earth, but they don't want humans on it, or they would not have attacked us as they have." He walked out of his bedroom for the staircase.

"Do you think we have a chance?" she asked him following him.

"I don't know," he said. "I just hope we're not the only people planning to find out what's happened to us."

"The more people out to attack the aliens the better chance of success we have," she said.

"Exactly," he said.

Ten minutes later Les parked his car in the parking lot of the village hall and walked into the police station. The nine others were there with bags and backpacks waiting for them and Hass, too.

"This team is going to need a captain and since I've had experience playing football I'm appointing myself," Rawlings said as if he were the leader.

"This isn't some damn football game we're going to, Rawlings," Level harshly said.

"I'm aware of that," Rawlings snapped at him.

"We've all got certain skills that can be of use to us against these aliens who've attacked Earth," William said. "And that means we work together as a unit not like some sports team obeying its captain."

"I agree," Nancy said. "Your win one for the team attitude isn't going to help us in what we've got to do, or may run into, Rawlings."

"How many of you have ever been in command of anything other than a kitchen, or a dress making social." Rawlings looked at Les. "Or a classroom?"

"I have," Level said. "I was second in command under General Winthrop at Strategic Command, and before that a battalion in the Middle East. And don't look down your nose at teachers, Rawlings.

It takes a lot more than the ability to catch a football to control and teach thirty or forty students."

"Yeah, a good loud voice," Rawlings growled.

"No, intelligence," Les said.

"So who's going to lead us?" Chester asked in a mousy sounding voice.

"Well, I'm telling all of you now if things don't go right with this group I'm breaking out on my own," Rawlings announced.

"I'll be with you," Chester said.

Rawlings turned to him and slapped him hard on the back with his left hand knocking Chester forward a few feet. "Good boy."

"You said, Hass you have weapons here we can use and there's a town west of here with military equipment in it," Judith said.

"I've six assault rifles I can let you have and fifty rounds per rifle. The rest I have to keep here to arm some of the men and women to control the village. People have been calling in and sounding like they were ready to fall apart," he said. "I've contacted a Chief of Police in the town of East Oak, Chief Morris, and told him what you all intend doing. He says he can give you some Humvees and more weapons."

"Where's it at?" Les asked him.

"Drive west on I-88 it's just south of I-88. There's a turn off to show you where to go. East Oak is just east of the Mississippi River."

"How do we get there?" Alex asked. "Drive our own cars?"

"I can let you have one of our patrol cars," Hass said. "I told Chief Morris you'd be coming in a village patrol car. I can't do more than that. I need the others to patrol the village."

"I'll drive my Chevy Suburban," Level said. "It can hold seven people. I'd like Les and Alex and Pedro with me if no one objects."

"Can Alice come along?" Les asked.

"That's five. Anyone else?"

"My Chevy Silverado can hold four," Rawlings said as he looked at Nancy with a grin on his face.

"I'll join you, Level, if you don't mind," Nancy said. She looked at Rawlings and rolled her eyes in disgust.

"Can I ride with you Rawlings?" Chester asked him.

"Sure can," Rawlings said.

"I'll drive the patrol car," Judith said.

"I'll ride with Rawlings," William said.

"If Judith doesn't mind I'll ride with her," Janis said.

"Happy to have you," Judith told her.

"Alright, let's saddle up," Rawlings growled.

"First we stop at a supermarket and take as much can food and dry food as we can carry, and water," Les said. "Then we stop at a drug store and stock up on medical equipment."

"We take only those drugs that are necessary for healing wounds and preventing infection," Level said.

"What if those places aren't open?" Nancy asked.

"Then we break in, and no shooting," Les said.

"The men should have the rifles," Chester said.

"You said your sons and husband were in the military, didn't you?" Les asked Janis.

"Yes, the Army," she said.

"Did your husband teach you how to shoot?"

"Yes, he did," she said.

"Then she gets one of the rifles. Level and I can have one apiece. The other three rifles go with Chester, Rawlings, and William," he said. "And one other thing, we're going to be passing through suburbs and towns where people are going to be in a state of shock. When they tell us to go away, we go away." He looked at Rawlings and added, "The last thing we need is some damn fool acting like some stupid Hollywood cowboy"

"All we'd do is end up killing each other," Alex said. "And the aliens have already done enough damage to us."

Everyone stood around looking at each other.

"Alright," Level said. "Let's go and we drive without lights"

"How do we keep in touch with each other if we get lost?" Alice asked.

"We've our cell phones," Nancy said.

"No, keep off those things," Pedro said. "These aliens may not be as stupid as we think. They may be monitoring all the frequencies. They might be able to pick up cell phone calls."

"Just stay close to the car in front of you," Les said. "And we shouldn't travel faster than fifty-five miles an hour."

"At that speed we won't reach this town of East Oak until sunrise," Rawlings complained. "We should travel as fast as we can, and if anything gets in our way we just rip through them."

"Rawlings, try thinking like something else other than a line man on a football team," Pedro said. "We don't want to kill anyone, and if we encounter the aliens we won't be able to tear threw them."

"I'm in charge," Level said. "And we drive at fifty-five miles an hour and we don't tear through anything. If you don't like my rules, Rawlings, then stay here or go out on your own. Is that understood?"

"All right," Rawlings reluctantly said.

"Now let's go while we still got some daylight left," Level said as he turned to Hass. "Can we have those weapons?"

Hass led them back to the arms room in the police station and handed out the rifles and ammunition. They got into the three vehicles and drove to the nearest Jewel supermarket, broke into it, and loaded up on can food and other nonperishables and as much bottle water as they could carry. Their next stop was a CVS Drug store where they found a female pharmacist locking up the pharmacy section and told her what they knew and what they needed. She gave them all the medical supplies they could carry along with instructions on how to use them. Les told her to go home and pray for them.

Ten minutes later they were on the road heading for I-88. Each vehicle was carrying enough food, water, and medical supplies for the people in them. There was silence in two of the vehicles except in Rawlings' Silverado where he complained they were being led by a pussy.

"We're being led by a man with military experience and intelligence," William said from the seat behind Rawlings. He was glad he didn't demand the seat next to Rawlings. He sounded like he had little sense of responsibility and acted on impulse at a time when such action was more of a threat to them than the aliens.

"I don't know about that," Chester said. He had the seat next to Rawlings. "Sometimes brute force is better than thoughtful action."

Rawlings grunted his approval and kept quiet. *Sooner or later this group of pussies is going to need a strong man like me to lead them. And then we're going to do things my way.*

They passed suburbs and towns where people were wondering around as if they were loss and police were trying to get them to go home. In three suburbs they could hear the police using a bull horn telling people to go back to their homes and wait for further instructions.

"These aliens, if we were attacked by aliens, are smart," Les said.

"What do you mean?" Nancy asked him.

"Destroy the political and military infrastructure of a society and all you've got are a lot of scared people wandering around and wondering what to do," he answered.

"And when the food and water run out, they'll resort to violence to stay alive," Alex said. "They'll turn on each other."

"The Aztecs are a perfect example of that," Les said. "Once Cortez destroyed Tenochtitlan the capital of their empire it collapsed like a house of cards in a strong wind. The political structure of their world had ceased to exist and their world collapsed."

"And the Spanish were masters of Mexico until 1821 when the Mexicans rose up and threw them out," Pedro said. He looked at Les. "Think that'll happen here?"

"History teaches us what mistakes we must not make when confronting a powerful force," he said. "Unfortunately Americans aren't known for their understanding of history. So yes it will happen here if we don't act intelligently."

"There aren't many cars or trucks on the highway," Alice said as she looked out the window.

"We should have made a decision not to stop and pick up anyone we encounter," Level said. "We can't afford any more people."

"We have about twenty-nine days," Alex said. "After that the power plants will start to shut down, and communications will end."

"That's important?" Alice asked.

"Yes," Les said. "If we can contact others around the world we can assure them there are still a lot of us alive and if we work together we can begin to put the world back together." He paused before he added, "If we can lay our differences aside and work together."

"And if we can do what we've got to do," Nancy said.

"Find these aliens and stop them before they can do more damage to the Earth," Alice added.

"And if we can't?" she asked.

"Then there will be worldwide chaos," Pedro said. "Distances will work against us. No one will know what's going on in other parts of the world. And people will do whatever they have to do to survive."

"So let's hope we can do something to prevent that," Nancy said.

"I'm glad Janis is in the patrol car," Level said. "She's keeping a nice steady speed."

"Think she can drive all the way to this town of East Oak?" Les asked him.

"I think she's got a good head on her shoulders," he said.

Les sitting in the back seat turned around and looked at Rawlings' Silverado following them. *But Rawlings is an emotional asshole. He has the intelligence of a Hollywood cowboy in a cheap western who thinks a six gun is the solution to the town's problems.*

Pedro saw him looking back and said, "So far so good."

"Yeah," Les said turning back to face the front. "Let's hope it remains like that."

"There are probably a few stray military units around the country somewhere," Level said. "I hope they're trying to keep order."

"Think we should try to contact one of them?" Pedro said. "I've got my laptop."

"I don't know," he confessed.

"Someone else must suspect what we do, or even know what's happened," Nancy said. "We certainly aren't the only people in the world who've managed to figure out that we've been attacked by aliens."

"The question is did they pick up that electrical spike that we detected," Alex said.

"If some military unit in the field did pick up that spike and located where it came from then they're headed for northern Nevada," Level said. "I just hope they're not being led by some gun ho fool who shoots first and asks questions later."

Les looked out the window at the lovely spring landscape and the few abandoned cars and trucks. "If they have satellites, and they would need them to do what they've done, the aliens can see every part of Earth."

"From the north pole to the south pole and every jungle, forest, plain, and desert between them," Alex said.

"So they can see everything that's happening day or night," he said.

"What's your point?" Level asked Les.

"They'll be looking for any organization that looks like a military unit," he said.

"Or acts like one," Alice added.

"And those will be the ones they would be most interested in destroying if they have satellites, because the aliens will interpret them as being the greatest threat to them" Les said.

"While on the other hand they're probably watching hundreds maybe thousands of people like us driving around trying to find out where they are," Nancy said.

"I doubt that," Les said.

"Explain yourself," Level told him.

"The aliens are probably well organized and are watching millions, who knows, maybe billions of confused frightened people running around trying to find out what's wrong," he said. "They may have even detected you, Pedro, and Alex using a weather satellite looking down at them. So they won't be expecting anyone to show up soon."

"But they will be prepared for anyone showing up," Level said. "We have to assume whoever these aliens are they've been watching this planet for years, maybe even centuries. That explains why they were capable of doing to us what they've done."

"So we have to approach this area in Nevada cautiously," Alice said.

"Like we're running to somewhere safe," Les said.

"Well thank God we've got electric powered cars and trucks so we don't have to worry about fuel," Level said.

"But with the technology they're probably got, they'll detect the electric engines in our cars and trucks long before we even get close to them," Alex said.

"You know a lot of hackers use the phone company to hack into corporations that do millions of dollars in calls every day to hide what they're doing," Pedro said. "I was a part of a project that developed a program to attract the hackers so we could use it to track them and arrest them."

"That's it," Alex said. "We let them know we're looking for them so they will try and find out who we are then get into their system and use it against them."

"Think that'll work?" Level asked him.

"Or we can go to this area in Nevada where we detected that spike like some dumb TV cowboys blasting away with as much fire power as we can get and hope for the best," Alex said.

"Like the great football player," Nancy said in a sarcastic voice.

"Considering their weapon technology we'd be dead in ten minutes," Les said. "Can you use your laptop to look for them, Alex?"

"We've got over a dozen weather satellites that have the ability to do detailed scans of the Earth," he said. "We can use them to do a detailed scan of that area in Nevada."

"No, don't do that. The aliens if they are there will detect such a scan," Les said. "Do a detailed scan of the entire southwest. That way they won't know exactly where we're looking."

"Anybody else got a laptop?" Level asked.

"I've got one in my bag," Nancy said. "And it's got the latest programs and chips in it. I bought it last year to study the fashion market."

"Can you get it?" he asked her.

"Just a few minutes," she said as she unbuckled her seat belt and turned around and started climbing over the back of the middle seat. "Pardon me everyone." Within a minute she was in the back of the van going through her bag. "Got it."

"Change seats with me, Pedro," Alex said as he unbuckled his seatbelt.

"Honk your horn, Level, so we can stop and let the others know what we're going to do," Les suggested.

Level honked the horn twice and began to slow down.

Within a minute they were all standing around Level's van listening to Alex's idea.

"That shit ain't going to work," Rawlings said. "We get them weapons from this East Oak town and go to Nevada and kick some alien ass."

"That will only get us all killed," William told him. "Their technology is probably far ahead of anything we've got, so, Rawlings, we've got to use intelligence and not brute force. If we can use laptops to get into their system, it may give us an edge."

"We don't even know if they've got computers like ours," Rawlings complained.

"Oh, they have computers," Les assured him.

"How the fuck do you know? You're nothing but a retired school teacher," he answered.

"Oh, you shithead -," Nancy screamed at him.

"Calm down, Nancy," Les told her. He turned to Rawlings and said, "In order to do what they've done to Earth, Rawlings, they would have needed computers similar to ours to get into our computers to locate the major political and military places on Earth."

"I still think -," Rawlings started to say.

"Shut up, Rawlings," Janis said. "My husband and my sons worked with military computers and they told me they were constantly changing codes to prevent people from doing what Alex is suggesting."

"We use your suggestion, Rawlings, and like William said we'll all be dead as soon as we get into Nevada, because they're going to know we're coming for them," Judith said.

"He don't even know if he can get into their system," Rawlings said.

"Can you?" Chester said breaking his silence as he looked at Alex.

"We detected that spike," Alex said. "And that was defensive. I can't guarantee anything, but trying certainly won't hurt."

"I've got my laptop," Janis said. "I always travel with it in case I want to contact my family." The hopeful expression on her face fell away and was replaced by a sad one.

"I've got an iPhone and it has everything in it a laptop has," Judith said.

"So are we all agreed on Alex' plan?" Level asked them.

"No, I don't agree," Rawlings said.

Chester put his right hand on Rawlings' left arm and said, "I think it's best for all if we go along with Alex' plan, Rawlings. Because right now it's the only plan we've got."

Rawlings glared at Chester and mumbled, "Alright for now I do."

"First we've got to get all the laptops working together," Alex said. "But I'll use mine to try and break into the aliens' computer system. Janis, you and Nancy watch what I do on your laptops and look for anything unusual."

"I'll do the same thing with my iPhone," Pedro said. He looked at the others. "Like Janis I always have it with me."

"Judith you drive the patrol car," Level said. "And let's get moving we've only half an hour of daylight left."

CHAPTER 8

It was dark by the time they stopped next to a metal sign on the left hand side of the two lane road that pointed to the small town of East Oak. There was no moon and the country for miles around was wrapped in a blanket of darkness.

"What do we do?" Judith asked Janis who was sitting in the passenger seat of the patrol car.

"I don't know," she said as she looked around.

"Let's hope there's someone around when we reach East Oak," Judith said as she started to turn left onto the road.

"Stay where you are!" cried a frightened male voice from the darkness.

Judith stopped the car immediately.

"Go back where you come from!"

"We come here to talk to someone," she replied hoping whoever was speaking didn't start shooting.

"Get the hell out of here before we start shooting," another male voice screamed.

"Please, listen to me," Judith cried out.

There was twenty seconds of silence.

"What the hell do you want?" the first voice asked angrily.

"We were sent here by Officer Hass from Oak Park," Level said in a loud voice as he leaned out the driver's window of his Suburban.

"Go away! We've got problems of our own. We don't need any outsiders!"

"We're not here to harm anyone," Level said. "But we need to talk to your Chief of Police Morris."

No one responded.

"People are afraid," Nancy said.

"They're terrified because they can't contact the outside world to find out what's happened," Les said. "And it's only a matter of time before people will become violent."

"Can you blame them?" Pedro asked. "They can't contact anyone in the government and they don't know what's going on fifty miles outside of their towns. They're living in a world of fear and confusion."

Rawlings looked in the direction of the voice and grumbled, "We ought to get out and kick some butt."

"We can't even see them, Rawlings, all we'd do is get killed in the process, and there's been enough death," William added. "The world these people have known all their lives no longer exist and they don't know why, and they're scared."

"What do you think we should do, Chester?" Rawlings asked him.

"For the moment we let Level handle things," he answered. "And we keep our opinions to ourselves."

William looked at the back of Chester's head in the dark Silverado and thought *at least he's using his brain something Rawlings may not have.*

"Please, let us talk to Chief Morris," Level said. "It's very important that we speak to him."

"The woman in the front car get out and walked across the road to the sign," the voice said. There was less anger and fear in it.

"Any false moves and you're all dead," the other male voice warned.

Judith nervously got out of the car and closed the door and walked across the dark road to the sign.

"Stop."

Judith stopped and said nothing. She heard the sound of footsteps approaching her.

"I'm sorry about this," a man said as he came out of the dark and stopped in front of her. He was wearing a pistol. "We don't know what's going on and we're scared as hell. Do you know what's happening?"

"May we speak with Chief Morris? We're not here to cause any trouble," she asked reluctant to tell him what she knew. "Officer Hass in Oak Park contacted him and told him we'd be coming here. He has equipment we need to find out what's going on."

"He said somebody might be coming from the Chicago area," the man said. "Go back to your car. I'll come with you." He turned around and said to unseen people. "You guys hang loose."

"Okay," she said and turned around and walked back to the patrol car.

"You others follow this car," the man yelled at those in the other two vehicles as he followed Judith. He got into the back of the patrol car before Judith got in the front seat.

"Who are you?" Janis asked him.

"Craig," he said. "I own a John Deere Store, and Lady, I'm scared. Do you know what's happened? We can't contact anyone in the government to answer our questions."

Judith got into the car.

"Take us to Chief Morris," Janis told him. "And we'll tell what we know."

"Drive straight ahead till you reach an intersection then turn right. Police headquarters are on the right a block from the intersection."

Judith followed his instructions and the other two vehicles followed her. Four minutes later they were parked side by side in a parking lot outside the East Oak Police Station. Craig led them into the station and into Chief Morris' office. He was sitting at his desk with his head down on the desk asleep.

"Chief," Craig said in a loud voice. "Those people from Oak Park you are expecting are here."

Morris woke up and raised his head and looked at Craig and the eleven people standing behind him. He sat up and ran his hands over his face. "Hass called me on the police channel and told me you'd be coming." He leaned back in his chair. "What the hell's going on? We can't contact anyone in Springfield, Chicago, or Washington. It's like those places don't exist anyone."

"They exist, but the people that use to live in them don't," Les told him.

He looked at Les and asked, "What the hell do you mean?"

Craig stared at Les like he was crazy.

"They exist but the people that lived in them don't exist anymore," Level said. "I'm Level." He introduced the others.

"How could those cities exist but no one in them exist?" Morris asked. "That don't make sense."

Level sat down in an empty chair and told Morris everything they knew.

"My God," Morris exclaimed half an hour later.

"This is what comes of sending them messages into space, saying come and get us," Rawlings said.

"Those messages never said that," Craig said. "I was a part of a high school project twenty years ago that wrote messages that were sent into space, and they never said come and get us."

"You're correct," Les said. "I'm not an authority on space -,"

"Then why you talking?" Rawlings said in a nasty voice.

Chester standing to the left of Rawlings pulled the cuff on the left sleeve of his jacket as a way of saying 'be quiet'.

Les ignored Rawlings and continued, "Considering what's been done to Earth I figure they've been watching Earth for years and there's something here they want, or they want the entire planet for themselves."

"That means they're way ahead of us in weapons," Craig said.

"And technology," Pedro added.

"And you're going to take this equipment Hass asked me to give you to go to Nevada and stop these aliens?" Morris asked in a disbelieving voice.

"The spike we picked up in Oak Park came from northern Nevada," Alex said. "While we were driving here we got into a weather satellite passing over that area and picked up another spike that's like nothing I've ever seen before."

"What do you mean like nothing you've ever seen before?" Craig asked him.

"Like it was a searching spike," Pedro said.

"What do you mean a searching spike?" Craig asked him.

"Instead of just jamming the satellite to blind it the spike slowly rose to a height of five thousand feet then spread out for over a thousand miles then disappeared."

"Searching for whoever was using that satellite to look down at them," Morris said.

"Yeah," Pedro said. "But we broke transmission before it could reach us and determine where we were."

Morris looked at Craig and nodded.

"What?" Level asked. He saw Morris' nod to Craig. "You've learned something."

"Six hours ago I picked up a distress call over the public frequency on my radio in my store," Craig said. "I repair farmers' tractors and they sometimes call me over my radio."

"Who sent the message?" Level asked him.

"A military unit somewhere in the southwest around northern Nevada," he said. "At least they identified themselves as a military unit. A battalion the caller said. He identified himself as a private and said his unit was on maneuvers when his unit was fired upon by people using electric weapons."

"I thought the Army had their own special radio waves," Alice said.

"They do," Level said. "If that private used a public frequency, it's because he couldn't contact anyone in the military using a military frequency."

"What did he say?" Les asked him.

"Me and Weaver are all that's left. We're wounded and they're coming for us," Craig said. "I recorded it. I usually record messages I get from farmers who need equipment from my store. That way I take what they need to repair their tractors."

"Could you give me a copy of that?" Alex asked him.

"You know about radios?" Craig asked him.

"Ex-CIA computer operator," Alex said. "I spent twenty years working in the Technical Branch."

"I've never heard of it," Morris said.

Alex smiled and said, "It's one of those CIA branches no one talks about. We spend a lot of time listening to terrorist talk."

Morris nodded, stood up, and said, "I'll take you to where I've got the stuff for you." He walked toward the door of his office and out.

The eleven people followed him.

"Eh, Chief, don't tell anyone about us unless we contact you," Les said. "If we should locate where the aliens are, we'll contact you over the public frequency."

"Okay," he said as he headed for the back of the police station.

"Contact all the towns and cities within a hundred miles of East Oak and tell them to get all the food, water, medical supplies, and weapons they can get their hands on," Level told them. "Tell them to get organized and use whatever radios you've got to spread the word."

"And do this immediately," Alex said. "Because within a month, maybe less, the power plants on this planet are going to start shutting down unless someone manages to keep them going. If someone can keep them going, especially the nuclear power plants, because once they've used up their cooling water they'll start to melt the reactors they're in. And that will only create more problems. And tell the people living close to them to get as far away from them as they can. If there are any technicians living next to those plants they'll know what to do to avoid a meltdown."

"You think things are going to get worse than they are?" Craig asked as he walked next to Les.

"Yes," Les said. "Unless people get organized and start acting intelligently fear is going to take over, and then chaos. We'll end up killing people the aliens haven't already killed."

Morris stopped in front of a wooden door and took keys out of his left pants pocket and opened it. He reached for the light switch on the right side of the door and turned on the lights. "How many people do you figure are already dead, or disintegrated?"

The room was filled with various kinds of weapons.

"Every major city on Earth has probably been hit along with every major military and political base," Les told him. "That would include every city with a population over a million and probably half those with populations over a hundred thousand."

"Jesus," Craig exclaimed. "That could be billions."

"And all those people were just disintegrated?" Morris asked him.

"Yeah, from what we saw in Chicago over the traffic cameras," Les said.

"What about you peoples' families?" Craig asked them.

"Dead I figure," Les told him. He was amazed that he could say that so calmly. *I've accepted my family's death.*

Rawlings walked rapidly over to a rack that contained six portable machineguns and picked up one. "Now this is more like it," he said.

"I guess we're luckier than you," Craig said, looking at him. "Most of the people in town have relatives in town or other small towns."

Les looked at Rawlings and said, "In more ways than you can imagine."

"East Oak had no political, military, or technical value, and neither do any of the other towns close to us," Morris said. "We're just farming towns with small industries."

"And not close to any place that's important," Janis said.

Chester heard what Les said and walked over to Rawlings and whispered, "Less machoism."

"Those are sunglasses," Nancy said as she walked over to a desk with over fifteen pair of glasses on them. She picked up one and said, "Heavy, too."

"They're basic night vision goggles," Level said walking over next to her. "Better than the older ones because they don't use electrical energy from batteries. They're solar powered." He picked up a pair and looked them over. "The glass in them is like the glass in those telescopes in orbit about Earth. It's designed to pick up the smallest rays of light and magnify it so the wearer can see like it's a cloudy day outside. We should all take a pair."

"Why?" Chester asked as he picked up an Army assault rifle.

"Because we should sleep during the day and travel at night," Les said as he walked to the table.

"Why?" Nancy said.

"Right now whoever these aliens are they're looking at a planet with a lot of terrified people left who are running around like scared chickens," Les said. "If they see us moving at night they may just think we're trying to find a safe place to run to without being seen."

"But they'll see us, if they are more advanced than we are," she said.

"Yes," Les agreed. "And let's hope they dismiss us as no more than scared people running in the dark."

Rawlings was checking the machine gun.

"That's not going to be of much use to us, Rawlings," Level told him. "It's too heavy when fully loaded and makes a lot of noise that can be heard almost a mile away."

"I can handle it," Rawlings replied.

"We should carry these," Janis said as she walked to a rack holding a dozen assault rifles with sound suppressers attached to the muzzles. "They're tactical weapons used by elite military units and make far less noise than that machine gun and are easier to carry."

"Have you ever shot one?" Nancy asked her as she walked over to her.

"Twice at the base my husband was assigned to," she said.

"What did your husband do in the Army?" Pedro asked her as he stood near the door looking around the room.

"He was in Ordinance Maintenance," she said. "I've fired these before though they're not the latest models."

"This is all surplus equipment," Les said as he picked up a pair of glasses and put them in the right inside of his jacket pocket.

"Jameson owns the military supply store," Morris said. "When he bought these weapons and the boxes of ammunition I insisted he let me lock them up in the station."

"Less chance of someone breaking into here and stealing them," William said.

"That's the idea," Morris said. "The last thing I needed was some fool getting his hands on a machine gun and a thousand rounds of ammo."

"I suggest we all take the light weight tactical rifles," Level said.

"Not me," Rawlings said. "This machine gun is my baby, and I'm going to carry enough ammo with me to blow down a mountain."

"Fully loaded that thing could easily weight over twelve pounds, Rawlings," Level told him. "These tactical rifles are good for close quarter fighting and weight a lot less than that machine gun when fully loaded."

"You take what you want, and I'll take what I want," Rawlings said as he walked to a stack of metal boxes and read the writing on the sides of them. "And two of these boxes of one hundred rounds of ammo."

Everyone was looking at Rawlings and his machine gun.

Les looked down at the table of night vision goggles and saw there were thirteen more on the table. He picked up another pair and stuck them into the left breast pocket of his jacket. Having a second pair somehow made sense to him, but he didn't know why? "Does Jameson's store have camouflage clothing?"

"Yeah, I'll take you all over there where you can take what you want," Morris said.

"Where is Jameson? We'd like to thank him for this equipment," Judith asked him.

"He and his wife are in New York City on vacation," Craig said.

"Well, they're not coming back," Les told him. "Are there heavy duty off road vehicles in town?"

"Jameson bought four out of date Humvees last year hoping to sell them to hunters, but he hasn't sold any," Morris said. "They're old and too expensive but they're electrically powered and built for off road driving."

"We should be leaving now," Alex said. "The sun will coming up in another five hour."

"Let's go to Jameson's store and get clothing and boots," Level suggested.

Twenty minutes later after they'd all, except Rawlings, taken the lighter short range tactical rifles, ten 9 millimeter semiautomatics, and a hundred rounds of ammunition each they were in Jameson's Army Surplus Store taking desert colored fatigues, boots, and hats. Les suggested they avoid the helmets even though they were made of plastic they had metal parts and could be detected by metal scanners. Half an hour later they had put everything they'd brought with them in their cars and vans into three of the Humvees.

"We should take these short range radios if we can access the citizen's band with them," Les said.

"What do we need with them?" Rawlings said.

"Rawlings, it's important that we be able to listen to what people are saying," he explained. "The last thing we want to do is run into a lot of scared people with weapons who may think we're the enemy."

"I agree with that," William said. "By now people know they can't contact the government so they're probably talking to each other."

"They can be used to contact people on the citizen's band," Craig said and told them what frequency to turn to.

"Okay, how do we divide up?" Level asked.

"The computer experts shouldn't be in the same Humvee," Les said. "Alex and Judith should ride with you Level while Pedro and Janis ride in another Humvee."

"Why don't you drive the second one, Les, and -," he looked around the group. "And Rawlings can drive the third one."

"I'll ride with Rawlings," Chester volunteered. "The rest of you can get into the first and second Humvees."

"I'll ride with you, Level," Nancy said.

"Me, too," William said. He didn't want to be in the Humvee with Rawlins and his machine gun. He considered him to be too irresponsible.

"I'll ride with Les," Alice said.

"Alright with everyone?" Level asked them

"We should keep off these radios and don't honk the horns on these Humvees unless it's absolutely necessary," Les suggested. "Do these Humvees have radios in them?"

"What's wrong, Les? You afraid of letting the aliens know we're coming for them?" Rawlins asked him.

Les turned around to face him and said, "This isn't some adventure, Rawlings. The only way we're going to save what's left of our world is to sneak up on the aliens and take over where they are and stop them from doing any more damage to Earth."

"We agree," Chester said.

"They have radios," Morris said.

"We can use the radios in the Humvees to find out what's going on in the outside world," Les said.

"Let's ride," Rawlings growled in a manly voice.

As they walked to their Humvees Level walked beside Les and said, "You realize this is probably a one way trip with no chance of success on our part."

"Yeah," Les replied. "Maybe we should just give up and wait to die."

"Do you really want to do that?"

"No, I want to fight back and kill whoever has done this terrible thing to our world," he said. He didn't add 'and killed my family' because it was too late for that.

As the others got into the Humvees, Craig walked up to Les and said in a soft voice, "You've got a problem, you know."

Les looked at Rawlings and knew what Craig meant and asked him, "Would you like to keep it here?"

"No," Chief Morris said standing on Les' left side. "We've got enough damn fools in East Oak. We don't need anymore, and good luck. Because you people are sure going to need it."

Five minutes later the Humvees left East Oak heading west for the bridge across the Mississippi River.

CHAPTER

9:30 p.m.

Rush walked in a quick march to the medical center on the fifth level of the compound with Theia right behind him.

The double doors to the medical center opened and Rush walked into the center and saw a soldier in his blue uniform standing at attention awaiting his arrival.

"Were you with Lieutenant Zack when he captured these two Earthlings?" he asked the soldier as he stopped next to him.

"Yes, sir, I was," the soldier replied.

"Tell me about them," he told the soldier.

"They are all that is left alive of a unit of eleven hundred men and women," the soldier told him. "Both suffered minor wounds to their bodies that can be quickly healed by our medicines. One is a man and the other is a woman."

"Take me to them," he demanded.

"Yes, sir," the soldier replied and did an about face and walked in the direction of the hospital room the two soldiers were in.

Rush and Theia followed him.

A minute later they entered a room where two people were lying in separate beds with bandages around on their stomachs. Zack and one of his men were standing on the left and right sides of the two beds with two medical officers in pink medical gowns standing at the head of the beds.

Rush walked up between the beds and looked to his right at a female with light tan skin who was asleep. He looked to his left and saw a young black male staring at him with an angry expression on his face and hard brown eyes.

"Who are you?" the black man asked.

"You do not question the Commander," Zack snapped at him.

The black man looked to his right at Zack and said, "Go fuck yourself."

Zack stared at him with a confused expression on his face.

"That was probably an insulting statement," Rush told Zack.

"What does it mean?" he asked the Commander.

Rush shrugged his shoulders to indicate he didn't know.

"I have monitored Earth communications for some time, sir," Theia said. "And I know what it means."

"Tell us," Rush ordered her.

"It means to go have sex with yourself," she answered. "It is meant to be insulting."

Rush laughed and said, "Such foolish people these Earthlings."

"It's a statement meant to degrade you," Theia said to Zack.

"You shall learn respect for your masters," Zack said as he drew back his left hand to strike the Earthling.

"Stop," Rush told Zack. "In time these Earthlings will learn who the new masters of this planet are."

"Like hell we will," the black man replied.

"If that statement means there will be others like you and your unconscious companion coming for us, do not put faith in it," Rush told him. "Ninety percent of the people on this planet no longer exist. And that includes your military forces, political leadership, and most of your technicians and scientists."

"You're lying," the black man replied.

"No, I am not," Rush told him. "Your world is now the world of the Overlord and the Warrior Class of Tabor. Those few that remain alive will become our slaves."

The black man's hard expression declined as he said, "Never."

"What is your name?" Rush asked him.

"James, Henry, Private First Class, serial number 447326644," he said.

"How long have you been in your planet's military forces?" he asked.

"James, Henry, Private First Class, serial number 447326644," Henry replied.

Rush nodded as he said, "You've been trained to give little information to opposing forces when captured. That is good. The destruction of any remaining military forces on this planet will be great sport of us."

"It's going to be a damn sight more than great sport for you," Henry replied. "You've attacked the wrong planet, fella."

"No we have not, Henry," Rush said. "We've been studying this planet for twenty years and we know your weaknesses."

"Is that how you learned our language?" Henry asked him.

"I am speaking Tabor," he said. "Your English just happens to be like Tabor."

"Why have you attacked us?" Henry asked.

Rush looked at him for a few seconds and decided why not tell him? There was nothing he or anyone on the planet can do to stop them. "To make your world our world as I have clearly stated."

"What happen they run you off your own world?" Henry asked him.

"Nothing in the galaxy runs the Tabor Warrior Class from anywhere," Rush told him. "We go where we wish and take what we wish from any world in the galaxy."

Henry grinned and said, "You're lying. You got kicked off your world by somebody stronger than you, or you fucked it up fighting wars. And now you need a new world."

"Do not speak to the Commander in such a disrespectful manner," Zack yelled at him.

"What are you going to do? Kill me?" he asked Zack as he looked at him.

"The thought of dying does not frighten you?" Theia asked him.

"I know I'm dead, but you people are not going to conquer Earth even if you have destroyed its military and political leadership," Henry told her. "Those who are still alive know the Earth has been attacked by aliens and right now they're getting ready to fight you people, whatever you are called."

"With what?" Zack asked him in a cold cynical voice.

"They'll make weapons and go back into the mountains, woods, and jungles and fight until you've been driven from Earth. The people of Earth will never give up. You should have stayed on your world wherever it's at and whatever you call it." The expression of Henry's face said he meant every word he'd said.

"Tabor is the name of our world and it will become the name of this world," Rush told him.

"Earth will become your grave and that of the Overlord's, too," he said.

Rush turned to one of the two medical officers in the room and said, "Take care of his wounds and that of his companion."

"Yes, Commander Rush," the man said.

"Come with me, Zack," he said as he turned around and walked toward the door"Shall I leave the guards in place, sir?" he asked Rush.

"No need. Where can they go in the compound we cannot go and find them?" he said as he walked out the door.

Theia, Zack, and the two soldiers followed him.

Rush stopped twenty yards from the door of the medical center and turned and said to Zack and the two soldiers. "Where were they when you attacked them?"

"Two hundred of their miles northwest of here in a place called Oregon," Zack answered. "They were in an unfortified camp near a small river."

"How did you attack them?" he asked.

"I used only two of our armored cars. I divided them, activated our armored vehicles defensive shields and attacked them from the south and northwest," he said.

"And you used only electrical weapons?" Rush asked him.

"Yes, sir," he said. "The vehicles they had were poorly armored and offered no resistance to our attack,"

"And they fought back?"

"Yes, sir," Zack said. "As if they did not expect to be defeated."

"Explain that."

"No matter how many were killed the others kept fighting even as they tended to their wounded. When one of their warriors was dead, the others continued fighting back even though it was apparent they could not win."

"You attacked without warning?" Rush asked him.

"Yes, sir, the Earthlings were not aware of the two cars until they started killing them," Zack told him. "I remained back in case they needed assistance, but they didn't."

Rush turned to the soldier known as Zig and asked him, "How long was it before they stopped fighting?"

"About ten of their Earth minutes," Zig said.

"And those two in the medical section were the only ones to survive?" Rush asked him.

"Yes, sir they were unconscious," he said.

"I remembered the order you gave, Commander, and called Lieutenant Theia and told her we'd taken two of them alive. She told me to bring them to the compound when I informed her they were the only two alive," Zack said.

Rush turned toward her but didn't say anything.

"Like you said, Commander, we needed to know more about the physical condition of the warriors of Earth," she explained. "I had them bring in their weapons that weren't destroyed in the fighting. They are very primitive compared to ours, but they can kill us."

Rush nodded and said, "I'll go and examine these weapons." He turned toward Zack. "Did you scan the area for any more of these warriors?"

"Yes, Commander for a distance of four hundred miles," he answered. "And they call themselves soldiers not warriors."

"Did you detect any more of them?"

"No, sir," Zack said.

"Did you dispose of the bodies?"

"I saw no reason to do that, sir, since there were no Earthlings around for hundreds of miles, but I did make sure those that we left were dead."

Rush turned to Theia and said, "I remember you telling me yesterday there was a message sent out by these soldiers."

"Yes, sir, but I do not know where the message was sent," she said.

"I detected numerous calls for assistance by the soldiers as they were being killed," Zack said.

"Have you detected any attempts by Earthlings to answer the messages?"

"None," Theia said. "But some of those messages may have been received, sir, and considering what we've done to the people of Earth there could be many more on their way here."

Rush nodded as he said to Zack, "Maintain a guard around the compound. Make sure those under your command are changed every two hours. I do not want tired guards on duty."

"How far from the compound should the guard be?" Zack asked him.

"At least ten Earth miles," he said. "And every time the guard is changed I want a report filed by the returning guards."

"I will obey," Zack replied as he stood at attention.

"Good, you may go," Rush told him.

Zack immediately turned to his left and walked off. The two guards followed two yards behind him.

"Our underground compound occupies an area of a quarter of a mile," Theia told him. "And there are five ways into the compound."

Rush started to walk. "Your point?"

"There are only twenty-six of us, sir, counting you, if Zack has ten guards on duty ten miles beyond the compound that will leave only fifteen of us inside the compound, sir. And two of the remaining personal are medical people, two are computer operators, two food supervisors of the food preparation robots, and two maintenance people to maintain our vehicles and weapons, sir. That will leave only seven guards to replace the patrolling guards," she explained.

"Yes, we are short of warriors," he said. He walked to an elevator and removed his communicator from its pouch and touched the call button on the plain black panel.

"Zack here, sir," Zack replied.

"Reduce the number of guards on patrol to two to an armored vehicle. I do not want them being overworked. No more than four hours for each patrol."

"Yes, sir," Zack replied.

Rush stood before the waiting elevator thinking. Then he spoke. "We must determine the intelligence of these Earthling soldiers. And the best way to do that is to allow those two the freedom to leave the compound."

Theia didn't reply.

"By allowing them to leave we can observe how they will act, and learn how to fight these soldiers as individuals," he finished. He looked at Theia. "Do you disagree?"

"No, Commander," she answered.

Rush looked at Theia's worried face. "Do not worry, Lieutenant Theia. In nine days the Overlord will arrive with half a million warriors on a fleet of a hundred ships to assist us in completing the conquest of this planet." He walked into the open elevator.

Theia followed him thinking *the battle on Tabor to get those ships had cost the warriors over half their strength, and there were probably many wounded among those on the ships. The fight to secure this planet may cost us many more warriors if these Earthlings are as violent as their past suggests they are.*

Henry looked at one of the men in the pink medical gown holding a small cell phone like device over Susan Weaver and asked, "Why do you want our planet if you have one of your own?"

The man looked at the other man and said, "I can handle them."

The other man nodded and left.

"What's wrong, you afraid to answer my question?" Henry asked him.

"We have left Tabor," the man said as he carefully moved the object from Weaver's head to her feet. "Your companion is improving. In a few hours she shall be healthy and capable of moving about on her own as you will be."

"We were both shot in the stomach," he said. "Wounds like that take weeks to heal."

"Not with the medicine we have given you," he replied.

"So you can travel through space and you have miracle medicines," Henry said.

"Excellent," the man said as he turned off his device and turned toward Henry. "We do not have miracle medicines. We are hundreds of years more advanced than you Earthlings are."

"Well, you're going to find out no matter how advanced you are conquering Earth will not be easy no matter how many of us you've already killed."

"We have killed over seven billion people on this world, and we did that in less than three hours. Gaining control of this planet will be no problem for us," he said as he moved the device over Henry's body and looked at the device. "Your wound has almost healed. If the remaining Earthlings are as healthy as you and this woman are you will all make excellent slaves for us Tabors."

"Don't count on us being slaves excellent or bad," Henry said. "We hate slavery and will fight like hell against becoming slaves, because we'd prefer death to slavery."

The man smiled at Henry's defiant statement. "In less than ten days the Overlord will arrive with a hundred ships and a half million warriors. And our weapons are more advanced than those that remain on this planet. And that includes your atomic bombs. Conquering the remaining Earthlings will take us only a few months."

"What type of world is Tabor?"

"It is a blue green world like Earth. There are some animals and plants on Earth that do not exist on Tabor, but they pose no problem for us," he said as he put the device in the pocket of his pink gown.

"So you're expanding your empire?" Henry said.

"Once we have completed the conquest of Earth we will begin to build our empire and spread it throughout the galaxy till it is ours," the man said.

"You're a doctor, right?" he asked him. Henry hoped that by slightly changing the subject he could get more information out of him.

"I am the senior medical officer in the compound, but like everyone in this compound I am a trained warrior," he said.

"So why didn't you start expanding your empire from Tabor? Why come to Earth to begin building your empire?"

"Because the government of Tabor was a government of peace loving fools," the man said. "They failed to accept the fact that all great advancements have been made as a result of conquest. Once we have Earth we will return to Tabor and add it to our empire."

"So you're a military doctor?"

"What does doctor mean?"

"You're a person who knows how to cure illnesses and injuries," he said.

"I am the best in my profession, which is why the Overlord chose me to come on this expedition," he said.

"Well, Doc, you're wasting your time," Henry told him. "This is one world you won't be able to conquer."

The man smiled at Henry and said, "Your defiance is as pathetic as your world's weapons are. We will succeed. You may get out of bed and walk around. It will help your wound heal faster."

"How about some food and water I haven't eaten in almost two days."

"I shall have them delivered here in two hours," he said as he walked toward the door.

"Hay, what's your name?"

"Senior Medical Officer Hayes," he said as he walked out the door.

Henry looked over at Weaver and said, "Hurry up and get better, Susan. The world needs us and we've only got nine days." He looked about the Spartan furnished room and decided to wait until he got some food in his stomach before he started moving around then decided, *to hell with that I've got to learn everything I can about this place.* He looked over at Weaver and thought, *and figure out a way to get out of this place and warn what's left of the world. And I sure hope I can take you with me, Susan.* He sat up in bed and thought about what the one addressed as Commander Rush had said. *No wonder no one answered our call for help. There was no one out there to hear the battalion's call for help.* He threw the light bed covers back off to his right and put his legs over the left side of the bed, put his feet on the floor, and stood up. He didn't feel weak or pain as he expected to feel after being shot in the stomach. He started to walk and was surprised that he walked like he'd walked before the battalion was attacked.

Henry walked about the large room for ten minutes before he walked over to the left side of Weaver's bed and looked down at her face.

Susan Weaver looked as if she was sleeping.

He started to pull back the covers on her bed and lift her gown to look at the wound in her stomach, but decided against it because it seemed like an invasion of her privacy. He turned around and looked around the room and saw a desk with a small TV screen on it. He walked over to it. "No keyboard. Damn thing is of no use to me." He turned around and mumbled out loud, "I wonder where the hell I am?"

"Fifth level medical section," answered the TV screen.

Henry spun around and looked at it. "Eh, did you say something?"

There was no response.

"What are you?" he asked.

"An information unit," replied the TV screen.

"Can you show me a diagram of what this place I'm in looks like?"

A diagram of the compound immediately appeared on the screen.

"Hold that," he said as he looked around the room for a closet. "Where is my uniform?"

"The clothing you and the female had on are inside the cupboard on the right side of the second bed."

Henry looked at the wall next to his bed. "I don't see any cupboard."

"The wall must be pressed," replied the TV screen.

Henry walked to right side of his bed and pushed the wall. Nothing happened. He walked around between Weaver's bed and his and pushed the wall. A door popped open an inch. He pulled it all the way open and saw his uniform and Weaver's hanging from metal coat hangers. They appeared to have been cleaned. On the floor was their equipment minus their weapons and iPhones. He pulled his uniform out of the cupboard and looked it over. Even the burned hole in it had been repaired. He threw the uniform on the bed and knelt down and picked up his backpack and put it on the bed and opened it and took out a pad of paper and a pen. He walked back to the desk with the pad and pen, pulled out the plastic chair, and asked, "Why were our uniforms cleaned and repaired?"

"The uniforms of all warriors who have survived wounds in battle are cleaned and repaired for the soldiers to use when they recover from their wounds."

Henry started drawing on the pad of paper what he saw on the screen. *These people are by the book soldiers, and that may be good for whoever is out there who can still fight.* He stopped drawing and turned around and looked at Weaver. *If we can get out of this compound alive.* A thought crossed his mind. "Am I being watched?"

"Wounded warriors are monitored until they die or are ready for battle again."

"What if they survive but can't fight again?"

"Such warriors are disposed of. The Warrior Class of the Overlord has no need for warriors who cannot fight."

"By the way, how large is this compound?" he asked.

"This compound is a quarter of a mile in circumference," replied the screen.

"Tell me how tall is it and any other facts about it."

"This compound has a height of six hundred feet with five levels. Each level has a height of fifty feet, with fifty feet of ground between each level. It is build one hundred feet below the surface of this planet next to an underground source of water."

"How long did it take the Tabors to build this place?" he asked.

"Two Earth days."

"Can you show me where it is?"

A picture of the northwest corner of Nevada appeared on the screen.

Henry leaned close and looked at it. *They sure chose the right place to build this compound. There's not a town within seventy miles of it in either direction.*

It took Henry five minutes to make a crude drawing of the entire compound and write down everything the information unit had told him about the compound. He made sure to mark the exits from the compound on his map then he returned the pad and pen to his backpack. He put everything back in the cupboard and got back in bed and waited for food and water to arrive.

The screen went off.

CHAPTER 10

Day 2 May 4, 1:30 a.m.

"It's one thirty," Alice announced from the passenger seat as she looked at the clock on the dashboard of the Humvee.

"Get one of those military flashlights and put your fingers over the front and push the blinker button twice through the windshield," Les told her as he drove.

"What's that going to do?" Janis asked him.

"Let Level know we want to talk to him," Pedro said as he reached behind the back of the second row of seats and pulled his backpack over the back of the seat and onto his lap. He took the flashlight out of his backpack and handed it to Alice.

"Push the button halfway up and then point the flashlight at the windshield and do as I told you," Les told her.

She did as he said.

When Level saw the flashing light he moved his Humvee over to the right side of the road and stopped.

"Aw, what are these pussies up to now," grumbled Rawlings as he moved to the right and stopped a yard behind Les' Humvee. "We ought to be driving like hell, and that pussy Level is doing only sixty miles an hour."

"When we get out and find out why they're stopping keep your fucking mouth shut," Chester told him in a calm voice.

"Who the fuck do you think you're talking to, Wimp, one of them pussies," Rawlings said as he turned to Chester.

"To a dumb jock who has managed to convince everyone you're nothing but a muscle bound idiot who thinks we're playing some damn football game," Chester told him.

"Now wait just a minute, Wimp, nobody talks to me like that," Rawlings warned him.

"Listen to me, Asshole. The world as we knew it has changed, and if we expect to survive the change we've got to start dealing with reality," Chester said as he opened the passenger door. "Just be quite and let me do the talking. Understand?" He got out of the Humvee.

Rawlings looked at Chester like he was crazy but said nothing as he got out of the Humvee.

They both walked up to Level's Humvee.

"We should start looking for a place to park and hide around four thirty," Les was saying.

"And we should turn off all the interior lights in these Humvees," William said. "This country probably has a lot of terrified people hiding in their houses with guns. They see a light they can't explain they just might start shooting."

"Yeah, I agree," Alex said. "So where should we stop?"

"Let's look at those military terrain maps we've got," Level suggested as he turned toward his Humvee.

The others waited silently while he got one of the terrain maps from his backpack and put it on the ground and used his flashlight as Les had told Alice to use Pedro's.

"What are those lines?" Rawlings asked as he stood behind Nancy looking over her right shoulder.

She moved away from him and got behind William.

"Terrain lines," Les answered.

"You learn that teaching history?" he asked him.

"No, thirty-seven years ago I was in a recon unit in the Army stationed in North Africa," he said. He was kneeling next to Level. "But maps are commonly used in history classes at all levels."

"What's that thick green area in Nebraska?" Judith asked as she stood behind Pedro

"A wooded area," Level said. "I estimate we're close to that area."

"Yes," Les agreed. "We've been driving since 9, and at the speed we've been traveling we should be close to the western Iowa border. And that area appears to be close to the North Platt country."

"It is," Level said. "And there's nothing around there but thick woods."

"How do you know?" Rawlings asked him.

"Twelve years ago I was on an infantry training exercise in that country," he said. "And there's plenty of fresh water in that country. None of it is polluted by industrial waste."

Pedro was looking closely at the map. "It looks to be about three hundred miles from here if we're close to Iowa's western border. If we drive at sixty miles an hour, we should be able to make it just before sunrise."

Level folded the map and stood up. "Alright we do sixty miles an hour. Keep a distance of five car lengths behind the Humvee in front of you. If somebody gets in trouble and needs help, flash your flashlights like Alice did."

"Why not let me lead?" Rawlings said. "I ain't afraid of speed like you people seem to be."

Level looked at Les.

"Alright, Rawlings," Les said. "Just remember sixty miles an hour and no faster, or we might lose you."

"Don't you folks worry I'll clear the path for you and keep you in sight, just hang onto my butt," he said and then turned toward his Humvee.

"He thinks this is just some damn football game," Nancy said as she started walking toward Level's Humvee.

"It won't be if we encounter any aliens," Alex said.

"Let us hope we spot them before they spot us," William said as he walked next to her.

"We must impress upon that man that where we're going might be very dangerous for all of us," Judith said.

"Easier said than done," William replied. "If you consider he isn't concerned in the least bit about the deaths of billions of people."

"Nobody is that inhuman," Judith said.

"Yes, there are," Nancy said. "And many of them have survived I'll bet."

"I don't find Rawlings' romantic attitude any more appealing that the rest of you do," Level said. "But so far he's with us."

They got into their Humvees and started following Rawlings.

Chester leaned over and looked at the speedometer on the dashboard. "You're doing seventy miles an hour. The agreed upon speed was sixty, so drop your speed."

"Why should I?" he replied as he pressed his foot down harder on the accelerator.

"Stop acting like some macho asshole, Rawlings, and start thinking," Chester yelled at him.

"Don't talk to me like that, Wimp," he snapped back at Chester. "I ain't impressed by you or them other pussies, and that includes them cunts, too."

Chester thought of pulling the small semiautomatic out of his right jacket pocket and pressing it against Rawlings' right temple, but he dismissed the thought. Rawlings may be a macho bonehead as far as he was concerned, but he was still smart enough to know if Chester shot him in the head while he was driving over seventy miles an hour the crash would kill both of them. Chester decided to appeal to Rawlings obvious desire to be a leader. "That's because you haven't considered the situation we're in."

"I know the situation we're in, Wimp," he said to Chester.

"The human race has had its day as masters of this planet," Chester told him. "The only ones that are going to exist in comfort in the future are those who can convince the aliens they need them."

"What the hell are you talking about?"

Chester looked at the speedometer. The needle was on eighty. "Slow down to sixty and I'll tell you."

For a moment Rawlings thought of ignoring Chester and increasing his speed to a hundred miles an hour. He'd always liked doing things his way, because he'd been taught by his Big Daddy that big strong men could do as they wished and would always be successful. His Big Daddy never bothered explaining to him why he'd spent his entire life going from job to job and never got rich which was his Big Daddy's idea of success. Rawlings dropped his speed back to sixty miles an hour.

"That damn fool is slowing down," Level said as he drew closer to Rawlings' Humvee.

"I suspect Chester has convinced him to do that," William said.

"Why?" Nancy asked him.

"Because I've dealt with men like Rawlings and Chester in the banking business for years," he said.

"What do you mean?" Judith asked him. She was sitting next to him. Nancy was on her left.

"Men like Rawlings think banking regulations applies to what they call men with no guts," he said. "And men like Chester who know how to control such men."

"Think we're going to have trouble with those two?" Level asked him.

"I don't know," William answered. "But it's best if we keep our eyes on them, because both are unpredictable."

Les couldn't see farther than the rear end of Level's Humvee, but he had seen Rawlings take off in his Humvee like he was in a race. "Keep your distance between Rawlings and Chester," he told Alice who was sitting in the passenger seat next to him.

"Why should we?" Janis asked him. She was sitting behind him in the second row.

"Rawlings has the mentality of a Hollywood cowboy. Shoot first and ask questions later," he answered.

"And Chester likes to be in charge," Alice said.

Les relaxed and said, "Glad you know that about him, Alice."

"Remember, Les, I live on the same block with him as you do," she said. "I know he's been trying to be the leader of the neighborhood for the last twenty years."

"I found that out ten years ago when I first moved into the neighborhood," Les told him. "I hadn't been in the neighborhood a day before he knocked on my door, introduced himself, and told me anything I wanted to know about anybody in the neighborhood all I had to do was just ask him. And I'll bet he could have told me, too."

"I wonder what they are talking about," Pedro said.

"Football, I'll bet," Janis said.

I wonder, Les thought.

"What do you mean convince the aliens we need them?" Rawlings asked.

"They need us," Chester corrected him.

"So what do you mean by that?"

"They may have the technology to kill billions of people on Earth and destroy our political and military systems, but they're going to need Earth people to control those that are still alive,"

"I don't get you," Rawlings said.

"I'm not surprised, Rawlings," he said. "You're a man who has spent his life running through life without a thought about your future. I, on the other hand, like to know what the future has in store for me."

"Are you talking about contacting the aliens?" Rawlings asked him in a shocked tone.

"Right now they probably know every move the human race is making to strike back at them, and they are prepared for them, too. So what I've got to do when we make contact with them is to let them know I want to work with them."

"How the fuck you're going to do that, Wimp?" Rawlings asked him.

He looked at Rawlings and said, "Consider this, which is better to be a slave, or to be an overseer of slaves."

Rawlings didn't say anything because he didn't know what to say.

"Overseers live far better lives than slaves." He looked at the confused expression on Rawlings' face and added, "They also have access to the prettiest slave women, too."

Rawlings grinned.

I knew this lummox thought threw his dick when he isn't thinking of making the game winning touchdown Chester thought as he saw the grin on Rawlings' face. He reached down with his left hand and patted his iPhone in his pants pocket. *Keep off the iPhones you said, Pedro. Well, I will until the time is right.*

CHAPTER 11

Henry was lying in his bed wondering what to do, and didn't know what time it was when he heard Susan moaning as she woke up. He got out of bed and walked over to her bed and stood next to it watching her moving her arms and legs under the bed cover as she woke up.

She saw Henry and asked, "What happened?"

"Get a good grip on yourself, Susan" he told her.

"What are you talking about, Henry?" she asked as she pulled herself up on her elbows.

"You remember the attack on the battalion?" he asked her.

"How the hell could I forget?" she replied. "Whoever attacked us shot the battalion to pieces in a matter of a few minutes." She looked around the room. "I was hit in the stomach. Worse pain I ever felt."

"We were attacked by aliens," he told her as he closely watched her face to see how she'd respond.

She looked at him with an expression of 'are you crazy'. "What the hell are you talking about?"

"You remember the two armored vehicles running through the camp with two guns in its moveable turret firing in all directions and two guns in the front and two in the rear of the vehicles?"

"I hit one of them in the front with an armor piercing RPG and it exploded harmlessly against it," she said. "I got shot in the stomach right after that."

"I was next to you and caught some of what hit you in my stomach, too," he told her.

Susan looked him over. "You don't look like you were hit."

"These aliens have remarkable medicine," he said as he lifted the long lose shirt he was wearing to show her the wound in his stomach that was rapidly healing.

"Your wound looks like it has almost healed," she said.

"And so has yours," he told her.

She stared at him for a few seconds, lay back down, and pulled her arms from under the cover and pushed it back and pulled up her shirt to reveal a bandage on her stomach. "I've still got a wound."

"But does it feel like it did when you were hit?"

She allowed her mind to move over her body before she spoke. "It feels like a bad stomach ache that's gradually going away. But I know I was hit bad."

"Me, too, and I felt just like you do when I woke up hours ago," he said.

She looked up at him and said, "You said we were attacked by aliens?"

"Yes."

"Then they are going to pay a terrible price for attacking us," she told him.

He shook his head.

"What?" she asked.

"Remember the Colonel sent out a call for help over every military frequency we had and received no answer?"

"Yes, I remember that. He eventually sent out a call on the citizen band frequency," she said. "But no one answered. After that I got hit."

"The aliens have taken down every military force on this planet along with all the political leadership. There are no governments left," he said. "According to them most of the people on this planet are dead over seven billion."

Susan stared at him with a face that gradually went white with fear. "No, you're wrong, Henry. They couldn't do that. They would have been seen long before they could do that. All the politicians and military leaders on Earth would have gotten together and drove them away."

Henry lowered his head and walked back to his bed and sat down on it. "I sure wish you were right, Susan. But I don't think you are."

"Maybe once we're better we can get out of here and find out the truth," she suggested.

"Maybe, but for now we should act like prisoners of war looking for a chance to escape, without looking like we're looking for a chance to escape," he told her as he lay down. "Food is being brought to us soon so just relax until it comes."

"Yeah," she said with the sound of defeat in her voice as she relaxed.

For an hour they lay silently on their beds. Susan not wanting to believe what Henry had told her, and Henry not believing what he had been told and had told to her.

They were both on the verge of falling asleep when the door to their room opened and a robot with a square metal body rolled into the room with a cart with plastic covered containers of food on food on it.

"What's that?" Susan asked.

"I am a serving unit," the robot answered.

"What the hell, it talks," she exclaimed in a shocked voice.

"And that food on the cart is for us?" Henry asked the robot.

"Yes."

"How do we know it won't kill us?" Susan asked.

"A biological analysis of you Earthlings indicates you are biologically like the Tabors and can eat Tabor food and drink without it harming you."

"Where did the food come from?" Henry asked.

"From the kitchen on the fourth level."

"Is that where the Tabor cooks are?" he asked.

"All cooks in this compound are robots supervised by Tabor Warriors."

"What about the other sixteen Tabor compounds on Earth? Do robots prepare food for the twelve thousand Tabors in each of them?"

Susan realized Henry was trying to get information from the robot.

"There is only one Tabor compound on Earth."

"Where is it?" she asked.

"In a place called Nevada. Do you wish this unit to place the food containers on the table?"

"No, you can just leave the cart. We'll help ourselves," Henry said.

"How many robots prepare food for the twelve thousand Tabors in this compound?" Susan asked as she sat up in bed and threw the cover back and put her legs over the right side of the bed.

"There are only twenty-six Tabors in this compound, and two cooking robots." The robot detached from the serving cart, and rolled around to the right and started for the door.

"The other five hundred thousand haven't arrived yet?" Henry asked as he got out of bed.

"That information is not available to this unit," it responded as it headed for the door.

"Stop," Henry said as he stood up.

The robot stopped and turned around to face Henry.

"Is there a washroom in this room?" Susan asked as she put her feet on the floor and stood up. She was surprised at the lack of pain in her stomach and how steady she was on her feet.

"That is unanswerable."

"Is there a place where the Tabors go to clean up and relieve themselves."

"The cleanup room is to the left of the second bed against the wall."

She turned around and looked at the wall to the left of her bed. "I don't see a door."

"Where the wall is segmented," Henry told her.

The robot turned around and rolled from the room.

"Come on," Susan said as she walked toward the segmented door on legs that felt as strong as they had been before she was shot. "We might as well wash up and eat."

Henry looked at her and wondered what she had in mind. *She certainly doesn't want to have sex.* Then he understood why she wanted him to wash up with her. He walked toward the segmented door.

Susan pushed the door and it slid to one side revealing a bathroom with a vanity that had two face bowls but no mirror above it, a glass enclosed shower, a toilet with a curtain hanging around it from a round brass rod, and bathtub. "All the comforts of homes we no longer have," she said as she entered the bathroom and walked to the face bowl on the right.

Henry walked into the bathroom and took the face bowl on the left. He raised the brass handle and water came out of a plain looking metal pipe. He moved the handle to the left then right till he learned which direction gave him hot water and which gave him cold water. He adjusted the handle till he got the temperature he wanted and took a short towel off the rack to his left.

Susan did the same as she looked around. "No soap."

Henry looked at the vanity and saw two drawers on the left side and opened the top one. Inside it was an instrument that looked like an electric razor and a plastic tube with the word 'cleaning cream' on the front of it. "Open the top drawer on your right. You'll probably find a tube with the word cleaning cream on it."

She did so and found the same thing. "What do we do with this? Wash our faces without using water?"

Henry looked around the faucet and saw what he thought was a device for stopping up the face bowl. He pushed it down and watched the face bowl fill with water. Then he squirted some of the liquid into the water and it became bubbly like it was soap. He put his left hand in it and moved it around. "Feels like soap subs." He pulled his hand out and smelled it. "That' what it is." He leaned forward and began to wash his face.

Susan did the same thing. As she washed her face she said to Henry, "You know they're watching us."

He washed his face without looking at her and said, "Yeah, but why? They know we can't go anyplace."

"Maybe we're like gold fish in a bowl," she said. "That may be why they kept us alive."

"Maybe, but that robot said we're biologically like them. So why watch us? They know we can't escape A guy by the name of Commander Rush told me while you were out all the Earth's military and political systems have been destroyed."

"I don't know," she said. "I'm hungry let's try their food."

"I drew a diagram on a pad I got from that screen on the table," he told her. "It's in my backpack."

They rinsed the cleaning cream from their faces and used the towels on the racks to dry off.

The face bowls automatically drained and a blast of warm air rose from the faucets.

They leaned forward to completely dry their faces and hands.

A minute later they had pushed the cart between their beds and were sitting on their beds tasting the food which looked like a vegetable and noodle combination.

"Taste like vegetables," Susan said.

"Not bad either," Henry said as he reached for a glass container that contained a pinkish and orange colored liquid. He poured some into one of the two glasses and tasted it.

"What does it taste like?" she asked him.

"Like nothing I've ever tasted before. Like a combination of fruit juices and it's good," he said.

"The future slaves of the Tabors were well fed," Susan said as she filled the remaining glass with the pinkish/orange liquid.

"My ancestors were slaves, Susan. And they fought like mad to be free, and I'm not about to let their efforts be in vain," he said. "How do you feel?"

"Fine," she said. "But I do feel the hole that was in my stomach, but it doesn't hurt."

"Me, too," he said.

"What are we going to do, Henry?" she asked him as she ate.

"Use our common sense and the escape and evasion training we've received," he whispered to her then got up and walked to the screen on the table. "What time is it?"

"The time is one thirty mountain time by Earth's method of determining time," answered the screen.

Susan got up and walked up next to him and said, "A talking TV screen."

"I figure it's some sort of computer," Henry said.

"Where are all the guards?" Susan asked.

"All the guards are at their posts or in their quarters."

"Where are those?" she asked.

"That information is not available to this unit."

"We couldn't be that lucky," Henry said.

"You said you got a pad out of your backpack and made a drawing of this place," she said.

"Yeah, it's in the closet between our beds along with our uniforms, underwear, and boots but no weapons, iPhones, or radios."

"So we relieve ourselves if we have to and get dress and take a walk around this place," she told him.

Henry nodded as he turned from the screen.

Ten minutes later they were dressed and ready to take a walk.

"Nice of them to leave our canteens," he said as he pulled his canteen out of its pouch. "Let's fill them with water and start walking."

"You fill them while I make a copy of that diagram you drew of this place," she said as she removed her canteen from its pouch and handed it to him.

He took the pad from his backpack and gave it and the pen to her and walked to the bathroom to fill their canteens.

A minute later they were ready to leave. They walked to the door the robot had entered and left by and started to push it when it automatically opened. They looked at each other a few seconds then walked through the open door into a semi-dark wide, long hallway. Without a word they turned to their left where Henry's diagram showed there were stairs. They saw nothing that looked like cameras but they were certain they were being watched, and they were correct. Every move and word they had made in the room they were in had been recorded and every move they were making now was being recorded.

Theia was in the control room at the top level and watched them walk to the stairwell, the door automatically opening, them entering and starting up the stairs for the first level. She knew when they reached level one, because she'd been given orders to watch them not to stop them, they would find an exit and leave. But where could they go on a world that had no political or military organizations?

They will contact others who are like them, and resist us if they can manage to avoid our patrols, she thought. Commander Rush was her commanding officer and like all Tabor warriors she obeyed his orders without question. But she thought he was being too lenient with these two Earthlings. Both had fought hard according to Zack and were captured alive only because they were wounded and unconscious. If she had been in charge, she would have ordered Zack to kill them. If these two met others like them, they would resist the Tabors attempts to turn them into slaves for the Warrior Class.

The last Overlord's lenience toward the government on Tabor had resulted in the government training soldiers that attacked the Warrior Class and destroyed their power base on Tabor. It had taken the government soldiers of Tabor fifty years of bloody fighting before they were powerful enough to force the Warrior Class to look for another world. And the Earthlings had a long and bloody history of fighting each other to be free. Such people would reorganize and fight back, and this time they wouldn't be fighting each other. All the skills they had learned fighting each other over the centuries they would use against the Warrior Class, and wouldn't stop fighting until they were all eliminated. The conquest of Earth would not be as easy as destroying their political and military systems.

She rose from her seat at the main computer console and walked toward the door that led to the hallway. *The fleet will be here in a little more than eight days and we can begin the destruction of any resistance to our dominating this planet.* She stopped at the opened door and turned around and looked at the large screen on the wall that showed Susan and Henry walking up the stairs to level one. *We will win because we will not make the mistakes the last Overlord made on Tabor.* She walked through the door to the elevator and pushed the call button to go to her quarters thinking, *there is no point in watching those two. Wherever they go we will be able to get them back in a few Earth hours.*

CHAPTER 12

4:30 a.m.

They had made better time than they'd expected on the two lane country roads and even the dirt roads that were devoid of cars and trucks, they'd avoided the expressways for fear of running into angry people with guns, and reached the wooded area in the North Platt of Nebraska at four thirty. They parked the three Humvees in a semi-circle and got out.

"Let's make some coffee," Rawlings suggested. "I'll look around for some wood to start a fire."

"The sun will begin to rise in about an hour," Alex said. "Coffee would be nice to have before we get some rest."

"No, fires till the sun's up," Les said. "A fire in the darkness could be seen for a mile."

"With magnifying binoculars it can be seen for five miles," Level said. "And we should assume the aliens have far better than that. Get those ground mats we have and lay them on the ground in front of the Humvee you rode in. One of us should stay awake after we've had coffee while the rest of us sleep. Reliefs should be every hour till we've all had at least eight hours of rest."

"I don't need eight hours of sleep," Rawlings said. "I can do good on just four hours."

"Then you stay awake and get some fire wood, but don't start a fire until the sun's up," William told him.

"I've never slept on the ground," Nancy said.

"Then you're about to have an experience," Level told her. "Clear the ground of stones and sticks as best you can in the dark and then roll your ground mat out. Get a blanket if you need one. And when you lie down cover your face and ears with a handkerchief or towel."

"Why?" Nancy asked.

"To stop bugs from crawling into your mouth, nose, and ear channels."

"Oh, God," Nancy exclaimed.

"I'll help you get wood," Chester said to Rawlings.

Rawlings walked off into the forest with Chester following him.

"Do you mind getting two ground mats out, Alice, while I clear a place for us?" Les asked her.

"You and Level are ex-soldiers," Judith said. "Show us what to do?"

"Will do," Level said as he began to move his feet around on the ground kicking stones and sticks to one side.

Les started doing the same thing. Alex, Pedro, and William, watched them for a few seconds then began doing to same thing. Within ten minutes they had cleared a space wide and long enough for all of them to lie on the ground with more than a foot of space between each person.

"What if we have to go to the washroom?" Nancy asked in a concerned voice.

"Let's get those entrenching tools and dig a slit latrine for the men and the women, Les," Level said. "You can all come along and see what we do so you can do it the next time."

"God, I use to make three thousand a day as a model, and now I'm reduced to shitting and pissing in a hole in the ground in the woods," Nancy moaned.

"You could be dead," Janis told her.

"Then I wouldn't have to worry about shitting and pissing in the woods," she replied.

"Let's see if there's a source of water nearby," William suggested.

"I wouldn't suggest wandering around in these woods at night," Les advised them. "You trip over something you could break a leg or some other important bone, and remember there aren't any doctors within miles that we know of."

"And if there are any close by they'll want to save their medical supplies for their families and neighbors," Pedro said.

"We'll dig the slit latrines on the other side of Rawlings' Humvee ten feet beyond the right side of the hood," Level said. "If you have to use the washroom, use your night vision glasses, and be careful where you walk."

Les and Level got their night vision goggles and the entrenching tools from the back of the Humvees they'd ridden in and walked to where they intended digging the slit latrines.

"We've become little more than cave men," Judith moaned as she and the others followed them wearing their night vision glasses.

"So will the rest of the world if some people out there haven't stopped whining and started thinking," Alex said. "If they can just keep the coal, solar, and nuclear powered power plants operating, they'll be able to maintain a resemblance of a modern civilized society."

Ten minutes later they all came back.

"If you've got to go walk straight from the front Humvee till you reach a wooden fence we set up, and wear your night vision goggles," Level said. "The women's latrine is on the right side. The men's latrine is on the left side. And gentlemen don't think because you don't have to sit down to pee you can just walk around to the other side of the Humvees and take a piss. We'll all hear and smell the odor, and we've got enough problems so use the slit latrines."

"Now would be a good time to go and go in twos," Les said as he walked back to his Humvee and put his entrenching tool in the back. "I'll put toilet paper on the hood of the second Humvee, and don't waste it." He closed the Humvee hatch, put toilet paper on the hood of the second Humvee and walked to where he saw a ground mat and knelt down. "This is mine I hope."

"Yes, it is," Alice said. "I put it next to mine. You don't mind do you?"

"No, because you people are the only family I've got," he said as he lay down.

"And you're the only family we have, Les," Janis said.

"Have Rawlings and Chester come back?" Level asked.

"I haven't heard them," Alex said. He was stretched out on his mat trying to relax.

"I hope you all have you side arms with you?" Les asked them.

"You don't think we're going to need them, do you?" Judith asked him. She was lying on her mat with a handkerchief over her face and ears.

"No, but if we do have to use them make sure you identify your target," he said. *Rawlings is a macho man who thinks this is all some great football game, and Chester is a man with a strong desire to lead. I hope they don't cause trouble.* He closed his eyes feeling guilty about what he thought of Rawlings and Chester. Like them or not they were in the same leaky boat with the rest. He was asleep in a few minutes.

"Let's go back," Chester said with an arm load of wood. "We've got enough wood."

"How you gonna make contact with them aliens?" Rawlings asked him.

"I don't have to make contact with them," he said. "Once we're in that part of northern Nevada Alex and Pedro detected that surge in they're going to detect us. And then I'll make my offer."

"What offer?" Rawlings was carrying large collection of branches on his left shoulder.

"To help them control what's left of the human race."

"What about those others," Rawlings asked him.

"Fuck'em," Chester answered.

Rawlings nodded his agreement with a big grin on his face.

They carried the firewood they had gathered back to the Humvees and dumped the wood on the side of the Humvees away from the others and settled down to their hour watch.

CHAPTER 13

The Warriors of Tabor didn't call their command rooms at the top of their ships the bridge, but the captain's control room. It was located not on the top of the five mile round, fifteen hundred feet tall ships, each story was sixty feet high with six inch thick ceilings and floors, but in front of the ship as if it was pulling the rest of the ship behind it. Antennae and radar scanners were on the top and bottom of the ships in the middle of the ships. The designer of their space ships had been an Overlord and didn't like the idea that he was a part of anything including the space ship he was on, because as Overlord he was separate and superior to all of the warriors of the Warrior Class and all other humans on the Planet Tabor.

Five hundred years ago Tabor was a world torn by wars between various warlords that controlled various parts of the planet called sections and they had been continuously fighting each other for three hundred years. The elected leaders of the Eastern Section of Tabor, the warlord of that sector allowed elections to give the people the illusion of political power, had decided the only way to end the continuous wars of Tabor was to create a class of men and women dedicated to fighting and provide them with the best weapons the scientists and technicians of Tabor could produce at the expense of the taxpayers of the Eastern Sector. And they had done exactly that within seventy years.

They had produced, through the process of cloning – hundreds of years ahead of Earth's primitive cloning methods in the twentieth century - in secret labs, a force of one million elite warriors Tabor had never had before. These warriors were physically and mentally fit men and women who were trained in the art of killing, and cared for nothing except fighting and victory in battle. They were given drugs that made them immune to disease and taught never to surrender which was dishonorable. Death in battle was the greatest honor a member of the Warrior Class could achieve. Growing old and dying of old age was a sign of weakness which no warrior wanted. Even suicide was considered to be better than death by old age, and very few died by old age or suicide.

Within fifty years the wars that been fought for three hundred years were brought to an end, but the planet was in shambles. Many of its plants and animals were dead. The skies were filled with pollution, and much of the water wasn't fit to drink unless it had been purified by an expensive process.

The political leaders created a single democratic world government and used the Warrior Class to enforce laws which helped them to establish law and order and to clean up the planet. They increased the population, which stood at three hundred million when the centuries of war ended, to a level where civilization could again take over and Tabor could again become a planet of peace loving men and women who could promote science and technology for the good of all. And they succeeded in their goals in a hundred and five years.

Learning, science, and technology advanced rapidly during those years. They achieved space travel then developed ships that could fly faster than the speed of light and sent ships to explore the galaxy, travelling to distant planets, including Earth.

But the Warrior Class which was six million strong and well-armed and experienced in the art of war and had never been a part of the general population realized that if peace continued as a way of life on Tabor they would become useless. So the commander of the Warrior Class gave himself the title of Overlord and announced to the political leaders of Tabor that he and his warriors were now masters of Tabor. And since they were the only ones who were armed and in excellent physical condition, they took over Tabor.

But they were warriors who knew how to fight and obey without question. They weren't teachers, scientists, technicians, or politicians. They had no knowledge or skills to govern a united Tabor. So the political leaders rather than face centuries of more war agreed with them and let the Tabor Warrior Class rule the planet while they served. And there was another hundred years of peace on Tabor with the Warrior Class as masters who did little more than train for war and act as police officers. They had little to do with the common people because they considered them to be inferiors and they despised the concepts of equality and freedom for all.

Knowledge expanded among the general population, and science and technology continued to advance. Tabor became a clean healthy planet with a growing population of healthy people.

At the end of the hundred year period of the Warrior Class rule the general population demanded police officers that didn't act like soldiers but obeyed laws that respected the rights of the individual. The political leaders convinced the Warrior Class to move into isolated areas of the planet while convincing them they were still masters of Tabor, and began the slow process of replacing the Warrior Class with an army made up of regular people and controlled by the elected government.

The Overlords soon realized they were gradually being phased out of existence and lead a revolt against the government plunging Tabor into fifty years of war. But this time the government forces were ready and won and the Warrior Class found itself facing extinction. Rather than have that happen the Overlords looked into space for a world similar to Tabor where they could go and establish their own world of Warriors. Using the knowledge about space the Tabor government had they learned of the existence of Earth and that it had an environment and gravity identical to that of Tabor. They demanded ships to go to Earth and conquer it.

The government refused their demand. The government knew Earth's political situation and didn't believe it was ready for contact by a more advanced space travelling peaceful civilization. And they knew what would happen if the Warrior Class went to Earth. They would conquer it and enslave the people of Earth.

The Warrior Class started another war to get what they needed.

While the war was being fought, the Warrior Class learned all they could about Earth. The most important thing they learned about Earth was that it was two centuries behind Tabor in science and technology, making it the perfect planet to conquer. Twenty-two years before they were ready to leave Tabor they sent a scout ship with one Warrior on it to Earth to learn where they had to strike first to dominate Earth and where an invasion force had to land to completely conquer Earth.

In the meantime, they conquered the most advanced parts of Tabor and built ships and equipment to leave Tabor. But time was against them as the forces of the government grew more powerful and won more victories. But the forces of the government were too late to stop the new Overlord, Zap Brangan, and the Warrior Class from building a hundred space ships in orbit about Tabor's moon.

A year before Zap Brangan was ready to leave Tabor he sent Commander Rush, his most trusted officer, to Earth on one ship with twenty-five chosen Warriors. They had the information the scout had secretly sent back to Tabor on where to land on Earth and establish a base to destroy Earth's military and political systems, so that Earth would be helpless and easy to conquer when he and the Warrior Class arrived. Commander Rush had been given weapons that would make it possible for him and his warriors to do what the Overlord wanted in a few hours once they had landed on Earth and established a base of operations.

The Tabor government learned of Overlord Brangan's plan from a spy working among the officers and made plans to stop him. Brangan's officers discovered the spy and killed her. But the Tabor Army attacked Brangan's ships with missiles and laser rays just as he was using shuttles to load his Warriors on the ships and damaged many of the ships before they could leave orbit. Overlord Brangan lost a quarter of his Warriors as they were leaving Tabor's moon with the one hundred ships they'd built. The bodies of the dead were floating in orbit about the moon as Brangan's force left.

When Rush had done exactly what the Overlord wanted, he sent Overlord Brangan a message telling him that he was successful. Earth was helpless and ready for conquest by the Overlord and the Warrior Class. But because of the damage done to his ships the Overlord's journey to Earth was slower than he liked.

Overlord Zap Brangan sat in the captain's chair looking at the large screen on the wall in front of the navigation console that showed the vastness of space and the many bright stars. He had a trouble look on his face.

"Do not worry, Overlord," the Captain standing next to Brangan and looking at his face told him. "We will succeed."

"I have no doubt about that, Captain," he replied in an assured voice. "Rush has never failed me and never will. Eighty to ninety percent of Earth's human population has been disintegrated along with most of its political and military leaders. Those that remain will be easily subdued and made to serve us. My only concern is our ships. They suffered heavy damage before we left orbit and I'm hoping they will be able to reach Earth before our engines fail."

"The damage was great and half of the warriors on board the ships were wounded in our escape," the Captain said. "But I have made sure the damage done to each ship has been repaired and the wounded are being taken care of. We have more than enough warriors to complete the conquest of Earth."

"But if there are people on Earth who know how to operate their missiles they may be able to launch enough of them with their nuclear weapons on them to destroy the fleet before we establish orbit above Earth."

"I am sure Commander Rush has made sure such people are dead. Without them their missiles with nuclear warheads will remain harmless in their holes in the ground," the Captain said.

"If one of their primitive nuclear bombs should explode next to the fleet the blast would be enough to render our ships useless, and we would all die in space," the Overlord said. His face mirrored his fear.

"We will reach Earth in eight days, Overlord," the Captain told him. "If there are still people on Earth who can launch their nuclear missiles, they are far from where the missiles are and in shock over what Rush and his command has done to their world. Our shuttle craft are in excellent shape, so we will be able to land a hundred thousand warriors on Earth in a few hours once we are in orbit above it and take control of those missiles before any of the Earthlings can get to them and launch them against us."

"Commander Rush said nothing about where those missiles were located," the Overlord said.

"They are useless to defend Earth, Overlord, no matter where they are located," the Captain said with the sound of certainty in his voice. "Once we are in orbit above Earth we shall locate those missiles and render them useless to any Earth resistance we encounter."

The Overlord stood up and turned around and walked toward the captain's control room elevator. "I have no doubt about that, Captain, but as Overlord I shall worry until we have landed and taken control of the Earth. I shall be in my quarters. Alert me if Commander Rush sends a message to the fleet."

"I will obey, Overlord," the Captain said coning to attention and waiting until the Overlord had entered the elevator and the door had closed. He relaxed and walked to his chair and sat down as he said to his first officer, "I want to know the exact condition of all our ships, Roy."

Roy from his desk looked at the analysis console on the desk and brought up a list of the Tabor ships on the computer screen in front of him and said, "Seventy of the ships are still not working at fifty percent level, Captain, but since we are travelling in a circle those ships that have over fifty percent efficiency have the others in their tractor beams. All the ships' life support systems are working properly, and all have enough food and water to last us six weeks."

"Are repairs being made on the damaged ships?" he asked.

"Yes, sir," Roy replied. "The repairs will be completed within two weeks after we reach Earth."

"The wounded?" the Captain asked.

"All of them are being taken care of. Within a month they will all be ready for battle again," Roy said.

"Do we have enough warriors ready to gain control of a portion of Earth we can use as a base to conquer the rest of Earth?"

"We have a hundred and fifty thousand, sir," he said.

"Very good," the Captain said. "Within two weeks after we've reached Earth the planet will be ours."

"Yes, sir," Roy replied as he looked over the console and checked to make sure everything he'd told the Captain about the ships in the fleet was correct.

CHAPTER 14

1:40 a.m.

"Where are we now?" Susan asked as she looked at the diagram she held in her left hand. With the exception of the bandage on her stomach she didn't feel her wound.

"Between level two and three," Henry said as he looked at his diagram.

"How do you feel?" she asked him as she followed him up the stairs.

"Okay, how do you feel? Your wound isn't bothering you, is it?"

"I can't even feel it," she told him. "All I can feel is the bandage over the wound."

"Yeah, me, too," he said.

"Doesn't it strike you as odd that people with such medicine and technology don't know we're in this stairway?"

"Yeah, and I'm wondering what sort of surprise we're going to run into before we get out of this underground complex," he said.

"Why leave us alone? Why keep us alive? Why give us food and drink? Why didn't they take our uniforms?" she asked him.

"Why let us leave the room we were in?" he asked.

"Because they want us to escape," she said. "The question is why do they want us to escape?"

"Because they want to learn more about how trained military people on this planet act," he answered.

"That's what I've been thinking," she told him.

"Well, Susan, let's not disappoint them," he said.

"This diagram you drew shows supply rooms on the second level," she said as she looked at it.

"I wonder what's in them," he said.

"I got a feeling we're dealing with very arrogant people," she said.

"Who expect success," he added.

"There's no way any army on Earth would let prisoners to wonder around like these warrior people are letting us do," Susan said.

"Maybe they've always been successful on Tabor and don't worry about prisoners," he said.

"Then why the hell are they here on Earth?"

Henry looked at his diagram. "We're nearing level two."

"You think we'll make it out?" she asked him.

"Yeah, because I've got a funny feeling there are guards outside waiting to catch us and take us back."

"But why do that?"

"Remember your escape and evasion training?" he said. "The best way to break a prisoner's resistance is to let them think they've escaped. Once they're caught again their will to resist will be less than before."

"Well, I'm not going to break," she assured him.

"We're at the door of level two," he said as he stopped in front of a metal door.

Susan stopped next to him. "Well, we've come this far." She reached forward with her left hand and pushed against the door.

It quietly slid to one side.

"I sure wish I had a gun in my hand," Henry said as he walked through the open door into a partial lit hallway like the one outside their hospital room.

They walked a few yards before they stopped and looked around.

"Nothing," he said.

"A setup if I've ever seen one," she said.

He looked at the diagram in his left hand. "Straight ahead to a wide corridor then up to level one and then to the right is the exit."

"And a grinning guard with a ray gun in his hand," she added.

They started walking. They walked in silence for ten minutes constantly looking around for the expected grinning guard with a ray gun.

"This is stupid," Susan said. "They fight a battle with our battalion and kill everyone but us then let us walk out of this compound."

"Naw, this was planned," he said.

"What are you talking about?" Susan asked him.

"How long have you been in a combat battalion?"

"About a year," she said.

"I've been in the Army almost two years, and I've always been in mobile armored infantry," he said.

"So what has that got to do with this situation?"

"Simple, they attacked our battalion and kill everyone but us because we were unconscious and wounded," he said. "These warriors want to know just how resourceful we can be. Let us escape after they patch us up to see just what we'll do."

"They know even if they have destroyed every political and military organization in the world there will be hundreds of millions of people left who will fight them," she said.

"They want to find out what they're going to be up against when they start the final conquest of Earth," Henry said. "And we're the lab rats they intend getting some information from by watching us because we're trained soldiers and have fought them in the past."

"So we get out and run and tell anyone we can find what type of aliens these Tabors are," she said.

"When you want to conquer a people you've got to study them, or you may run into something you didn't expect," he said.

"Henry, if what they've told you about knocking out the governments and military of Earth is true they've already conquered us,"

"But there must be at least a billion left out there who are willing to fight like hell rather than become the slaves of these warriors," he said.

She thought for a few seconds before she said, "They can't afford a long drawn out war, and the survivors need to fight such a war to stop them from taking over our planet."

"There must be hundreds of millions of people still alive who know how to run the technology and industries of Earth, and these Tabors want to make sure they can handle them. So they arrange to let us go to get some idea of what they might run into."

Susan didn't respond because she agreed with him.

They walked until they reached stairs that went up to level one then walked up the stairs to a corridor that went in the direction of the exit on Henry's diagram. They turned in the direction of the exit and walked for what they estimated was an eighth of a mile making sure to keep a wall on their left side before they saw a wide, high wall directly in front of them. They walked up to it and stopped.

"Why have a road go up to a wall?" he said as he looked over the wall that was sixty feet high.

Susan looked to her left then looked up at the top of the wall where it joined the ceiling. "It's segmented at the top and on the left side, probably on the right, too."

Henry looked over the wall. "Yeah, it is. This wall probably rises when a large vehicle wants to get out and in."

"Let's see if we can get out," she said as she stepped forward and touched the wall.

For a few seconds nothing happened.

"Trapped like rats in a cage," she said.

The wall began to move up on silent hinges. Warm desert air rushed into the compound. Without a word between them they both walked rapidly through the open wall out into the desert. Henry turned to his right and walked quickly.

"Be careful," Susan told him. "We don't have night goggles."

"Let's keep moving until we can find a good place to hide," he said. "I've got something I want to tell you."

There was no moon but the dark sky was clear and filled with numerous twinkling stars, but their vision was limited to a few feet in either direction. As they walked they began to feel the heat of the desert. After ten minutes they found some boulders with thick desert plants growing around them. They carefully moved in among the boulders listening for the sound of rattle snakes. When they were sure there were no snakes or other animals around they stopped and sat down.

"Take off your pack and search all your clothing for anything unusual," Henry told Susan as he removed his backpack.

"Looking for tracking devices," she said as she did as he said.

Five minutes later she said. "I didn't find anything that's not supposed to be on my clothing."

"Check the bottoms and heels of my boots to see if they've been loosened and replaced," he said as he leaned back and held up his feet.

She knelt in front of him and checked the soles and heels of his boots. "If they have been removed and tracking devices put in them they've done a good job of resealing them."

"Sit down," he said as he got up on his knees and checked the soles and heels of her boots.

"So what's this you've got to tell me?" she asked after he'd checked her boot soles and boot heels and sat next to her.

"We should go back into that compound and see if we can get into one of them supply rooms," he said, leaning close to her so he could see her face.

Susan stared into his face and didn't say anything. She was thinking.

"I know it sounds crazy, Susan, but we don't know a damn thing about the type of weapons these aliens have, just that they're better than anything we've got. And if the rest of the people on Earth are going to have a fighting chance to stop them from taking over our world they've got to know what we're up against," he said hoping she'd agree with him. "And I don't think they'd expect us to come back."

"We got no food, no weapons, no way of contacting anyone, and only a limited amount of water, Henry, and we're in a desert," she told him.

"And we don't know what direction we're facing now that we're out and there's no moon," he added. He looked around into the darkness and said, "We don't even know if they're watching us at this moment."

"Sounds crazy, Henry. It sounds fucking insane, but I'm game if you are," she said. "But I don't suggest we go back the way we got out."

"According to that screen in our room this compound is a quarter of a mile in circumference," he said. "We should be able to walk to the other side and rest a few hours before sunrise."

"If the sun isn't going to rise within an hour," she said as she stood up. "But let's go."

Henry stood up and they started walking away from the exit they'd left for the other side of the compound.

"Why?" Susan asked him.

"Why what?" he asked her.

"Why can't they afford a long drawn out war?" she asked him.

Henry thought as he walked then said, "Because they don't have the forces available to them."

"What about those five hundred thousand on those one hundred ships you told me about?" she asked him.

Henry thought for a few seconds then said, "The best I can think of, Susan, is there's something wrong with them and maybe their ships, too."

"We've got to get some of their weapons and get away to contact somebody so we can tell them and we can fight back," Susan said.

Henry didn't reply because he agreed with her.

Zack was in the bedroom of his quarters awaiting a call from one of the two patrols outside the compound telling him they'd spotted the two Earthlings and were following them. When no call came after two hours, he got out of bed and walked out the bedroom to a table with a computer on it and said, "On."

"Working."

"Show me the two humans in the medical section."

A picture of Susan and Henry appeared on the screen. He watched them eating then getting dressed and leaving their room. He watched them walk up the five hundred feet of steps to the exit and leave by the overhead door. He looked at the time they had left the compound on the screen. *An hour and a half has passed since they left the compound. They should have been picked up by the patrol outside scanning for them.* He picked up his communicator on the table and asked, "Sergeant Raw, have you picked up the Earthlings who left the compound?"

"No, Lieutenant, but we saw the ramp open and them leaving and the ramp close," he said. "But they moved among some large rocks and plants and then we lost visual contact of them."

"They are probably using the rocks and plants to hide their movements," he said. "Widen your search area and continue your scan until you are relieved within an hour. If you have not found them when your relief comes, inform them of what they are supposed to do."

"Yes, Lieutenant Zack," Raw replied.

Zack ended the call and put his communicator back on the table and walked back into his bedroom and lay on the bed. *I will replace the next relief.*

CHAPTER 15

Day 2 May 4, 7 a.m.

"Alright everybody time to wake up," William called out as he stood next to the rear of the second Humvee. "Coffee's up."

Alice woke up and looked at Les lying on his back sleeping peacefully. She and he had been on watch two hours ago. She reached over and shook his right shoulder waking him up.

He opened his eyes and looked at her and for a moment he felt as if everything was like it had been two days ago. Then he remembered everything that had happened and sat up.

"Coffee's up," she said as she smiled at him.

"Yeah, coffee," he said as he got to his feet.

Level got up, stretched, yawned a deep yawn and said, "Let's find a place to wash up before we have coffee."

"Is that necessary?" Pedro asked. He'd been awake for ten minutes lying on his ground mat looking at the sky and thinking about the surge they'd picked up back in the Oak Park Police Station.

"In the field hygiene helps keep disease at bay," he said.

Janis got to her feet and stretched and said, "He's right. We don't want to get sick without any hospitals close by we can go to."

"There are towns around here we can go to if we need medical help," Rawlings replied.

"You're right, Mr. Rawlings," Nancy said. "But will they be willing to share their limited supply of medicine with us? And don't say we can just barge in a take what we want."

"We've got plenty of fire power," he told her as he stood up.

"The last thing we want is to start killing other Earthlings," Les said. "So let's get our towels and soap and find a place to wash up, and try not to put a lot of soap in the stream or river. Earth has enough problems with pollution."

"I agree," Chester said as he stood up.

Rawlings looked over at him on his left side and decided not to say anything. The time would come soon enough for him to take over.

Alex got to his feet. "Let's spread out and keep in groups of twos. Whoever finds a nice place to clean up sends one back to tell the rest of us."

"Coffee's on the other side of this Humvee," William said as he turned around and walked back to the small fire.

Within forty minutes they'd found a stream and separated in two groups the men in one and the women in the other. Twenty minutes later they were sitting on the ground around the small fire drinking coffee.

"Things don't look so bad now that we've got coffee in us," Judith said.

"It is as far as I'm concerned," Nancy said. "I'm a tea person."

"Sorry we didn't get any tea, Nancy," Les said.

"Forget it. I should have told you I prefer tea," she told him.

"So what do we do until sundown?" Alice asked.

"Get on our iPhones and laptops and find that place that surge came from," Janis said.

"I suggest we use just one," Alex said. "We don't want to drain the batteries in them even if they are solar powered."

"We should each eat something at noon and again a few hours before sundown," Les said. "We don't want to waste what little food we've got."

"Maybe we can find some game and have a nice meal before we leave tonight," William said.

"Any hunters among us?" Alex asked them.

No one said anything.

"I'll take my machine gun and find something," Rawlings offered.

"That thing will tear any animal you find into pieces," Janis said. "I suggest we use the assault rifles for hunting. They have excellent range and make very little noise."

"So who goes hunting?" Nancy asked.

"I'll go," Les volunteered. He didn't want to sit around thinking about his family. He had never believed in mourning over the death of loved ones because it didn't help the living and the dead certainly didn't need any help. Better to get on with life and remember those who were gone.

"A couple of rabbits or deer would be quite nice," Judith said.

"Or a few snakes," Les said. "Even poisoned snakes are supposed to be good eating if you remove their heads."

"Ug," Alice replied.

Les walked to the third Humvee and opened the door and got his assault rifle from between the seats and checked to make sure it was loaded. "I'll be back in two hours if I can't find anything worth killing," he said as he slammed the driver's door and started walking into the woods. He'd gone about twenty yards when Alice caught up with him. "I thought you didn't like the idea of eating snake?"

"I don't, but I will if I have to, especially if I'm real hungry," she said.

They walked in silence for ten minutes before she spoke. "Things have really changed for us, haven't they?"

"Get used to it, because the world we knew of buying food in supermarkets and clothes in clothing stores is a thing of the past," he said. "I don't know what we're going to do if we find these aliens we think are in Nevada, but as of right now we're back where our ancestors were two thousand years before Jesus was born."

"They knew how to survive in a world without stores and conveniences that we've gotten used to," she said.

"Yeah," he agreed. "And I sure wish to hell we had one of them with us."

"You think we're on a fool's errand?" she asked him.

"I think those who were disintegrated are a lot better off than we are," he told her.

They got lucky and killed two rabbits a quarter of a mile from the camp and brought them back.

"Cooking pot's ready," William said as he saw them walk into the camp. "I started getting it ready when I heard your first shot."

"You heard my first shot?" Les asked him as he dropped the two rabbits on the ground.

"Yeah."

"I must have been at least a quarter of a mile away," he said. "I didn't think the sound would carry that far."

"The sound suppresser isn't tightly attached to the muzzle," Janis said. "Always make sure the sound suppresser is screwed tightly to the muzzle."

Les turned around to face the woods and grabbed the thick muzzle of the rifle and turned in to the left till it couldn't turn anymore. "Thanks."

"Who's going to skin and clean those rabbits?" Judith asked.

"We should all help to get used to doing it," Level said as he picked up the two rabbits. "Somebody get a sharp knife."

"Maybe we can make clay pot and pans to cook in," Rawlings said as he stood up.

"Those things aren't as easy to make as they appear to be," Les told him. "Ancient people knew you had to build ovens first then heat them up to make clay pots that could be used for years."

"Well, at least I'm going to lose some weight," Alex said as he got up and went to the Humvee he'd been in for a knife.

Three hours later they had all eaten the two rabbits and were sitting around on the ground with satisfied looks on their faces.

"I hope all of you have toothbrushes, because we all need to get in the habit of brushing our teeth after every meal," Les said. "A tooth ache is the last thing we need among us."

Level looked at his watch. "Let's clean up and get some rest. We should be leaving around sundown."

"We continue toward northern Nevada?" Janis asked.

"Yes," Pedro said as he sat crossed legged with his laptop on his legs. "Because I've gone over the record of that surge we picked up back in Oak Park, and it definitely came from there."

"So we're just going to drive into northern Nevada and start looking around?" Nancy asked.

Level turned to Pedro and said, "Type CZ7138BG54."

Pedro looked up at him. "Why?"

"That's a top secret government code for accessing most of the satellites in orbit around Earth," he said.

"You think it'll work?"

"If the code hasn't been changed," Level answered.

"Including the military satellites, too?" William asked him.

"Those, too. Since the collapse of the Warsaw Pact and the Soviet Union all the major nuclear powers wanted to make sure some damn fool didn't get into a satellite and start launching missiles. So they set up a system where they could check with each other to make sure their missiles were secure." He looked at the startled faces. "Each nuclear power controls its own missiles."

"I thought you got out of the Army ten years ago," he said. "Wouldn't they have changed the code by now?"

"Maybe," Level said.

"If it doesn't work, type Silent Eyes," Alex said. "The CIA doesn't change its codes that often."

"That's why some hacker is always getting into their computers," Rawlings said.

"No they don't," Alex said. "When someone hacks into the CIA's computer system it's because some former agent talked." He looked around at the others. "Like now."

"You still work for them don't you?" Les asked him.

"I'm a damn good computer operator if I do say so myself, and I do. The CIA pays well for part time workers. Be sure to capitalize all the S's and E's."

Pedro used the code Level had given him. The others got up and walked to the stream with their toothbrushes. Fifteen minutes later when they came back he said, "I accessed a low level weather satellite passing over northern Nevada and got a picture of a desert area based on the coordinates of that surge. But there's nothing there."

"So we're headed for an empty desert," Rawlings said.

"Maybe not," Les replied.

"What does that mean?"

"To do what these aliens have done would have required a lot of set up time," he said. "And they wouldn't have wanted to be visible."

"They're underground," Level said. "And I doubt if we'll get any more surges from them unless they're stupid."

"What do you mean?" Chester asked him.

"That surge that we detected may have been an automatic response of a computer trying to hide their location," Les said. "Send up another surge and they say 'here we are'."

"Why are they hiding considering the damage they've already done to Earth?" Judith said. "And they certainly know they've done a lot of damage to Earth."

No one said anything.

"Well, doesn't somebody have something to say?" she asked.

Level and Les were looking at the ground thinking the same thing. "They don't have enough men to finish us off," they both said as the same time.

"They're waiting for reinforcements," Janis said. "My husband use to tell me a first strike is always followed up immediately by a massive assault to finish the enemy off before they can set up a defense. That way few casualties are suffered by the attacking force."

"The aliens who attacked Earth are no more than a reconnaissance in force to prepare the way for a larger attacking force," Les said.

"What's a reconnaissance in force?" Alice asked.

"A large military unit scouting an area with a lot of fire power," he explained.

"But they've tipped their hand. They should have waited until they were ready to take over the Earth before they attacked," Level said.

"They've never read Sun Tzu. Never attack your enemy unless you are prepared for a major battle," Les said.

"Who the hell is he?" Rawlings asked.

"An ancient Chinese general who wrote the book The Art of War," Les told him. "Attack the enemy before you are ready for battle and you alert him to your intentions allowing him to prepare for your final attack."

"I really don't think that applies to our situation," Chester said. "The Earth has already been made defenseless."

"But not conquered," Alex said.

"They destroy our political and military systems, but don't announce to the rest of us they've come to conquer Earth and make it theirs because they're not ready?" Nancy asked.

"That could be the reason why they're hiding," William said.

"What do you know?" Rawlings asked him. "You're just a banker."

"Rawlings, every banker knows that before you move to support the takeover of a company you make sure you've got everything you need to succeed, or you're just going to waste a lot of time and money," he said as he looked at him. "And time and money carry equal weight in the world of business. He who moves too slow with too little money loses. If what Les and Level have said is true, these aliens moved too fast."

"But would they attack without sufficient forces to control the Earth?" Les asked.

"They've got a problem that forced them to attack us when they did," Alice said.

"But what sort of problem that would make them do such a thing?" Nancy asked.

"If we find out where they are in Nevada, we'll find out if we aren't killed first," Les told her.

"Let's clean up, get some sleep, and have coffee and a fruit bar before we leave tonight at seven," Level said.

"The sun doesn't set until a little after seven," Chester said. "I thought moving in the darkness was the best move."

"They've picked up those satellites moving over them and they probably know by now somebody is looking for them," Pedro said. "But they don't know who we are or where we are."

"Let's move," Rawlings said as he stood up. He wanted everyone to think he was with them even though he was only thinking about himself. As much as he disliked Chester, Chester was right. Better to be a slave overseer than a slave.

"Foolish Earthlings," Rush said as he looked at the large screen on the wall of the control room. He was sitting at his desk. "They think they can use their primitive satellites to locate us."

"It would be best, Commander, if we didn't underestimate them," Theia said. "According to our computer those two weather satellites that have passed over this area and scanned it have given them a general location of the compound even if they can't see the compound."

Commander Rush stood up. "You give them more credit than they deserve, Theia. In less than eight days our fleet will arrive and we will complete the conquest of this planet." He turned from the desk and started for the door. "I think I shall go outside and enjoy some of the sights of this planet."

"Be careful, sir," she said. "We have not been able to locate those two Earthling soldiers we allowed to escape."

"Do not worry about them, Theia," he said as he walked out the door that opened for him. "They aren't a serious problem."

Where could they have gone when they left the compound? She thought after Rush left the control room.

CHAPTER 16

May 4, 4:30 a.m.

Henry and Susan had walked a quarter of a mile since they started walking and were now walking in a circular manner keeping to thick desert brush and boulders looking for a door. When the sun started to rise they got their barring's and knew they were walking north.

"I'm glad we ate that food the aliens gave us," Susan said as she walked next to Henry. "I feel great, and I don't feel like I was ever wounded."

"I wish we had some binoculars," Henry said as he looked around.

"Yeah, they would be nice to have," she agreed with him. "I wonder how many patrols they have out."

"That robot that brought us food said there were only twenty-five warriors in the compound," he said as he was thinking. "They'd need medical personal, maybe as many as two or three, and two or three technicians to man the computers in that underground compound."

"That would leave them only twenty warriors to guard the compound and look for us," she said. "Figure two warriors to one of those armored vehicles they've got that would mean they would have only ten patrols. And those patrols would have to be changed every four hours to avoid having the warriors getting bored and careless."

"Assuming they don't have drugs to keep them alert for twenty-four hours," Henry agreed with her. He saw a flat piece of ground a few yards ahead of them. "So there are probably four patrols out looking for us."

"Henry that ground a few yards in front of us looks flatter than the rest of the ground around us," she said.

"I see it," he said as he slowed down and began to look around.

"We've been heading in a northern direction for at least half an hour," she said.

"You tired?"

"A little," she said. "We've been walking since about two in the morning."

"Yeah, I figure we may have walked around the entire compound if it's a quarter of a mile in circumference, and we need rest," he said. "But first let's look over that flat piece of ground."

They stopped a few yards before they reached the flat ground and looked it over for a few minutes.

"What do you think?" Susan asked him.

"Could be another one of those ramps -," he stopped speaking and looked at a narrow grove in the ground. "See that narrow grove?"

"I see it and it's straight," she said.

"Could be the result of rain water during the rainy season," he said as he looked at it.

"No, it isn't, rain wouldn't make a grove that straight," she said as she looked at the direction the grove was going. "That grove moves to the left and right. It connects to two other groves of equal width. They're about four feet apart."

"And they connect to another grove behind us," he said looking behind. "We may have found another exit door like the one we used."

"We got out by a ramp, and this is more of a door," she said as she looked at it.

"They would need a way for people to walk out of the compound without opening a ramp every time someone wanted to go outside," he said.

"Let's find someplace to hide and rest," she suggested.

He looked to his left and saw a cluster of four seven foot boulders thirty feet away. Two were leaning against each other and two were standing up straight with thick three feet tall woody brush growing around them. "Over there looks like a good place," he said, pointing to it.

"Let's go," she said leading the way.

"Wait," he said as he knelt down and picked up four rocks and stood up and threw them one by one in the area between the boulders.

She knew what he was doing was driving out any animals in the opening between the boulders. She knelt down and picked up five rocks and threw them.

They didn't see any animals running from the boulders, and carefully approached them. Once they reached the woody brush they moved carefully around them hoping they didn't surprise any snakes. Once between the boulders they looked around.

"A depression about four feet long and half as wide," Henry said.

"That's why there's such thick brush growing here," Susan said.

"What do you mean?"

"During the rainy season this depression fills up with water," she said as she looked for a place to sit down and placed her hands on the ground. She sat down. "The ground has a damp feel to it."

"This is early May. Spring even in this part of America," he said, sitting down next to her. "I figure the rainy season is just about over."

She turned to face the direction of the groves they'd seen in the ground. "You get some sleep while I watch. I'll wake you up after the sun goes down."

"Where could they be?" Rush asked as he looked at the large screen that showed the outside area around the compound for a distance of twenty miles.

"Maybe they're hiding somewhere?" Dram said.

"No, our scan of the area is complete," Rush said.

"Pardon me, Commander, but our satellites were never adjusted for an in-depth scan of Earth's wild areas," Theia said. "They were programmed only to locate Earth's significant military and political areas because once they were eliminated we would face very little opposition from the isolated forces remaining."

Rush nodded his agreement as he said, "Those two Earth soldiers have no weapons and no food, and only the water they carried in their water containers. Wherever they are they are of very little danger to us."

"There are sources of ground water five miles from the compound, sir," Dram said. "We chose this area two years ago to land on and build the compound because it was dry on the surface with available sources of excellent underground water."

"The Commander knows that, Dram," Theia told him.

"I meant no disrespect, Lieutenant," Dram told her.

"None taken," she replied.

"I just meant that maybe the two Earth soldiers could have gone looking for a source of water to replenish what's in their water containers," he said.

"How soon will it be before the patrols are exchanged?" Rush asked ignoring Dram's explanation.

"By Earth time nine a.m.," Theia said.

"And Zack is sending out only two patrols with two warriors to a vehicle?" he asked.

"For a period of four Earth hours, sir," she said. "To allow the others time to eat, clean up, and rest."

"Leaving only nine warriors in the compound," he mumbled as he thought *I should have asked the Overlord for fifty people to come with me instead of twenty-five.* "How long do you and Dram spend in this control room?"

"Twelve hours each, sir," she answered.

He sighed and said, "Well, the escape of those two Earthlings mean nothing. They have no weapons and no way of contacting any Earthlings out there who may have detected the presence of this compound from our spike." He looked at Dram then at Theia. "You two do not expect trouble before the fleet arrives, do you?"

"No, sir," Dram replied. "There are no Earthlings left who can threaten this compound."

"Even if we are attacked by a large force of Earthling soldiers, sir, we would be able to hold them off till the fleet arrives," Theia said in a positive tone. She had convinced herself the two escaped Earthlings meant nothing to their plan to take over Earth now that it had no major military or political organizations to threaten them with. "But we should conserve energy to avoid draining our solar batteries."

"Reduce surveillance within the compound since we are the only ones in it, and raise the solar array when the star of Earth shines on this part of the planet to recharge our batteries," he ordered as he stood up and turned toward the door. "I will get a communicator and do a patrol outside the compound in case those two Earthlings are hiding around outside."

"Yes, sir," Theia and Dram said at the same time as Rush walked toward the door and out the control room when the door opened.

"Are you tired, Dram?" Theia asked him as she stood up.

"I have been awake for ten hours, Lieutenant," he replied. "But I think I can stay alert for another four hours. Relieve me then."

"That I will," she said and turned around and left the control room glad for another four hours of sleep.

These Earthlings have nothing left that can threaten this compound, Dram thought as he suppressed a yawn. *If I get tired I can take ten minute rest periods every hour.* He shut down all the interior cameras and the alarm systems. The last thing the exhausted guards in the compound needed was a high pitched alarm going off. Anyway there was no threat to the compound. No Earthling knew where it was. He decided to reread the glorious history of the Warrior Class, and brought up a written history of it on the computer screen in front of him.

8:30 p.m.

The sun had disappeared behind the western horizon at seven thirty and the land was cloaked in darkness. The dark clouds in the sky hid the stars from view and Henry had the feeling he was inside a giant closet with the door closed. He looked into the darkness and wondered. *What are we going to do if we can get back inside? Damned if I know.* There was only one thing Henry could do. Sit and watch and wait and pray that something happened that would somehow help them. What that might be he decided to leave to fate.

Susan replaced him on watch at ten thirty and ended of doing what Henry had done. Waiting and watching and trusting to fate. At eleven fifty she placed her hands over her mouth to suppress the sound of a deep loud yawn, and ignored the trembling of the ground. She assumed it was the result of her yawn. But the ground continued to tremble after her yawn had passed. Suddenly the ground underneath her and Henry began to rise.

I've never heard of Earthquakes this far east.

The rising ground woke Henry up. "What's going on?"

"The ground is moving," she told him as she stood up.

He jumped to his feet and grabbed his backpack and asked, "Why?"

She looked in the direction of the rectangular groves on the ground and said, "They're doing it."

He put his backpack on his back and grabbed hers and said, "Let's move to the edge of these boulders."

She grabbed her backpack from him put it on her back and moved to the western edge of the boulders.

"Grab one of the thick branches on that brush," he told her as he moved toward the largest and thickest brush. "Be careful not to put your hand around a thorn we've got enough troubles."

They both ran forward and grabbed a branch of the thickest brush and held on as the ground rose to a height of thirty feet and stopped.

"I hope those boulders don't fall on us," Susan said in a loud voice.

Henry looked around them and on the sides and said, "I don't think they will."

"Look, Henry, if this is an earthquake -," she was cut short when a four wheeled vehicle shot out from under ground and moved west at an incredible speed. "That door was a part of an overhead door."

"Come on and be very quiet," he told her as he pulled himself up and over the brush and dropped down on the edge of the raised ground in a stooped position.

Susan moved as quickly as he did and stopped next to him. "What do we do?"

"Pray for luck," he said as he watched the vehicle move out into the darkness.

The ground began to decline.

"Over the side," he told her as he moved to the edge of the raised ground and grabbed the edge and threw his legs over the edge.

She did the same thing. "When do we release and drop?"

"Just before it closes," he said.

"And pray we're not hundreds of feet in the air," she added.

"Keep your knees and ankles loose and land on your feet and roll back on your backpack to absorb most of the impact."

When it seemed the edge was close to hitting the ground and cutting off their hands, they both released the edge and dropped to hard smooth ground not more than five feet below them. Both landed on their feet in a crouched position so their ankles and knees would not absorb all the impact and rolled back on their backs with their backpacks absorbing all of the impact.

Susan rolled over on her stomach like Henry did and looked at Henry. "Are you alright?"

"Yeah," he said as he lay flat on the ground.

"What's next?" she asked him as she lay on the ground.

"Listen," he said.

A loud hissing sound filled the cavern as the ground moved back into place. A second later there was a metallic clicking sound as the ground was locked back into place.

"Let's find a corner," Susan suggested as she got to her feet and looked around in the darkness. "Over there on the right looks good."

"You see a place to hide?"

"No, but laying here in the middle of this ramp, if this is a ramp, doesn't seem like a smart thing to do," she answered him as she ran off to the right.

Henry followed her till they reached a smooth wall and both lay down on the floor.

"What next?" she asked him.

"Just lay here till those warriors come and say 'you've returned'," he said.

"Great plan," she said as she looked around. "Sure wish I had a better one."

A light came on in the ceiling casting a dim light around the cavern allowing them to look around.

They both lay still for what they estimated to be ten minutes.

"No warriors," he said as he looked around.

"Or these assholes have a sick sense of humor," she said.

"Let's move," he suggested.

"Down the ramp," she suggested as she got to her feet.

Henry rose up and started walking. Susan fell in beside him.

"If this were an American compound, there would be a guard shack on the side of this ramp with cameras in the ceiling," she said.

He didn't say anything as he looked around.

They walked in silence till they reached a wide rectangular segmented wall with two wide high doors cut into the stone.

"An elevator I bet," Susan said.

"Yeah, and a big one too," he said.

The single light in the ceiling behind them flashed twice and the soft sound of moving metal filled the cavern.

"They're coming back," Henry said.

"Maybe they saw us," she said.

"Over here on the left," he said. "There's a dark corner."

Both moved rapidly to the dark corner and stood silent with their backs against a wall as the light went out and the ground at the far end began to move up. Less than a minute passed before a vehicle moved down the dark ramp and toward the elevator door. They heard nothing as the doors of the elevator opened and the vehicle moved into it. The elevator doors closed and a whooshing sound came from the elevator.

When the whooshing sound stopped, Henry said, "I don't think they're looking for us anymore. That armored car was the relieved patrol returning."

The ground closed with the same metallic clicking sound and the dim light in the ceiling came back on.

Henry reached into his pants pocket and took out the diagram he'd drawn and looked at it in the dim light. "We came out the eastern end which was a hill, and this part is just flat ground."

Susan had taken her diagram out of her pants pocket and was looking at it. "Get your pen out and mark W on this part of the diagram and E on the other part."

He did as she suggested and marked both sides with a W and an E. Then he put an N on the left side of the diagram and an S on the right side. He handed his pen to her so she could put the same marks on her diagram.

"These SR's on the diagram might mean supply room," she said.

"Maybe, according to what I got off that screen in our hospital room," he said.

"Well, according to this there's one not far from where we are," she said as she looked at the diagram.

"I see it," he said. "It's off to the right."

"Then let's go," she said as she moved to the right.

They crossed the fifty foot wide ramp and walked up to a door like all the other doors in the compound flat against the wall. They both pushed against the door and the door moved back and to the left. They walked into it not knowing what to expect and not caring because they had nowhere else to go. As soon as they entered the room, the lights in the ceiling sensing their body heat and movements came on. What they saw surprised them and they both moved into the room away from the door which closed behind them.

"This is an arms room," Susan said.

Henry walked toward a rack of rifles and reached out and touched one.

A clicking sound occurred and the metal bar restraining the dozen rifles on it moved down to the floor. "Looks like our rifles," he said and pulled the one he'd touched from the rack.

"This room must be seventy or eighty feet in width and length, too," Susan said as she walked over to a stack of boxes and read the sign on one of them. "Dry field rations."

Henry walked over to her and looked over the ten foot stack of boxes. "I wonder what's behind them."

"Let's see," Susan said and walked around behind the boxes.

Henry followed her.

They saw a plastic table with what looked like iPhones on them.

Henry picked one up and looked it over. "I wonder if this is some sort of iPhone."

"Probably is," she said as she looked at a lower shelf on the table and saw smaller boxes on it. "Let's see what's in them."

They both knelt down and in doing so they were blocked by the stack of boxes on their left and in front of them.

The overhead doors were all built with electric eyes in them that opened immediately upon detecting the electric eyes on the vehicles. With only Dram and Theia as control room operators Rush had decided to build the doors to respond to electric current. That way when Dram or Theia were in the control room they wouldn't be constantly bothered opening and closing the overhead doors for the patrols. Their most important job after the compound had been built was to activate the satellites' disintegration rays and destroy the political and military structure of Earth. And they had done exactly that. Any further resistance from Earthlings in their primitive war machines could be easily handle by Zack and his men, which they had demonstrated with Susan and Henry's battalion.

Dram woke up in time to see the patrol returning to the compound. Then he'd gotten up and gone to the cleanup room to wash his face missing the blinking light on the computer console that indicated someone had entered a supply room. When the door of the supply room closed the blinking light went out. When Dram returned to the computer console he said, "Replay everything that happened while I was away?"

The computer showed the blinking light that indicated a supply room door had been opened and closed.

"What warrior entered the supply room on the level one western section?" he asked the computer.

"None," replied the computer.

Dram wondered what could have caused that. "Turn on the cameras in the supply room on level one western section and scan the room."

The camera came on and began to scan the supply room.

Henry and Susan were on their knees looking through the smaller boxes on the table when the camera scanned the room showing only what was stored in the supply room.

"These look like batteries," Susan said as she looked at one of the square shaped objects in the box she'd opened.

"If no warrior entered that supply room, computer, what could have caused the light to blink indicating the room had been entered?" Dram asked.

"No explanation," replied the computer.

Dram thought for a few seconds then decided it was static electricity. *Earth has more water than Tabor and moving water produces static electricity that sometimes is reflected from the upper atmosphere and bounced back to the planet's surface. We must in the future adjust our equipment to deal with that.* "Turn off the camera."

The camera went off and Dram leaned back in his chair and wondered what could he do for the next three hours to avoid going to sleep? *Think about how many Earth slaves I will have once our control over this planet is complete.*

CHAPTER 17

May 4, 4:40 p.m.

Level was standing behind Pedro looking at the screen of his laptop. "Can you get a picture of that area that surge came from?"

"Yeah, I've got it in the hard drive," he said as he brought up a picture of the area the surge came from.

Level knelt down behind him and looked at the screen. "Can you magnify that area?"

"Sure," he said and increased the size of the picture till it dominated the screen.

Level stared at the picture and said nothing.

"See something that's out of place?" Janis asked him.

"I see what looks like tire marks," he answered.

"That's nothing," Rawlings said. He was sitting on the ground across from Pedro. "Those tire marks were probably left by some bikers riding around the area."

Level didn't say anything.

Les got up and walked over to him and knelt behind Pedro and looked over his left shoulder at the tire marks. "There're quite a lot of them, too."

"There are quite a lot of motor bike riders," Chester said. "Haven't you seen reports by the environmentalists about how those bikers are damaging desert vegetation?"

Les leaned forward over Pedro's left shoulder and looked at the tracks. "Excuse me," he said as he stared at the tracks. Some of his Army recon training came back to him. "Look at those tracks, Level."

Level looked at them. "They're going around in a circle."

"So a bunch of doped up bikers rode in a circle," Rawlings said.

"Come over here and look," Les told him.

Rawlings got up and walked behind him and Level and looked down at the tracks. "They're just biker tracks."

"But they're real clear tracks, and they're close together," Pedro said.

"As if they were made only hours ago," Level said.

"By a four wheel bike and they don't meander," Les said. "Bikers don't ride in perfect circles. They wander all over the place."

"How large an area would you say that circle is?" Level said.

"Wait," Pedro said as he brought up a legend of area.

Les and Level looked at the legend.

"That area is at least fifty miles in circumference," Les said. "Why would bikers ride around in a circle fifty miles in circumference?"

"Eh, Les, look at those short tracks coming from the center to the circle," Level told him.

Alice, Janis, Judith, and Alex were standing behind Les and Level leaning over and looking at the screen.

"Yeah, I see them," Les replied.

"How long would you estimate they are?" Level asked him.

"Using the legend I'd say they're at least ten miles long," he said as he looked at them. "And there are four of them all coming from the center of that circle of tire tracks and the same length." That caused him to think of what he'd learned as a recon man when he was in the Army. "A smart guard walks in his tracks to make sure anyone finding them wouldn't know how many guards are out there."

"Didn't a wind storm swept over the southwest a week ago?" Alice asked as she looked at the tracks.

Les and Level turned around and looked at her.

"I heard about it watching the news seven days ago," she explained with an expression of foolishness on her face. "The news said the winds were blowing at forty miles an hour."

"So some bikers went back there after the wind storm passed and rode around in a circle," Rawlings said.

"So why would they ride ten miles to the center of the circle and turn around and ride back?" Judith said. "Were they on some geological survey?"

Level turned around and looked at the laptop screen again. "No. The government, especially the Department of the Interior has excellent maps of the US. That's no geological survey."

Les put his left index finger over the area the four separate tracks came from. Saw only the first two digits of his finger covered the area in between the separate tracks. "That center area is about a quarter of a mile in circumference."

"Four separate tracks going east, west, south, and north, and joining that circle," Pedro said.

"How many days ago did you see that news report, Alice?" Les asked her.

She thought for a few seconds and said, "Seven days ago."

"Those tracks wouldn't be as clear as they are if they had been made seven days are," Les said. "The wind would have covered up some of them with sand or dirt, or blown them away."

"That area is a perfect place to establish an underground command post," Level mumbled. "The closest towns east, south and west are nearly a hundred miles away and the only thing that's closer than that north is a highway with small towns along it."

"Why do you say it's the perfect place?" Chester asked he was standing in the back looking at the screen.

"It's close enough to the US Strategic Command."

"That doesn't make sense," Rawlings said.

"Wasn't there a hot line established between all the nuclear powers in the late 60's so the nuclear powers could talk to each other if there was an accidently launch of a missile?" Les asked.

"That's why that area is a perfect place for aliens to establish an underground command," Level said. "They could tap into the frequencies of the Strategic Command and get the location of every major military command post on Earth and all the important political centers by simply listening for a few days."

"The nuclear powers didn't talk to each other for three days at a time?" Nancy asked.

"No," Alex said. "Everybody was scared shitless of an accidental nuclear war then so everybody talked to each other on a daily basis."

"That's not going to stop an accidental nuclear war," Rawlings said. "Any moron working at those nuclear stations could go crazy and launch a missile."

"No," Level said. "Everyone knew the names and mental stability of the officers on the other side in a position to launch a missile. Like Alex said everybody was scared of an accidental nuclear missile launch. Because if one missile was launched there was no guarantee someone else might not think 'to hell with it' and launch all their missiles. By constantly talking to each other we were capable of reducing that possibility to less than ten percent."

"Aw, them damn Commies would have launched an atomic war and not given a damn about anything but their narrow minded political beliefs," Rawlings said.

"That's why once or twice a year the leading generals and admirals would meet and talk to each other," Level told him. "And, Rawlings the Commies went out of business in the 1990's."

"Aw, there're still enough of them around to cause trouble," Rawlings said.

"You should read something else other than the sports pages in the papers," Chester told him. "Russia has been a republic for over thirty years with a higher standard of living than the Commies ever gave the people."

"Well, we know where to go," Les said standing up. "Let's get some rest and leave after seven."

"I agree," Nancy said. "I slept well on the ground last night and today. We should stop for a rest stop and change drivers once every six hours after we leave."

"Good idea," Chester agreed. He looked at Rawlings added, "And this time no speeding. If aliens did make those tracks we don't want to rush into any of them."

"Would be nice if we could make paper maps of that area," Les said as he stood up.

"I've got it on the hard drive," Pedro said.

"And can you guarantee when we get close to that area the aliens aren't going to be able to pick up your laptop's electrical frequency?"

"There are maps in my Humvee. I took a number of them when we stopped in East Oak," Level said as he stood up and walked toward his Humvee. "We can mark that area on those maps."

Ten minutes later they were all lying on their ground mats looking at a darkening sky. Judith and Nancy had agreed to stay awake on guard twenty yards away from where their camp was.

"What do you think, Les?" Alice asked him as she lay next to him. She'd moved her mat an inch closer to him to feel safe.

"What do you mean?" His mind was a blank because he didn't want to think about the family he'd never see again. He didn't even want to think there was no way of finding their clothes and giving them a proper burial.

"Think we got a chance against those aliens?"

"We know more now than when we started," he told her as he thought *what we need is a miracle.*

Within a few minutes everyone was asleep.

Before he drifted off to sleep, he was lying ten feet from Rawlings' right side Chester thought *I've got to figure out a way to contact them aliens when we get close to them.* He turned his head and looked at Rawlings and smiled. *Perfect.*

CHAPTER 18

"Maybe they are batteries for those cell phone devices," he told Susan.

"Let's find out," Susan said as she reached for one of the boxes and opened it and took out one of the smaller boxes. "This cardboard feels funny."

"It's from another world," Henry told her. "It may not be made of plant fibers."

She opened the end of the box and turned it upside down and a small round thin clear glass chip the size of a half dollar slid out of the box in a paper holder and landed on the floor.

Henry turned the iPhone device he held in his hand over and looked at the sides and back. "I don't see any place where we can remove the back."

Susan pulled the chip out of its holder and the bottom of the iPhone device in Henry's hand flipped up and a tray slid out of it. "The presence of the battery activated that device," she said.

"Put it in," he told her.

"Hope this thing doesn't blow up in our faces," she said as she placed the chip in the tray and the tray closed and the bottom part of the iPhone device closed. "What now?"

Henry turned it right side up and saw on the black screen the words 'this communicator in now operational'. "Good thing these Tabor warriors speak a language similar to English or we'd be lost trying to figure out how their equipment works."

"So it's operational. What can it do?" she asked in a voice that had the slight sound of disappointment in it.

'This communicator can access all the computers in the main control room,' appeared on the screen.

"Can it tell us what's in this compound?" Henry asked.

'Yes,' appeared on the screen.

"So let's find out," Susan suggested.

"How many computers are in the control room?" Henry asked.

'One main computer and three others that can access information from the main computer, and those in the armored vehicles' appeared on the screen.

"What can the computers in the main control room do?" he asked.

"They control every part of the underground compound," answered the communicator in a loud voice.

"The damn thing speaks," Susan said.

"Tone down the sound," Henry said.

"This communicator does not understand last command," replied the communicator.

"Reduce the volume of answers coming from the communicator," Susan said.

"To what level?"

"To minimum level," she said.

"What level is that?"

"Reduce volume to lowest level," Henry said.

"Done," replied the communicator at a level so low they couldn't hear it.

"Show various sound levels," Susan said.

Ten numbers appeared on the screen in vertical form with the lowest number one in bright white.

"Go to level five in volume," he said.

"Done," replied the communicator in a volume they could hear.

Henry looked up at the table and took another communicator from the table and a box like the one the chip had come in from the box next to them and opened it and pulled out the paper tray with the chip in it. He handed the communicator to Susan and took out the chip and slid it into the base of the communicator when it opened and started it. She adjusted the sound to level five.

"I wonder if we can set our own frequency?" she said.

"Can we put our own frequency in these two communicators?" he asked the one in his hand.

"Cannot answer," replied the communicator.

"It doesn't understand frequency," she said then asked, "At what electrical current are you operating at?"

"00700350," replied the communicator.

"Eight digits," he said. "Does all the electrical equipment in the compound operator on that current?"

"Yes."

"Can a different electrical current be given to a communicator that would allow the operator to communicate with others without the computers in the compound knowing it?"

"Yes."

"Would that delete the original electrical level?" she asked.

"Cannot be answered."

"How many different electrical levels can be put in a communicator," Henry asked.

"Three hundred."

"When were we attacked?" Henry asked Susan.

"Around one thirty in the afternoon on May 3," she said.

"Enter a new operating electrical current, but keep the original ones," Henry said.

"Will do," replied the communicator.

"Enter electrical current 12345679," he told the communicator.

"Done."

Susan put the same electrical current in the communicator she held. "Have we been recorded coming into this compound?"

"No."

"Why not?" He asked.

"All the visual and audio recording devices were turned off," the communicator answered.

"Why? She asked.

"To conserve energy according to the main computer in the control room."

"Has there been any signal sent to indicate we're in this room?" he asked.

"Yes."

"Shit, they know we're here," Susan said.

"How many warriors are on their way to this storage room?" Henry asked the communicator.

"None."

"Why not?"

"All warriors are in their quarters or on duty or patrol outside the compound," the communicator said.

Henry looked around the wall of boxes surrounding them on three sides and said, "Whatever recording device they've got in this room didn't record us because we were hidden by these boxes."

"They created blind spots when they put this equipment in this room," she said.

"And that's to our advantage," he said. "Turn off the recording device in this room and don't let the main computer record what was done."

"Impossible. The main computer in the main control room records everything that happens in the compound."

"Is the recording device on?" he asked.

"No."

"Can it be activated by movement?" Susan asked him.

"Cannot be answered."

"If we start moving around will the recording device start recording?" he asked the communicator.

"Yes."

"We're trapped behind these boxes," Susan said in a depressed voice.

Henry held up his left index finger and said, "Wait. When we start moving will that set off an alarm?"

"Do not understand alarm?"

"Will the main computer notify whoever is in the main control room we are in this storage room if we start moving?"

"Wait," replied the communicator. Two seconds passed before the communicator said, "The main computer in the main control room has not been set to notify the operator in the main control room there is movement in the storage rooms."

"These warriors may be centuries ahead of us in technology, but their security systems are a joke," Susan said.

Henry started in her face and said nothing. He was thinking.

"What?" she asked him.

"That doctor in our hospital room told me that they came from Tabor and were going to make Earth their new Tabor," he said. "He said there were one hundred ships heading for Earth with five hundred thousand warriors on them lead by someone called the Overlord and they'd arrive in less than ten days."

"So you've already told me that," she reminded him.

"We escaped over twenty-four hours ago, Susan," he told her.

"We've got less than eight days to let the world know what's coming for it," she added.

He looked down at the floor and said, "Yeah, a world that has a history of states fighting each other, a world that has no major political or military organizations left."

"Well, we've got to do something," she told him in an angry voice.

"We find out what's in this storage room, take what we need, and get out of this compound and tell the world what's coming for it. Five hundred thousand warriors and advanced technology isn't going to be able to completely conquer Earth even if they've already done us a lot of damage. If we can take some of this equipment out of this room to someone who can duplicate it, the world has a chance."

"Then let's get busy," she suggested as she stood up.

Within an hour they'd learned how the weapons in the storage room worked, gotten two large canvas like bags and loaded them with three rifles, six handguns and electric ammo packs for each weapon, medical supplies, and a dozen communicators with batteries.

"Henry, these boxes contain pills for purifying water," Susan said as she looked in two boxes they had opened but ignored because they contained only bottles of pills.

"Susan, we've gathered close to two hundred pounds of equipment in the last hour, and have no way of getting it out of this compound except on our backs," he told her.

"But these are small bottles and what if they can purify polluted water?" she said.

"Okay, take six of them, and let's find a vehicle of some kind we can use to get out of this compound, because I figure time is rapidly turning against us," he told her.

She sat her canvas bag on the ground saying, "If this storage room was at this end of level one that's should be a garage of some sort nearby."

Henry took the communicator out of his pants pocket and asked, "Is there a place at this level where vehicles are placed?"

"Behind the door at the other end of this storage room," said the communicator.

Henry looked around and saw the door a few yards ahead of him, "Let's go. Susan."

She put six bottles of the purifying pills in her canvas bag, closed it, and pulled it up on her back over her backpack. "I hope we find a big one."

Henry did the same thing with his canvas bag and got up and walked up to the door and stopped and asked, "If I open this door, will it be recorded in the main computer?"

"Yes."

"And if there's a Tabor Warrior in that room he'll be notified."

"Yes."

Susan walked up to his right side. "We don't have much of a choice, do we?"

He ignored her question. "Do all the vehicles in this compound have a tracking chip in them?"

"Cannot answer that."

"Do they have a way of being located?" Susan asked.

"All vehicles in the compound have a locator in each of them," replied the communicator.

"Can they be removed?" Henry asked it.

"No."

"If they are damaged will the vehicle still operate?" he asked.

"Locate chips are not a part of the power system of the vehicles."

"Let's go," he said as he walked to the door and pushed against it.

The door immediately opened and slid to one side, and the moment it did that it registered on the main computer in the control room.

Dram was tired, but alert and saw the blinking light on the computer screen on the wall above him. "What is that light?"

"A door to the vehicle room has been opened."

That's probably Trak or Bull running a check on the vehicles. Rolling around in this sandy country has probably filled the air intakes with sand. He ignored the blinking light and stood up and decided to walk around to avoid going to sleep. He looked at the clock on the screen. It read three a.m.

As soon as they entered the garage the lights came on revealing six armor cars similar, but smaller, than the ones that had attacked their battalion. They walked to the closest one and put their heavy canvas bags on the ground and pushed on the door on the left side of it. It popped open outward. Henry pulled it open and looked inside it. When he did the lights came on inside.

"Automatic lights," he said as he looked over the inside of the vehicle. "There are two seats inside, one for a driver and a gunner."

"Let's get these bags inside and figure out how to disable that locator," she said.

Henry turned around and took her bag and his and put them inside then took off his backpack and put it inside and climbed inside over to the driver's seat. "This thing's got a steering wheel just like a regular car."

"How do you control the speed?" she asked as she removed her backpack and tossed it inside and climbed inside over to the gunner's seat and sat in it. "Comfortable."

Henry looked down into the foot well and sat two pedals. "One for acceleration and the other for braking. But I wonder which is which?"

"The pedals are interchangeable," said a voice.

Both immediately looked toward the open door expecting to see a warrior with a weapon pointed at them. There was no one at the opened door. Henry leaned back and grabbed what looked like a handle and pulled the door shut.

"Make the right pedal the accelerator and the left for breaking," Susan said.

"Done."

"Every piece of electrical equipment in this compound talks," Henry said. "Where is the locator?"

"In the center of the steering wheel," replied the computer in the vehicle.

Henry looked at the steering wheel and saw nothing but a curved plastic center like that found on Earth cars. "How do I get to it?"

"Push on the center of the steering wheel," said the computer.

Henry pushed on the steering wheel and the center flipped up. He saw a dull looking square piece of glass in the center. "I hope this is the locator," he said as he put his index and thumb of his left hand on it and pulled on it. It did not move.

"How can I disconnect the locator?" he asked.

"Turn it to the left."

Henry turned it to the left.

"The locator has been disconnected," announced the armored car's computer.

"Well, here goes nothing," he said as he looked at the dashboard and saw a small blank screen. "Start the car, and display on the screen how to get out of the compound."

The engine started with a soft hum and a picture appeared on the screen showing how to leave the compound.

"Do you want automatic drive or self-drive?" asked the computer.

"Drive it yourself, Henry," Susan told him. "It might tell that main computer what we're doing, and it could bring us back."

"Shut down automatic drive," he said.

"Done."

He looked at the gearshift and saw three letters on the panel next to it. D for drive R for reverse, and S. "I wonder what S stands for on this gearshift?"

"Stationary."

He shifted the gear into D and the vehicle began to move forward. He looked at the map displayed on the screen on the dash board and headed in the direction that indicated the ramp. "Find out how that gun works," he told Susan.

"That's exactly what I'm doing, Henry," she told him. *I just hope I don't need to do any shooting.*

A minute later they were approaching a solid wall of stone.

Susan was looking through the target finder of the gun on the top of the vehicle at the approaching wall. "I don't think we're going to get out of here, Henry."

He didn't say anything he was too busy praying that wall would suddenly move.

They were ten feet in front of it when it began to move down in their direction.

Henry stopped the vehicle and reversed it two feet.

The wall was slowly and silently lowered to the level of the floor with an apron a few feet in front of the vehicle.

"My God, these warriors must have been here on Earth for years to build this place," Susan said as she watched the wall stop level with the floor.

"Just two days according to that robot food server. The question is how did they manage to do it without anyone knowing about it?" he said as he started driving forward again.

Within less than a minute they were moving toward the ramp they had used to get into the compound. As they reached the end of the ramp the dim light inside the compound went out and the stone overhead door facing them began to rise.

"We've been spotted," Susan said.

"Yeah, right now an alarm is going off in that main control room."

There was no alarm but the computer did announce, "The overhead door on the west side of the compound is opening."

Dram stopped walking and looked at the screen and saw what was happening. He wasn't sleepy any more. "Show that door."

The overhead door appeared and the armored car Susan and Henry were in appeared on the screen.

"Who is inside that vehicle?" he demanded.

There was no answer.

"Show the inside of the vehicle," he ordered the computer.

A small camera that was a part of the center roof light of the car came on showing Henry driving and Susan in the gun seat.

"The Earthlings," he exclaimed as he picked up his communicator on the desk underneath the computer screen and said, "Theia, wake up the Earthlings have returned and they are taking one of our armored cars."

Theia was usually a lite sleeper, but she was very tired and didn't wake up when Dram's voice came over her communicator on the table next to her bed.

"Loud ring," he said as he rushed to the console and started pushing buttons to close the overhead door.

But he was too late.

Henry was driving up the ramp when he saw the overhead door starting to close.

"They're closing the door," Susan said.

Henry responded by slamming his right foot down on the accelerator and the car shot forward at sixty miles an hour. He reached the end of the ramp and the car shot out of the underground compound with an inch of solid rock just above the top hatch of the car. The car hit the ground and bounced once on its large plastic tires before it hit the ground again and moved away from the closing overhead door at a speed of over seventy miles an hour.

"They can't locate us because the locator is off, Henry," she said. "But they can follow our tracks."

"Not if I can find a stream," he said. "Show the surrounding terrain."

A map appeared on the dashboard screen showing all the terrain around for a hundred miles. They appeared on the map as a green dot. He saw it. "There's one about twelve miles southwest of us."

"Let's hope there's water in it," Susan said.

"We've got to find a place to hide this car once we get in that stream and we can't hide it in the direction we're going," he told her.

"Let's make it to that stream before sunrise and then head east zigzagging to avoid leaving a clear trail," she suggested.

"We've got to tie some brush behind this car to cover our tracks," he said.

"Let's just reach that stream then work out a plan for covering our tracks," she told him.

Henry silently agreed with her and kept driving as fast as he could, and he was surprised at how the car didn't bounce as much as he expected.

Susan turned around in her seat and looked through the two view slots behind her. "No one's after us, Henry. We've got a chance."

"Let's hope our luck holds," he said.

A thought passed through Susan's mind and she said, "Can the main computer see what's in this car?"

"Yes," replied the car's computer.

"How?" Henry asked as he drove.

"A camera in the light in the center of the car," answered the computer.

"Can you turn it off?" Susan asked.

"Yes."

"Then do it," she said.

"Done," replied the computer.

"When we find a safe place to stop, we've got to figure out a way of disconnecting that camera," Henry told her.

"Let's just hope they aren't sending one of those heavier armored cars after us," she told him. "It may be faster than this one."

"Then let's hope," Henry said.

CHAPTER 19

Theia finally woke up and reached for her communicator on the stand next to her bed. She looked at the screen and saw the call was coming from Dram and that told her it was a serious call. "What's wrong, Dram?" she asked knowing the moment she mentioned his name his communicator would be the only one in the compound to be contacted.

"Those two Earthlings returned to the compound and somehow managed to get inside, and now they've got a small armored car and have left the compound," he told her. "I tried locking the overhead door but they were near the end and escaped before it closed."

"I shall be there in a short time," she told him as she jumped out of bed and started to get dressed. She should have told him to contact Commander Rush, but if he did Rush would hold him responsible for everything that had happened and kill him. A good commander always did his own killing, because it told the warriors of his command he or she was in charge. And considering how few warriors were on Earth, they couldn't afford to lose anyone, especially a skilled computer operator such as Dram. If he was dead the responsibility of controlling the computers in the compound would be hers alone. And she knew she couldn't survey the main computer in the control room herself. Such a job would require almost twenty-four hours of surveillance, or the main computer would have to be given complete control over the compound, and like all computers Warrior computers sometimes malfunctioned.

True to her word she rushed into the main control room with her uniform improperly buttoned and her short hair in disarray. Something not permitted by warriors on duty. "Let me see the recording," she demanded as she walked to the computer console Dram was sitting at and stopped behind his chair.

He hit replay and everything the cameras had recorded were shown on the screen.

"I had no way of knowing -," Dram began to say.

"Be quiet," she ordered him as she watched the replay. When it ended she leaned forward and pushed a button on the console that notified Commander Rush something serious needed his attention.

"I will take responsibility for what has happened," Dram said in a strong proud voice.

"You will be quiet until I tell you to speak," she ordered him. "Turn on the exterior cameras and put them on maximum range, especially those going south."

Dram did as he was ordered.

Five minutes later Rush walked into the main control room looking like he was ready for inspection by the Overlord. He stopped in the center of the control room and waited for an explanation as to why he was summoned.

Theia stood at attention two feet in front of him, apologized for her appearance, and explained what had happened.

Rush turned to his right and looked at Dram and said in a cold voice, "I should torture you to death."

"Excuse me, sir," Theia said. "But the fault was not Dram's but the limited number of warriors we have here on Earth. We have all been working for twelve or more hours every day since we arrived on Earth two months ago to build this underground compound in this isolated part of Earth while at the same time avoiding detection by the primitive electrical equipment of this state. And carefully surveying the military installations and political organizations of their most advanced states the scout gave us and avoiding detection so we would know exactly where to strike and when. We are all very tired, sir, and in need of a long period of rest."

He turned his head back to face Theia and asked, "Are you implying, Lieutenant, that I made a mistake in not asking for more warriors to carry out my orders?"

"No, sir, I am not," she said in a strong voice. "But we are all very tired and tired warriors make mistakes through no fault of their own."

He thought over what she had said for a few seconds before he said, "I want to see everything that was recorded in that section of the compound for the last four hours."

Dram jumped to his feet and said, "Please, sir my chair."

Rush looked at him with angry eyes and took the seat offered.

Theia sat in her regular seat next to Rush and began a replay of everything that had been recorded in the western section of the compound. After two hours Rush yawned a loud yawn and said, "I see nothing in the replay that explains how those two Earthlings managed to get back into our compound."

"Sir, you never completely explained your purpose in letting them escape," Theia told him. "Not that a Commander of your quality has to explain anything to anyone under their command."

"I expected them to contact the nearest group of surviving Earthlings and tell them resistance was futile. If they had told any Earthlings they met what happened to their military unit when attacked by only two of our armored cars those they told would immediately realize the foolishness of resistance and given up making our conquest of this planet far easier than the Overlord expected."

Theia and Dram said nothing.

"But I -," he paused for a minute before he continued. "I underestimated those two Earthlings. Instead of running to the nearest Earth settlement to tell what happened to them they came back into the compound by the western section." He leaned back in Dram's chair and said, "Computer, replay the part showing our patrol leaving."

The computer replayed the part he requested.

"There," he said as he saw two dark figures dropping down into the ramp area just before the ramp closed. "They were close to that overhead door and felt the ground move when it opened and saw the patrol car leave and dropped inside before the door closed. That's how they got back inside."

"I assume blame -," Dram began to say.

"Silence, Dram, the Commander is thinking," Theia yelled at him.

Dram didn't say another word.

"The cameras recorded them because all the cameras at the ramps automatically record anything entering or leaving the compound," Rush said.

"Pardon me, sir, but Dram saw the blinking light indicating the supply room in that section had been entered, and activated the camera to show what was in the room," Theia said. "But the two Earthlings weren't seen because they were knelling down behind the boxes of supplies in the room."

"Yes, but how did they manage to get one of our armored cars and leave the compound?" Rush said.

"They apparently found communicators in that supply room, sir, and all our communicators are programed to give information about all our equipment the moment they are operational," Dram said.

Rush nodded his head as he said, "You are correct, Sergeant Dram. And now they will make contact with other Earthlings and show them what they've got." He thought a few seconds before he said, "Our mission here as gotten a bit more difficult."

"We could send warriors out after them," Theia suggested.

"No, as you've pointed out, Theia, we are all tired and need rest. If the Earthlings don't get themselves organized quickly, in less than eight days, the Overlord will arrive with everything we need to destroy all remaining resistance on Earth." He pushed his chair back and stood up and walked toward the door. It opened. "I do not think we need to worry anymore about Earthlings getting into the compound. Those two who've managed to acquire some of our equipment will be too busy trying to reach other Earthlings to tell them what they've seen and know and got. And that will take them some time, probably a few days. And those they tell will take more days to get themselves organize and come for the compound, and by then the Overlord and the fleet will be here." He stopped and turned around. "You two need not remain in the control room. Put your communicators on alert status. If the main computer records anything unusual it will immediately alert you." He turned around and walked out the door.

Dram turned toward Theia and said, "Thank you, Lieutenant for saving my life."

"Do as the commander has ordered," she told him and left the room.

CHAPTER 20

Day 3 May 5, 3 a.m.

They had taken US 80 and had been on the road since seven thirty p.m. May 4 and were already three quarters of the way through the southern part of Wyoming. They hadn't seen any vehicles on the road and no lights off in the distance to indicate there were houses in the darkness with people in them. But they knew there were. Because of what had happened many people were too afraid to turn on their lights at night. Even though there was still electricity for the lights. No one was sure if a friend or foe would show up if they saw lights on in a house, and no one was willing to take the chance.

The three Humvees had kept a steady speed of sixty miles an hour and had stopped only once at midnight so the drivers could be exchanged. Rawlings hadn't wanted to let Chester drive, but Chester told him to use his head. Both of them were going have to be alert when they made their move to take over the group. Rawlings was asleep five minutes after he had gotten into the passenger seat and strapped himself in.

At five a.m. they crossed into Utah and were approaching Salt Lake City when Les who was sitting in the front passenger's seat suggested turning on the radio to find out what was happening in the world.

"You think there's someone out there on the radio?" Janis asked him.

"I've got a feeling people have been on radios, cell phones, and computers demanding to know what's happened since we became aware of what happened," he said. "I'd like to know if I'm right, and how they're handling it."

"Would be a good idea," Pedro said. "Maybe somebody else knows what we know and are trying to reach this area in Nevada."

Les leaned forward and turned on the radio. It wasn't necessary for him to search for a station. All of them were broadcasting similar messages. He found one that was strong and listened.

"What we know listeners is that since midnight of May third, no government on this planet exists because none have answered any of the thousands of calls we here in the United Kingdom have sent out. And we've been broadcasting on the strongest transmitters we've got outside of London, with our most powerful receiver on trying to receive messages from anywhere in the world. We have had contact with some smaller towns on the various continents and the people in them are telling us exactly what we are telling you. There is no one alive in any capital city on Earth. Nor are any of the military installations operating. Some people in some countries have checked the capitals and military bases close to their towns and find nothing but clothing without people in them. We know that what has happened to us is not the result of the actions of any government on Earth. The technology to do what has been done to Earth is far beyond any nation on Earth. We know this disaster is not the result of some bacteria or virus, because no government of people on Earth could be so inhuman to produce such a thing. We, therefore, can assume only one thing. The Earth has been attacked by aliens who have a weapon that causes flesh to disintegrate. Any human or animal caught in this weapon's range of fire is immediately disintegrated. We can therefore assume their plan is take Earth for themselves. Those of us who have survived cannot allow that to happen. We have estimated that the attack on Earth occurred at the same time all over the Earth. We have chosen 5 p.m. May 3 Greenwich Mean Time as zero hour of the alien attack."

The speaker cleared her throat and continued. "We must get ourselves organized and fight back. We must stop fighting among ourselves and put our insignificant differences aside. We still have the ability to communicate with each other and we must use that to organize ourselves by countries then by continents. We must gather food, medicine, weapons, and let each other know what's happening wherever we are. We must let these aliens who have attacked us know this is our world and shall remain our world." The speaker paused.

"We are beginning to get information from other parts of the world of people who are organizing themselves to resist, and will pass it to others who can contact us. We must keep our communication systems operating, because it is the only way we can work together to defeat these aliens, and let them know we of Earth all stand together. If anyone out there listening to me has any skills in communications please report to those areas where power is supplied to the communication systems of the world to keep them operating. Only by working together will we succeed in preventing the aliens from taking control of our world and killing the rest of us, or turning the survivors into slaves. Please contact this station if you've heard me. We are broadcasting on a general news frequency. I'm sorry I can't give you more. We are sure the aliens are listening. We must stand together if we are to save our world."

"What do you think?" Alice asked everyone in the Humvee as she drove.

"I think those aliens should have moved faster, because now people are not in shock anymore and are beginning to get organized," Janis said.

"And by now the aliens know that," Pedro said.

"Why make a big attack on Earth then do nothing?" Les asked.

"What are you talking about?" Pedro asked him.

"When you attack a well-armed enemy, you overwhelm them as quickly as possible before they can get themselves organized and fight back," he said.

"You're right," Pedro said. "They attack Earth with a weapon that disintegrates people on the night of May third and then nothing."

"Maybe they didn't know how well organized and armed this planet was?" Alice said.

"No, they knew that or they wouldn't have attacked the major cities and the major military installations and destroyed the people in them in one day," Pedro said. "I figure they've been studying us for years and knew just where to hit us."

"If those aliens are listening to those broadcasts, they're going to strike again," Janis said.

"They're listening," Les assured her.

"So they know we're prepared to fight them to the death," Janis said.

"Uh huh," he replied as he looked out the window at the passing dark landscape.

Pedro was sitting on the left side of the second row of seats. He leaned forward a few inches and looked at Les' face. "I haven't known you very long, Les, but in the short time that I have known you, I know you have something on your mind when you have that expression of deep thought on your face. And I can see your face even in the darkness. So let us all know what you're thinking."

"They didn't bring enough soldiers, so they are waiting for reinforcements," he mumbled.

"What?" Alice asked him as she threw a glance in his direction.

Les looked at the clock on the dashboard. "It's nearly five thirty and the sun will be up in ten or twenty minutes." He turned around and looked east through the back window and saw a sliver of light on the horizon. "It's rising now."

"Chester is driving so he'll stop soon," Janis said.

She was right. Chester started to slow down a minute later and turned to the right onto a dirt road and headed for a group of trees around the dirt road. He stopped among the trees. Alice stopped next to him and Level stopped next to Alice. Everyone in the first and third Humvees got out and walked toward the center Humvee.

"This looks like a good place to spend the day," Level said as he stood next the front passenger door of his Humvee looking around at the tall trees with new fresh green leaves on them.

Nancy, William, Judith, and Alex walked over to him.

"Nice and leafy," Nancy said. "With soft grass on the ground, too."

"I've always thought that west of the Mississippi River the rest of America was nothing but hard sandy mountainous country with very little grass," Judith said.

"You've watched too many Hollywood cowboy movies," Nancy told her.

"We were listening to the radio and heard from a station in Britain outside London that people know we've been attacked by aliens," Alice said as she walked up to Level

"What did they say?" Level asked her. There was deep interest in his voice.

"They're encouraging people to get organize and contact each other so they can resist the aliens," she said.

"They also said that they've had contact with other people by radio and they all report that every government on Earth no longer exists, and neither do the armies," Alice said.

"Les thinks the aliens haven't brought enough soldiers to finish Earth off, and they're waiting for reinforcements" Pedro said.

"Earth is already finished," Rawlings said.

"Not as long as there are hundreds of millions of people still free and capable of fighting back," Alex said.

"Why do you think the aliens don't have enough soldiers, Les?" Level asked him as he walked over to the group.

"According to that radio report we heard from Britain, the aliens attacked us on May third around midnight central time in America," he said as he stopped among the group. "They said no government on Earth exists, or any military. Now I figure there were probably a few military units out training somewhere that avoided being destroyed."

"So what does that matter?" Chester asked him.

"Why haven't the aliens made an announcement telling us they've destroyed our ability to resist them? Why haven't they issued demands telling us why they attacked us and what they want?" he asked. "They must know our communication systems are still working."

"They're probably still trying to learn the various languages of Earth," Chester said.

"They should have known that before they attacked," Rawlings said.

Everyone in the group looked at him because his statement made sense.

"They probably do," Level said. "You never attack an enemy unless you know the enemy's strengths and weaknesses, and knowing the enemy's language is a must." He looked at Les and said, "You think they don't have enough soldiers to finish the job, and neither do I."

"If there were alien space ships in orbit about Earth, they would have been seen by the various observatories and reported. Or picked up by the all the radar stations on Earth before they attacked, and that certainly would have been on the radio," Les said. "But it wasn't because there are no alien space ships orbiting Earth."

"What are you saying?" Level asked him.

"I think a small group of them landed on Earth so they could destroy every government and all the major military forces on Earth and then they sat down and are waiting."

"Waiting for what some superman to show up?" Rawlings growled.

"No, Rawlings, for reinforcements," he answered.

"You don't know that," Rawlings told him.

"Start thinking, Rawlings," Les told him. "They knock out all the governments and major military forces on midnight of May third, and this is May fifth. And there's been nothing done to Earth since May third."

"What say we make ourselves a breakfast of bread and coffee and listen to the radio while we eat," Level suggested.

"That sounds great," William said. "I'd like to know what's going on in the outside world beyond what we learned at East Oak."

"I'll look for a stream where we can get water," Les said. "No sense in using up what little water we have." He started walking for the back of his Humvee.

"I'll come with you," Alice said as she followed him.

"I think those two are getting close," Janis said to Nancy.

"I think we're all getting close since all we've got left is each other," she replied.

"Yeah," Rawlings said as he grinned at Nancy.

"Not you," she said as she turned around and walked away. "I'll get the coffee and bread in my Humvee."

"Let's get some fire wood," Chester told Rawlings. Once they were far enough away from the others so they couldn't be heard Chester said, "Stop acting like some lecherous asshole or they're going to figure out what we're planning to do."

"Whatever you're planning to do that bitch Nancy belongs to me, understand," he told Chester.

"You can have her mother for all I care, but until I can make contact with the aliens, we act like we're a part of the group," he told Rawlings.

And when we do, I get rid of you, Wimp.

Within an hour they'd started a fire made coffee from water from a spring Alice and Les had found and were eating campfire made toast and drinking coffee listening to the radio in Chester's Humvee. Most of the stations they heard were issuing cries for help. Every ten minutes they would switch to a different station till they found one that was broadcasting about what people were doing and listen to that one. After an hour of listening, Alex spoke.

"The aliens would be real stupid if they aren't listening to those broadcasts," he said.

"We've heard six different broadcasts," Les said. "From Africa, Europe, South America, Asia, and Australia, and they've all said they've had contact with people in other countries. But none have mentioned any more attacks."

"Like you said, Les, the aliens are waiting for reinforcements," William said. "Campfire toast is real good." He popped the last piece into his mouth and chewed and swallowed it.

"But why?" Janis asked.

"Why what?" Chester asked her.

"Why attack us then sit on their asses and wait for reinforcements?" she told him. "Why not just wipe out all resistance now before people can get themselves organized and start fighting back?"

"Maybe that's the way they do things on the world they come from," Pedro said.

"Attack then wait for resistance to arrive then attack again and wipe that out, too," Judith said.

"I think they're following the orders they were given," Nancy said.

"What do you mean?" Chester asked her.

"They're given orders to destroy all political and military organizations on Earth, and every major city, and they've done just that. Now they're waiting for some superior officer to show up and take charge."

"Not one of those broadcasts reported seeing space ships in the air," Les said and then became silent again.

"Maybe the people making them don't have access to telescopes," Rawlings said.

"All the really large observatories are located in areas far from cities where the glare of city lights don't interfere with watching the sky at night," Les said. "That would mean most of the people in them have survived and have contacted those stations that are broadcasting."

"And if they haven't reported seeing space ships in orbit about Earth that means there are none up there," Alice said.

"The aliens here on Earth would have needed a space ship to get here," Nancy said. "And if there isn't one in orbit about the Earth where is it on the dark side of the moon?"

"Yes," Alex said. "Because the way the moon and Earth rotate we can only see one side of the moon. The dark side of the moon has been photographed many times, but only by manned capsules or satellites."

Level nodded his understanding of what Judith meant. "Wait for resistance to develop and then rush in with a lot of firepower and destroy it."

"Whatever reason they have for not following up on their initial attack we should try and find out before we do anything once we find this place in Nevada," William said.

"Don't we have radios?" Nancy asked.

"Yes, we do, two to each Humvee," Pedro said.

"Why not let the world know we've located a place in Nevada where we think the aliens are?" she suggested.

"No!" Les said sharply. "Do that and if the aliens are there and listening we tell them we know where they are."

Chester agreed. "I agree. As long as they think they're safe wherever they're at they're not going to attack anymore."

"What do you mean attack anymore?" Rawlings said. "Whatever ray they hit us with they probably don't have anymore. They used it all up on one major attack. That's why they're sitting on their asses and not doing anything."

"To destroy all life in the major cities and military organizations in one day suggests whatever weapon they used is in orbit about Earth," Les said.

"Then why didn't those hundreds of satellites we've got up see them and let the world know?" Rawlings said.

"Because they have some sort of cloaking device that prevents our satellites from detecting them," Alex said. "But why weren't they seen by the telescopes on Earth?"

"They probably were," Les said. "But there are so many satellites up there whoever saw them probably thought they were put up by a nation on Earth."

"Aw, you're all just blowing hot air," Rawlings said.

"Camouflage has been used in warfare for centuries, Rawlings," Les told him. "Don't let the enemy see you until you are ready to attack is one of the oldest rules of warfare, and those who've managed to use it skillfully have usually won the battles and the war."

"What I don't understand is why wasn't the space ship that brought these aliens to Earth been seen or detected?" Nancy asked. "Don't we have satellites orbiting the moon?"

No one said anything, but they all looked at her.

"You people are talking about observatories and such things and no one in any of those observatories saw the ship that brought the aliens to Earth?" she continued.

A minute passed before Alex spoke.

"Stealth," he said.

"That's for hiding from radar," Chester told him.

"But what if these aliens have the ability to bend light away from their ships so they can't be seen even by a telescope?" Alex asked.

"That's the only explanation," Les mumbled.

"Why don't we all get some rest and start for this place in Nevada after sundown," Chester suggested. "Standing around here coming up with ideas that we can't prove isn't worth a damn." He turned to Rawlings and said, "Let's clean up."

Rawlings without a word of protest started gathering the tin cups and metal coffee pot they'd used to make coffee.

The others silently went to their Humvees for their ground mats and blankets.

"We'll take first watch," Chester said as he and Rawlings walked off with the cups and coffee pot in their hands for the stream Alice and Les had gotten water from.

When they reached the stream two hundred feet away, Chester gave Rawlings the cups and coffee pot saying, "Wash these and do a good job. I'm going to try and contact the aliens." He walked off among some bushes and took out his iPhone and sat down on the ground thinking, *I hope these damn fool aliens are listening and understand English.* He turned on his iPhone and said, "Hello, aliens, answer if you can hear me. You're going to need my help. Danger is coming your way."

The two cars patrolling ten miles beyond the compound had been ordered by Zack to keep their communicators on so he could contact them and to keep the radios in their cars on and monitor all Earth broadcasts. It was a good way for them to avoid getting bored and sleepy.

"These Earthlings are foolish to think they can resist us," Sam said as he drove.

Zig snorted an agreement and said nothing as he looked out the target finder at the countryside. *This Earth is a beautiful planet. I will enjoy killing any Earthling who attempts to resist us.* He looked at the radio below the target finder and noticed it was on the all-electric current band. On that band they could pick up any calls from the compound for them and any broadcasts on Earth.

"Hello, aliens, answer me if you can hear me. You are going to need my help. Danger is coming your way." Chester's call was picked up by the car's radio.

"Did you hear that, Zig," Sam asked him.

"Yes, I did, and it was recorded," he said as he pushed a button on the radio locking in on the signal. Then he adjusted a nob until he got its location. "It is coming from a spot in a wild area a little over five hundred Earth miles from here."

"Then it is not from the other patrol car," Sam said.

"No. Contact the compound and tell them what we have received," Zig said.

Sam immediately called Zack.

"Have you seen the Earthlings who escaped with our car?" Zack asked him.

"No, sir, but we picked up a call from an Earthling," Sam said.

"To you?" Zack asked in a surprised voice.

"No, sir, it was a general call," Sam said.

"Let me hear it," Zack demanded.

Sam transmitted the call to Zack.

Zack listened and thought, *why would an Earthling be calling us and telling us we're in danger?*

"What should we do, Lieutenant?" Sam asked him.

"You have a location of the call?"

"Five hundred Earth miles from our position," he said.

Zack wondered should he tell Rush about the call or make his own decision? Warriors who acted without orders and brought victory to the Warrior Class were always rewarded with promotions, and for a long time he'd wanted to become an Assistant Commander. Commander Rush had the authority to promote him, and he'd be second only to Rush who was second to the Overlord. He decided to take a chance. "Answer the call, but do not give away your position."

"Yes, sir," Sam said. "Zig, we have been ordered to answer the call."

Zig took his communicator out of his pocket and punched in the location numbers on the communicator's small screen then said, "Earthling, I have received your call. Explain yourself."

Chester nearly dropped his iPhone when he heard Zig's reply. He quickly got control of himself and said, "A group of people have located the position of your base and are preparing to attack you. I can help you in exchange for your support."

"Stay with them and keep your communicating device on," Zig replied. "We will contact you."

"I will," Chester said and ended the call. He put his iPhone in his pants pocket and walked back to where Rawlings was finishing washing the cups and coffee pot.

"Did you contact them?" Rawlings asked him.

"I said I would, didn't I," he answered in a smug tone.

"When do we make contact with them?" Rawlings asked him.

"We don't. They'll make contact with us," he said. "Keep that machinegun of yours handy we're going to need it real soon."

Zig immediately contacted the compound and reported his contact. Zack told Commander Rush what he'd done, and within two minutes he was ordered to reply to the Earthling's message but to be careful. Rush was not about to make the mistake of underestimating an Earthling again.

"I have already done that, Commander," Zack said.

"Excellent, Zack," Rush said. "I shall report your initiative to the Overlord and you shall be rewarded with a promotion."

"Thank you, Commander Rush," Zack replied with the sound of pride in his voice.

CHAPTER 21

"What time is it?" Henry asked Susan as he drove.

"No idea," she answered. "How close are we to that stream?"

He glanced at the map on the dashboard screen. "We're about a mile away."

"We must have left that compound an hour ago," Susan said as she turned to her left and looked through a view slot at the eastern horizon. "I can see the sunlight coming over the horizon."

He took a quick glance out the view slot on his left. "Yeah, I see it, too, must be close to six in the morning. Have you seen any of those alien cars close to us?"

"No, and I wonder why?"

"Well, you can bet they know we got some of their stuff and an armored car and escaped," he said as he drove. "This thing has a wonderful suspension system. I can hardly feel the bumps in the ground, and we're rolling over some rough ground."

Susan didn't say anything because she was looking over the ten inch wide four inch high screen on the panel in front of her.

"Did you hear me?"

"There's a control panel of some kind in front of me with a screen," she said as she saw a large brown button in the center of the panel.

"Don't touch anything," he told her. "We may blow up."

If we do that'll solve our problems, she thought as she raised her right index finger and moved it toward the button. She hesitated a second then shrugged her shoulders and thought *what the hell* and pushed the button.

The panel lit up and a screen came on with a list of options on it.

'Target finder, wide scan, high intensity scan, long range scan, map, vehicle identifier.'

She pushed long range scan and watched the screen change to a view screen with scales on it to determine distance to objects. She looked at the small scale near the center of the screen and touched it with her index finger.

The objects pictured on the screen suddenly grew twice as large as they first appeared as if they had suddenly gotten closer.

Susan looked through the target finder of the gun and saw the objects were much closer with the small words 'in range' appearing across the objects. She looked down and touched the smallest scale on the screen and the objects on it grew much larger. She looked through the target finder and saw the small objects in the target finder. "I touched that screen, Henry, and it's a small computer with magnification abilities. I can see miles in front of me."

He heard her but didn't say anything because he was thinking.

"Did you hear me, Henry?" she asked him.

Then he realized something. "All our vehicles have Global Positioning Systems in them that other vehicles can pick up, don't they?"

Without hesitating a moment she pushed the brown button turning off the screen. "Damn, I may have told them where we are." She said.

"Or where we were," he said. "But I wouldn't worry about it, Susan, because if they've got satellites in orbit they know exactly where we are."

"They're probably using ours," she said.

"Probably," he agreed.

"So going through that stream to cover our tracks may not do us any good," she said.

"May not, but it won't hurt to try," he said. He looked at the map on the dashboard screen and wondered if he was giving away their position by having it on. He reached over and turned it off. "When we reach that stream, I'm heading west then north if it divides where I can get into some mountains."

"Let's hope this car has mountain goat abilities, or we may have to abandon it," she said.

"That's the very last thing I want to do," he said. "There are a lot of people out there who are still alive and willing to fight back, and they're going to need a lot of information about those aliens and this car has some that could be of value." He looked ahead through the view plate in the hatch and saw the stream. "That stream's just ahead."

Henry entered the stream heading in a southwesterly direction. He traveled in that directing for ten minutes before he pulled out of the stream and headed west toward some mountains whose name he didn't know or want to know if they hid the car.

It was noon before they found a large, wide overhanging rock to hide the car under and stopped.

"We need water, food, and rest," Susan said. Her body felt as if she had pushed it to the limit and it was ready to stop working.

"I'm exhausted and my mind is empty of ideas," Henry said as he leaned back in the seat and let his sore muscles relax. "I'll take the first watch."

"No, you've been driving since we escaped that compound," she told him. "I've managed at least about forty minutes in cat naps." She reached up and unlocked the locking bolt on the hatch and pushed it open. Warm spring winds rushed into the car through the opened hatch. "I'll take the first watch outside. I'll wake you when I can't go any longer without sleep." She climbed out the hatch onto the top of the armored vehicle, closed the hatch, and dropped to the ground and found a spot where she could see and hear but not be easily seen or heard.

Henry leaned back in the driver's seat and felt along the sides for a lever to recline the seat. He felt one on the left side and pushed it forward. The back of the seat rose to a ninety degree position. He pushed it backwards and the seat moved back ninety degrees forming a narrow bed. He lay back and looked around the spacious car. *God, where are we going to find someone to help us? Everything that can fight these aliens is dead or destroyed.* He closed his eyes and within seconds was asleep.

Theia had been awake for hours and had noticed the direction the stolen armored car had been heading until Susan and Henry had turned off the dashboard computer screen. *So they are two hundred and three miles away heading toward the west coast of this continent. They will find nothing there that can threaten our position. What I've learned from monitoring their radio broadcasts indicates there is nothing but disorder, confusing, and fear among the survivors. It will take them months to get themselves organized enough to present any serious resistance to us, and by then our ships will be in orbit above Earth and will have located every group of these fighting back Earthlings and destroyed them. What will be left will amount to no more than terrified Earthlings running and hiding from us. We have won.*

CHAPTER

Day 3 May 5, 7 p.m.

They had all finished eating a meal of canned baked beans and water, they thought it best to conserve as much of their coffee as possible, and were all ready to leave.

"Think we should leave now?" Janis asked as she looked in the western sky. "There's still almost an hour of daylight left."

"Yes, I think we should leave," William said. "We're in the Rocky Mountains and we don't want to be driving fast in these mountains without lights. And we shouldn't travel faster than fifty miles an hour."

"From those radio broadcasts we've heard here in America there must be hundreds of small communities around with people in them who'd be willing to help us," Nancy said. "Why don't we stop and ask them for help?"

Chester didn't like hearing that but he kept quiet.

Rawlings was in the backseat of his Humvee making sure his machinegun had a thirty round magazine in it and a second one taped upside down to it.

"Would be nice to have more people with us and more food and medical supplies," Alex said. "You can never tell what we're going to run into when we reach this area in Nevada."

"How far are we from it?" Les asked.

"No more than three hundred and fifty miles if our estimates are correct," Level said. He was standing at the hood of his Humvee with the map on the hood looking at it.

"So what do we do when we reach this area?" Judith said. "Go barging in shooting?"

"No," Les said. "I'd recommend we look it over before we make any moves. We want to know what we're getting into."

"Do we really have time for that?" Pedro asked. "Remember, Les, it was you who suggested these aliens are probably waiting for reinforcements. Suppose they show up while we're looking over this area?"

"We'd lose any chance we had of driving them away," William said. "Anyway wherever this alien area is it certainly isn't above ground, so we'd have to find out where it is then how to get into it and stop them from completing their conquest of Earth."

"I hate to say this," Alice said. "But we didn't put much planning into this expedition, did we?"

Everyone looked at her and said nothing.

"Standing here and talking about what we're going to do if we find this alien place, and how poorly we've planned isn't doing anything but wasting time. Which I don't think we have a lot of if there are reinforcements coming to help the aliens."

"She's right," Les said. "I think we should move now. We should reach this area before sunrise and then start making our plans to do whatever we can do to save what's left of Earth."

Level looked around. "Is everybody ready?"

No one said anything they just started getting into their Humvees. They were on the road in ten minutes driving at fifty miles an hour.

CHAPTER 23

11 a.m., May 6

Susan and Henry had each gotten eight hours of sleep and had eaten some of the alien food and drank some water. They were standing in front of the armored car looking at the map of the western part of the United States on Henry's communicator.

"Where do you think we should go?" Susan asked him.

"Your guess is as good as mine," he said.

"There's no doubt the aliens picked up those transmissions given out by those computers in this car," she said. "The question is do they know where we are now?"

"I figure they've got a pretty good idea, but not an accurate one," he said. "And I don't think they're out looking for us at least not this far from their compound."

"Why would you think that?" she asked him.

"When you were asleep in the hospital room we were in, I talked with the doctor of that compound and he said there were a hundred ships heading for Earth with half a million warriors on them. He said they would arrive in ten days."

"That was on the third," Susan said. "We have a little over seven days to contact someone to stop them from completing their conquest of Earth."

"So we got to go someplace where we can make contact with people who'll help us stop them," he said.

"But where do we go?" she asked with the strong sound of failure in her voice.

"I don't really know, Susan. I don't even know what's going on in the outside world. For all I know we could be the only soldiers left alive on Earth."

"There has to be someone out there who is still capable of fighting back, someone who'll help us," she said. "Someone we can work with."

Henry looked at her and thought for a few seconds. "That commander said they'd killed ninety percent of the people on Earth, but he may have been lying for all I know. But there has to be a lot of people who know we've been attacked by aliens and are out there preparing to fight back. Our problem is we don't know where they are."

Susan looked at the communicator on the hood of the armored vehicle and said, "Maybe we can get a radio broadcast from somewhere using these things. They're more advanced that anything we've got so they should be able to pick up Earth broadcasts."

"Can we access Earth broadcasts with a communicator?" Henry asked the communicator.

"This unit is capable of scanning all electrical currents," answered the communicator.

"Access one now and give us its location," Susan said.

A second passed before they heard a broadcast.

"The damage the alien attack has done on Earth has been extensive, but there are people all over the world organizing in groups to fight for our world. On every continent we've heard from people who say they will fight. There are people who are keeping the power plants operating so we can have energy to talk to each other. More information will be forthcoming from this station as soon as we get it. Do not despair. Do not give up. This is our world."

A spot appeared on the screen of the communicator showing where the broadcast was coming from.

"That's east of here," Susan said.

"Bring up a map of the area where the broadcast is coming from?" Henry said.

A map immediately appeared on the screen with a blinking blue light to indicate the source of the broadcast.

"I wonder where that's at." Susan asked.

"From a town that wasn't a target of the aliens. It was probably too small and of no military or political value to them. And it looks to be less than five hundred miles away from us."

"Show us a larger map," Susan told the communicator.

A larger map of the area appeared on the screen showing roads.

"These people did a great job of mapping this planet," Susan said.

"Commander Rush said they had been studying this planet for twenty years," he said. "Communicator is this map coming from your main computer?" He leaned close to the screen and looked at a road.

"Yes."

"That's a major highway," he said.

"And it's running west over fifty miles south of where that compound is," Susan said. "And it's in Nevada."

"Nevada is mostly a wide open state with few people in it," Henry said. "So what major road runs through the northern part of it?"

Susan stared at the map for a few seconds then said, "When I was a little girl, my family and I drove from our home in Rhode Island to San Francisco, and the highway we used was US 80. It starts somewhere in Ohio and continues west to San Francisco. It goes through some very lovely country."

Henry looked at the map and nodded. "So what do you think?"

"I figure this highway has to be US 80," she said. "And it's running at least fifty miles south of that alien compound, and that's in northern Nevada."

Henry looked at the map on the communicator and agreed with her, "US 80."

"We know the broadcast came from a town that was probably too small for the Tabors to attack," she said. "So I suggest we go north till we reach US 80 then head east."

Henry stared at the blinking blue light and said, "Looks like that broadcast came from somewhere in Utah south of US 80."

Susan looked at the map. "Most of western Utah is unoccupied country because of the Great Salt Lake and that Great Salt Lake Desert."

"I'd say it came from someplace southeast of the Utah Test and Training Range and the Dugway Proving Ground," he said. "I've been to both places and that's pretty barren country."

"So we head in that direction, but we should go forty or fifty miles north of the compound and then head south when we are fifty miles east of it, and hope we encounter somebody who hasn't given up hope," she said. "And we drive fast, because time's running out for us."

"We can take turns driving, and we pray those Tabor patrols aren't very far east," he said.

"I'll drive you get some more sleep," Susan told him.

"Off," he said to the communicator.

Five minutes later they were heading northeast for US 80.

"They have ten of our communicators and batteries and weapons and food and medicine, and we cannot locate their position," Rush said as he sat in the chair next to Theia.

"The armored car cannot be traced if the computer in it is not operating and it does not have to be operating to drive the car, and communicators cannot be traced if they are not operating the radio, Commander," she said.

"I am aware of that," he told her.

"There is one other thing, Commander," she said as she looked at the large screen.

"What is that, Lieutenant?" he asked.

"The communicators can be given a different electrical current than the ones we have are on. If that has been done, they can use them without us knowing where they are."

Commander Rush nodded as he said, "I should have known the arrogance of that soldier concealed an intelligent mind. That can be corrected once the Overlord arrives with the rest of the Warrior Class."

"There is no danger to our operation," Theia said.

"None whatsoever, Lieutenant, now that Zip has made contact with an Earthling willing to work with us for a safe position in the new world we will created on Earth," he said. He looked at the time on the right hand side of the screen. "Zip should be making contact with those Earthlings in a few of their Earth hours."

CHAPTER 24

Day 4 May 6, 12:01 a.m.

"We've been driving for five hours," Rawlings said. "When do you think we'll make contact with those aliens?"

"I don't know," Chester said. "Whenever we make contact we must be ready."

Rawlings drove silently for twenty minutes before he said, "I've got an idea."

Chester didn't reply. Rawlings ideas were of no interest to him. Making contact with the aliens was the only thing on his mind and he knew when he made that contact he had to appear to be in control if he was to impress them. *Anyone who has the ability to do to Earth what these aliens have done is not about to make me their main contact with other people if I'm just one of eleven people and not in charge.*

"I said I've got an idea," Rawlings repeated.

"Okay, let's hear it," Chester said in a voice that sounded uninterested.

"We should stop in a few hours because one of us is sick," he said. "And the other one can act like they're helping him. Then I get the machine gun and take over."

Chester looked at him in the dark Humvee and thought, *the Neanderthal has a brain and it works, occasionally.* "Great idea, Rawlings, they won't be expecting anything."

"Now we got to move fast," Rawlings said. "Level is former military and that school teacher Les has had military training, too.

They suspect anything and they're going to start reaching for them assault rifles of theirs."

"I understand that," Chester said as he looked at the clock on the dashboard. "I suggest we stop around three. By then they should all be tired and ready for a rest break. They won't suspect a thing. And you act like the sick one."

"Three it is then," Rawlings said.

May 6, 12:01 a.m.

By ten a.m. Henry and Susan had reached US 80 and were traveling east at eighty miles an hour.

"I wonder if this thing has a radar unit that can scan the road in front of us," Susan asked as she drove.

Henry had slept two hours and was feeling refreshed. "Probably does, but I wouldn't recommend turning it on. It can probably be detected by that main computer and the other vehicles the Tabors have out on patrol."

"How far are we from that broadcast we picked up?" she asked him.

He looked at the communicator in his left hand. The blinking light was closer to them. "We've gone over two hundred miles, so I figure from this map we're probably less than two hundred miles away by road."

"You know, Henry, with the exception of Las Vegas, Reno, and Carson City, Nevada has mostly small towns scattered over wide areas," she said.

"Your point," he said.

"Some of those small towns should have picked up that broadcast we heard and maybe others and are ready to defend themselves against the Tabors," she said. "Maybe we should stop at a few."

"Susan, we're driving in an alien vehicle, and the Tabors probably know where every town within a few hundred miles of their compound is," he said. "They may even been have monitoring them with our satellites. They spot us going into one of them towns they're going to send two or four of those other heavily armored vehicles that attacked us to those towns and do to them what they did to our battalion. And there's probably nothing but retired soldiers and civilians in them with little or no military training and no equipment beyond hunting rifles."

"So what do you suggest we do when we reach the spot where that broadcast came from?"

"We hide this armored car somewhere and hope the Tabors don't find it then make contact on foot," he said. "Even a town full of scared people are going to hold their fire when they see two American soldiers walking toward them."

"We hide it about a mile away," she suggested.

"Alright," he said.

May 6, 2:57 a.m.

Rawlings glanced at the clock on the dashboard. "Okay, it's three to three. I'm pulling over."

"Remember we've got to be quick," Chester told him.

"Quick is my middle name," Rawlings said as he slowed down and moved toward a side road on the right.

"What's wrong?" Alice asked as she saw Rawlings' Humvee slow down and moved to the right side of the road.

"I don't know," Pedro said. He was sitting in the front passenger seat. Les and Janis were on the back seat asleep.

"Rawlings is pulling off to one side and Alice is following him," William said as he reduced the speed of the Humvee and moved to the right side of the road.

Rawlings turned onto another side road and drove another two hundred feet before he stopped among some boulders. He turned around and grabbed the machinegun and put it on the floor next to the right rear passenger door and opened the driver's door and jumped out and ran around to the right side of the Humvee and opened the right rear door and grabbed the machinegun and ran off into the darkness. He left the engine running.

"Wake up," Alice yelled as she stopped two yards behind Rawlings' Humvee and turned off the engine.

Les and Janis woke up.

"What's happening?" Janis asked.

"I think something is wrong with Rawlings," Alice said as she opened the driver's door and got out. "He got out of his Humvee and ran into the darkness."

William stopped two yards behind Alice's Humvee and everyone inside got out and walked around to the right side of Rawlings' Humvee.

Chester jumped out of the Humvee after making sure he had his nine millimeter in his right pants pocket and moved to the front of the Humvee stopping three feet in front of it.

Les saw Chester's move and felt something wasn't right. He started to remove his nine millimeter Glock from his right jacket pocket but left it and turned around and got another one from the box behind the seat and stuck it in the front of his belt after making sure it was loaded, the safety was on, and pulled his shirt out of his belt and let it cover the weapon. He didn't know why he did that, but he decided not to say anything. He stayed in the Humvee as Alice and Janis and Pedro moved toward the right side of Rawlings' Humvee.

"What's wrong?" Level asked in a concerned voice.

"This!" Rawlings yelled as he walked out of the darkness with the machinegun in his hands pointed at those standing next to his Humvee.

"What the hell is wrong?" Alex yelled in an angry voice as he looked in Rawlings' direction. He could just barely make out in the semi-darkness Rawlings was holding the machinegun.

Rawlings raised the machinegun over the roof of his Humvee and pulled the trigger firing a dozen rounds into the air. "Does this answer your question, Boy?"

Everyone suddenly stopped and looked in Rawlings' direction.

"What are you doing?" Pedro demanded.

"Isn't it obvious?" Chester asked pointing his nine millimeter at them.

"No, it isn't," Nancy said.

"Get out of the car, Les," Chester yelled.

Think of something Les thought as he opened the right rear door of the Humvee and started to get out. He put his right foot on the ground and felt a large stick under his foot. He deliberately fell out of the Humvee on the ground. "Oh, hell!" he screamed as he fell on his right side and rolled away from the stick onto his back. "My ankle!"

"Aw, isn't that a shame, Rawlings," Chester said with a big grin on his face. "The nigger has hurt his ankle."

"Don't call him that!" Alice yelled at Chester.

"What the hell are you two up to?" Nancy demanded.

"Simple. We're joining the winning side," Chester said. "Watch Les, Rawlings."

Rawlings turned the machinegun in Les' direction and said, "Get up real slow, nigger, and don't make no false moves." "I can't without help," Les said as he rolled over on his left side.

"Then you're not worth a damn to us anymore," Chester said.

"Don't harm him," Alice screamed as she moved toward Les. "Let me help him."

"Get him on his feet or he ain't never going to get up," Rawlings told her.

She rushed over to Les and grabbed him under his right arm. "Let me help you."

"There's a stick next to me," Les said. "Get it and give it to me so I can use it to stand up."

Alice reached down and got the stick and put it in his right hand.

Les was thankful the stick was long, at least six feet, and thick enough to support his weight. *I wonder what I can do with this.* He raised himself on his left knee and with Alice's help got to his feet using the stick as a crutch. Alice helped him limp to the right fender of the Humvee and lean against it. "What are you two doing?" he asked in a voice with the false sound of pain in it.

"All of you turn around and put your hands on the cars," Chester said. "And if one of you tries to be a hero you'll become one less problem for us."

"You rotten piece of -," Pedro growled at them.

"Do as they say," Level said cutting him off.

They all turned around and put their hands on the Humvees.

"Now I'm going to move behind each of you and remove those automatics I know you've all got," Chester said. "Rawlings, move to an angle so you don't shoot me if you have to start shooting."

Rawlings did as he was told saying, "I've got you covered."

Chester moved down the line removing automatics from their pants pockets and tossing them on the ground in a pile a yard behind him. When he reached Les, he reached into Les front right jacket pocket pull out his automatic and tossed it where he'd tossed the others. He backed a yard away and knelt down and picked up the nine semiautomatics and carried them to his Humvee, opened the right rear door and tossed them on the floor. "Now what we're going to do is make a campfire and heat of some of those cans of baked beans and Spam we've got and have ourselves a nice meal until the new owners of Earth arrive."

"You women do the cooking," Rawlings said. "I want to make sure all of these men are where I can see them."

"You're a fool, Chester," Les told him.

"No, what I am is a man who tried to be friends of with you and those other fools on the block," he yelled at Les in a voice filled with hate. "But what did I get? Rejection from everyone on the block because they didn't know I was a good friend and neighbor offering them my friendship."

"You were nosy and obnoxious," Alice said.

"You didn't want to be a friend to anyone, Chester," Les told him. "All you wanted to do was be a leader in the neighbor."

"I should have been the neighborhood leader. I'm the one that organized all the block parties," he said. "You never even attended any so what the fuck do you know?"

"I know that I'm not very good at parties, so I tend to avoid them," he said. "But I always signed and contributed money to all the block parties, and I never complained about the noise."

"You never organized any block parties," Alice said. "Caroline and Mona and their children did that."

"I told them what to do," he yelled at her. "If they had listened to me the block parties would have been the best in the village."

"Is that what this is all about?" William asked. "No one followed your advice on how to organize block parties?"

"Block parties are for the children that live on the block," Pedro said. "All adults do is cook and sit around drinking beer and complain about the government."

Chester looked at William and said, "What this is all about, William, is being on the winning team."

"Let's cut this stupid talk and call the aliens," Rawlings said.

"I can assure you they won't have anything to do with you two," Level said.

Les thought that was an unusual statement for Level to make. He assumed it was because of what was happening.

"I think they will," Alex said as he looked at Chester's face. "By working with these two they'll learn some Earth people will do anything for money."

"No, they won't," Janis said. "They haven't done what they've done to Earth to make a deal with those two."

"How could they call them?" Alice asked.

"By an iPhone," Alex said. "Remember we agreed not to use our iPhones because the aliens might be able to pick up the frequencies and locate our position."

"But why are you doing such a terrible thing?" Nancy asked. "Why would you two want to work with the aliens that attacked us?"

"To be on the winning team," Les said. He was desperately trying to think of something to do that wouldn't result in any of them being killed or wounded.

"Nice to know, Nigger, you can remember what I said," Chester said with an evil grin on his face.

"Is that sort of language necessary?" William asked him.

"I'm in charge. If I do it or say it, it's necessary," Chester told him. "Rawlings, I'm going to find a good place to start a fire so the women can cook us all a nice hot meal."

"Don't worry, Buddy, I've got my eye on them, if one so much as farts they're dead," Rawlings assured him.

"I'll be back in a few minutes," Chester said as he turned around and walked into the darkness.

"Which one of you made contact with the aliens?" Les asked.

"Does it matter, teacher," Rawlings asked him.

"Yes, it does. If I'm going to die because you and Chester decided to sell out the human race, I'd at least like to die knowing who made the first move."

"We both made contact at the same time," he lied.

"The last time we made camp," Les said. *A stick against a machinegun a yard behind me is a guarantee of death.*

"You got it, Boy," Rawlings said.

"I think you two are going to get one hell of a surprise when the aliens show up," Level said.

"Sure are," Rawlings agreed. "They're going to see how smart Chester and I are."

"They're going to kill you right after they let you kill us," Nancy told.

"Not so, Sugar," he said. "We're going to be in charge of every man and woman on this planet working as overseers."

"Once they've gotten complete control of this planet, you two will be useless to them," Pedro told him. "Any intelligent form of life who can do to Earth what they've done is not about to trust two Earthlings who've sold out their world and the human race."

"Rawlings, I found a place," Chester called back. "Let the men get food and coffee and pots out of their Humvees and bring it to the sound of my voice."

"You heard him, you guys," Rawlings said. "The cripple can just hobble to the camp spot on his own. Don't fall, Les, I ain't about to take pith on you."

Five minutes later they were walking in the direction of Chester's voice. When they reached the spot where Chester was he said, "Drop the food on the ground and Level you and Alex start gathering fire wood. And I better be able to see you."

Level and Alex walked off and began gathering fire wood.

"What are we going to do?" Alex asked him in a whisper.

"Damn little against a machinegun with a clip in it that holds thirty rounds," he whispered back as he began to gather wood. "But whatever we do we had better be damn fast about it."

Twenty minutes later they were sitting around a campfire watching the six cans of bake beans they had put in the pot over the fire boil. The odor was very appealing but none of them were thinking about food.

Les was sitting close to the fire with the point of his stick near the fire so it began to smoke. Chester and Rawlings didn't notice it.

CHAPTER 25

Day 4 May 6, 5:30 a.m.

Henry had increased the magnification of the target finder on the screen till he could see everything thirty miles in front of him and around him when he turned the target finder around. When he saw the light of a fire in the distance he didn't understand why it was there. "Do you see what I see?" he asked Susan.

"What?" she asked.

"Go to magnification ten on that screen in front of you," he told her.

She was going over ninety miles an hour in the darkness and didn't want to release the steering wheel for fear of running into something. "Eh, can you transfer it to my screen. I don't want to take my eyes off the road I'm doing over ninety miles," she told him. Then she said, "Magnification ten."

The magnification on her screen increased to ten times its normal range and she saw the light of the fire. "That's a campfire," she said. "You can tell by how it flickers and how small it is."

"But who would have a campfire out here after what's happened?" he asked as he stared at the fire.

Susan didn't say anything she was too busy driving and staring into the dark hoping to avoid any objects that could damage the car they were in.

"It looks to be about thirty or forty miles from us," he said. "Maybe it's just a fire accidentally started."

"Think we should head for it?"

He looked at the communicator in his left hand. "We're about a hundred miles from that broadcast." He thought of something. "Susan, they may be able to pick up our location from these screens."

"Turn off!" she yelled and her screen immediately when blank. "We should head in the direction of that fire. That could be someone who managed to locate the Tabors underground complex using satellites."

"Off," he said to his screen. "Okay, head in the direction of that fire."

"We should reach it in less than an hour at our speed," she said and increased the speed of the armored car. "Whatever type of fire it is we park this vehicle somewhere we can get back to it real quick before we check out that fire."

"I agree with you, Susan," he said. "But I'm a little sick of fighting a war with aliens all alone. I feel like saying the hell with it and going off somewhere and hiding for the rest of my life."

"I'd like to do exactly that, Henry," she said. "We've lost our families, friends, and neighbors and everything else we value. Where do you come from?"

"Seattle, Washington," he said. "And there's a major navy base close to it so there's no one left alive on the base or city. These Tabors would have never missed such a target."

"All we've got left is a world that's in pretty bad shape if what those Tabors told you is right," she said.

"I just pray to God we've still got a chance of stopping those Tabors," he said.

"We've got six days left, Henry. Maybe we can perform a miracle," she told him not believing they could.

"Yeah," he agreed, but he didn't believe it.

"We are outside our patrol area," Sam said as he drove.

"Yes, we are but I have the location on the communicator the Earthling used," Zig said. "We shall approach them long before the star of this system begins to shine over this part of Earth."

"I suggest we approach slowly," Sam said. "These Earthlings can be devious."

"I agree. We shall come within a hundred yards of them then dismount and approach them on foot without them knowing we are close and watch them for a while to determine if they are part of some military unit trying to catch some of us."

"How far are we from the location," Sam asked Zig.

"Fifty-five Earth miles," Zig said. "Slow down we do not want to rush up to them."

Sam dropped his speed by one half.

For an hour they had sat silently around the fire staring at Chester and Rawlings. None of them knew what to say to change their minds.

"How could you even imagine doing what you are intending to do?" Janis asked Chester breaking the silence as she sat on the ground opposite him across the fire.

"Common sense," Chester said. "Considering what these aliens have already done to Earth what are our chances of stopping them from completely taking over the Earth? And I'd rather be an overseer of slaves than a slave."

"You could join a resistance movement and hide in the back country and continue fighting for Earth," Judith told him.

"And live like a wild animal?" he asked her. "Whoever these aliens are they're going to need Earth people to tell them how to control those that are still alive on this planet and those are the people they're going to treat well."

Les noticed that Rawlings was sitting opposite him across the fire with the machinegun lying on his lap and looking into the pot of cooking baked beans. He inched the tip of his stick closer to the fire until it was burning. Chester was sitting on Rawlings' left side and wasn't paying any attention to Les, and Rawlings hadn't noticed Les moving the stick into the fire.

But Pedro did. He was sitting on William's left side wandering what Les was up to if he was up to anything.

"You two have no idea how much of a traitor you two are, do you?" Level said to Chester.

"Does it really matter?" Chester told him in an angry voice. "There are no more nations. Earth belongs to the aliens, treason is a concept that doesn't exist anymore, and I'd rather work for them than become one of their slaves."

"I suppose you agree with him, Rawlings?" Nancy asked him.

He straightened up and looked at Nancy and said, "You bet I do, Girlie, cause I've always been on the winning team."

"This is not a football game, Rawlings," William angrily snapped at him. "This is an attempt to find out who those aliens are that attacked us, and to stop them from doing any more damage to Earth and save lives."

"And to take our world back," Alice said. She was sitting next to Les wondering why he hadn't said anything.

"What did you tell them when you contacted them?" Alex asked.

"That I could be of help," Chester answered.

"That we could be of help," Rawlings corrected him.

"Yes," Chester nodded. "That Rawlings and I could be of help to them in controlling the remaining humans on Earth."

Les looked at the burning tip of the stick he held in his left hand and thought, *when I move I've got to move very fast. I sure hope I'm up to it.*

Pedro's frown faded when he realized that Les was planning something to help them get away and the only way to help him was to distract Rawlings. "You've never been on a winning team in your life, Rawlings."

"What are you talking about?" Rawlings growled at Pedro.

"I'm a sports fanatic," he said. "I'm one of those types of people with a big screen TV in his basement game room who watches six different games at the same time, and can keep up with all the plays."

"So what?" Rawlings replied.

"I'm one of those people whose basement game room is devoted to sports of all kind, even soccer," he said. "Most people in the world call it football."

"Bullshit," Rawlings snapped at him. "A bunch of faggots running around in short pants kicking a ball around a green field. That ain't football. Football is what we Americans play a rough game for rough men like me."

Les looked up and saw Rawlings and Chester sitting on the opposite side of the fire from everyone else. He looked back at the tip of the wooden stick and saw the tip was burning. *I hope it's getting hard enough to do what I've got in mind.*

"We must be pretty close to that campfire," Susan said as she looked through the view slot of the armored car. The glow of the fire seemed much brighter now.

"No more than a few miles," Henry said looking through the target finder at the glow of the campfire. "Three miles at the most I'd say."

"At ninety miles an hour we should be there in a few minutes," she said.

"I hope there's someone at that fire we can work with," Henry said.

Susan looked off to her right and saw an even spot where she could leave the highway onto the rough terrain. "I'm reducing speed and moving off the road," she told him.

"Okay," Henry said. "I'll look for a place to park this car and we can get out on foot."

"I can see the glow of a small fire three miles ahead of us," Zig told Sam.

"We must contact Zack," Sam said.

Zig did so. The Commander answered his call.

"How far are you from the location of the contact?" Rush asked him.

"We are less than four Earth miles away, sir," Zig answered.

If that were some military unit from this state they would have detected the presence of Zig and Sam before they got that close. "Have you detected any electrical scans of your car?" Rush asked him.

"No, sir, no electrical scans for over a hundred miles in any direction," Zig answered.

"How far out is your detector scanning?"

"One hundred miles," he said.

"And you have not been detected?"

"No, sir."

"Stop when you are a mile away and approach on foot. Use your communicators to scan an area of ten miles around you," he said. "If you detect nothing that could be a trap make contact with the Earthlings. Disarm them, secure them, and bring them back to the compound."

"Yes, sir," Zig replied.

"Keep your helmet communicators on open so I can see and hear what is being said and done," Rush ordered them.

"Yes, sir," Zig said and put his helmet communicator on open and activated the face plate so it functioned like a camera.

Sam did the same thing.

Rush put the computer on standby and looked at the screen that showed the exact position of Sam and Zig. He saw exactly what they saw. "There is no danger," he said more to himself than to Dram who was on duty.

Dram didn't respond.

"It's the most popular sport in the world," Nancy said. "And soccer players aren't all gay. Most are straight."

"They're all a bunch of faggots," Rawlins growled at her.

"Not tough guys like you were, huh?" William said wondering why they were discussing sports instead of trying to talk Rawlings and Chester out of what they were doing.

"You're right there, Boy O, and I'm still a tough guy," Rawlings told him.

"You can't do this, Chester," Level said. He was trying to think up something he could say to Chester that would make him change his mind. "What we were going to do may not have saved the human race from extinction but to willing join the aliens is a crime against humanity."

"Humanity is finished, Level," Chester said. "What Rawlings and I are doing is making damn sure we're not finished with them."

"You're despicable," Janis said in as nasty a voice as possible.

Judith just glared at them with hate in her eyes.

"How soon will it be before your alien masters arrive?" Alex asked.

"Partners," Chester corrected him. "And they should show up within a few hours."

Pedro shook his head and said, "You're the same fuck up you were when you played for the Seattle Seahawks, Rawlings."

"You don't know what you're talking about, Wetback," Rawlings yelled at him. "I was the best they had. Just like I was when I played for the Miami Dolphins and the Dallas Cowboys. No defensive line stopped me, and no one ever got pass me when I was on the defensive."

"Bullshit," Pedro told him. "You were shit!"

"You don't say that to me, you wetback son-of-a-bitch!" Rawlings yelled at him leaning forward like he wanted to jump Pedro and smash his face into a blood pulp.

"Calm down," Chester told him.

"Like I said, Rawlings, I'm a sports freak, but I've never played any sports pro or amateur, but I know about you. You played for the Seattle Seahawks from September 3 of 2010 till October 4 of that year, and then you were thrown off the team."

"That's a fucking lie! I was transferred," he yelled.

Pedro shook his head hoping whatever Les was planning he'd do it soon. "You refused to take orders. You thought because you were big with a lot of muscles you could do as you wished. You never even knew the plays because you never studied the playbook, and because of that Seattle never won a game when you were on the field. And you only played three games before you were cut from the team."

"You don't say that shit to me," Rawlings screamed at him as he started to rise up on his feet with the machine gun in his left hand.

"And you never played for the Miami Dolphins or the Dallas Cowboy, because Seattle put the word out that you couldn't obey orders," Pedro said as he stood up to confront Rawlings. "No team in the NFL wanted a damn thing to do with you."

"You shut your fucking mouth, Motherfucker!" Rawlings screamed at him.

Les looked at the burning tip of the stick and thought, *now!*

"That campfire looks like it's only a few hundred yards away," Susan said as she eased the armor car between two large boulders and stopped.

"And just south of us," Henry said as he opened the hatch of the car and climbed out.

As soon as they were both on the ground, they checked the electric pistols they carried to make sure they were ready to shoot then separated ten feet and walked toward the campfire making sure to walk as quietly as they could.

"We are close enough," Sam said as he stopped his vehicle. "We should approach on foot."

Zig said nothing as he opened the hatch of the armored car and got out.

They stood shoulder to shoulder for a few minutes scanning the land around them for half a mile and seeing everything as if it was day and not night. Then they took out their communicators and scanned for ten miles. Certain there was no danger they put their communicators in their pants pockets and started walking forward holding their rifles in front of them as if they were on parade. Making noise didn't concern them. There was nothing on Earth they couldn't kill.

CHAPTER 26

Without a word Les pulled both of his feet together under him and lunged forward with the tip of the burning stick pointing at Rawlings' stomach.

Rawlings was so busy screaming at Pedro he was a liar he didn't notice what Les was doing until the tip of the burning stick plunged into his stomach. Then he howled in pain and threw the machine gun he was holding in his left hand back to his left hitting Chester in the face with the barrel and jumped to his feet grabbing his stomach.

Chester fell backwards on his back screaming in pain. The automatic in his right hand flew out of his hand behind him.

Les pulled the tip of the burning stick from Rawlings' stomach and pulled it back and using it like a baseball bat and hit Rawlings' on the left side of his head with the still smoking bloody tip as hard as he could as he yelled, "Run!"

Level, Pedro, Janis, Judith, Alice, Alex, Nancy and William all jumped up and ran back into the forest.

"Find someplace to hide," Level yelled to them as he ran. "And get down on the ground and be quiet."

The blow knocked Rawlings to the ground on his right side howling in pain.

"I'll kill you, you fucking nigger bastard," Chester screamed as he rolled over on his left side.

Les started to plunge the burning tip of the stick into Rawlings again, but decided against it as he saw Rawlings recovering from his painful wounds faster than he'd expected and turn on his left side and reaching for the machine gun. He dropped the stick and turned around and dashed into the dark forests as fast as he could run. He ran in a zigzag manner with his arms stretched out in front of him waving them from side to side hoping he didn't run into any objects that could hurt him. He didn't know how far or long he ran, a half minute at the most, before he noticed the ground was beginning to decline under his feet. He slowed down when his hands touched a tree and he ran around behind it and threw himself on the ground knocking some of the wind out of his lungs.

The others ran directly away from the fire in a group as Les had done and continued running until they encountered some bushes less than fifty yards away that slowed them down.

"Get down behind this and stay quiet," Level said as he threw himself over the top of the bushes and landed among them.

Alex, Pedro, and Alice threw themselves down on the ground just in front of the bushes. Janis, Nancy, and Judith did the same thing. William was to the right of Level behind the bushes lying down, and like everyone else afraid.

Rawlings felt intense burning pain in his stomach and a nasty burned bruise on the left side of his face and he was filled with rage. He ignored the pain in his stomach and on the left side of his face as he rolled over on his left side and saw the machine gun. He grabbed it with his left hand and jumped to his feet as pain raced through his stomach. "You're so fucking dead, nigger!" he screamed as he turned the weapon in the direction everyone had run and squeezed the trigger waving the weapon from left to right and back again.

Chester jumped to his feet a few seconds after Rawlings did holding his gun and started firing the semiautomatic in the direction he thought Les had run.

Over thirty slugs tore through the dark forest cutting branches and leaves off the trees and brush.

Everybody stayed down except William who rose up on his knees to look around in the darkness to see if he could see the others. Two slugs hit him in the chest. A third hit him in the forehead and not a sound escaped his lips as he fell to the ground dead.

Les pulled the semiautomatic from the back of his pants and put a round in the chamber and waited. To challenge a machine gun with an semiautomatic handgun wasn't only foolish, but deadly even though he could see Rawlings and Chester standing in front of the fire shooting at them.

Susan and Henry were less than a hundred yards from the fire when they heard Rawlings' scream and a moment later Chester screaming he was going to kill Les. Less than thirty seconds passed before they heard Rawlings' screaming "You're so fucking dead, nigger." They both froze in their tracks and waited. When they heard the machine gun and semiautomatic firing both dropped to the ground in a prone position with their electric handguns pointing in the direction of the firing. They kept quiet.

Sam and Zig were closer to the fire than Henry and Susan because they hadn't been walking in a slow, cautious manner as had Henry and Susan. They pointed their weapons in the direction of the firing and waited. Warriors didn't fall and hide they stood up and fought.

Rawlings fired the remaining bullets in the clip in the machine gun and knelt down on his left knee to switch the empty clip for a full one.

"Don't," Chester told him as he ejected the empty fourteen round clip from his semiautomatic and got another out of his jacket pocket and slapped it into the butt of the handgun and jacked a round into the chamber.

"I going to kill that fucking nigger!" he screamed. "Don't no black motherfucker stabs me with a stick and runs off and lives."

"No, we may frighten away the aliens coming for us," he said. He looked at Rawlings' stomach wound. "It doesn't look that bad."

"It feels like my guts are on fire," he screamed at Chester. "And that nigger is got to die."

"You want to make contact with the aliens don't you?"

"Yeah, but I want that nigger dead," Rawlings screamed at him.

"He's probably already dead, and the rest, too," Chester told him. "Nobody could survive the firepower you and me put into that forest."

"I want to see his bleeding nigger body," Rawlings yelled as he made sure the full clip was in the machinegun and pulled the bolt back putting a round in the chamber. He was trembling with pain and rage.

"You shoot anymore and those aliens aren't going to make contact with us," Chester warned him.

"My guts are on fire," he said as he let the muzzle of the machinegun fall to the ground and he looked down at his wound. "Jesus Christ, it hurts like hell!"

"Stay where you are and no more shooting," Chester said. "I'm going to get a medical kit out of our Humvee."

Rawlings sank to his knees and grabbed his wound and moaned in pain while Chester went to one of the Humvees for a medical kit.

Sam and Zig had heard everything Chester and Rawlings had said.

"Those are the two Earthlings waiting for us," Sam said.

"Yes," Zig agreed. "And that loud noise was one of their metal shooting weapons."

"The nigger must be an Earthling who opposed them making contact with us," Sam said.

"Speaker," Zig said and his helmet went to exterior speaker mode. "Maximum level two."

'Done,' flashed on the faceplate of his helmet.

"Earthlings," he said. "Can you hear me?"

Level, Les, Alex, Nancy, Janis, Judith, Pedro, and Alice heard him and didn't respond. They stayed where they were lying and remained quiet.

Henry and Susan heard him and also stayed down and quiet.

The sound of Zig's voice surprised Chester and he froze.

Rawlings had heard him too, but he was in pain and didn't care. All he wanted was the pain in his stomach to stop and to find and kill Les.

"Yes, I hear you," Chester said after he recovered from his momentary shock.

"Stay where you are and do not move if you value your lives," Zig said.

"I need help," moaned Rawlings.

"It's coming," Chester told him. "Just don't move and put that machinegun down."

Rawlings dropped the machinegun to the ground and moaned loudly as he held his stomach and stayed in place.

Les remained still and quiet and prayed the others did the same thing.

Level thought *foolish bastards to think they can deal with the Tabor,* but he didn't make a sound. The others also remained quiet.

Susan and Henry lay still and quiet with their weapons pointed in the direction of the fire and wondered what the hell was going on.

Zig and Sam approached the fire as if they didn't have a care in the world and stopped a few feet beyond the middle Humvee and looked around. They could see everything for over four hundred feet as clearly as if they were only a foot away. When they were sure there was no danger to them they walked over to the front Humvee where Chester stood and stopped on the side of the Humvee he was at.

"You are the Earthling willing to help us control this planet?" Sam asked him as Zig looked at Rawlings on his knees moaning in pain.

"Me and the man on the ground can help you take control of Earth and the surviving Earth people," Chester told him. He couldn't see their faces behind their faceplates. "My name is Chester Brown and the other man is Samuel Rawlings and without our help you'll find yourselves in a continuous war with the people of Earth."

"The Commander will determine whether you can be of value to us," he said.

"Where is your commander?" Chester asked him wondering if this alien looked like some horrible monster behind his helmet's face plate.

"Where I am is not your concern, Chester Brown," Commander Rush said.

"He can see me?" Chester asked.

"I can also see you injured companion," he said. "Is the area safe?"

"Yes," Chester said.

"I am not speaking you, Chester Brown," Rush said.

"Yes, Commander," Zig said. "The area is safe."

"What were those loud noises I heard?"

"These two Earthlings using their metal firing weapons against other Earthlings," Zig answered.

"Are they close to you?" Rush asked.

"No, Commander," Sam said. "They have run away into the thick plants close to us."

"Gather the two Earthlings and take them to you vehicle and bring them to the compound," he ordered. "Give them medical aid if they need it."

"Shall we bring their weapons with us?" Sam asked.

"Secure them in your vehicle and bring them," Rushed ordered.

"Give me your weapon," Zig said to Chester.

Chester handed him his semiautomatic without a word of protest, hoping he hadn't made a mistake.

"Go to your injured companion," Sam ordered him.

Chester dropped the medical kit on the hood of the Humvee and turned around and walked over to Rawlings. Sam and Zig followed him.

"Help me," Rawlings moaned. "I'm in a lot of pain. My guts are on fire."

"Put him on his back," Zig said to Chester as he put his rifle on his shoulder and reached behind his back and removed his medical kit from the back of his belt.

Chester knelt down next to Rawlings and rolled him over on his back.

Sam stood guard as Zig knelt down next to Rawlings and ripped his shirt open to expose the burned bleeding wound. He looked at Rawlings' wound for a few seconds before he opened his medical kit and took out a plastic bottle and flipped the cap back.

"That's not going to kill him, is it?" Chester asked. He didn't really care if it killed Rawlings or not. Now that he'd made contact with the aliens Rawlings wasn't of much use to him.

"Your bodies are biologically identical to ours and our medicine is superior to yours," he said as he pushed the top of the plastic bottle three times spraying a cool, clear liquid onto Rawlings' wound. He looked at the burn on the left side of Rawlings' face and sprayed some of the cool liquid on it avoiding his eye.

Within seconds Rawlings' pain ended and the spray formed a clear bandage over his wounds. "Damn, they don't hurt no more."

Zig stood up closing the plastic bottle and returned it to his medical kit and the medical kit to the back of his belt. "Get up we must return to the compound. The commander wants to speak with both of you."

"How did you learn to speak English?" Chester asked him as Rawlings got to his feet.

"We are speaking Tabor," Sam answered as he picked up Rawlings' machinegun.

"It's similar to English," Chester said.

"Come," Zig said as he turned around and started walking back toward his vehicle.

Chester and Rawlings walked behind him and Sam followed off to their left two yards behind them carrying Chester and Rawlings' weapons.

Chester and Rawlings didn't think of the weapons inside the Humvee, and Sam and Zig weren't interested in any more Earth weapons.

My God, was all Les could think as he heard them talking and walking off.

Susan and Henry stayed where they were and remained silent until they heard Zig's and Sam's vehicle moving off over the rough terrain and brush.

Les and the others remained where they were for over fifteen minutes before Level rose up on his knees and looked in the direction he'd heard the sound come from. He lay back down and waited another five minutes before he said in a whisper, "Who's alive?"

"Me, Alex" Alex said.

"I am, too," Nancy said.

One by one they all answered except William. Les was the last one to speak. "Stay where you are all of you," Level told them. "I'm going forward to find out if they've really gone."

"Be careful," Alice said from her hiding place. She hoped Les was okay. She had grown fond of him and didn't want to lose him.

Les moved forward on his belly till he could see the fire and smell the bake beans cooking in the metal pot.

Level stood up and walked slowly toward the fire looking around for anyone and stopped when he was a few yards away from the fire. He couldn't see anyone.

Henry and Susan were lying on their bellies looking in the direction of the fire and listening and remained quiet.

Level saw no one and didn't hear anything. All he could smell were the beans cooking in the pot. He took his handkerchief out of his back pocket and leaned down and grabbed the pot by the handle and set it off to one side. Then he stood up and looked around and listened for any sound. When he heard none, he said, "They've gone."

Susan and Henry heard him and looked at each other wondering what they should do. Susan made a motion for them to stand up. Henry shook his head against it.

Alex got up and walked to the fire with a feeling of safety. "They've gone?" he asked Level as he stopped next to him.

"Yeah, with those aliens," Level said.

"That means they're going to tell the aliens about our plans," Alex said.

"They will. It's safe. You can all come out now," Level yelled back into the woods at the others.

One by one they all rose from their hiding places and stood up and walked to the fire.

"Where's William?" Judith asked.

"I don't know," Pedro said. "He could be hurt in the woods somewhere."

"When Les stabbed Rawlings with that burning stick and yelled run, I just started running," Nancy said. "I was so scared."

"Brilliant on your part," Level told him.

Alice walked up to Les and looked him over. "You okay?"

"I'm fine how about you?"

"Yes, thanks for what you did."

Les looked around and said, "Let's get a flashlight and go find William. He might be hurt and need help."

Janis walked to the last Humvee and opened the door and looked inside for a flashlight. She found one on the rear seat, she took it, and came back to the others saying, "We all ran in the same direction, I think, so William shouldn't be too far from where we hid."

"I'll go with you," Les offered.

They walked off into the woods in the direction they had all ran. They walked for fifty yards before Janis stopped and said, "Oh, my, this is terrible."

Les was standing next to her as she shined the light down on William and looked at the bullet holes in his body. "Yeah, let's go tell the others."

Five minutes later they walked back to the fire and told the others about William.

"Are you sure he's dead?" Alice asked them.

"Shot twice in the chest and once in the forehead by slugs from a heavy caliber machinegun," Les told her. "He's dead."

"Let's get a blanket and wrap his body up and bury it when the sun comes up," Pedro said as he walked toward the Humvees.

Susan put her electric gun in her left hand and gently hit Henry with her right hand.

He knew what she meant. They should help. He motioned with his left hand they should wait a moment.

"So what do we do now?" Janis asked.

No one said anything for a few seconds because no one had an answer to her question.

"We bury William get some food in us and continue as before," Les said. "And this time we do it without two traitors among us."

"I agree," Alice said.

The others looked at her.

"What else can we do?" she asked them.

No one said anything.

"Go home and wait for these aliens to come and put slave collars around our necks?" she asked them.

"Now that Chester and Rawlings are working with them, they are going to know everything that we know," Pedro said. "They're going to know we traced that spike we picked up in Oak Park to a certain spot in Nevada, and that we're headed there."

"And they'll be waiting for us, too," Level said. "And where we least expect."

Susan looked at Henry in the dark and made a face indicating she thought they should say something.

He looked back and nodded and whispered, "You say something. Your voice may not frighten them."

She started to get up but Henry stopped her.

"Don't make a target of yourself," he told her.

She nodded and said in a loud voice while lying on her stomach, "Maybe we can help you?"

CHAPTER 27

As soon as they heard Susan's voice all of them dropped to the ground. Level cursed himself for not getting a weapon from the Humvee where Chester and Rawlings had put them in.

Les dropped to his stomach with his weapon pointed in the direction the voice came from.

"Eh, we're like you," Susan said while still lying down. "We're people from Earth."

"You are?" Alex responded in a surprised voice.

"Yes, we are," Henry said. "We're going to stand up and come into your camp. Please don't shoot us. We've already been wounded once."

"Come on," Level said.

Les cocked the semiautomatic and prayed these were not some more aliens.

Henry stood up and put his weapon in the holster on his right hip and raised his hands high above his head. Susan did the same thing.

"Don't shoot us," Susan said. "We've got our hands up, and we're not holding weapons."

"Come ahead," Level said as he looked at Les and whispered, "Keep them covered."

"Don't worry," Les assured him. After Chester and Rawlings' actions he was ready to kill anyone who seemed a threat to them, human or aliens.

Susan and Henry walked forward till they were three yards from the fire and could be clearly seen by the eight.

"You're American soldiers," Janis said when she saw their uniforms. She started getting up.

"Yes. Our unit was attacked by those aliens a few days ago, and we were wounded and captured," Henry said. "We were the only survivors."

Les and the others stood up. Les was pointing the semiautomatic in their direction.

"Look, Mister, could you point that automatic in another direction," Susan told him.

Les nodded and put the safety on the automatic and lowered the hammer back in place. He put the semiautomatic in his jacket pocket.

"You're the ones that sent out that message a few days ago?" Nancy asked them.

"Our unit was on maneuvers over a hundred miles west of here when we were attacked hours after sunrise," Susan told her as she and Henry slowly lowered their hands.

"Your message was picked up," Les said.

"You said, Young Man, you were wounded and captured," Alice asked Henry.

"Yes, ma'am, we were," he said as he smelled the odor of the bake beans.

"How did you get away?" Alex asked them.

"Eh, are those baked beans?" Susan asked as she pointed at the pot.

"Yes, they are," Janis said. "Are you two hungry?"

"Yeah," Susan said with a grin on her face. "All we've had since we escaped from the Tabors' compound is water and some of their food we took. Those beans smell good."

"You ate alien food?" Nancy asked.

"They did feed us while we were in custody," Henry said.

"Somebody gets some plates for them," Level said. "We need to listen to these two."

"Are those others coming back?" Pedro asked them.

"No, they've gone back to their compound," Henry said.

"How do you know?" Level asked him.

"We weren't very far from them behind some brush, about seventy feet, and we heard them talking," he answered.

Alice rushed off toward the Humvees to get plates and spoons and cups for everyone.

"And they didn't know you were that close?" Pedro asked him.

"We got into position behind some thick brush maybe twenty minutes before they approached your fire and remained quiet," Susan said.

"What do those aliens look like?" Judith asked them.

"Like us," Henry said. "Except they are in excellent physical condition, and are warriors from the planet Tabor."

Alice came back with plates, spoons, and cups for everyone and passed them around.

"What about William?" Nancy asked. "Do we just forget him?"

"No," Level said. "We eat and listen to them, then give him as decent a burial as we can."

"Sit down, everybody," Alice said as she approached the hot pot with a cloth in her left hand and a large ladle in her right hand.

Everyone sat down around the fire and Alice served everyone. "I'm sorry this is all we have right now. We weren't expecting to eat even these beans."

Henry and Susan began to eat without saying a word.

"Mind telling us about yourselves?" Les asked them as he held a plate for Alice to fill for herself.

"Yeah," Susan mumbled as she continued to eat like a person who hadn't eaten in days.

It took Henry and Susan ten minutes to eat and tell them what had happened to them over the last two days.

"You two have been very lucky," Pedro said.

"But not the men and women in our unit," Susan said as she ate.

"How many were in your unit and what type of unit was it?" Janis asked them.

"We were a part of the Tenth Infantry Division, Second Brigade First Battalion. It was a heavy weapons battalion," Susan said.

"How many of you were there?" Level asked them.

"Eleven hundred combat troops and one hundred medical and KP staff personal with fifty armored light tanks and sixteen personal carriers," Susan said.

"And when were you attacked by the aliens?" Les asked.

"Around noon," Henry said as he took his canteen off his belt. "We were trying to contact the Brigade when they attacked us. They killed our outposts who were a mile beyond the camp without us knowing, and tore into us."

"How many were there?" Level asked.

"Two heavily armored vehicles with, I think, two men in each one," he said after a swallow of water. "They came at us from the east and west. It took them less than ten minutes to destroy all our armored vehicles and kill everyone but Susan and me."

"Didn't you fight back?" Level asked him.

"Hell yes, with everything we had, even though most of our ammo was for training we did have some live ammo and used that against them," he said. "It was a waste of time. RPGs, antitank rounds, and armor piercing ammo were all useless against them."

"They raced around among us shooting in all directions and hitting us like we were targets on a wooden board," Susan said.

"What are RPGs?" Nancy asked.

"Rocket Propelled Grenades," Susan told her. "We used training ammo as well as live ammo against them, and didn't even scratch the surface of their armored vehicles."

"And you two were the only survivors?" Les asked her.

"Yes," she answered. "I was wondered first and slipped into unconsciousness. Henry was still fighting when I passed out."

"And you?" Level asked Henry.

"Shot in the stomach like Susan. I passed out a second later," he said.

"You said you were captured?" Alex said looking over them both.

"Yes, both of us," Henry said. "We were both wounded and woke up in a hospital room, or what the Tabors call a hospital room."

"All this occurred three days ago?" Janis asked in a disbelieving voice.

"Yes, it did," Susan said as she put her empty plate on the ground and took out her canteen. "I don't blame you for not believing us. I wouldn't if I were you. But all of what we've told you happened three days ago when they first attacked Earth is the truth."

"Why would they take you prisoners and treat your wounds?" Les asked.

"To find out more about our bodies," Alice said.

"I heard one of those aliens Chester and Rawlings went off with say we're biologically like them," Nancy said.

Les fell silent as he began to think.

"How did you get those uniforms and escape?" Level asked.

"These are our uniforms," Henry said as he pointed to the center of his jacket at a patch job on a round hole. "See that's where I was wounded. The Tabors patched it. Susan's got the same patch on her clothing."

"And they fed you while you were in their custody?" Alex asked them.

"Yeah," Susan said. "It was good tasting food, too."

"It was?" Judith asked in a surprised voice.

"Yes, but we didn't so much as escape as they let us go," Susan said.

"They let you escape," Level said as if he was hearing it for the first time.

"Yes, they did," Henry said.

"Sorry we didn't give you water," Alice said.

"That's alright," Susan said. "Those beans were real good."

"Why would they do that?" Pedro asked. "Why not just leave you two to die on the field of battle?"

"Because they wanted to know more about us," Les said.

Level looked at him not understanding Les' statement and said, "They already know a lot about us, Les. That's why they were capable of knocking out our military and governments."

Les nodded as he said, "But they don't know about us as individuals, about our moral character. They don't know what type of resistance we'll put it when they begin the final conquest of Earth. They don't completely understand our intelligence and how we use it. So they captured these two while they were unconscious, took them back to where they're operating from, fix them up, and then let them go to see how predictable they are."

"Yes, that makes sense," Level said. "These two are trained soldiers. If they reacted in a predictable manner, then crushing all resistance against them will be easy once they learn how we act under stress."

"We reacted according to our training and they tore through us like a sharp knife through wet tissue paper," Henry said. "We fired everything we had at them, and didn't even scratch them even though we hit them numerous times."

"Their armored cars have some sort of invisible shield about them that stopped our rounds from reaching the vehicles," Susan said.

"Well, we've known their weapons are better than ours," Les said. "So if we're to stop them from conquering Earth we've got to beat them."

"Is there anyone else with you guys?" Susan asked them.

"Just us, soldier," Level said. "And now there are fewer of us."

"Oh, that's wonderful," Nancy said. "If these two join us we go from eight untrained civilians to ten with two trained soldiers."

"Things look pretty bad," Susan said. "But we may have a slim chance of beating them."

Everyone looked at her and waited for her to explain herself.

"There are only twenty-five of them in that compound," she said.

"Twenty-six counting Commander Rush," Henry added. "But more are coming soon."

"How soon?" Janis asked him.

"Counting today," he looked at his watch. "And it's almost five thirty. Six days."

"How many are coming?" Les asked him in a voice filled with fear of the answer.

"Half a million according to Rush on one hundred space ships," he said.

"Good Lord!" Level exclaimed as his expression changed from a positive one to one of defeat. "If twenty-six of them knocked out the political and military systems of Earth, a half a million on a hundred space ships can completely wipe out the human race."

"And they'll have complete command of the sky," Les added.

"We don't have much time," Judith said.

"Don't have much time?" Alex repeated. "My God, Judith, we've got six days to do the impossible and we don't know where this compound is or how to get into it."

"You two escaped from it so you should know where it's at," Pedro said.

"Yes, we did, and we know exactly where it's at, and we drew diagrams of the inside of the compound," Susan said.

Les stood up saying, "At the moment we're all there is to stop these aliens from taking over the world, and we can't call for help because there's no one close enough to help us. So let's stop wasting time and bury William and get started."

"We may have an edge," Susan said.

"What are you talking about?" Alex asked her.

"We escaped then got back inside the Tabor compound from another way and got six of their communicators, some weapons, medical supplies and food, and an armored car, but not like the ones they attacked us with," she answered.

"Communicators?" Pedro asked her.

"Yes," Henry said. "And we can access their main computer with them."

"Now that's very nice to hear," Alex said. "Where are these communicators?"

Henry reached into the large pocket on the left leg of his pants and pulled out the one he was carrying and handed it to Alex. "Be careful their technology is way ahead of ours and they might be able to track that here even though we put in our own special code."

Alex looked it over a few seconds and said, "Your special code prevents them from accessing this communicator?"

"Yes, it does and Susan's, too," he said. "But we didn't put the code in the others."

"You and Pedro and Judith and Janis look over that thing while the rest of us get blankets and shovels and bury William," Level said.

"How far is this compound from here?" Les asked them.

"A little over a hundred and eighty miles, and there are patrols around it," Henry told them.

"We know that," Janis said. "Why don't we show them what we've got then work out a plan of attack on this compound?"

"Sounds good to me," Pedro said.

"They come from the planet Tabor and they are of a Warrior Class," Henry told him.

"By now they've told their commander about Rawlings and Chester, and those two are telling them about us, and where we are," he continued.

"Okay, let's get busy," Level said.

Two hours later they had buried William in a clearing and placed heavy stones over his grave to stop animals from digging up his body, and had a simple service for him. His grave was marked by a circle of stones one of which had his name and date of death on scratched it. Then they moved the Humvees and the Tabor armored vehicle forty miles closer to the compound.

CHAPTER 28

Day 4 May 6, 8:23 a. m.

Rush was standing looking at Chester and Rawlings wondering if these two Earthlings could really be of use to him while his medical officer worked on Rawlings.

After a few minutes the medical officer stepped back and turned around to face Rush and said, "Their injures are of a minor nature, Commander Rush. They should be fully recovered in a few hours."

"Mine didn't feel like no minor injury," Rawlings said as he lay on the medical table in the medical section of the compound. "They hurt like hell, especially that hole in my stomach."

The medical officer turned around and looked at him. "Stomach wounds always hurt the worse, but our medicine has cured you." "You people are just like us," Chester said as he lay on his back on a table next to Rawlings and looked around.

"No, better," Theia said.

"In what way?" Chester asked her. "You look just like we do."

"Yes we do, but your world's diseases do not affect us the way they do you," she answered.

"Then you're going to need us," Chester said.

"Why should we need you?" Theia asked him.

"Because we know what's coming your way," he told her.

"And what is coming our way?" Rush asked breaking his silence.

"Nine people are coming here to destroy you," Rawlings answered. "And they've got a lot of fire power."

Rush looked at Zig and asked, "Did you or Sam detect the presence of other Earthlings?"

"No, Commander, we did not," Zig said. "All we heard was screaming then the sounds of people running away, and two of their metal firing weapons shooting into the woods."

"They were hiding," Rawlins told him. "And once they've recovered they will come here."

"And do what?" Theia asked.

"Get into this compound and destroy it," Chester said. "And they have the ability to do that. They already know where this compound is, and they have the ability to get into it."

"When should we expect them?" Commander Rush asked.

"Probably after sundown," Rawlings said. "Maybe around midnight."

"Captain Hayes, take these two to a room where they can rest and bring them food and drink," Commander Rush told the medical officer. He looked at Chester and Rawlings and said, "We will speak later." He turned around and walked out of the medical room.

Theia, Sam, and Zig followed him.

"You and Sam have done quite well, Zig, thus proving you are more than deserving of the title of Tabor Warriors. You may retire to your quarters for food and rest," Rush told him.

"Thank you, sir," he replied and both walked off toward an elevator.

He turned to Theia and said, "Your opinions concerning this matter."

"We are secure in the compound, sir," she said. "But we must recognize our weaknesses."

Rush started walking toward an elevator and said nothing. Theia walked beside him.

"What are our weaknesses, Lieutenant Theia?" Rush asked her as they walked.

"Those two Earthling soldiers have six of our weapons, six communicators and an armored car which we cannot access, they know where the compound is, and we do not know where they are," she said as she walked beside Rush. "We must make the assumption they know what the inside of the compound is like, and they will join with the Earthlings that attacked those two and return to the compound because they know they have less than six days to capture this compound and turn our weapons in orbit against the Overlord and the ships and Warriors with him."

"Captain Hayes told me he told those two soldier Earthlings when the Overlord and the fleet would arrive. I should have punished him for that," he said in a voice that had the sound of anger in it.

"No, Commander," she said. To have said nothing would have meant she agreed with him and no Tabor Warrior admitted their superior could make a mistake. It would result in instant death since any Tabor reaching the level of Commander, especially one trusted by the Overlord, was incapable of making a mistake. "Your decision not to punish him was the right decision, Commander. As for the Earthlings coming here to the compound if they want to try and stop us from gaining complete control of Earth, they must be able to get into the compound. They won't be able to get into the compound, Commander, but we will learn more of their individual battle skills than we already know. When they attempt to get into the compound we can kill them outside, and all resistance to our making this world ours will end."

"Nine people are really no threat to us. This compound is impregnable from the outside," Rush said more to himself than to Theia as he stopped in front of an elevator. "But they could be a nuisance. So what must we do to prevent that?"

Theia stood next to him and said nothing. It was not her place to tell him what to do. Only answer his questions when he asked them of her.

The elevator door opened and he entered followed by Theia.

"To the control room," he said.

The elevator door closed and the elevator started to rise.

"My command is tired and in need of rest, so I cannot assign more warriors to patrols," he said as he looked at the floor and thought.

When the elevator reached the top and the door opened he walked out saying, "I must make those nine Earthlings think they can enter this compound and destroy it. Theia, issue an order to the two patrols outside not to stop any Earthlings they see headed for the compound. The patrols are not to be seen or heard. Just report the direction the Earthlings are coming from when spotted, and how many of them there are."

"Yes, sir," she said as she walked to a computer and sat down and issued the order.

"Once they are within five miles of the compound the patrols can attack them and hold them in place till two more patrols can be sent out to kill them," he said. "And make sure the patrols are changed every four hours."

"Yes, sir," she said.

"Put all security systems on full alert," he said.

"Yes, sir," she said as she issued his orders.

"And you and Dram must be alert," he said as he started for the elevator.

"I will make sure of that, Commander," Theia replied.

CHAPTER 29

6:55 a.m., May 6

Pedro suddenly drew back from the communicator he was holding in his left hand.

Judith was sitting next to him and saw on the screen of the communicator what had caused him to draw back as if he was shocked by what he saw. "Eh, Susan and Henry, can these communicators pick up messages sent from that compound?"

Henry was sleeping.

"Yeah," Susan said in a sleepy voice. The meal of baked beans she had eaten over an hour ago had relaxed her and she was ready for six or eight hours of sleep.

"Why do you ask?" Level asked her. He was sitting on the ground looking at a paper map of the area.

"Because we just received a message ordering the patrols outside that compound not to stop any Earthlings they see approaching the compound," Pedro said.

"I got the same message on this communicator, too," Alex said as he looked over the communicator.

Les was lying on his back looking at the morning sky and wondering why he'd never appreciated it before. *Because there were more important things to appreciate than a morning sky before Earth was attacked.* He heard what Judith had asked. "Didn't Henry say they'd put a special code in those communicators?"

"Yes," Judith said. "And apparently the Tabors haven't discovered it."

Les sat up. "Maybe they're not looking for it."

"Even though Susan and Henry managed to get back into that compound and steal some of their equipment?" Nancy asked.

No one said anything. They were all trying to think up an answer to Nancy's question.

Level looked up from the map he'd been looking at and said, "Because they didn't think Henry and Susan were smart enough to understand the complexity of their equipment."

"Their technology is way ahead of anything we've got so they wouldn't think we'd be smart enough to master theirs," Les said. He started to get up.

Alice, lying next to him, grabbed his right arm and stopped him. "Les, you need to get some sleep."

"We all need to get some sleep," Level said. "Alex, you're the former CIA computer expert. Why don't you work with that communicator you've got while Pedro and Judith get some sleep?" He looked in Nancy's direction. "Can you stay awake another two or three hours with Alex while the rest of us sleep?"

"No problem," she said as she got up and walked over to Alex and sat down next to him. "I'll just look at what you're doing and make a few suggestions if you don't mind."

"I don't," he said. "Pedro, put your communicator on sleep mode and get some sleep. I'll wake you in three hours and tell you what I've done."

Pedro nodded his agreement and pushed the sleep mode button on the communicator.

"Do you mind if I sleep next to you?" Judith asked him.

"No, company is welcomed," he said as he put the communicator into his inside jacket pocket and lay down on the mat he was sitting on.

Judith did the same.

"So what are you going to do?" Nancy asked Alex.

"These communicators work on the same electrical communication principal that our iPads, laptops, and iPhones work on," he answered her. "The only difference is they are way ahead of ours in performance, but the operating principal is the same."

"So what are you going to do?" she asked him again.

"Try and get into that main computer Henry told us about," he said.

"Be very careful," she advised him.

He looked at her and smiled as he said, "Yeah, what's left of the world is depended upon the Tabors not knowing what I'm going to do." He started touching keys on the communicator. "But I don't think it's going to be that hard if the Tabor's haven't discovered the code Susan and Henry put into these communicators and they can access what's in their main computer."

"How are you going to do that?" Nancy softly asked him as she watched what he was doing.

"Back tracking that message this communicator just received," he said. "And if I can do that without being detected I may be able to get into the Tabor's main computer, and find out where those patrols are."

"How do you know they won't detect what you're doing?" she asked him.

"Nothing ventured nothing gained, and let's hope they don't," he said as he worked.

Nancy watched him touching keys on the keyboard and then watched the response that flashed on the screen for ten minutes. Then Alex stopped and watched and read the messages that appeared on the screen.

10:55 a.m.

Nancy yawned and asked Alex, "They don't know what you've done, do they?"

"No, I don't think so," he said as he shut the communicator down and put it in his pants pocket. "Will you wake Pedro?"

She got up and walked over to Pedro and shook his left shoulder waking him up.

"How long have I been sleeping?" he asked as he rolled onto his back and looked her in the face.

"Four hours, and you're going to be very proud of Alex," she said.

Pedro got up and walked over to Alex and asked, "What have you done?"

Alex was lying on his back on his ground mat and looking up at the blue sky. "Gotten into the Tabors' main computer and put in a program."

"They don't know it's there?"

"No, they don't," Alex said. "Slipped it right in under their noses if one of them was watching that main computer."

"Will it let us get into that compound?" he asked Alex.

"No, but I know exactly where it's at, and I've accessed all the security cameras in and outside the compound," he said. "I'm tired. I need at least six hours of sleep."

Nancy got her ground mat and walked over to Alex and spread it on the ground next to his. "I'm tired, too," she said as she lay down next to him. "I'm glad it's warm. I won't need a blanket."

"What do you want me to do?" Pedro asked him.

"Just keep an eye on that communicator you've got," he told him. "If any Tabor patrols get within five miles of us you'll see a map and a blue dot flashing on the screen telling you where they are."

"If any Tabor patrols get that close to us it means they detected what you did," Pedro said.

"It does, good day."

Pedro walked off and sat next a tree and took the communicator out of his pocket.

Judith woke up and noticed Pedro wasn't sleeping next to her. She saw him and got up and walked over to him. "What are you doing?"

"Keeping an eye on this communicator like Alex told me to do," he replied.

"There's a small stream not far from here," she said. "I'll got get some water and make coffee."

5 p.m.

Alex and Nancy woke up and found everyone awake and sitting around a small fire talking.

"Is there any fresh coffee?" Nancy said as she stood up.

"Just made a fresh pot," Level told her.

"Good," Alex said as he stood up. "I need to wash my face."

"There's a small stream about two hundred yards east of us," Judith told him. "Don't forget to take your towel."

"Don't need one. I'll let the wind dry my face. It'll help refresh me," he replied as he turned east and started walking.

Nancy fell in beside him. "I've gotten used to living outdoors."

Twenty minutes later they walked back to the group.

"Pedro told us what you've done, Alex" Henry said. "That was real smart of you. Now we can get into that compound."

"No we can't," he said as he sat down and took an empty tin cup, looked inside it to make sure it was clean, and handed it to Nancy. "All I did was get into their main computer and accessed their security cameras. We can't get into that compound, and any attempt to do so will only let those Tabors know we're in their computer. And if they learn that we're finished." He picked up another cup and checked it to see if it was clean then reached for the coffee pot and filled his cup and Nancy's cup.

"So what good did you do getting into their main computer?" Level asked him.

"They'll send out patrols every four, six, or eight hours, and we'll know," Susan said.

"So what?" Alice asked. "They'll know when those patrols come and go and they'll be able to see them, too."

"So will we and we can avoid them," Henry said. "The trick is to be able to get into the compound behind one of the patrols."

"They'll be scanning all around those patrols that come and go," Level said. "They'll spot us trying to sneak in behind a patrol."

"How far out from the compound are those patrols?" Les asked Alex.

"Ten miles and they patrol in a circle, and they probably keep in touch with each other, too," he said.

"Can those communicators record when a door opens or closes in that compound?" Les asked.

"Yes, they can," Alex said.

"Can you control what the security cameras see?" he asked Pedro.

"Should be if Alex's program in their main computer is working," Pedro said.

"It is," Alex assured him. "But we can't control the security cameras. We can only see what they see and hear and record."

"So why not wait until the replacement patrol leaves and the other returns then when the security cameras show an empty area we sneak inside?" he asked.

"That's a good idea," Level said.

"Maybe not," Alice said.

They all looked at her.

"All I know about computers is how to use them," she said. "But won't those cameras record what's behind the returning patrol? Anyone around that main computer is going to see whoever enters behind the returning patrols. And that door is probably going to close right after the returning patrol enters the compound."

"Yeah, they will," Henry said.

Les looked at her and said, "Smart as well as lovely."

She smiled at him and said, "Thank you."

"Can you delay the closing of a door that opens to let a replacement patrol leave?" Susan asked.

Alex looked at her and mumbled, "Probably."

"We have a diagram of that compound that shows the entrances and exits," Susan said. "If we can get close enough to one of those entrance/exits when it opens, we might be able to slip in right after a patrol leaves and before the other returns. That's how Henry and I got back in."

"We're talking about a delay of only a few seconds," Henry warned them. "Any longer and they'll know something is up."

"So we'll have to be real close to one of those doors and be ready to move real fast," Level said.

"But first we'll have to know what door the returning patrol is going to use," Les said. "We just can't afford to sit on our asses outside one of those doors and hope it opens."

Level nodded in agreement with Les. "More than likely two patrols won't use the same doors to leave and enter. What does your diagram show about those entrance/exits?"

"There are four," Susan said as she reached into her shirt pocket and took out the piece of paper with the diagram on it. She opened it and spread it on the ground.

The others gathered around her and sat next to her or looked over her shoulders.

"Military experience tells me that it's always best to have patrols coming and returning from different exits," Level said. "Which means one patrol is going to leave by the north or east exits and the returning patrol will enter by another entrance/exit."

"That means as soon as the relieving patrol leaves an exit it will close, and won't reopen until another patrol is ready to leave," Les said.

"Henry and I got back inside after a patrol had left," Susan said. "We jumped in seconds after the relieving patrol had left, and we had to hide when the returning patrol retuned."

"And they probably know that now," Janis said. "And they've probably changed how patrols enter and leave."

"That would be a smart move on their part," Susan said.

"They would be stupid if they didn't have a satellite scanning the area around that compound for a couple of hundred miles," Les said as he looked over Susan's left shoulder.

"If they had why didn't they catch Susan and Henry leaving and returning to that compound?" Alex said.

No one said anything.

"Because they didn't have a satellite looking down at their compound when they were allowed to escape," Les said.

"That's stupid, Les," Nancy said.

"No, he's right," Susan said. "They had attacked the Earth and destroyed every major military and political organization on Earth. Why should they have been worried about us when they allowed us to escape? They knew there was nothing around their compound to threaten them. They would have been scanning the rest of the Earth for any signs of resistance."

"We did what they didn't expect," Henry said. "We returned by a different entrance and stole some of their equipment. But now they've got a satellite looking down at their compound and scanning for hundreds of miles. Because they know we're coming back because of those two men who turned against you guys. They see any vehicles they don't control approaching that compound and they'll go on the alert."

"Then we get within twenty miles, hide the Humvees and that armored car Henry and Susan stole, and walk to the place," Les said.

"They'll see them long before we get that close with a satellite," Henry said.

"Can we blind their computer to our vehicles?" Alice asked.

"No!" Alex said in an emphatic voice. "We can't afford to do any more to their main computer until we get inside that compound. The program I put into their main computer is small, but it can be detected if we start using it to blind their satellite to what's approaching them."

"Then how the hell do we get close enough to get into that compound?" Janis asked.

"We could put plants on the Humvees and that armored car and drive real slow," Judith said. She was standing behind Susan.

Level looked at her and nodded his agreement. "She's right."

"Whatever satellite they've got looking down at that compound can probably detect anything metal moving toward it," Pedro said.

"What if we put some of that canvas we've got over the Humvees and that armored car and then put dirt over them and then put plants on top of the dirt?" Alice suggested.

"Oh, they're not going to be able to tell plants moving toward that compound?" Pedro asked.

"If they've programed their satellite to look for metal objects moving toward the compound, it may not register the movement of four vehicles that look like plants moving toward the compound," Level said.

"One," Les said.

"What?" Level asked him.

"One vehicle," he said.

"Which one?" Henry asked him.

"That armored car because it's got that cannon on it and it can destroy or at least damage one of their armored cars," he said. "We cover it with canvas and dirt and put plants on top of it and move real slow, no faster than a few hundred feet every ten or twenty minutes."

"There are ten of us, Les," Alice reminded him.

"I know that," he said. "But we can't afford to attract attention slowly driving the Humvees and that armored car to that compound. But one that's been camouflage to look like a tree might get us close enough so we can walk the rest of the way."

"How long a walk are you talking about?" Janis asked him.

Les thought for a few seconds then said, "Twenty miles and at night."

"How fast should we be driving the armored vehicle?" Henry asked him.

"We can't cover more than a couple of miles an hour, and we can't move in a straight line. To do so might attract their attention."

"Listen, Les and you others," Susan began. "We've got a time element to deal with. Those one hundred Tabor space ships show up with a half million warriors on them, and it's all over for everyone on Earth who is still alive."

"We're about a hundred and fifty miles from the compound," Henry said. "If we can cover a hundred and thirty miles in twenty hours we should be able to walk the rest of the way at night if we start right after sundown."

"And the chances of us being picked up by that satellite of theirs will be very slim," Susan said. "But what entrance should we use to get inside?"

"We get close to one of the entrances of that compound, hide, and watch on the communicators the ramp to open. Then we sneak in," Henry said. "But we could be waiting throughout the day."

"How many days have we got before the other Tabors show up?" Level asked.

Henry looked at his watch. "It's seven now. Five and a half days."

"Five of us get rifles only from the Humvees and put them in the armored vehicle and make us a light meal while the rest of us start camouflaging that armored vehicle," Les suggested as he stood up.

"What about the weapons we took from the compound?" Susan asked them.

"Do you know how to use them?" Les asked her.

"Just the electric pistols we've got," she said. "But the rifles probably work on the same principal as the pistols."

"And we don't have a lot of time to learn how to use them," he said. "So we use weapons we know how to use. We can leave those Tabor weapons in one of the Humvees"

"So let's move our asses," Nancy said as she started walking toward the Humvees.

CHAPTER 30

7:15 p.m., May 6

"We've made it, Rawlings," Chester said as he lay on his bed looking at the pink ceiling. "Once we help these Tabors kill those assholes coming here, we'll be accepted by these Tabors."

"Yeah," Rawlings said. His stomach wound didn't hurt at bad as it did when they first arrived in the compound. "Where do you think we should help them rule Earth from?"

"Someplace where we can convince the people they must do as we say if they want to live comfortable lives," he said.

"How about Trump Tower," Rawlings suggested. "I've been there and I like it."

"No. We must be somewhere in the country where the only people around us will be country bumpkins that will do as we say," Chester said. "The problem with big cities is the people in them tend to think they're smarter than everyone else."

"Well, where?" Rawlings asked.

"For the moment let us think of how we're going to help Commander Rush kill those nine assholes," Chester told.

"That nigger Les is mine, understand?"

"I could care less what you do to him," Chester told him. He closed his eyes. "It'll probably take them two or three days to reach where this compound is. So we've plenty of time to come up with a plan that'll convince the Tabors we can be depended upon. I'm tired I going to get some sleep."

"You told them those assholes will arrive around midnight," Rawlings reminded him.

"Yeah, I know, and if they don't, that will make Commander Rush nervous and improve our position with him," he said.

"How the fuck is that going to improve our position with him?" Rawlings asked him.

"He'll think they're coming slow because they've got something planned, and he can't think like an Earthling, but we can," Chester said. "Be quiet now, I'm sleepy."

"Good idea," Rawlings said as he closed his eyes.

Level and Les will probably figure out a way to get pass any patrols these Tabors have got around this compound, Chester thought. *When they do, I'll tell Rush where they are and I can help them kill them all.*

CHAPTER 31

8:30 p.m., May 6

"Well, what does it look like?" Level asked the others as he looked at the camouflaged Tabor armored car.

"Like a pile of dirt on four wheels with a lot of brush growing out of it," Nancy said as she looked at the camouflaged vehicle.

"It really does, doesn't it, Les?" Alice asked him as she stood next to him.

"Yeah," he said. "Let's hope it looks like a small hill with plants on it from a satellite thousands of miles above Earth."

"Remember these Tabors are years ahead of us in technology," Pedro said as he looked at the vehicle. "Those satellites they've got going around Earth may be able to tell the difference between a real pile of dirt with brush on it and a fake one."

"I hope not," Janis said as she looked at it.

"If it can't all the Tabors will see in that computer room of theirs in a pile of dirt with brush on top of it," Susan said. "You guys did a good job for civilians."

"We're not going to be able to move more than five miles an hour, and not in a straight line," Henry said as he looked at it. "Even if their satellites can't tell the difference between a moving pile of dirt with brush on top of it and one that doesn't, it may be able to spot a pile of dirt with brush on it moving in a straight line."

"You said we had five and a half days before the rest of the Tabors show up," Les said.

"Yeah, an hour and a half ago," Henry told him.

"How far are we from that compound?" Level asked him.

"About a hundred and fifty miles," Susan said. "And moving at five miles an hour in a zigzag pattern is probably going to take us five times as long to reach that compound as it took us to reach here. And it took us two days to get here after we left that compound."

"If they do detect this thing moving toward them, let's pray they think it's some sort of weird plant," Alice said.

"A zigzagging pile of dirt with plants on it," Susan mumbled as she shook her hear. "We're going to need all the luck there is."

"Let's eat and move out," Les said.

They all turned around and went to the small camp fire and sat down.

"Only bread and coffee," Judith said. "There are some canned vegetables and over a dozen packs of those military meals on wheels if you want more, but it'll take time to open the cans and packages."

"Time is one thing we don't have a lot of," Level said as he sat down and reached for a tin cup of coffee.

"Five miles an hour in a zigzag pattern might take us more than forty hours to reach the place where that compound is," Nancy said. "So whatever zigzag pattern we follow we can't zigzag backwards."

"We should remember this is May and this far south the sun isn't going to set until after seven-thirty and will start to rise again a little after five," Alice said. "That means we'll only have approximately ten hour of darkness to move in."

"And we'll have to stop for fourteen hours," Les said.

"And at five miles an hours we'll be able to cover no more than thirty miles a night at the most assuming we don't zigzag too much," Judith said. "That means it'll take us at least four days to reach the area of the compound and we have only five days."

"And then we'll have to walk another twenty miles," Alice added. "And with the exception of Henry and Susan the rest of us don't look like we can walk twenty miles in one night."

"We won't be that close to the compound in four days if we do a lot of zigzagging," Susan said. "Maybe we can cut down on some of the zigzagging."

"Is there any way we can tell when a satellite moves overhead?" Les asked.

"If it moves," Pedro added.

Les looked at him.

"They're ahead of us in technology, Les," he said. "A Tabor satellite could be in a fixed position looking down at that compound. And if it is we aren't going to be able to tell its overhead without tapping into their main computer. And if we do that, they'll know exactly where we are."

"Can ours stay in a fixed position?" Nancy asked as she ate her bread and drank her coffee.

"No," Alex said. "But we do have satellites that can move back and forth." He looked in the direction of the armored vehicle and began to think as he ate his bread and drank his coffee.

"Look, people," Level began. "We've got two choices. Try to do something to stop those other Tabors from showing up, or run and hide. Things aren't going to be in our favor if we move toward that compound in that camouflage vehicle, but it's all we've got and we'll just have to take our chances and pray Lady Luck is on our side."

"So let's finish up and get ready to go," Henry said.

Ten minutes later after cleaning their cups, putting everything away, and putting out the small fire the ten of them were standing on the right side of the vehicle.

"Is this thing big enough to carry all of us?" Nancy asked.

"Six of us should be able to squeeze inside," Susan said. "The other four will have to ride on top."

"Those on top can hide under the canvas," Les said. "Just make sure not to knock any of the plants off it."

"Okay, who gets inside?" Level asked.

No one said anything.

"Henry or Susan can do the driving," Nancy said. "And four of us can get inside with them."

"So who's getting inside?" Level asked again.

"Pedro and Alex because they're the computer experts, and Alice and Janis," Les said. "Level, Nancy, Judith, and I can ride on top the whole way."

"I can ride on top," Alice volunteered.

Les looked at her and said in a pleading and demanding voice, "Inside, Alice. Please."

She understood his concern for her safety and said, "Okay, and when we stop I can switch places with Judith, if that's okay with everyone?"

No one said anything.

"Okay, let's mount up," Level said.

Susan got in the driver's seat and Henry got in the seat behind the gun. Alice and Janis squeezed into the back behind him next to a rack of batteries.

"What are these batteries for?" Janis asked.

"They're used for the gun," Henry told her. "The Tabors have only electric weapons."

"We forgot about our assault rifles," Alice said as she looked around the tight interior. "It's nice that the Tabor's painted the inside of the armored car white. It gives it a feeling of roominess."

"Yeah, you did, didn't you?" Henry said as he looked around the inside of the armored car and raised his seat and stuck his head out of the hatch. "There's no room in here for those rifles of yours."

"Damn," Level said. "We can't carry them on top with us. They've metal parts on them. Those satellites of the Tabors may pick them up."

"So we carry only our side arms," Les said. "We can put them under our shirts in front and pray that satellite doesn't have x-ray abilities. Make sure you've got your night vision glasses and binoculars especially those on top."

They all called out they had their night vision glasses.

"Let's get some extra ammo clips, and semiautomatics for those inside," Level suggested as he turned around and walked for the Humvees. He came back six minutes later with ten extra ammo clips for the semiautomatics, six extra semiautomatics, and ten full canteens of water and two sets of binoculars. He gave the clips to Les and Judith and Nancy and handed six of the canteens and six semiautomatics to the people inside. He gave Les one of the binoculars and kept the other one himself.

It took Les and Level a few minutes to slip under the canvas on the back and front of the armored vehicle after they'd helped Nancy and Judith under the canvas on the sides. A minute later Susan started the engine of the armored car.

"Eh, this computer in this armored car can pick up signals from that satellite, can't it?" Alex asked as he looked at the computer screen in front of him.

"It probably can," Henry said. "But it may also allow that satellite to detect where this armored car is, too."

"You said you got that diagram from a computer screen in the room you and Susan were in, didn't you?" Alex asked.

"Yeah," Henry answered.

"Do you know if the Tabors knew what you were doing?"

"Probably."

"How did you get that diagram?"

"I asked the computer screen in the hospital room we were in to show me a diagram of the compound," Henry said.

"Then you had the screen download the information on you iPhones?"

"No, they took our iPhones and radios," he said. "I drew a diagram of that compound."

"Do you think this screen is verbally activated?"

"We didn't have time to check it out."

Alex moved around to get into a comfortable position and said, "Show me where the satellites are?"

A picture of Earth appeared on the screen with twelve satellites as bright spots appeared on the screen.

"Stop that!" Susan yelled at him. "They might pick us up."

"I don't think so," Alex said.

"And why not?" she demanded.

"If they didn't pick you up when you took this car, I doubt if they can pick us up now."

"And why do you think that?" she asked him.

"Because those communicators you and Henry put a code in is preventing them from knowing where this armored car is," he said. He thought for a few seconds before he said. "The communicators are the only way they've got for communicating with each other, and they enable the Tabors to control whatever armored car they're in."

"We disconnected the tracking chip in this vehicle," Henry said. "That's why they don't know where it's at."

"Well, that's one good thing for us," Pedro said.

"We're ready!" Level yelled from his position on the front of the armored car.

Susan started driving slowly.

"If that's true then we should be able to control the speed of this car with one of those communicators," Pedro said.

"You think so?" Susan asked.

"Try it," Pedro suggested.

Susan took out her communicator and said, "Car speed five miles per hour." She looked at the small computer screen in front of her and saw the word 'done' appear on it. "It works," she said.

"Tell it to go a few yards left or right every five hundred yards," Pedro suggested.

She did so and the words 'instructions accepted' appeared on the screen. "It's doing it," she said.

"Have it change direction and distance right or left every mile," he said. "That way if they have a satellite up it'll record the movement of this car as irregular."

"And that's going to convince them this isn't their armored car returning home?" Nancy asked.

"I don't know," Pedro said.

"That's not reassuring," Nancy said.

Janis looked at her watch and said, "Sitting in these cramped positions are going to put pressure on our bladders. So could we stop after a four or five hours to relieve ourselves?"

"Alright with you guys?" Susan asked the others.

"A great idea," Alex said as he studied the small screen. "Control over their soldiers, or warriors, is apparently an important thing to these Tabors and these armored cars must be their support vehicles for their main attack vehicles."

"Tell those on top about stopping," Alice said.

"We're going to stop every four or five hours," Susan yelled out the open hatch above her.

"They're moving," Alex said as he watched the bright spots on the computer screen.

"What's moving?" Les asked from outside.

"Those satellites," Alex said. "Every two hours one of them passes over where Susan said the compound is."

"What about the others?" Pedro said. "They should have overlapping scans."

"They do and that means the area that compound is in is being scanned every second by one of those twelve satellites," Alex said.

"Well, let's hope they don't pay any attention to this moving pile of dirt and plants," Henry said.

CHAPTER 32

2 a.m. May 7

They stopped at two in the morning among some rocks and everyone got out or off the armored car and stretched their legs and relieved themselves.

"How far have we gone?" Les asked as he walked around in a circle.

"Less than four and a half miles," Susan said walking beside him.

"That puts us at about a hundred and forty-five miles from that compound," Alice said as she walked around behind Les.

"We should be able to make three more miles before sun rise," Level said.

"Not with all the zigzagging we're doing," Susan said. "We will probably make another mile and a half."

"And this is the fifth day," Pedro said.

"Maybe we should go a little faster," Nancy suggested.

"No," Level said. "Any faster and we might attract attention."

"Maybe she's right," Les said. "We're well over a hundred and forty miles away. A mile faster will bring us closer to the spot where we have to walk."

"And how far can people our age walk in the darkness?" Pedro asked.

"Maybe fifteen miles," Nancy said.

"And then there's the problem of waiting for one of those entrances to open," Judith said. "By the time we get into that compound those ships could be here if we can get into that compound."

"And we're screwed," Susan said. "But I don't recommend going any faster."

"We should reduce the zigzagging by a few hundred feet," Les said.

"That will reduce the mileage we have to cover," Henry said. "But not by much."

"Well, let's move," Level said. "We aren't getting any closer standing here debating our problem."

"You get inside, Nancy," Alice said. "I can ride outside." She looked at Les to see if he would disagree with her.

Les didn't say anything. He understood places would have to be switched.

"I'll ride outside, too," Pedro said. "Alex is the one who should be on the inside. He's the computer expert. And that'll give those inside a little more room."

"Doesn't mean shit," Alex said. "I don't dare use the computer in this armored car to do more than I've done."

"Let's move," Level said.

Nancy, Janis, and Alex got inside while Les, Level, Alice, Judith, and Pedro got under the canvas. Two minutes later they were moving.

"I'm going to sleep," Pedro announced.

"Don't fall off," Alice warned him.

Ten seconds later they were moving again.

2 a.m.

Dram walked into the computer room and stopped behind Theia's chair and said, "I've come to replace you, Lieutenant."

Theia stood up and stretched and said in a tired voice, "I shall be in my quarters sleeping."

"Have the patrols reported anything?" he asked as he waited for her to move away from the chair.

"No, all is quiet, Sergeant," she said as she got up and walked away from the chair. "Call them once every hour to make sure they are alert. And be sure to monitor their movements."

"Yes, Lieutenant," he replied as he moved to the chair and sat down. "Shall I check the position of the Overlord's fleet?"

"I have already done that," she told him. "They are within a half billion miles of the orbit of this systems' farthest planet. At the speed they are traveling they shall arrive in orbit about this planet in six days."

"That will make them a day late," Dram said.

"I know," she said. "But once they enter this system they must move farther away from the large gas planets of this system to avoid being caught in their intense gravitational pull. Some of the ships in the fleet suffered damage leaving Tabor and have to be towed by the other ships. The towing ships don't have the power to pull the others pass those large planets at maximum speed. Come close to those gas giants and the damaged ships could suffer more damage."

Dram pushed a button on the console and brought up a picture of the solar system. He looked at it for a few seconds before he said, "The four inner planets are all lining up."

"The fifth and largest planet in this system has the strongest gravitational pull. The fleet must move millions of miles from it to avoid its gravitational pull," Theia said as she walked to the door. "One of our satellites is in a stationary position over the compound. The other eleven are in orbits over the former target areas."

"Is it necessary to keep that one in a stationary orbit?" he asked.

"No. You may move it every hour to scan other areas of this continent," she told him as she walked to the door and the door opened. She turned around and said. "Be alert for anything that is not usual."

He turned around in the chair to face her and asked, "Do you believe what those two Earthlings told the Commander about other Earthlings coming here to stop us from achieving our goal?"

"The Commander does so be alert for anything that does not seem normal thirty miles outside the compound," she said as she walked away.

The door closed.

Dram turned to the computer and said, "Replay everything that has been recorded over the last six hours."

The computer began the replay.

He looked carefully at the replay and saw only one thing that attracted his attention. A group of plants that were moving in a zigzag manner toward the compound, but it was still over a hundred and forty miles away. *Moving plants*, he thought. *There is much more to learn about this planet and the life on it than we've already learned.*

Dram didn't bother to notice the group of plants sometimes moved against the wind.

5 a.m.

Les' shirt was soaked in his own sweat and dirty and beginning to smell. *Stinking is something people don't do when they have hot water and soap to bathe with on a daily basis.* He raised the edge of the canvas he was lying under and saw the darkness outside was beginning to look a little brighter. *The sun's coming up.* "We'd better look for a place to hide," he said in a loud voice. "The sun will begin to rise in a few minutes."

Henry heard him through the open hatch. "He's right, Susan," he said. "Let's look for a hiding place. We've got maybe ten minutes before there'll be enough light for us to be seen."

"Eh, there's a wooded area half a mile ahead of us next to a stream," Alex said.

"How do you know?" Susan asked him.

"This computer screen has a very detailed map of the Earth on it, and I'm looking at a map of where we are," he said then quickly added. "Don't worry I don't think the Tabors know about us."

"You don't think," Susan said.

"Yeah, from what I've been able to determine about this computer screen the only way the Tabors will know about us is if I try to contact that main computer of theirs," he said. "Otherwise this screen is limited to this armored car."

"Where is that map coming from?" she asked him.

"It's a part of the computer's program," he said. "All their vehicles probably have maps like this one on their computers."

"Let's pray you're right," Susan said. "Which direction should I go?"

"Sort of wonder to the south twenty feet and then go straight ahead," he said.

"I sure hope you're right, Mr. Alex," she said as she turned slightly to the right.

"Just Alex, if you please," he said.

"I would like a nice cool spring to bathe in and wash my clothes in," Alice said. "I haven't had these clothes off in over five days. God, I must stink."

"I can assure you, you do," Janis said from inside the armored car. "Because it stinks in here, too."

"Bath time coming up," Susan said.

Twenty minutes later they stopped under a grove of thick, leafy trees twenty yards away from a stream.

Level and Les were the first out from under the canvas and walking toward the stream.

Les smiled when he saw the stream was filled with moving water. "This is a good spot. This stream is moving so the water is probably safe."

Level looked around and said, "If no one knows we're here."

"I'll look around a bit then come back," he said as he checked the semiautomatic he carried to make sure it was loaded and the safety on. He took a pair of binoculars.

"I'll come with you," Pedro said. "Two sets of eyes are better than one."

"Take binoculars both of you," Nancy told them.

Level gave Pedro his binoculars.

They both walked off separated by ten feet looking around as if they expected some aliens to show up. After half an hour they were sure they were alone and returned to the group.

"No one around for miles," Pedro said.

"Oh, great," Judith said. "Now I can take a bath and wash my clothes."

"Bath downstream," Henry told him. "We don't want to pollute our drinking and cooking water."

"Come on, ladies," Nancy said. "We can wash each other's backs and keep an eye out for any aliens that might show up."

"We forgot one thing," Alice said as she walked over to Nancy.

"What?" Janis said joining her and Nancy.

"Towels from the Humvees," she said.

"It's warm out," Susan said. "We can wash our clothes first, hanging them on tree branches to dry then bathe."

The five women walked off.

"We'll have coffee and beans ready for you when you get back," Level told them.

"Coffee and beans," Alex said. "I do hope that's not going to be our diet for the rest of our lives."

"Better than raw meat," Pedro said. "And that's probably what some people on Earth are reduced to eating now."

"Four thousand years of learning how to cook raw meat and the human race has slipped back," Level said as he shook his head.

"Things aren't that bad," Henry said. "We still have records of all human progress in libraries and museums. We stop these Tabors and we can start rebuilding civilization again. We won't have to start from scratch."

Les was sitting on the ground listening to them but not paying much attention. He was tired, dirty, and hungry and nothing much mattered. He stretched out on the ground saying, "When the ladies are finished, waked me if I'm asleep."

"We will," Alex assured him.

Les closed his eyes and relaxed allowing some of the exhaustion to leave his body. As it did so a thought passed through his mind. *How did the aliens know where to attack this planet to render it helpless?* He considered it to be a worthless thought that would have normally passed from his mind, but the thought lingered in the back of his mind like a bad taste in his mouth he couldn't wash away with a strong mouth wash.

CHAPTER 33

Dram was bored. There was nothing on the computer screen to indicate there was any threat by Earthlings to the compound. There were no Earthlings moving toward the compound for hundreds of miles in either direction. Those on this continent they called North America who had survived the attack were hiding someplace or trying to organize their communities to deal with the attack that had destroyed their government. Those two Earthling soldiers they had allowed to escape had made fools of them by returning to the compound by the western ramp and stealing an armored car and some equipment, but everything was safe and quiet now.

He decided to scan those areas that had been attacked to determine if there were any attempts by survivors to locate where the attack had come from and respond. Earthling weapons were primitive compared to theirs, but they could still kill Tabors. Even their atomic bombs were deadly if they could be launched at those outside the compound, but they would have no effect on the compound it was too deep in the ground.

For an hour he scanned every area on Earth that had been attacked. All the people in the political and military areas of importance on Earth had been disintegrated. Not one national or state government on Earth had survived the attack or any of the leaders in the major cities. Every major military area had been devoid of all life except plants. All that remained were small governments at the county and local levels and small military units that weren't at the areas that had been attacked. And they were working with the small governments to control panic among the billion or so people on Earth who had survived.

Dram smiled as he said, "Our spy did an excellent job of locating and identifying the areas for us to attack. The Overlord will reward our spy for the spy's great contribution to our victory. I wonder who this spy is."

The computer heard Dram's statement and answered. "Forerunner is the Tabor who supplied this unit with the information necessary to carry out a successful attack on Earth."

"Forerunner, your reward from the Overlord will be great," Dram said. Then he decided to play 'battle' a popular computer game among the Tabor warrior class. Before he began playing the game he brought up a recording of that collection of plants that were moving toward the compound. He watched it for ten minutes before he thought *that must be a very rare form of planet life on Earth. It must be a product of evolution in this desert environment. It moves when it needs moisture.* He stopped the recording and began playing 'battle'.

"We've been in this fucking alien hole for over twenty-four hours, and nothing's happened," Rawlings grumbled.

Chester didn't bother to look at Rawlings because he was looking at the far wall and thinking. *They're up to something, but what?"*

"Did you hear me?" Rawlings asked him.

"How are your wounds?"

"All healed," he said. "But that's not what I mean."

"What you mean is why hasn't that commander come here and offered us a deal," Chester said.

"That's exactly what I mean," he said. "By now he should be interested in what you told him."

"Maybe he's checking out what I said," Chester said. "Remember I told him the nine would be here by sundown."

"Yes, and they should have arrived hours ago and they haven't." Rawlings grumbled.

Chester didn't respond. He was wondering why Les and Level and those other seven hadn't arrived.

"Maybe those two alien soldiers who helped us scared them off."

"No. They believe they must get inside this compound to save the Earth from these aliens," Chester said. "They're still coming they come up with a plan to make us look like fools to these Tabor."

"They've already got Earth," Rawlings told him.

"They've done a lot of damage to Earth and killed maybe billions, but they don't have the Earth and they can't come out of this compound to complete their control of Earth because there are too few of them."

"There are no more governments or armies," Rawlings said. "If that don't mean they've got Earth, I don't know what else would."

Chester looked at Rawlings and said, "Listen to me, Rawlings, and listen carefully."

"I've been doing that," he replied.

"They've knocked out every government and military organization on this planet, but they haven't conquered it." He paused and looked around the room knowing they were being watched and listened to. "Because some state and local governments still exists."

"No they don't because we couldn't get in touch with Springfield in Illinois and neither could that Chief of police in East Oak."

"Well, the county and local governments still exist and so does the communication system, and that means the Internet is still operating. And by now everyone with common sense knows Earth was attacked by aliens. They're getting organized all over the world, and if these Tabors keep sitting on their asses in this compound they're going to find thousands of people attacking this compound real soon."

"A bunch of damn civilians," Rawlings snored. "These Tabors can blow them to pieces within minutes."

"There are probably millions of military people still alive all over this planet, and they're getting themselves organized with weapons.

The major airports may be damaged but they are still usable and there are still planes that can fly," Chester said. He raised his voice. "And if we were capable of picking up a signal that told us where this compound was others have, too."

Rawlings nodded his understanding of what Chester had said. "We better figure out some way to let that Commander guy know that."

Chester looked around the room they were in and saw no way of contacting Rush.

"So how do we do that?" Rawlings asked him.

Chester got out of bed and walked to the door and pushed it because he saw no doorknob.

The door remained closed.

Chester began banging on the door and yelling. "We have to talk to the man in charge. There are people on their way here to attack this underground complex and kill all of you."

"The two persons in medical are banging on the door and screaming to talk to Commander Rush," the computer said to Dram.

Dram turned on the intercom to the room Chester and Rawlings were in and listened. After a few minutes he spoke. "There is no one coming here to attack the compound. Be quiet or I will send a medical rob into your room to silence both of you."

"I'm the man who called and warned you two days ago about the people coming," Chester said. "You have to talk to me."

Dram thought for a few seconds before he said, "I shall inform the Commander when he is available."

"When will that be?"

"Do not question me, Earthling," Dram told him and turned off the intercom to their room.

"That's just great," Rawlings said. "We've got to sit here on our asses and wait for a fucking commander to be available. I wonder what the fuck he's doing. Getting some pussy I bet."

Chester walked back to his bed and sat down. "Don't worry. The moment Level and that group attack this place they'll come running to us and we can make our demands."

"And if Level and the others don't attack?"

"Oh, they will, Rawlings," he said as he lay down. "They won't get very far, but the commander of this place will know they're going to have trouble with resistance sooner or later. Then they will come to us."

CHAPTER 34

May 7, 8:45 a.m.

The five men got a chance to clean up an hour after the women had finished. Les thought the water was surprisingly comfortable and not cold as he thought it would be this time of the year when he got into the stream. He suggested they take off their boots and wade around in the water with their clothes on and let the water do some of the cleaning for them. After ten minutes of wading around in the five foot deep stream they stripped their clothes off, hand washed them as best they could, hung them on some of the trees near the bank to dry, and then got back in the water.

"Nice ain't it?" Alex asked him.

"Excellent," he replied. He hadn't felt this good in days and that was a bit disturbing. He had the feeling he should be deeply depressed over the death of his family. *I've accepted their deaths. And considering the mess the world is in it is better they are with God and not here.* He relaxed as he let the cool water wash over his body then he thought of Alice. *I wonder if she would be willing to be my friend for life if we succeed. She still may have family or relatives alive somewhere. Maybe I do, too.*

"Water this far south is always nice to swim in this time of the year," Pedro said.

"You come from this part of the country?" Henry asked him.

"No, New York born and bred," he said. "Got a good job offer from Com Ed in Chicago years ago, and packed up my family and left."

"Why?" Level asked him. "You couldn't get a compatible job in the Big Peach."

"Like I said I got a good job offer," he said. "Plus my wife -," he stopped speaking for a minute while he thought of the family he'd never see again. "She didn't like the cost of living in New York and was glad to get out of it."

"I don't want to seem like the odd one," Alex said. "But considering what's happened I think we should stop thinking about the past, because for us it's dead."

"Don't you think about your family?" Level asked him.

"Whenever I have a quiet moment to myself, and I tell myself they're gone. Dead. And there's nothing I can do about it."

"None of us are ever going to forget about what we've lost," Les said. "No matter how long we live."

"I think about my job in the -U. S. Strategic Command in the Sierra Nevada Mountains," Level said. "I loved walking outside during the winter when there was a blizzard."

Henry was treading water on his back and he glanced at Level then went back to enjoying the water.

"How long were you assigned there?" Alex asked him.

"Ten years," he said. "And I loved every minute of it."

Les flipped over on his stomach and started to swim. He swam for half an hour then floated.

After an hour they got out, walked around to let the warm sun dry them off, got dressed, washed the mud off their feet, and put their socks and boots back on and returned to the camp.

Les had a cup of coffee then lay down on his ground mat and went to sleep. He didn't wake up until Henry shook his shoulder and told him it was sundown.

"And four days left at midnight," he said as he got up.

"We have to stop zigzagging," Alex said. "If we want to reach that compound before time runs out."

"We'll have to go faster," Susan said.

"I don't recommend we go any faster than we've gone so far," Level said. "If we do we will be spotted."

"And if we don't we won't make that compound before time runs out," Henry said angrily. "Remember we agreed to stop twenty miles short of it and walk." He looked around at them. "Susan and I can make twenty miles in a few hours, but you people look like you'll need a lot more time than a few hours."

"We've no choice," Les said. "We have to go faster, but we should still zigzag."

"You all know by now if they have a satellite in a stationary orbit over that compound they've already seen us," Alex said.

"That's why I suggest we continue to go slow," Level said. "If they've seen us, they won't know exactly what we are. Remember we're dealing with people from another world. Things will seem different to them on this world."

"How far are we from that compound?" Les asked Susan.

"About a hundred and thirty-three miles," she said.

"How fast do we need to go to be within twenty miles of it in the next two days?" Pedro asked her.

She did some quick figuring and said, "If we can cover forty miles a night, we should be within twenty miles of it in three days."

"After we make that twenty mile walk, we'll have less than a day to figure out how to get inside that compound," Nancy said.

"And Heaven knows what we'll run into once we get inside," Janis said.

"A lot of angry aliens," Judith said.

"So we have to make better than forty miles a night," Alice said.

"Fifty miles a night would put us within twenty miles in less than two nights," Susan said.

"And that would give us plenty of time to walk the twenty miles," Les said. He looked at Level. "Like it or not, Level, we're going to have to go much faster if we want to have a chance at success."

Level shook his head and said nothing.

"Okay, let's mount up and get going," Pedro said. "I'll be on the outside."

"Me, too," Alice said.

"Alright," Les said. "Everyone on the outside make sure you're hold on tight. And, Susan, try and give us a safe flat ride."

"I'll do the best I can driving over this rough terrain," she promised.

"What are we going to do if we do get inside that compound?" Nancy asked as she crawled under the canvas.

"Let's get inside first then figure that out," Pedro told her as he crawled under the canvas on the front.

Five minutes later the others had packed up and they were moving. The only benefit of being on the outside traveling faster was a cool breeze.

CHAPTER 35

May 7, noon

The door to the room Chester and Rawlings were in opened and an armed guard entered.

"Get dressed, Commander Rush wants to talk to you," the guard said.

"Both of us?" Chester asked as if he expected to be the only one Rush would want to speak with.

"Yes," the guard answered.

"About time," Rawlings grumbled.

"Where are our clothes?" Chester asked him.

"In the room between your beds. Push the door and it will open. I will wait outside," the guard said.

"Damn nice of you to give us some privacy," Rawlings replied.

The guard left the room but the door remained open.

"Cut the smart ass remarks, Rawlings," Chester told him as he got up. "We're in no position to piss off this Rush guy."

"Alright, I'll cool it, until he pisses me off."

"Even if he pisses you off respect his position," Chester said as he turned to the door between their beds.

"What's he going to do if I do piss him off?"

"Kill us both and probably slowly," he told him as he pulled their clothes off the hooks on the wall they were hanging on.

Five minutes later they were following the guard down the hall to an elevator.

"This is a big place you've got here," Rawlings said as he looked around.

The guard didn't respond.

"How long it take you guys to build this underground place?" he asked.

"Considering their technology, a few months at the most," Chester told him as he looked around at the smooth stone walls and diamond cut floor to prevent slipping.

The guard stopped in front of two elevator doors and said, "Elevator."

"Humans that speak English must be quiet common in the galaxy," Chester said.

The elevator door opened a second later to reveal a plain looking steel elevator with a metal bench at the back for sitting down.

"The language you call English is similar to ours. Go to the back and sit down," the guard said as he waited for them to enter.

Chester entered first with Rawlings behind him and sat down.

The guard entered after they did and faced them and said, "Commander Rush's level."

The door closed and the elevator began to move with Chester and Rawlings feeling it move. Ten seconds later the door opened.

The guard walked out and stopped against the far wall and said, "Come out and turn to your left. The door at the end of the walk will open."

Rawlings and Chester did as told and walked to a steel door that opened when they were five feet from it.

"Electric eye," Rawlings said as he looked above the top of the door and saw nothing but stone.

"A heat sensor in the door," Rush said from the chair behind the desk he was sitting at. "And it took only two of your Earth days to dig the hole for this compound and five more to put our equipment in it and set it up."

"Must be real small," Chester said as he entered the office and looked around.

The office was fifteen feet by twenty with plain stone walls, floor, and ceiling. The only furniture in it was Rush's desk and three chairs in front of his desk. A metal pitcher and four metal glasses sat on the right side of the desk. An electric pad was in the center of the desk.

"It's a quarter of a mile in circumference and six hundred feet in depth with five levels. Each is fifty feet high," Rush said.

"And just below the surface," Chester said.

"You are the intelligent of the two," Rush said. His face was expressionless.

"Why you say that?" Rawlings demanded.

"Because he is trying to determine how far below the ground this complex is and how many warriors are in it."

Chester walked to one of the chairs and sat down without being invited. "That means you only have a few hundred men at the most in this complex, and that's not enough to stop what is coming your way."

Rawlings sat next to him.

"There is nothing coming our way," Rush said as he nodded at the guard he could leave.

Rawlings turned around and saw the guard leave and the door close behind him. He turned around and grinned at Rush. "You better play it straight with us, Boy-O, because you're all alone in this room with us now."

"If that means you are a threat to my life, you are mistaken," Rush told him.

"Yeah," Rawlings replied as he stood up and flexed his muscular chest.

Chester suspected there was something between them and Rush that would prevent them from reaching him. He decided not to warn Rawlings not to be foolish. It was time this dumb jock realized the position they were in.

Rawlings took two steps toward Rush and lunged at him like he was going for a guard on a defensive line in a football game. He hit an invisible force field that knocked him backwards into the chair he had been sitting in, and the chair fell backwards with Rawlings in it.

Chester didn't bother looking at him or shaking his head at Rawlings' stupidity.

Rawlings landed hard on his back with his legs in the air. The impact knocked the wind out of his lungs. "Oh, hell!" he gasped.

"How did you manage to build this compound without being seen by someone?" Chester asked him.

"This area is somewhat isolated, and we worked at night," Rush told him. "And your spy satellites may be excellent for spying on your fellow Earthlings, but easily blinded to our activities."

"And someone chose this part of Nevada for you long before your space ship reached Earth," Chester said.

"We of the Warrior Class always prepare well before we move to attack an enemy," Rush said.

"When you used your weapon to destroy all the major military and political centers in the world you gave away the position of this compound," Chester told him. "Your computers obviously detected us scanning the world to find out what was left and blocked us. And we detected where it came from."

"That is of no interest to me," Rush told him.

"It should be, because like I said in that room we were held in there are people coming to this compound to attack it. If we detected that spike, others did, too. And they know what's happened to the world is not the result of some nation on Earth, but an alien attack. You've got maybe two days at the most before thousands of people start for this compound. And they are going to be traveling fast with airplanes and nuclear weapons."

"We will destroy them," Rush told him.

"Maybe some of them, but not all of them. And all it'll take is for one of the planes heading this way to get through and drop its a-bomb. And no matter how deep this compound is the damage will be great."

"We are aware of you atomic bombs and we know their limitations," Rush said.

"Great enough to shut down whatever defensive systems you have. Then soldiers who have survived your attack will come within a few days. And your problems will be too great for you to handle."

Rush stared at him with a blank expression.

Rawlings set up and mumbled, "What hit me?"

"You ran into some sort of electrical force field," Chester told him as he looked down at him. He looked back at Rush. "You've got reinforcements coming, don't you?"

Rush said nothing.

"No matter how many you've got coming you're going to be fighting to control this planet for centuries unless you've got someone who can convince the people resistance is foolish."

"And you are that person?" Rush asked him.

"Rawlings and me," Chester answered.

Rush looked at Rawlings sitting on the floor with a dazed expression on his face. "Then you should instruct your companion to be more intelligent."

"Don't worry, I will."

"This meeting is over," Rush said.

Chester stood up. "Remember, Mr. Rush, you don't have a lot of time before the first attack."

The door opened and the guard entered the office.

"Take them to more comfortable quarters," Rush told the guard.

"Get up," Chester told Rawlings.

Ten minutes later they were in a room that looked like a basic hotel room.

"Why the fuck didn't you do something?" Rawlings demanded of Chester as he sat on one of the two beds.

"Because I'm not stupid," Chester said from the chair he was sitting in. He looked at a desk on his right with a TV on it. "I hope I can find out what's occurring in the outside world." He got up and walked to the desk.

"I don't like your implication," Rawlings yelled at him.

"Rush believed me," he said as he sat down in the chair behind the desk. "Can I get information from the outside?"

"Yes," replied the TV screen.

"A talking TV screen," Rawlings said.

"No, a talking computer," he said. "Those others are going to be here within a day or so, and somehow they're going to figure out a way of getting into this compound. And that's when Rush is going to realize how much he needs us."

"How do you know that's going to happen?"

"Because those coming here aren't stupid, either."

CHAPTER

Fifth day, 9: 30 p.m. May 7

"Hay, I just picked up an energy surge on this computer!" Alex yelled.

"What did you do?" Susan yelled at him.

"Not a damn thing," he answered. "The energy surge was displayed on this screen."

"Where did it come from?" Les asked him from his position outside.

"From inside that compound," he answered. "That means they haven't accessed my program inside the computer in that compound." He looked closely at the information on the screen. "But this energy surge occurred hours ago, at twelve-fifteen to be exact if the information on this screen is correct."

"Why would you pick it up if it occurred hours ago?" Henry asked him.

Alex thought for a few seconds before he replied, "Because the computer is sending information to all the Tabors wherever they are, and this armored car is still listed as part of their equipment. And that main computer had to look for it."

"Somebody in that compound is making sure everyone knows what's going on inside the compound," Henry said.

"You don't send soldiers in the field information until it directly affects their performance in the field," Susan said.

"You put information from that communicator you used to get into their computer into the computer in this armored car, didn't you?" Pedro asked him.

"Yes, I did," he said.

"So your program is just alerting you to what's going on in that compound," Pedro told him. "Phone company and cell phone company computers are always doing that."

Alex didn't reply.

"Is he right?" Henry asked Alex.

"Yes, he's right. Software companies are always sending out the latest updates to computers that have their software in them," he said. "They do that because it's good for customer relations."

"So what caused that power surge? And what type of power surge was it?" Susan asked.

Alex didn't answer her.

She waited a minute before she asked, "Did you hear me, Alex?"

"Yeah, I heard you. Power surges occur on our computers only when a powerful outside electrical source hits the computers. But now days all computers have surge protectors in them that blocks the surge from reaching the computer."

"These Tabors have more advanced computers than we do," Level said. "So why did you pick up a power surge from inside the compound?"

"Because there was a use of power in that compound the computer recorded and sent to every Tabor computer on this planet," Les said. "How far have we gone?"

"About twelve miles," Susan said.

"What time is it?" Judith asked.

"Nine p.m.," Level said.

"We've been moving since eight-thirty," Nancy said.

"And twelve miles isn't very far in an hour," Alice said.

"Settle down everyone we've got eight hours of darkness ahead of us," Janis said.

"We're making good time," Nancy said. "We should be able to cover forty-eight miles at the speed we're traveling before sunrise."

"And the ride outside hasn't been bad at all," Alice added.

"We should take a ten minutes break at midnight," Level said. "Agreed?"

"Agreed," Susan replied.

But why that power surge? Alex asked himself. He was sure they hadn't detected his program in their computers. He touched replay on the screen and watched a rerun of the power surge. *And it wasn't a very large one, and lasted only three seconds.*

May 8, midnight fourth day

At midnight they stopped among some large boulders and everyone got off or out and stretched their legs and relieved themselves.

"We should have covered twenty-four miles," Nancy said.

"And according to Susan we were only a hundred and fifty miles away when we started," Judith said. "So we're a hundred and sixteen miles closer. If we can cover another twenty-four miles we'll be only ninety two miles away when we stop."

"Looks like we may make it," Janis said.

"Maybe not," Les said in a gloomy voice.

"What do you mean, Les?" Alice asked him.

"This is the beginning of the fourth day," he said. "If we cover another forty-eight miles tomorrow night we'll still be forty-four miles away, and that'll be the third day. If we start at sundown on that day we can cover twenty-four miles before we have to stop and walk."

"Maybe we can go a little faster?" Pedro suggested.

"That I don't recommend," Henry said.

The others looked at him.

"These Tabors are warrior and they'll have patrols out at least twenty miles, and those patrols will probably have radar or what they consider to be radar. They'll pick us up the moment we enter their patrol zone."

"That's why we have to abandon the armored car," Susan said. "There's too much of a chance of it being detected. Our weapons we can hide under our clothing until we need them."

"And then the twenty mile hike in the darkness," Henry said. "That's going to take us at least a full night. We'll have one day left when we reach that compound, and we don't know how long it'll take us to get inside."

"If what you and Susan said about that fleet of space ships showing up, we won't have much time to spare," Janis said.

"We'll just have to hike faster," Level said.

"And if someone falls out? Do we just abandon them?" Les asked him.

"We've already lost three of us," Pedro said. "Two because they're traitors and one killed. No, I don't want to abandon anyone in this desert. Enough people have already died."

"Chester and Rawlings were picked up by two of those Tabors," Susan said.

"And by now they've talked and the Tabors know we're coming," Les said. He didn't want to say the odds are against us. They had enough problems without making everyone feel they were on a hopeless quest.

"Then let's stop talking and start moving," Alice said.

Within a minute they were moving again. Susan didn't tell anyone but she drove half a mile faster and reduced her zigzagging to twenty feet.

Les settled down and tried to get some sleep even though he knew he couldn't on the bouncing armored car. So he thought about everything that had occurred except the death of his family. He kept running into a mental block when he thought up to the last twenty-four hours. *Can't think right because I'm scared we're going to fail. I sure hope I can walk twenty miles at night.*

CHAPTER 37

May 8, 1 a.m.

Lieutenant Theia watched as the two replacement patrols left. Like all Tabor warriors in the compound she had no fear of failure because she knew there were no military forces left on Earth that could threaten them. Commander Rush had told her what Chester had said and had warned her to look for anything that was unusual. And so far she hadn't seen anything that was unusual. She had put the satellite in a moving orbit about Earth looking for any flying aircraft that might be headed for the compound, and so far she had seen three hundred aircraft flying around the continents. But none were headed in the direction of the compound. To be sure she had accessed their radios and learned they were no more than supply planes carrying medical supplies and food to where they were needed.

These Earthlings may be a primitive and barbaric type of humanoids but they do have the ability to unite when their world is threatened. It is good that the person we sent to this planet years ago got us information on their military installations, or we would have had great difficulty in destroying the important installations on this planet. Once the fleet arrives we will destroy all resistance on Earth in a few years. Those that remain we can use as sport while we hunt them down and kill them. She switched to the satellite that was tracking the fleet in deep space. *They have passed the planet these Earthlings call Pluto. They will follow a straight course directly to Earth now.* She brought up a picture of the solar system and didn't like what she saw.

The five inner planets, Mercury, Venus, Earth, Mars, and Jupiter, were lining up in a straight line. And that meant the fleet would have to come close to Jupiter. Many of the ships had been damaged in the battle escaping Tabor, and were being towed by the other ships. They would have to increase the speed of the fleet if they hoped to avoid Jupiter's tremendous gravitational pull. The fleet could avoided the problem of Jupiter by moving ten million miles away from Jupiter, but that would have added an extra day on their trip to Earth and require recalculating their course.

"I am worrying about nothing," she said softly and turned off the computer. She switched to receiving and began listening to broadcasts from around Earth. After half an hour of listening she said, "Computer, make a note for Commander Rush."

"Ready."

"The Earthlings are aware that their world was attacked by aliens and they are now preparing to respond. They picked up the spike we sent out to prevent them from accessing our computers, but they have located the general area the spike came from. Within a few days they may have the ability to locate the compound, and will attack. Lieutenant Theia. Send the note to Commander Rush's communicator, but do not awaken him"

"Will comply."

5 a.m.

"I'm looking for a place to stop and hide," Susan announced.

Alex and Janis had been dozing and woke up when they heard her.

"Good," Henry said. "I'm tired and those on top need to get off and stretch their legs."

"I need to do that, too," she told him.

"Directly ahead on your left about a mile is a cut between two hills. That'll be a good place to stop," he told her as he looked at the computer screen in the armored car.

She saw the two hills and headed for them. "Good place to hide, too. The sides of those hills are vertical. Not too high, either. We can put someone on top of them and see everything for miles."

Forty minutes later they were parked between the two hills and everyone was out walking around.

"What about breakfast?" Level asked.

"We made fifty-one miles," Susan said. "That puts us ninety-one miles away. So if we're going to start a fire I suggest it be a small one. Those Tabor patrols may have the ability to see the smoke from a large one."

"I just want to sleep on something that is not moving," Les said.

"Me, too," Alice said. "I didn't get a wink of sleep riding on the outside."

"I didn't get any sleep either," Susan said. "So I'm going to find a cool place to sleep."

"Who wants to take first watch on the tops of these two hills?" Henry asked.

"I'll take the first watch," Alex said. "Sitting in that armored car for almost eleven hours has made me feel all cramped."

"I'll join you," Nancy volunteered.

"Reliefs should be every two hours," Level said.

"Wake me in two hours whoever is awake," Les said.

"Me, too," Alice said.

In five minutes Alex and Nancy were each on a hill with binoculars, Level had made a small fire for coffee, and everyone else was lying on their ground mats sleeping or trying to sleep.

"A penny for your thoughts, Les," Alice said as she lay on her left side looking at him.

"They're not worth that much," he said as he lay on his back looking up at the clear blue sky. "And the only thing valuable about pennies now is the copper in them."

"You look worried," she said.

"I heard something recently that I'm trying to remember but can't seem to," he said.

"Was it important?"

"I don't know because I can't remember it," he said. "So whatever it is it's apparently not important." He looked at her. "Get some sleep. You must be very tired from hanging onto the outside of that armored car."

She laughed and rolled onto her back. "Believe it or not I've gotten used to it. Good morning."

"Good morning, Alice," he said and closed his eyes.

The Overlord was sitting in his command chair looking at the large screen in front of the navigation desk. The expression on his face said he wasn't happy with what he saw. "Is there no way to avoid passing close to that giant gas planet?"

"We are capable of passing it by ten million miles which would put us far enough away from its gravitational pull so that it wouldn't affect the fleet," the Captain told him. He was sitting in the captain's chair a few yards to Brangan's right.

"Would such a change in course affect the damaged ships?" Brangan asked.

"No, Overlord, it would not, but it would add an extra day to our voyage," he said. He looked at Roy and said, "Give your report to the Overlord about the ships, Roy."

Roy stood up, turned around and faced the Overlord standing at attention. "The damaged ships would be able to make the change in course, Overlord. All life support systems are working properly."

Brangan nodded and started to speak.

"May I continue, Overlord?" Roy asked.

Brangan looked at him and said, "Continue."

"While the ships are capable of making the change, Overlord, half our warriors have suffered wounds and the ships are overcrowded. The air they are breathing is not healthy though breathable. Twenty percent are seriously wounded and require an environment where there is clean air and water. Adding another day to our voyage could result in many of them dying."

Brangan thought about what he said for few seconds then said, "We will stay on our present course. We will need every warrior if we are to completely subdue Earth."

"Yes, Overlord," the Captain said. "You should know, Overlord, that our present course will bring the fleet within a million miles of the giant planet. We will have to use extra power to pass the planet, but its intense gravitational pull will nevertheless slow us down. But once pass it we can increase speed and still make Earth orbit in three days."

"And there will be no damage to the ships?" he asked.

"No, sir," the Captain said.

"That is acceptable," Brangan said.

7 a.m.

Les looked east and saw Alice sitting on a rock behind a cactus scanning the land with her binoculars. *Good woman.*

Two hours later Janis and Level had relieved them and they were sitting on the ground Indian style drinking coffee. Les was looking at the map of the area they were heading for.

"We can make fifty miles tonight," he said. "And then twenty-one miles on the night of the ninth and on the tenth we start the twenty mile walk."

"Think you can make it?" Alice asked him.

"We have to." He looked up at her and asked, "What about you?"

"If I'm with you, I can," she said.

"You like me don't you?"

"You're all I've got left in the world," she said.

"You're all I've got left in the world, too, Alice," he told her. "So we make it together. But do me a favor, okay?"

"What?"

"If we, or I should say when we get in that compound there's going to be killing. Stay behind me."

"Okay, but you do me the favor of not taking chances," she replied.

"Alright," he said, knowing he was going to do whatever he had to do to punish the aliens for what they had done to him and his world. "There's just one problem I don't think we've thought of."

"What's that?" Susan asked him.

"What the hell do we do if we do get inside that compound?"

"Go to the top level where the main computer is," she told him.

"Alright, we get control of that main computer. How do we stop a fleet of one hundred space ships from reaching Earth?" he asked.

"First let's get inside that compound and that room where the main computer is," Pedro said. "Then we can figure out how to stop one hundred space ships from reaching Earth."

"Maybe we should contact them and tell them Earth is closed until further notice," Nancy said.

The others laughed.

CHAPTER 38

May 8, 4:30 p.m.

"Maybe we should start now," Henry said as he looked at the sun in the western sky. "It's not dark yet but we could go slow and gain a few extra miles."

"He's right," Susan said.

They were all sitting around the cold remains of a small fire. They had finished their evening meal of bake beans and coffee and crackers.

"Wouldn't hurt," Alex said.

"I don't agree," Level said. "All we need is for that satellite to spot us moving and we're finished."

"Day or night that satellite can spot us," Henry said.

"We're camouflaged," Nancy said. "They won't notice us if we start moving during the day."

"My guess if we've already been spotted," Les said. "And our zigzagging has confused them."

"How would that confuse them?" Level asked him.

"When these aliens looked over the Earth to determine what they had to attack first they weren't looking at plants. I think they've already seen us, and they don't know what type of plant life moves in a zigzagging manner."

"Tumbleweed," Alice said.

"What about tumbleweed?" Level asked, looking in her direction.

"Tumbleweeds move," she said.

"They break off from their roots when dry and move with the wind," Pedro said. "And I'll bet they know how the major winds on Earth move."

"That dumb jock and Chester have probably told them about us," Nancy said.

"Let's hope they have," Les said.

"And why should we hope they have?" Alex asked him.

"Because the Tabors are probably looking for three Humvees not one of their own armored cars disguised to look like a collection of moving plants," he answered.

"So what is it? We move now or talk?" Henry said.

Les turned around and looked east. "Dusk is in the east, maybe if we move the Tabors won't pay any attention to us if that satellite sees us."

"That's taking a chance," Level reminded them.

"We've got three days left to reach that compound and get inside it and figure out how to do something to stop those other Tabors from reaching Earth. The sooner we reach that compound the more time we'll have to do what we've got to do, so let's take a chance," Les said in an angry voice.

"Then let's go," Henry said.

They were moving within two minutes.

"Les, what exactly do we do when we get into that compound?" Level asked from the rear of the armored car.

"Damned if I know," he replied. "We can figure that out once we get inside that compound." The thought passed through his mind that he should be remembering something of importance. It annoyed him that he couldn't remember it so he dismissed it from his mind. *If it were important I'd remember it so to hell with it.*

10 p.m.

They stopped and got out and off the armored car to stretch their legs and drink some water.

"That early start helped us," Susan said. "We've traveled twenty miles."

"That's good," Level said as he looked up in the night sky and stretch his back. "Let's hope some satellite the Tabors control hasn't spotted us."

"We're now only seventy-one miles away from that compound," Janis said.

"Don't you all think we should be making a plan of attack?" Judith said. "My late husband use to say 'always have a plan of action before you reach your destination'."

"I think if we get there within the next twenty-four hours we should wait until one of the patrols leave then get into the compound," Janis said.

"Yeah, but which one of the exits should we wait at?" Henry asked her.

"We should use the one you and Susan used to get back into the compound," Alice said.

"They may have that guarded," Pedro said.

"It doesn't matter which one we use, they are all going to be guarded," Les said. "Henry, you said there were only twenty-six of them in the compound."

"That's what the doctor told me," he said.

"And they've got patrols out looking for us," Les continued.

"But how many patrols?" Level asked.

"Maybe four," Susan said. "Four armored cars and two men per car."

"That doesn't leave them many men left to guard the compound," Nancy said.

"Let's assume at least four armored cars with two men to a car," Les said. "That would leave them only eighteen people in the compound."

"And not all of them are going to be awake if we try getting in at night," Pedro said.

"But where will those that are awake be?" Alice asked.

"My program that controls their cameras will let us know that," Alex said.

"When you activate that program will they know it?" Les asked him.

"Yes, if they've ordered their main computer to display all programs that have been activated."

"Come on, let's go," Susan said. "We've got about twelve hours of darkness before the sun starts to rise."

"We should start thinking of how to get pass those patrols?" Henry said.

"We can do that while we're moving," Level said.

They were moving within minutes.

Commander Rush walked into the main control room and looked at the display on the screen. "Any sign of any Earthlings coming for us, Sergeant Dram?"

"There are none, Commander," Dram replied.

"Is there anything unusual happening out there?"

"No, sir, everything is quiet." Dram decided not to mention the group of plants he had seen moving a day ago. He didn't consider them to be important. "But the computer is picking up numerous transmissions between various parts of Earth."

"That is understandable," he said. "Their world has been attacked and suffered greatly with the loss of their leading political and military centers. These primitives are getting themselves organized to strike back at us. But within three days it will be too late for them." He decided everything was going as planned. "I shall be in my quarters. If you see anything unusual notify me immediately."

"I will, Commander."

Rush left the control room.

Dram thought of putting the satellite in a stationary orbit over the compound and looking for those moving plants, but decided against it. It was more important to listen to any plans the Earthlings were making to determine if they knew where the compound was. He switched to receiving and sat back and relaxed.

"Your brilliant fucking plan has stalled, Chester," Rawlings complained loudly.

"Not really," he said as he watched the news on the TV.

"Why do you say that?"

"Because the news from outside clearly indicates people are preparing to fight back, and our quarters have been updated."

"That don't mean shit!"

"Rawlings, stop using your head as a battering ram like some dumb jock," Chester told him. "These aliens have destroyed every major political and military organization on Earth, but they remain in this elaborate hole in the ground. Why?"

"Maybe they like living in holes in the ground?"

"They don't have enough men to come out and take over. This group here represents the first wave. Their job was to render Earth helpless and that is exactly what they've done. Now they are waiting for the second wave to arrive so they can finish the conquest of Earth."

"And if that happens we're up shit creek because they're not going to need us to control people still alive."

"You're right there."

"So your brilliant fucking plan has failed, and these aliens don't need us," Rawlings yelled at him.

"But what if Level and his group attack this place before the second wave arrives?"

"That group of fucking wimps? They're probably running for home."

"No they are still coming and when they arrive these aliens are going to need us," he said. "So relax everything is going as I planned."

CHAPTER 39

May 9, 5:43 a.m.

They stopped in a sparely wooded area near a small muddy looking river and got out and off.

"How far have we come?" Les asked Susan the moment she crawled out of the driver's compartment.

"Forty-one miles," she said.

"And we have two days left," he said. He turned to Alex. "Is there any way of determining the patrol pattern of the Tabor patrols?

"I've been working with the computer in the armored car, and I say no. The only way to find out where those patrols are is to log into their main computer in the compound, and once we do that they'll know exactly where we are."

"I suggest when we start moving again we head for the southern exit of that compound," Henry said. "It'll only add an extra mile to our journey."

"Why there?" Janis asked him.

"We left by the eastern exit and returned to the compound by the western exit," he said. "They may not expect us to try for the southern exit."

"If they're smart they'll be expecting us at all the exits," Level said.

"If they believe we're going to attack them," Les added.

"Have you forgotten Chester and Rawlings?"

"No, I haven't, but I'm hoping after what they've done to the world they may think they are safe. Or at the very least we represent an unimportant threat to them."

"If they think that we may have an edge," Susan said.

"What do those exits look like?" Judith asked.

"They blend into the surrounding terrain," she said. "You can't see them unless one opens."

"Remember we saw groves cut into the ground, Susan?" Henry reminded her.

"Yeah, we did, didn't we," she said. "So we look for groves that are straight and join with other straight groves, if we see any that'll indicate an overhead door."

"So we have to pray we find some straight groves in the ground at night to find an exit," Alice said.

"Eh, you're all going to think I'm crazy, but why not get closer than twenty miles before we start walking?" Nancy said.

They all looked at her.

She didn't say anything.

"Explain," Level told her.

"Well, so far we've avoided being spotted by them, so why not get as close as ten or even five miles before we abandon this armored car. The walk would be shorter and we'd have more time to look for those groves," she explained.

"Those exits are at least an eighth of mile away from each other, Nancy," Susan told her. "We'd have to divide up to be able to watch all of them."

"No we won't," Pedro said.

"We're listening, Pedro," Henry told him.

"The communicators we've got can pick up the opening and closing of those exits right?"

"That's right," Henry said. "Those Tabors don't know the special code we put in the communicators we've got so it wouldn't be a problem for me -." He looked at Alex. "Or for Alex to watch his communicator to see what exit is opening."

"But what if we're not at the right exit?" Janis said.

They all looked at each other because no one had an answer for her question.

"They probably change those patrols at a certain time every so often," Alice said.

"Considering the few people they've got, I'd say once every four hours," Henry said. "That way the men in those patrol cars would be able to get enough rest."

"According to you they have twenty-six people," Nancy said.

"Yeah, but only about twenty of them are soldiers the rest are medical personal, I think," Susan said.

"And computer people," Pedro said. "And let's assume they change them once every eight hours. So that would mean there are two of them leaving only twenty-two regular soldier. And eight of them would be out on patrol."

"Didn't we decide the patrols wouldn't be called in until the replacement patrols are sent out?" Les said.

"Yes, we did," Level said.

"So using those communicators we should be able to learn when a patrol leaves and returns. If we could reach one of the exits as a patrol is leaving we'd have a few minutes to get inside before the returning patrol enters."

"No, they're not going to leave an exit open. They open and close only when a patrol is leaving or returning," Susan said. "What we'll have to do is slip inside after the leaving patrol leaves and without them seeing us."

"All ten of us?" Alice asked.

Les nodded his head as he said, "Yeah, all ten of us because we have no other choice."

"So we get as close as five miles and using the communicators we watch to see what exit opens. And we walk toward it making sure the returning patrol doesn't see us. Then we wait until the patrols are exchanged and slip in after the replacement patrol leaves."

"Assuming the returning patrol uses the same exit," Level said.

"It may mean hours sitting and waiting and remember time is something we are rapidly running out of," Judith said.

They all looked at each other waiting for someone to come up with a better idea, but no one did.

"What about the patrols?" Susan asked.

"What about them?" Level asked her.

"Before we can get into that compound we've got to get pass those patrols," she said.

"She's right," Alex said. "So how do we do that without being seen?"

"If they have four patrols out they'd be separated by miles if they're patrolling twenty miles beyond the compound," Henry said.

"Those tire marks we saw on the ground a few days ago indicated they were patrolling an area ten miles beyond that compound," Nancy said. "Maybe we should look for one. We've got binoculars and night glasses."

"That'll take more time," Janis said.

"How far do we have to go?" Les asked.

"A little over sixty miles," Susan said.

"Those of us on top will have to start looking for a patrol when we're within thirty miles of that compound," Les said. He looked at them to see if they agreed with him.

"We haven't much choice, do we?" Alice asked.

"Let's get some coffee and crackers in us and get some rest," Level said.

Half an hour later they had eaten, posted two guards, and the rest were lying on their ground mats trying to get some sleep.

CHAPTER  40

May 9, 6:45 .p.m.

"We've got forty-one miles left to go if we stop twenty miles from the compound," Les said.

"Let's get as close as ten miles," Susan said.

"It means we'll have to be alert for one of those patrols once we get within twenty miles of that compound," Henry said.

"If we see any we'll tell you," Les said.

"We can use those view finders to look for them," Susan said. "They can be magnified, but not the one on the gun because it's covered."

"Drive carefully," Level said.

They left fifteen minutes later.

11 p.m.

"We've reached the twenty mile limit," Henry announced to those inside the armored car. He rose up and told the others outside through the canvas and dirt the same thing.

"Maybe we should stop," Level said.

"No," Nancy said. "We haven't seen any patrols and we need to reach that compound with plenty of time to see the patrols coming and going. Let's go another ten miles."

"Let's hope one of those patrols hasn't spotted us," Level said. "Because if they have we'll be moving into a trap."

"Let's go," Janis said. "We've got nothing else to lose but our lives."

Henry dropped back down inside and said to Susan. "Keep going another ten miles. You guys on top keep your eyes open for the patrols."

Susan continued driving.

"Let's look for anything unusual," Les said to those on the outside.

"It's so dark we can only see a few yards," Janis said.

"Put on your night vision glasses and listen for any unusual sounds," Les told her. "I'll use the binoculars I've got. You use yours, Level."

"Like the sounds we're making?" Nancy asked as she got her night vision glasses out of her shirt pocket and put them on. "Boy, I can see a long way in these."

"I'm reducing speed to five miles an hour, Henry," Susan told him.

"I should turn on the computer to see what's around us," he said.

"Leave that damn thing alone!" Alex snapped at him. "We're too close to that compound. They pick up the computer being turned on at this distance they'll know it's us."

Les heard him and thought *a diversion is what we need. But what can we use to create a diversion?*

An hour later Susan said, "We're within fifteen miles. Should I keep going?"

"Yes," Les said. "I haven't seen any of those Tabor patrols."

"Maybe not," Level said.

"If one of those patrols had spotted or heard us they would have attacked immediately. We should try and get as close as possible."

"What if they've been ordered not to attack us if they see us, but let us get closer?" Level asked him.

"Then let's just pray we haven't been spotted," Les replied.

"Have any of you seen tire marks on the ground?" Alex asked from inside the armored car.

"I did," Les said. "About ten miles behind us, but I didn't see any patrols."

"That means we're probably inside their patrol area," Henry said. "Lady Luck's been with us so far."

"What time is it?" Alice asked.

"Midnight," Janis said from inside the armored car.

They quieted down.

"Ten miles," Susan announced an hour later.

"And no trouble. I don't see anything around us that says those Tabor patrols are near," Nancy said as she looked around the country side. "We should get closer."

"I can't see anything that looks like a patrol," Les said as he scanned the country side with the binoculars. "What about you, Level?"

"Same here," he answered looking around with his binoculars.

The two Tabors patrolling the eastern side ten miles out were tired. They had been out for two hours and hadn't had but four hours sleep when they were in the compound.

"I am glad the Overlord choose this planet," the Tabor in the passenger seat said.

"Why?" asked his companion.

"I like the star patterns in the night sky," he said as he looked up at the stars.

"Why?"

"They remind me of Tabor."

"You don't miss that world of equality lovers, do you?"

"No I don't," he said then laughed and said, "God no."

The driver burst out laughing along with his companion.

"How foolish of those equality lovers to believe there is a god," the Tabor said.

"We of the Warrior Class are not so stupid as to believe such nonsense," the driver said. "Any human with intelligence knows that anyone who can become the Overlord is supreme."

"That is right," the other man said. "Only he could have developed a plan to get information on this world from the Tabor government and then send us here to conquer it."

"Yes, only a supreme being like the Overlord could convince those democracy loving equality lovers to believe he was changing the Warrior Class into a class of peaceful people while building a fleet of space ships and escape that mad world."

"With the Overlord as our leader we are indestructible. We can master anything."

"When are we to be relieved? I'm tired," the other man asked.

"In another two hours," the driver said. "Seen anything that says any Earthlings are near the compound?"

"No, nothing," his companion said. "You think the Overlord will reward us with land grants on this Earth?"

"And with Earth slaves to work the land for us," the driver said then yawned. "I will sleep well when I'm off duty."

May 10, 1:35 a.m.

"We're four miles away," Susan said.

"We should stop," Janis said from her cramped position on the floor.

"I agree," Alex said. "We've pushed our luck in this armored car as far as we should push it."

Susan stopped the armored car between two tall cactus plants, and climbed out.

Henry was already on the ground with Janis coming down the side of the armored car and Alex following her. Those on the outside had gotten off the moment the armored car stopped.

"Okay, we should carry as much of the food and water as possible, along with the medical kits, and our weapons," Level said. "You and Susan, Henry, should stay close to us since you don't have night glasses."

"We should stick close together. Stay within sight of the person in front of you. We don't want to lose anyone," Nancy said.

"Susan or I should take the lead since we've some idea of what the terrain looks like around that compound," Henry suggested.

"Here, Susan, take my glasses," Alice said and took them off and handed them to her.

"I'll bring up the rear," Henry said.

Alex took his night vision glasses out of his inside jacket pocket and gave them to Henry. "So you can see what's behind us."

"I don't think we have to worry about the patrols, because we're inside their patrol area," Susan said.

"Let's hope they didn't spot us and let us through," Alice said.

"Yeah, because if they have we'll all be dead in ten seconds," Susan agreed.

After they got everything they needed and put them in the backpacks they had, they started walking with Susan in the lead and Level behind her and Les behind him. Alice was following Les holding on to the tail of his jacket. Janis, Judith, and Pedro and Nancy were next in line with Alex behind Nancy and Henry bringing up the rear. None of them said anything as they walked. Those with night vision glasses looked for the Tabor patrols and the others listened for the sounds of wheels crunching on the ground. Les and Level scanned the area with their binoculars looking for a patrol.

An hour later Alex breathing heavily asked, "How far do you think we've come?"

"At least three miles at the speed we've been walking," Henry said from the rear. He could hear Alex's heavy breathing. "You okay?"

"Yeah, I'm alright," he said then laughed a short laugh. "For years I've been planning to lose ten pounds and I think I've lost more than that since I began this adventure if you can call it that."

Les looked back at Alice. "How are you doing?"

"Fine so far how are you doing?"

"Like you, fine so far."

"We should take a ten minute break to catch our breaths," Level said. He wasn't breathing heavily.

"Would be nice," Nancy said.

"Okay, let's stop," Susan said and stopped and sat down on the ground.

The others stopped and sat down in a circle with their backs to each other.

"Isn't this rattle snake country?" Janis asked.

"Much of the southern part of America is rattle snake country," Les said. "But I wouldn't worry about them if I were you."

"Why shouldn't we worry? Those things are poisonous," Judith said.

"Because there is no danger from them unless you hear a rattling sound," Henry told her. "And considering the vibrations we've been making as we walked any rattle snakes around us have moved as far away from us as possible."

"Alex, didn't you say we shouldn't use those communicators this close to the compound because they might be detected?" Nancy asked him.

"Damn, she's right," he exclaimed.

"That means we won't be able to use them to determine when an exit is opening," Janis said.

"We'll have to go to that southern exit and trust to luck," Alex said.

"Everybody take a swallow of water," Pedro said.

After ten minutes and a few swallows of water they got up and started walking again, but this time much slower. An hour later, 3:45 a.m., Susan stopped.

"What's wrong?" Les asked her as he stopped.

"We should be right outside that southern exit," she said.

"The ground was flat where we entered the western exit, Susan," Henry said.

"With trees growing on top of it," she added.

"Why flat ground with tree growing on top," Janis asked.

"So when they leave the compound they don't have to go down any hill," he answered.

"So let's walk around in twos and look for flat ground," Les suggested. "Alice, stick with me. Alex you stick with Henry."

"Stay close so we can hear each other without screaming," Level said.

They started walking around in twos ten minutes later they came back together.

"What did you find?" Level asked them.

"All the land is flat around here," Les said.

"Sure is," Janis said.

"What about you others, see anything odd?" Les asked.

"There's a small hill a few yards to the north of us," Nancy said.

"That figures," Henry said. "They wouldn't want flat land all around their compound. A hill would help hide their comings and goings."

"I didn't see any hills on that map of this country I was looking at in that armored car," Alex said.

Les looked at the hill and said, "That's probably the result of all the dirt and rock they took out of the ground to build that underground compound of theirs."

"Did anyone see any groves in the ground?" Henry asked.

They all said they didn't.

"I wonder why?" he asked.

"Maybe opening and closing of those exits spreads dirt over the groves?" Pedro said.

"Yeah," Henry said. "Maybe that does happen."

"So let's get on top of that hill and wait," Susan said.

They all walked to the hill and up on the incline and sat down.

"Now be quiet and don't make any foolish moves if you hear something," Susan told them.

"And if you feel the ground moving don't jump up and start running, because it won't be an Earthquake but an overhead door opening," Henry said.

They became quiet and sat still. Level was sitting off by himself a yard away.

Les began thinking about what he wanted to remember but couldn't. What annoyed him was he couldn't understand why he was trying to remember something he couldn't remember. If it was important he'd remember it. *Stupidity!*

An hour of silence passed. The desert was quiet as if it was asleep.

"Did you hear that?" Nancy asked.

"Hear what?" Judith asked her.

"The sound of rocks moving," she said.

"I didn't hear a -," Janis started to say when she heard a soft grinding sound and the ground began to tremble.

"We're in the right place," Susan said as she stood up.

"Sit down," Henry said. "We don't want them to see us."

Susan sat back down.

The ground stopped trembling and the grinding sound was replaced by a soft whooshing sound as air escaped from the ground thirty feet in front of them. A dull light that didn't go more than five feet came out of the ground as a wide long part of it rose up then the light went out. A few seconds passed before an armored car came out of the ground and moved off into the darkness at a rapid speed.

"Now," Henry said as he moved toward the opening in the ground.

Janis, Judith, Nancy, and Alex followed him as he ran to the edge of the open ground. Alice was behind Alex and Pedro was behind her. Susan and Les followed as they ran side by side for the opening.

"Be careful," Les said as the others jumped down from the left side of the ramp onto the apron and began to move back into the compound.

Susan and Les jumped together and landed side by side on their feet. That's when Les remembered what he had been trying to remember. He turned around to his right and looked back and saw Level standing on the edge of the open ground aiming his semiautomatic at him and Susan.

"Jesus!" he exclaimed and pushed Susan out of the way and pulled his weapon out of his jacket pocket and fired wildly at Level. "I just remembered."

Susan staggered forward yelling, "What the hell are you doing, Les?"

Level ducked down to avoid Les' shot and fired five rounds at him and Susan. All five rounds missed them and slammed into the smooth stone wall to their left.

"What the hell is going on?" Henry angrily yelled back.

"Level is a Tabor," Les answered.

"That's bullshit," Alex said.

"Then why did he try to kill Les and me?" Susan asked him.

"Let's get off this apron," Pedro suggested. "That overhead door might start closing or the returning patrol may show up."

"Which way do we go?" Judith asked.

"Back down the corridor," Henry said as he began running down the corridor.

"They probably heard the shooting," Janis said.

"Let's hope not," Alex said as he was reaching into his pants pocket for the communicator. He turned it on and accessed the security cameras of the compound.

The overhead door began to close.

"They'll open it when the other patrol returns," Nancy said.

"Let's hope they haven't seen or heard us," Alice said.

"Stick together two of us don't have night glasses," Les said.

Alex brought up a picture of the southern exit on the communicator. "They haven't seen us. But we've got to get out of this corridor and find a place where we can talk."

"We're near the top and that control room shouldn't be too far from here," Susan said.

"Look for doors on the sides," Henry said.

"There should be some sort of garage at the end of this ramp," Les said.

"Alex, what do you see?" Nancy asked him.

"I've got the southern exit and there's nothing on the communicator," he said.

"The lights are out maybe the cameras can't record anything," Judith said.

"The lights may be out but what I'm seeing on the screen of the communicator is an empty corridor."

"Maybe you're looking at another corridor."

"No, at this one and they can't see us," he said. "Apparently their cameras can see in the dark."

"I've found a door on the right side," Nancy said.

"Move toward her voice," Les said.

"Open it," Janis said.

"We don't know what's behind it," Alice said. "We could walk into someone's apartment."

"Wait a minute, please," Alex said as he worked on the communicator.

They stopped on both sides of the door and waited for Alex.

"Got a diagram of this corridor and what it connects to," he said. A few seconds passed before he said, "This is an empty room." He reached down for the handle, but didn't feel one. "Farther down on the left is a garage with those cars in it."

"Let's hope opening that door doesn't register on some computer in that control room," Alice said.

"We don't have much choice unless we want to stay in this corridor," Les said. "And we've got to make it to that control room in the next few minutes."

"We've got time," Judith said.

"No we don't, because right now Level is calling that Commander," Susan said.

Alex looked for a doorknob and didn't see one. "There's no way to open this door. There's no doorknob."

"Push against it, and it'll open," Susan told him.

Alex pushed against the door with his right shoulder.

The door opened.

They all rushed inside. Pedro turned to close the door, but it closed automatically.

"What now?" Janis asked.

"Find out where that control room is, and quickly," Nancy said.

"Remember Rome wasn't built in a day," Alex said as he worked on the communicator.

"At the moment how long it took to build Rome isn't our major concern," Nancy told him.

"Where's the other communicator?" Pedro asked.

"Here," Henry said as he reached into his pants pocket and took it out and handed it to Pedro.

"We shouldn't be using all of those communicators," Nancy said.

"Too late for that, now," Alice said.

Pedro moved to Alex. "What did you do?"

Alex showed him. "If that control room is at the top it must not be very far from us if that diagram Henry drew was accurate."

"It was. I got it off that computer of the hospital room Susan and I were in," Henry assured him.

Twenty seconds later Alex and Pedro said at the same time, "We've got to go back into that corridor and move right down it till we reach the end."

"What's there?" Alice asked them.

"A door that connects to a hallway that has two elevators and a stairwell in it," Pedro said.

Henry led the way back into the corridor with Les behind him and the others following him.

No one said anything until they reached the door at the end of the corridor.

"What's it like behind this door?" Les asked.

"An empty hallway," Alex said looking at the communicator in his left hand.

"I'm in a computer than says it's the control computer," Pedro said.

"Do they know?" Judith asked him.

"I don't know what they know," he said as he worked on the small keyboard of the communicator.

"What are you doing?" Alex asked him.

"I'm trying to get a picture of the hallway beyond this door because it goes in a circle. And to see if I can I can order the computer to replay the recording of the hallway, then we can enter."

An idea dawned upon Alex. "Computer."

"Yes," replied the computer over the communicator in his hand.

The others looked at him as if he was crazy. They could see an expression of success on his face.

"Don't display anything on the main screen but recordings made ten minutes ago," he said.

Two seconds passed before the computer said, "Done."

"That's all you'll see on those communicators," Susan said.

"No, we'll see what's really being recorded," he said. "But not someone in that control room."

"Is it safe?" Henry asked him as he reached the door.

"Yes, I think so," Alex said.

Henry opened the door and entered the hallway. "No one's here."

The others quickly followed him and let the door softly close.

"Where is that control room?" Les asked.

"A little more than fifty feet just above us," Pedro said.

Janis moved toward one of the two elevators.

"Leave those elevators alone," Les said. "We use the stairs. We get in one of those elevators its movement might be registered on that main computer and we could be trapped in it."

"Show this stairwell computer," Alex said.

"How does it know where we are?" Nancy asked him.

"It doesn't," he said. "But it knows where this communicator is."

A dark empty stairwell appeared on the small screen of his communicator.

"It's safe," he said.

"Where are they?" Nancy asked.

"They're all probably asleep if they're not on duty," Susan said.

"Opening the door to that stairwell might also register on the main computer," Alice said.

"We don't have a choice," Henry said as he moved to the stairwell and opened the door and looked in. "Empty."

"Does this stairwell stops in the main control room?" Janis asked.

"Yes, it does," Pedro said as he looked at the communicator in his hand.

"And there will be someone on duty inside there," Susan said.

"We go slow and quiet. When we reach the top, I'll burst into the control shooting," Les told them.

"I'll be with you," Henry said and started up the stairs with Les following him.

CHAPTER 41

Level was angry as he got to his feet, but he didn't show it on his face and all he thought as he put his weapon in his pocket and removed his iPhone from his other pocket was *I must not fail the Overlord*. He pushed two buttons on the keyboard of his iPhone waited a second and pushed two others. *They will not have gone very far.*

The number he had dialed began to ring. It rang for ten minutes before it was answered.

"Who are you?"

"The Earthlings are inside the compound," he said in angry voice. "Awaken all your warriors and lock all entrances to the control room."

"I don't take orders from someone I don't know."

"Who are you?" Level yelled over his cell phone.

"I am Commander Rush. Who are you?"

"I am the Forerunner, fool! Do as I say."

"The Forerunner may have inadvertently let his identity slip during his time on this planet, and you could be any Earthling who may have heard it," Rush said.

"If you don't want to die a painful death, fool, do exactly as I say now," Level yelled at him.

"I am a Tabor Warrior and threats of a painful death don't cause me fear. No warrior is afraid of any form of death as long as they die in the Overlord's service."

"Are you afraid of being labeled a failure by the Overlord?"

"I have the trust of the Overlord."

"Overlord Brangan will kill you slowly and enjoy watching you die if you don't do as I say immediately."

It was forbidden for Tabor warriors to mention the Overlord's name. And no Tabor Warrior ever did so unless given permission by the Overlord.

"I shall allow you into the compound," Rush said thinking, *this man could be the Forerunner.* "Then I will have your DNA checked to verify you are the Forerunner. What exit are you next to?"

"You are wasting time! They have already accessed your main computer."

"What exit are you next to?"

"The southern exit!"

"I shall have the overhead door opened for you," Rush told him and turned off his communicator.

Level knew it was a waste of time to yell at Rush. All he was doing was following the standard Tabor safety procedures. And that wouldn't do him or the Tabors any good if Les and the others got into the control room, because he knew the great weakness of the Tabor computer system. "Order all your patrols to return to the compound immediately you are going to need them."

He received no response.

When the overhead door began to open he jumped down on the apron and ran into the corridor knowing none of them would be there. *What did I do to tip off Les?*

The corridor was lit up, but none of them were there.

What would I do if I were them? He thought as he ran down the corridor for the door to the hallway where the elevators were. He pushed the buttons on his iPhone to summon Rush and said, "Lock down all the elevators and all the doors to the stairwells, and do it now!"

There was no response from Rush.

If they get into the control room and get access to the main computer they will learn how to control the satellites and the laser rays on them. For the first time in the twenty years Level had been on Earth he was afraid of failure.

Les led the way up the stairwell quietly taking two steps at a time and making sure not to misstep and fall with the fear of failure in his mind.

Henry was a few steps ahead of him.

Within two minutes Les and Henry were standing on the landing at the top of the stairwell facing a door that had no sign on it.

Henry looked at the closed door and thought, *no need for signs on doors since they all probably know every inch of this place. God be with us.*

Henry looked at Les, saw the look of determination on his face, and nodded.

Les nodded back that he was ready.

Theia was sitting in the chair facing the main computer and looking up at the screen on the wall. She was tired, but alert. She had heard the sounds of the shooting and wondered what they were since she'd never heard an Earth gun fired.

Rush's voice came over the intercom in the main control room. "Theia, this is Rush. Lock all the doors to the main control room."

She wondered why he would issue such an order, but she would obey it.

Henry was standing on the left side of the door and Les on the right, and both heard Rush's order over the intercom. Without a second thought Henry pushed against the door with his left hand and it opened, and Les rushed into the main control room.

Theia was reaching for the button which would lock all the entrances into the main control when she heard the door open. She wondered who would be so foolish as to the burst into the control in such a rude manner. She turned around and looked in the direction of the open door and saw Les followed by Henry, and jumped to her feet.

"Hands up!" Les yelled at her as he rushed toward her as if he was a police officer bursting in on criminals involved in a criminal activity.

"Who are -," she started to say then yelled, "Earthlings!"

Henry didn't say a word as he ran pass Les, dropped low, and slammed his right shoulder into her stomach.

The blow knocked Theia back into the desk three computers with screens and keyboards sat on and knocked the wind out of her doubling her over in pain.

Les ran up to her and using the butt of his weapon he slammed it down on the left side of her temple as hard as he could and knocked her down her on her knees. He'd never hit anyone like that and didn't care what damage he'd done to her.

Pain rushed through Theia's head and she felt like passing out, but she fought the urge and got to her feet. She was confused and couldn't properly focus her eyes.

Henry had straightened up and grabbed her by the collar of her uniform and pulled her away from the desk as he backhanded her on the right side of her head with the blaster he held as hard as he could.

Theia dropped to the floor unconscious bleeding from her right ear.

The others had rushed into the control room before the fighting had stopped. Alex and Pedro and Janis rushed toward the desk with the three keyboards and computers. Judith and Nancy ran over to Theia before she hit the floor pointing their weapons at her.

Alice closed the door saying, "How can we lock this door?"

"This unit can lock the door that is unlocked," answered the computer.

"I knew it!" exclaimed Alex.

"A verbal computer," Janis said.

"Are there any codes in the computer?" Pedro asked.

"Codes do not compute," replied the computer.

"No codes?" Janis said.

"How do we lock this door and the elevator doors?" Alice repeated. "There are two elevator doors next to this door."

"Lock all stairwells doors and elevator doors leading to this room," Alex said.

"All doors and elevators to the main control room are locked," said the computer.

Les and Henry started running around the glass column in the center of the room looking for anymore Tabors.

"There are two elevators on this side of the room and two other doors," Les said.

"What are those doors for?" Janis asked the computer.

"One is a door that leads to the stairwell behind it. The other door leads to stairs that lead to the outside door," answered the computer.

"There are three other doors in this room beside those doors," Henry said.

"Let's see what's behind them," Les said.

"Keep an eye on that Tabor woman," Henry said as he and Les moved toward one of the two other doors.

"If she moves, kill her!" Les ordered.

Alice walked over to Theia and pointed her weapon at her chest. "After what this bitch and her warrior friends have done to Earth, I won't hesitate a minute."

"Let's check those other doors," Nancy said to Judith.

They moved toward the doors.

"One of you stand on one side of the door and one of you push on it to open it while the other prepares to shoot inside," Susan said as she dropped her backpack on the floor and rushed to join Nancy and Judith.

Henry and Les opened the door they had gone for.

The light inside immediately went on.

"A bedroom with two beds in it," Henry said as he looked into the room and saw a door at the far end of the room. "Let's check it."

It took the five of them less than a minute to check all the doors in the control room.

"The bedroom contains a bathroom with hot and cold running water, and another door that has a closet behind it when you push it," Les said.

"One room is a storage room with boxes of what looks like food," Judith said.

"And this one is a room filled with what looks like guns and some boxes," Nancy said, standing at the open door.

"What type of guns?" Susan asked her as she walked over to the room.

"I don't know. I'm not that familiar with guns," she said.

Susan walked into the lit room and began looking at the weapons. She walked around the room picking up the guns and looking them over.

"Let's fill our canteens with water, before the Tabors cut off the water to this room," Les said.

"No need to do that, but you may do so to be on the safe side," Alex said as he worked on the keyboard and looked at the screen on the desk.

"Why do you say that?" Judith asked him.

"This computer I'm sitting at connects to the main computer in that glass column in front of us and it controls everything in this compound including the flow of fresh water, air, and the removal of waste." He brought up a program on the computer screen in front of him than explained how waste was disposed of.

"They recycle everything that can be recycled and burn for energy that which can't," Janis said. She read the program on the screen in front of her explaining how waste was handled. "And when they burn things they don't produce any harmful pollutants."

"Ships traveling billions of miles through space can't afford to waste anything," Pedro said. "And they've applied that same principle of handling waste on planets."

"All that is nice to know, but how do we stop those one hundred ships with half a million warriors on them headed for Earth?" Henry said.

"Computer, show the location of the Tabor fleet headed for Earth," Alex said.

A picture of the solar system appeared on the large screen above his head showing the exact location of the fleet and its speed.

"That bright dot is the Tabor fleet?" Nancy asked as she looked at the screen.

"That's it," Alex said. "All one hundred of them, and they're travelling in a circle."

"Looks like they're close to a planet," Les said as he looked at the screen. He saw the speed the fleet was travelling at the bottom of the screen. "And they're traveling at a speed just below the speed of light. How long will that take them to reach Earth at that speed?"

"That planet is Neptune," Pedro said. "And at their speed they'll reach Earth in a little over sixteen hours."

"So what do we do to stop them from reaching Earth?" Alice asked.

Les looked at Theia. "We've got to find a way to tie that woman up."

"Why not use her uniform?" Nancy suggested. "It looks strong enough to hold her."

"Anybody got a pocket knife?" Alice asked.

Les took his out of his pocket and walked over to her and handed it to her. "Judith and Nancy help her. One of you point your gun at her head in case she wakes up."

Judith and Nancy walked over to Theia and knelt down and rolled her on her stomach and took Les' knife from Alice and began cutting the legs off her uniform. They quickly tied her hands and feet tightly with only one of the legs of her uniform. The other they used as a gag.

"That should keep her quiet and still," Nancy said.

"I don't know," Judith said looking over Theia. "She's pretty muscular. She may be able to break lose and attack us."

"That's why one of us has to watch her at all times," Alice said. "I'll take the first watch. One of you can relieve me in two hours."

Susan walked out of the arms room holding a barrel in her left hand. "There's nothing in that room but parts of weapons, and boxes. No ammunition that I can detect."

"They're probably electric weapons and need batteries to make them operate," Henry said from the couch he was sitting on.

"So why have them here?" Susan asked.

"Our problem is how to stop that fleet from reaching Earth," Les said. "Not weapons without batteries."

"Yes, and I think I know how to stop them from reaching Earth, but it's going to take time to do that," Alex said.

"How much time?" Les asked him.

"At the moment I don't know."

"Let's secure this room, because right now Level's made contact with his buddies and they're planning to break in here and kill all of us," Henry said.

"A room this important should have extra security," Pedro said. He started to type a question on the keyboard, but stopped and asked, "Computer, what other security is there for this room?"

"There are steel blast doors two feet thick at every entrance."

"Computer, close the blast doors," Janis said.

"Blast doors are closing."

"We're safe until those ships arrive," she said.

"Enough time for Les to explain how he knew Level was a Tabor," Henry said.

"He made some statements while we were bathing in that stream that caused me to think," he said as he walked to Commander Rush's chair and sat down. "And one to Chester I paid little attention to."

"What statements?"

"When Chester and Rawlings were holding their guns on us, Level said, 'I can assure you they won't accept you,'" he said. "How would he know that if he wasn't one of them?"

"I remember that," Alice said. "But what other statements did he make, Les?"

"Remember when we were swimming in that stream a few days ago?" Les asked the men.

"Yeah, I remember that," Henry told him.

"He said it had taken the human race four thousand years to learn how to cook raw meat some time earlier. Anyone with a minimum knowledge of the history of the human race would have known that was wrong."

"When did humans learn how to cook meat?" Nancy asked him.

"It was a knowledge passed down from the ancient ancestors of humans," he said. "Homo-Erectus knew how to make fire and cook meat, and that was a million years before the Cro-Magnons, the first modern humans, appeared on Earth."

"Yeah," Pedro said without turning from the computer. "He also called New York the Big Peach. Everyone should know it's called the Big Apple. Why I don't know?"

"He also said the U. S. Strategic Command was located in the Sierra Nevada Mountains, and I thought that was really odd, but I didn't say anything at the time," Henry said. "Any officer in the U. S. Military who had worked there would know it's located on the eastern side of the Rocky Mountains in Colorado near the base so weather won't close it down, or earthquakes on the west coast won't affect it."

"And that he loved walking outside the command during blizzards," Les said. "I'm no expert on the Sierra Nevada Mountain's weather, but I don't think anybody would be foolish enough to go outside in any mountains during a blizzard."

"He was sent to Earth years before the attack so he could locate the most important military and political places to attack to render

Earth helpless to defend itself when the Tabor Fleet showed up," Susan said. She was sitting on the floor near a wall.

"That's how they were capable of knocking out all the major military bases and political systems on Earth. They knew where everything of importance was, because Level had spent years locating them," Nancy said. "And when those here arrived he gave them that information and where to build this underground compound."

"If Level was one of them, why encourage us to look for this place," Janis asked.

"Because he was with us when Alex and Pedro detected that spike," Les said. "His purpose was to get us here, kill us, and tell the Tabors to stop using spikes to hide this compound."

"How could they build this place without anyone knowing about it?" Judith asked. "They must have moved thousands of tons of dirt and rock."

"This is isolated country," Les said. "There aren't any towns close to this part of Nevada for almost a hundred miles. And with their technology they could punch a hole in the ground in a matter of days and pile the dirt and rocks up to form that hill we were sitting on."

"But someone would have seen a space ship bringing in the equipment to build this place," Nancy said.

"Technology again," Susan said. "They probably cloaked their ship in some way so our radar and satellites wouldn't detect it, and brought down the equipment and started digging this hole out of the ground. A week to maybe ten days would be more than enough time for them to dig this hole."

"Two days to dig this hole in the ground and another three to bring down their equipment. And two days to set it up," Alex said as he read the computer's answer to how long it took them to build the place.

"So where is the ship that brought these twenty-six?" Susan asked.

"In a stationary orbit on the dark side of the moon," Janis answered.

"Why didn't all those telescopes on this planet see their ship?" Alice asked. "It had to be in orbit while they brought down their equipment."

"They may have thought it was a satellite," Nancy said. "There are probably hundreds up there in all sizes."

"Or they have the ability to turn light waves away from their ship, blinding our telescopes to it," Henry said.

"And the Tabor ship captain would have been smart enough to avoid coming close to that international space station up there," Judith said.

"You think the technology of bending light and cloaking their ship would have applied to a shuttle craft?" Nancy asked.

Everyone looked at her.

"Well, they certainly didn't use a space ship to bring down all this equipment?" she said.

"Yes, to your first question, Nancy," Pedro answered.

"So whoever is on that ship is going to know within minutes we're in this control room," Nancy said.

"But if they've got cloaking devices why can we see their ships in space on this screen?" Judith asked.

"Why hide their ships from their own radar or from the rest of the world for that matter when they arrive? Can you imagine the fear that would sweep this planet if the few remaining telescopes still operating saw one hundred alien ships in orbit about Earth and told everyone?" Janis asked.

"After what's been done to Earth, a lot of people would just give up," Judith said.

"What about that ship that brought these Tabors here?" Les asked.

"So how do we stop those ships from reaching Earth?" Alice asked.

"Give us a little time," Alex said. "Janis, Pedro and me are working on the answer. And this is the only computer in this compound, but it can handle all our questions at the same time."

"I don't mean to upset anyone," Judith said. "But we've got to stop those ships from getting into orbit about Earth. Even if we manage to destroy them when they reached Earth they would fall on Earth and cause a lot more damage."

"How big are those ships?" Susan asked.

"Five miles in circumference," Janis answered.

"My God, if a hundred ships that size fell on Earth it would -," Alice began saying.

"Wipe out ninety percent of all life on Earth," Les said interrupting Alice.

"Shit we need a miracle," Henry said.

"No, just time," Alex said in a calm voice as he worked.

"What about that ship that brought these Tabors here?" Les asked again.

"Computer, where is the original Tabor ship?" Susan asked.

"Original Tabor ship does not computer," replied the computer.

"Who is on the ship that brought these Tabors here?" Nancy asked.

"The ship is on automatic pilot," replied the computer.

"Let's hope the ones in this compound can't contact it," Les said.

"No, they can't," Janis said.

"How do you know?" Susan snapped at her.

"Because they need this computer to contact it," she said.

"Where is it?" Les asked.

"On the dark side of the moon," Alex answered.

"So how much time do you three need to stop that fleet of Tabor ships?" Henry asked.

"Don't know," Pedro answered.

"What are you three doing?" Susan asked.

"Getting complete control of the floor underneath this control room, and learning about the weapon systems within this compound," Janis replied.

CHAPTER

May 10, 5: 20 a.m.

Theia's failure to answer meant there was something wrong in the control room.

Rush turned his communicator to the number of the patrols and said, "All patrols report back to the compound." Then he called Level. "Forerunner, where are you?"

"In the hallway outside the corridor," he said. "And if you are calling me, you fool, that means the Earthlings have made it into the control room."

"The officer on duty there has not responded to my order to lock all doors to the control room," he said.

"That officer is dead or rendered useless to us," Level told him. He pushed a button calling an elevator. "I am going to the floor the control room is on."

"I will meet you there with the warriors in the compound," Rush told him.

"Hurry! We are running out of time," Level said.

"We have plenty of time to break into the control room and regain control of it," Rush told him. "But not if they have control of the laser weapons in the hallways."

"By now they have complete control of the main computer and everything in this compound, including your laser weapons that cover the hallways," Level said.

"That is impossible. The main computer will not respond to their demands."

"That computer has no codes in it to prevent them from controlling it."

"What are codes?"

"Special words or numbers to stop people from gaining control of someone else's computer," Level said. "We have no such codes because as Tabor Warriors we do as we are told and have no need of codes. These Earthlings are different."

"Then we must overwhelm them with force," Rush said.

"You don't have enough warriors for that," Level said as he walked into an elevator. "Take me to the control room."

The elevator didn't move.

"They have complete control," he said in a defeated tone.

"It will do them no good," Rush said. "The fleet will arrive in a day and we will destroy the compound from the top down. We will prevail."

Level was thinking as he walked out of the elevator.

"Your silence says you agree with me, Forerunner," Rush said.

"They are learning all they can about the fleet," Level said. "If they learn how to operate the satellites they may be able to destroy the fleet."

"I have two Earthlings here we may be able to use to force them to open the doors to the control room," he said.

"Chester and Rawlings," Level said.

"Those are their names."

"Where is the nearest conference room?"

"It is two levels below the control room to the right of the elevator."

"Have them taken there and how do I get there? The elevators aren't working and the doors to the stairwells are probably locked."

Rush started pushing buttons on his communicator.

"Did you hear me?"

"I have regained control of the elevators. They will not go to the control room or the level under it, but they will go to every other level in the compound," Rush told him.

Level walked back into the elevator and pushed the down button for level three. The door closed and the elevator began to move down. Three seconds later the door opened and he walked out of the elevator and walked to his right.

Chester and Rawlings were asleep in their separate beds when the door to their room opened and two armed guards walked in and over to them.

"Wake up!" yelled the guard shaking Chester's left shoulder.

The other guard angrily hit Rawlings in the stomach with his left hand knocking him awake.

"What the fuck was that for?" Rawlings yelled at him.

"Get up and come with us," the guard told him.

"For what?" Rawlings asked. "Is that Commander of yours going to agree to our demands?"

Chester noticed their angry expressions. "Get up. Somethings happened."

Five minutes later they walked into the conference room and saw Level sitting in a chair at the round table. Rush sat across the table from him.

"What the fuck are you doing here?" Rawlings yelled at him.

Chester grinned and said, "He's one of them, and the others are inside this compound."

"It must be a great source of satisfaction to you, Rawlings, to know your friend has a brain that works," Level said.

"What the fuck does that mean?"

"You can afford the luxury of being a dump jock, because Chester does the thinking for both of you," he answered.

"Wait a minute, motherfucker, you don't talk to me like that," Rawlings growled angrily at him.

"Be quiet, Rawlings," Chester said as he walked to a chair and sat down. "They're in some room in this compound that allows them to control this compound, aren't they?"

"No," replied Rush.

"Bullshit!" Chester said.

Rawlings took the chair next to Chester with a confused look on his face.

"I have enough warriors to overcome them wherever they are and carry out my mission," Rush said.

"You may have a lot of men, but you can't over power them and time is running out for you," Chester said. "If you want our help, I want to know everything."

Level looked at Rush and said, "Tell him."

"In one of your Earth days our fleet of a hundred ships will arrive with a half million warriors on them. Taking complete control of this planet will take us less than a day."

Rawlings grinned and said, "It's the fourth down, they've got control of the ball, and they're deep in your territory."

"That is an adequate explanation of our situation," Level said. "What you must understand is if you fail us your deaths will be slow and painful."

"And yours aren't going to be all that quick and painless," Chester said.

"There is no way they can stop us from succeeding," Rush told him.

Chester looked at both men and thought *they've got a serious problem.* "So what do you want us to do?"

"Convince them they cannot win," Level said. "There is no way they can stop the fleet from arriving, and when it does if they are still in control of the room they're in they will beg for death before we grant them death."

"Their situation is hopeless," Rush said.

"Let them talk to their friends," Level told Rush.

Rush took his communicator out of his pocket and typed on it a second and placed it on the table and said, "Speak."

Level turned to one of the guards and said, "Get every laser tool the compound has, and bring them to the third floor. And get every warrior in the compound to help you including the ones returning from patrol."

The guard looked at Level and asked, "Who are you and what does floor mean?"

"Level," Rush told him. "And tell all the others the man who gave you an order is the Forerunner."

"Yes, Commander," the guard said then to Level, "Forgive me for asking who you were."

"Your mistake is understandable," Level said.

The guard left immediately.

"So they've got control of your control room," Rawlings said with a big grin on his face.

Everyone in the control room heard Rawlings.

"They're going to use Rawlings and Chester against us," Alice said.

Theia groaned and raised her head from the floor.

"She's awake," Nancy announced.

Those in the conference room heard her.

"Theia is still alive," Rush said softly to Level.

Level nodded.

"You fools can't win," Chester said. "Even if you do have control of the control room the Tabor Fleet will arrive in less than a day and blast into that room killing all of you. So why be fools? Face facts Earth has new masters and the only thing we can do to live descent lives is to work with them."

"I've never liked you, Chester, because you're such an obnoxious person," Les said. "Now you're a traitor to your world."

"And you, too, dumb jock," Nancy said.

"Who said that?" Rawlings demanded.

"The one you called girly."

"You gonna be mine, bitch, when this is all over. Do like you're told and you'll have a nice life under me."

"I'd rather be dead."

Les got up and walked over to Alex and whispered, "Can you shut down the intercom system."

"Talk to Pedro or Janis," he said. "I'm busy."

Les turned to Janis and whispered his question.

"Yes, I can," she said and typed 'shutdown intercom system' on the keyboard.

Level, Rush, Chester, and Rawlings heard a click.

"What does that sound mean?" Level asked Rush.

"They have shut down the intercom system," he answered.

"There's no way we can talk to them?" he asked.

"Only if they have a communicator."

"They have eight but only two with them," Level told him.

Rush leaned toward his communicator and said, "Establish contact with the communicators in the control room."

Henry's communicator buzzed. He took it out of his pocket and looked at the screen to see who was calling him. "It's them."

"Turned down the volume," Les told him.

Henry did so as Alex told the communicator on the desk next to him to do the same thing.

"Well," Judith asked.

"They can't hear us," Alex said.

"So what have you guys learned?" Susan asked.

"There are twelve Tabor satellites orbiting Earth, and they have a weapon that's a disintegrator," Janis said as she looked at the small screen on the desk in front of her. "Set at disintegrate they can disintegrated living objects made of flesh in the areas they swept."

"What else can they do?" Henry asked.

"They have lasers in them on the other end that can cut through a mountain of stone like it doesn't exist," she answered.

"How the hell can a satellite do such a thing?" Les asked.

"I don't understand exactly how they operate, but the source of power for them is the sun," she said. "They each take a ray of sunlight and magnify it a billion times and convert the energy into a powerful ray of light."

"A laser weapon?" Judith asked her.

"Yes."

"We can use that to destroy that fleet of ships," Susan said.

"Maybe," Pedro said.

"What do you mean maybe?" Nancy snapped at him.

"One of those satellites is incapable of harming even one of those ships, because they've all got some sort of protective electrical shield about them according to this computer. But combined they could cut through their protective electrical shield like a lawnmower through grass."

"And do what?" Henry asked him.

"Shut down their power source," he said.

"Well, get them together," Susan said.

"They're in an orbit forty thousand miles above Earth, and the Earth is a little less than twenty-five thousand miles in circumference," he said.

"So what?" she yelled at him.

Pedro turned around in his chair to face her. "It means, Susan, those satellites are over five thousand miles apart. And it'll take us a few hours to bring them together."

"Start doing it now," Les said. "Because they're planning how to get pass the blast doors and get into this control room, and if they do we don't stand a chance of survival. There are nine of us and twenty-six of them."

Pedro turned around to the computer. "Okay."

"Will they be able to detect what we're doing in here?" Henry asked them.

"Yes, using their communicators," Alex said. "Computer, shut down all transmission from the compound to the fleet in space, and to all communicators."

"Done."

"What about listening to us in here?" Henry said. "That's what I meant."

Theia was awake and listening to everything they were saying.

"Give me a few seconds," Pedro said as he worked on the computer. He stopped and leaned back in his chair.

"Well?" Henry asked him.

"Those communicators operate independently of the long range transmission system and the computer in this room, but they won't be able to warn their ships about us in here because the communicators can't transmit a message beyond a million miles. But they can still use them to talk to each other."

"Now there is just them outside this control room and us in it," Alex said.

"Can the computer detect what's going on outside this room, Alex?" Les asked him.

"Ask one of the others I'm very busy."

"Doing what?"

"Tracking that fleet of Tabor ships."

"Why?"

"Because in less than six hours it will be a million miles from Jupiter."

"Who gives a fuck about that?" Susan growled at him.

"We do, because if those satellites can be brought together and hit that fleet with a powerful laser ray it will destroy their power source and they'll be caught in Jupiter's powerful gravitational pull."

"They'll be a million miles away," Susan told him as she looked at the large screen. "They'll be able to repair whatever damage we can do to them."

Alex nodded and said, "Yes they will be able to start repairing their ships engines. But Jupiter is a thousand times larger than Earth with a gravitational pull more than twice that of Earth's. Without a power source they'll be caught in its gravitational pull and helpless."

"The momentum of the ships will carry them pass Jupiter even if their engines are shut down," Nancy said.

"No," Alex said as he typed on the keyboard. "A laser blast from those twelve combined satellites will not only shut down their engines, but bring them to a complete stop."

"And that fleet will be instantly sucked into Jupiter," Susan said in a relieved voice.

"Within an hour is my guess," he said. "But understand one thing all of you."

"What's that?" Henry asked him.

"We get only one shot."

"Well, for God's sake, Alex, don't miss," Judith told him.

Theia using her strength tore the restraints from her wrists and sat up and tore those from her ankles. She ripped the gag from her mouth and screamed, "They're going to use the satellites to destroy the fleet!"

Alice turned quickly toward her with her weapon in her hand saying, "You should have stayed down, bitch."

She shot Theia twice in the stomach.

Theia fell on the floor.

Alice took a few steps toward her and aimed at her throat and fired once.

The bullet tore through Theia's throat and into her spinal cord killing her instantly.

"Well, we don't have to worry about her anymore," Nancy said.

CHAPTER 43

Everyone in the conference room heard Theia over Henry's and Alex's communicators.

"How long will it take them to bring the satellites together?" Level calmly asked Rush.

"Two hours if they have begun now and another two hours to properly alien them on the fleet if they know where the fleet is," Rush said with a look of deep concern on his face.

"Locating the fleet will be easy since they have control of the main computer," he said.

"Yes," Rush said.

"Then we must not waste any more time."

"You need us," Chester said.

"What can you two do?" Level asked him.

"Convince them they're wasting their time that it would be better if they just gave up and accepted their fate."

"I hardly think that will work," Level told him. "Les and those others are very determined to save what is left of their world and destroy our fleet and kill us."

"Then you need us to slow them down," Rawlings said.

"How are you going to do that?" Rush asked him.

"We can distract them while your people bring up those lasers and cut through the doors and get into the control room," Chester told him.

"Then do that," Level told him.

"Hay you in the control room," Chester said. "Give it up. You can't win."

"Should we reply?" Judith asked.

Nancy picked up the communicator next to Alex and said, "We got into this control room, didn't we?"

"And you are trapped with no food or water," he said.

"What happens to you if we do win?" Susan asked him.

"I don't recognize your voice," Chester said.

"I'm one of two soldiers who survived an attack on our unit by the Tabors and escaped from this compound," she said. "And now my fellow soldier and I are back for revenge."

"A woman soldier," Rawlings snored in a disagreeable voice. "They're the worse thing to happen to the American Army."

"No that's wrong, but if you had been in the Army it would have been pretty bad for the Army," Henry said.

"Les, you're the most intelligent one among them," Chester said attempting to appeal to his intelligence. "You know your situation is hopeless. The Tabors will break into that control room hours before you can align those satellites."

Les got up and walked over to Theia's body and knelt down and went through her pockets and found her communicator. He looked at it for a few seconds then pushed the off button. "Now they can't hear us unless we talk loud. Let's get rid of this body before it begins to stink and figure out some way to stop them from getting into this room."

"Why don't we open one of the elevator doors and dump it in there, and then send the elevator to the bottom?" Henry said as he stood up and walked to Theia's body.

"Can one of you do that?" Les asked.

"Yes, we can," Janis said. "Use the second elevator on the other side of the room. I'll open the blast door."

Henry picked up Theia's feet and Les took her shoulders and carried her to the other side of the room When an elevator door opened they tossed her body inside.

"Close it," Henry said.

The door closed and the elevator started for the bottom while the blast door closed again.

"Okay, what can we do to stop them from getting into this room?" Les asked as he and Henry walked back around to the other side.

"If they've got blasters, they'll use them on us once they've cut through one of the blast doors," Henry said.

"Can we see what they are doing?" Susan asked.

"Look at the big screen," Pedro told her.

They all, except Alex, looked up at the big screen.

"What floor are we looking at?" Nancy asked.

"The third floor," he said. "The second floor, the one underneath this control room, they can't get in."

"They've got five men at each elevator door," Henry said as he looked at the screen. "If they're smart, and they are, and they can get up to this floor they'll cut through the four elevator blast doors and both stairwell doors. We'll be overpowered in ten seconds or less."

"And Earth will be theirs forever," Judith added.

Les sat down in a chair and leaned back and relaxed. *To come so far only to fail would be terrible.*

"Tell me don't important military rooms have weapons in them?" Nancy asked.

"Yes," Susan answered.

"Then why doesn't this room have weapons?"

"It probably does," Judith said. "We just haven't discovered them."

"Suppose this place had been detected before the attack?" Les said.

"Contact would have been made with it, and they would have been asked why did they come to Earth?" Susan said.

"And if it was learned their intentions were to conquer Earth?"

"America would have attacked them with everything it had."

"And the rest of the world would have joined America," Judith added. "These people would have been up to their necks in thousands of soldiers from all over the world in a few days."

"And twenty-six warriors wouldn't have been enough to stop them," Les said. "But if they have some sort of backup weapon they could stop anyone from getting into this compound they would have had a chance."

"What backup weapon? And if there is one why didn't it stop us?" Susan asked him.

"Because it hadn't been activated because they didn't expect us," he told her.

"Alright," Nancy said. "There is a backup weapon system. Where is it, and how can we use it to stop them when they cut through the blast doors?"

"Robots," Judith said.

"Are there any robots in this compound?" Les asked.

"Yes, because one brought us food when we were in that hospital room," Henry said. "And that doctor said the cooks in this compound are robots."

Les looked at Janis, Alex, and Pedro. "If one of you can spare the time find out about these robots."

Janis started working on finding out about robots. "They're cleaners and cooks," she said a minute later.

"That's all?" Judith asked.

"That's all," Janis said. "I'll keep looking for such a weapon."

Les looked at Susan then at Henry. "If you two were going to have a backup weapon in this compound, where would you put it?"

"Right where it would do a lot of good," Henry said. "On the surface where it could stop attacking forces on the ground or in the air."

"There are four cameras on the surface," Janis said. "And they can see things a hundred miles off."

"That's a hell of a range in the air," Susan said.

"That's not very far for a fighter plane," Alice said.

"No, I mean if they were weapons they could knock everything out of the sky coming for them at a hundred miles off."

"You know the nice thing about laser weapons," Les said.

"They have an unlimited supply of ammo," Susan said.

"As long as they have electrical energy," Alice said.

"And they do," Pedro said as he read what was on the screen of the computer in front of him. "Behind this round wall of glass we're facing is the main computer and a generator, or what we'd call a generator. And it is capable of producing billions of volts of electricity in a second."

"This wall of glass goes in a circle," Les said. "And that's how electricity is produced by turning wheels in opposite directions."

"Those cameras on the surface have cross hairs in a circle," Janis said.

"Lasers!" Susan, Henry, and Les exclaimed at the same time.

"And they're inside the cameras," Les said.

"How long have we been in this place?" Alice asked.

"That's not important now, Alice," Les said.

"Yes, it is because the moment we got control of this control room they called in their patrols," she told him.

"Lock the overhead doors," Susan said.

"Give me a second," Pedro said.

"Well, I've started moving those satellites together," Alex said as he leaned back in his chair. "In two hours they'll be on the opposite side of Earth facing the direction that fleets coming from."

"Overhead doors locked," Pedro said.

"Two of those armored cars are approaching the compound," Janis said.

Les and Susan and Henry moved behind her chair. Alice stood behind Les and looked over his left shoulder. They saw two armored cars approaching the compound from two different directions zigzagging to the right and left.

"See if you can target them," Susan told her.

Janis typed 'target approaching armored cars' on the keyboard.

"The main computer is verbally operated, Janis," Susan told her. "Don't waste time typing."

"Sorry, I'm not use to handling computers that respond to voice commands," she replied. "They are targeted."

The armored cars began firing at the cameras.

"They know or suspect we know about the lasers in the cameras," Alice said.

The cameras on the surface began firing. One of the armored cars was hit with the first shot and was cut in half.

"Damn those lasers are powerful," Janis exclaimed.

"The cameras are shooting at us," the second car called in.

"They know about the lasers," Rush said. He leaned forward and said to his communicator, "Abandon your vehicles."

There was no response to his order.

"Respond! Abandon your vehicles," Rush said to the communicator.

"You're wasting your breath. They've been destroyed," Rawlings said.

"Are there cameras within the compound that have lasers?" Chester asked.

"Yes, as I have said," Rush said.

"Then shut them down now."

"Impossible with those Earthlings in the control room," Rush answered.

"Have your men bring up all the electric grenades," Level told Rush. "We'll blow open the stairwell doors and attack up the stairs."

"What if there are cameras with lasers on them in the stairwell?" Rawlings asked.

"There are none. I didn't have enough cameras to cover the corridors, hallways, and stairwells, too," Rush replied. "My warriors will throw grenades into the hallway under the control room and destroy the cameras before they can use them against us."

"Have them all attack at the same time," Rawlings told him. "That way you can overpower them before they can do any more damage with the lasers."

"If they can't see what we're doing they won't be able to respond. Have the warriors shoot out the cameras in the areas where they are," Level said.

Rush issued the order.

Level reached for Rush's communicator and said, "Les, listen to me."

CHAPTER 44

Les heard Level over the communicator on the desk next to Alex. "Why does he want to talk to me?"

"Those warriors are shooting out the cameras in the hallways and corridors on the third and fourth floor and probably the fifth floor, too," Janis said.

"They're blinding us to what they are doing," Henry said.

"Les, answer me," Level said. "By now you know you can't see anything that's going on in this compound below the level under the control room. There are only nine of you and over twenty of us."

Les walked over to Alex's desk and picked up the communicator. "What's five from twenty-six?"

"So you've killed Lieutenant Theia and the patrols returning to the compound," he said. "But you are all trapped and there is nothing you can do to stop the fleet from arriving."

"We'll think of something," he said.

"As a former history teacher you should know a trapped force has two choices surrender or die fighting a battle that's already been won by the besieging force."

"The battle isn't over," he said.

"We can sit and wait until the fleet arrives then use the power of the lasers on the ships to break into that control room and kill all of you."

"We can shoot back," Les replied.

"The lasers in the cameras on the surface have limited range. The blasts will not get pass the upper atmosphere. And we can signal the fleet to change course in case you've decided to use the satellites against the fleet."

"And how are you going to do that without the ability to transmit a message?"

"Don't be foolish, Earthling," Rush said. "We've spare transmitting equipment in the storerooms of the compound. And they are being assembled as we speak."

"This control room is a hundred feet underground with a stone roof fifty above it and we control the fifty feet below it and that hallway on the second floor. How are you going to get a message through two hundred feet of dirt and rock?"

"You Earthlings have such limitations on your transmitting equipment, we Tabors don't," Rush told him.

"Stop being stupid, Les," Rawlings said. "You know you can't win."

"Tell me, Mr. Rawlings, what's going to happen to you and Chester if we do?"

"A question," Henry said.

"Who is speaking?" Rush asked.

"The soldier who got out of this compound then got back in it and stole some of your equipment," Henry said. "Why didn't you bring more warriors with you?"

"That's if of no importance," Rush told him.

"I was right when I said you Tabor Warriors got kicked off your home planet and now you've come to Earth to establish a new home," he said.

"We Tabor Warriors are planet conquerors," he said.

"Bullshit!" Susan said. "You got your asses kicked off your home planet and Earth was the only place you had left to go. And now you don't have that."

"Who are you?"

"The female soldier," she answered.

Level turned off the communicator. "We must begin the attack on that control in the next ten minutes."

"What do you think?" Alice asked Les.

"We're going to be attacked soon," he told her.

"Can lasers shoot through smoke?" Judith asked.

"I think they can," Henry said.

"I hope so because if I were them I'd blind us to what's going on outside this room and the floor beneath," she said.

"The moment we see smoke in that hallway under this room, we start the lasers on those cameras shooting," Susan said. "How many cameras are in the hallway?"

"Two at each end of that round hallway underneath us," Pedro said.

"The moment we see any movement we start shooting those lasers," she said. "If we can hold them off for two hours, Earth wins."

"Have only one laser shooting in the hallways," Henry said. "They may think we can control only one camera at a time. And that'll give us a very slight chance of winning."

"Alex, is everything ready?" Les asked him.

"In less than two hours the satellites will be assembled," he said as he looked up at the large screen.

"How do you know?" Judith asked him.

"Look at the large screen," he said. "I've programed the satellites to transmit pictures of what's happening to them and that fleet of Tabor ships."

They looked up at the screen and saw twelve big round satellites moving toward each other.

"How big are those things?" Alice asked.

"Twenty feet round and forty feet long," he said. "But we've may have a problem."

"The ships may see them and guess what's going on," Les said.

"Yes, even though I have them facing Earth," Alex said.

"To convince them they are there to protect the fleet," Janis said.

"I hope so," he said.

"So you'll have to turn them around to face the fleet when it comes time to shoot those ships," Nancy said.

"Risky, but I had to do something to convince those ships the satellites are no threat to them, because they will see them," Alex said.

"Where are the ships?" Les asked.

"Show position of the ships," Alex said.

A picture of a large bright spot appeared on the screen next to a larger duller spot millions of miles to the right of the bright spot.

"That bright spot is the ships?" Alice asked.

"Yes," he said. "The larger dull spot off to the far right is Uranus."

"How much of an area are those ships covering?" Nancy asked.

"They're in locked positions five miles apart and considering their size, I'd say their covering an area of twenty-five thousand miles," Alex said.

"It looks like they're coming straight at us," she said.

"They are," he said. "The five inner planets are almost lined up, and they are using them as a guide to Earth."

"Do they have the ability to travel faster than the speed of light?" Judith asked.

"More than ten times according to the main computer in this control room," Janis said.

"So why is it going to take them almost sixteen hours to reach Earth?" Nancy asked him.

"I figure some of those ships aren't working properly and they're being towed by those that are. Plus common sense says traveling faster than the speed of light in a solar system isn't smart. You might run into a planet or meteorites. There are always a lot of them passing through this system. And those ships have to get pass the asteroid belt which is pretty thick with billions of asteroids in it." Alex answered her.

"Maybe the asteroids will hit those ships and destroy them," Alice said.

"No chance of that," Alex said. "Contrary to public belief there are vast spaces between those asteroids. And by now the commander of that fleet knows where those spaces are. That fleet can pass right through the asteroid belt and not even scrap the sides of their ships, but that's not what's going to slow them down. It's towing the damaged ships pass Jupiter that'll slow them down. Once they get a few million miles pass Jupiter's gravitational their speed will increase and they'll be here in a few hours."

"I don't get it," Susan said. "Why would towing ships in space slow them down? There's no gravity in space."

"The towing ships are probably suppling power to the damaged ships," Alex said. "And that reduces the amount of power for speed."

"What's the total amount of time we've got before you turn those satellites around and shoot at them?" Henry asked him.

Alex looked at the clock on the small screen on the desk and said, "Maybe four hours, maybe less."

"Let's hope we can hold out that long," Alice said.

Les reached out and took her left hand with his right and said, "We have to if Earth is to be free to rebuild."

CHAPTER 45

"When will the Overlord contact you?" Level asked Rush.

"When they reach the fifth planet from this system's star," he answered.

"Come let's begin the attack on that control room," he said as he stood up.

"These two should come with us," Rush said.

"We're not soldiers," Chester said.

"You are what we tell you are," Level told him.

Chester reluctantly stood up asking, "What can we do?"

"Are the lasers in place?" Rush asked over his communicator.

"They are, Commander, on the third level and I impatiently wait revenge against those Earthlings for killing Theia," Dram said.

"Your impatience is about to be rewarded, Dram," Rush told him as he walked out the conference door behind Level.

"You two wait in the hallway," Level told Chester and Rawlings. "And don't question my orders."

Chester and Rawlings walked out into the hallway and leaned against a wall.

"Let me see a diagram of this compound," Level told Rush.

Rush brought up a diagram of the compound on his communicator and let Level look at it.

"They have something planned for us so we must do what they wouldn't expect," Level said as he pointed to the diagram. "Send two warriors to reach of those points and tell them to move up as fast as they can and be quiet. Then send two to one of the air ducts on both sides of the control room. While they are shooting at those in the hallways those at the air ducts can go up them using the ladders in them and attack them from the air ducts."

"The noise of the battle will cover any noise those in the ducts make," Rush said and issued the order.

Janis looked at the screen in front of her. "What do you think they are going to do?"

"First they'll send two men up the stairwells one behind the other in standard cover formation," Susan said. "When they reach the door at the floor below this one, they're going to cut through that door."

"And throw in smoke grenades to partially blind us then move to the doors of the stairwell that leads up here," Henry added.

"Then what?" Nancy asked in voice filled with worry.

"Use their lasers to cut through the blast doors. Then the killing starts," Susan said.

"I've never killed anyone before," Janis said.

"Let me have your seat," Susan told her.

Janis got up and Susan sat down.

"Show me how to control those lasers," she asked Janis.

"Those on the third floor don't work anymore," she said. "But the ones on the floor below this control room do. Just tell the computer to point at a target and shoot, I guess," she said.

"They're going to go through the stairwell on the other side of that floor the same way you said, Susan," Les said.

"I know," she replied.

They all, except Alex, watched patiently as they waited for the attack to begin.

A minute passed before they saw smoke drifting into the hallway from the stairwell door on the second floor. Ten seconds passed before they saw through the smoke a door on each side of the second floor open and two round objects flying into the hallway that immediately exploded and filled the hallway with a dense white smoke.

"They're probably wearing helmets with face plates that will allow them to see everything without the smoke clouding their vision," Henry said.

"I know," Susan said.

"You should start shooting the lasers on the cameras now," Judith told her.

"Not yet."

"Why not?"

"Why waste ammunition?" Les said. "She's going to wait until they're in that hallway under this room and then start shooting."

"Not exactly," Susan said with a determined look on her face.

Four Tabors, two on each side of the hallway, threw two more smoke grenades into the hallway filling the hallway with a smoke so dense it looked like a white cloud. Then the four Tabors rushed into the hallway moving very fast.

"Damn they're fast," Pedro said barely making out the Tabors.

"They've been trained to be fast and ruthless," Susan said.

"Why are they running into the hallways?" Nancy asked. "Why didn't they just continue up the stairs till they reached the blast doors?"

"They are in the hallway of the second level," Dram said. "I request permission to join them, Commander."

"Permission granted," Rush said.

Dram immediately rushed forward up the first stairwell to the door.

"Is Dram one of your best?" Level asked him.

"No, he is trained as a warrior and he is good, but he works as a computer operator," he answered.

"Who is your best warrior?"

"Zack and he is the lead on the opposite side."

"We will need Dram now that Theia is dead once we're in the control room. Have him bring up the rear as support," Level said.

"Dram, support the group you are with," Rush ordered.

"I will obey, Commander."

"What are those long metal tube like things I saw them carrying a minute ago with the bulge at the end that look like weed-whackers?" Alice asked.

"Lasers," Les said. "And they can probably cut through the steel of the blast doors of this control room in a matter of seconds."

They watched the smoke moving as the Tabor warriors moved through it to an elevator on each side of the hallway.

"What they're doing doesn't make sense," Henry said.

"They're going to attack us from the stairwells and elevators at the same time," Pedro said.

Les turned around and began to walk around the room. He didn't know what he was looking for but he knew they had to do something soon. "Sure would be nice if we could hear what they were talking about."

"Impossible if they're using the radios in their helmets to talk to each other and Level and Rush," Pedro said. "They operate independently of the main computer."

"Yes, yes, I know that," he said as he came around back to the others and looked at the screen of the computer Susan was sitting in front of.

"It looks like they're cutting through the elevator doors on the second floor," Susan said.

"Shoot them now that we know they're in that smoke," Nancy said to Susan.

"Not yet," she said.

They watched as the smoke moved around as doors were pushed open and two round objects were thrown through the doors into the elevators on both sides of the second floor. The round objects exploded with a bang and the second floor was filled with a dense smoke so thick they could barely see anything.

"They're in the stairwell, Susan, start shooting," Judith told her in a loud voice.

Susan ignored her and waited.

The four warriors ran into the hallway below them and moved toward the stairwell doors.

Thirty seconds pass before Susan said, "Fire the lasers of the cameras at the far end of the hallway, fire in a circular pattern from the ceiling to the floor for ten seconds."

The lasers began to fire and the smoky hallway was filled with the sounds of screaming warriors as the lasers hit the bodies of the four warriors that were in the hallway.

"Damn," Les exclaimed as he turned around again and looked at the ceiling of the control room and then at the floors.

"What?" Henry asked him.

"Air vents! Look at the screens covering the air vents on the floor," he said. "They're large enough for a man to get through, and there are four that lead into this room. And there may be ladders in them."

"Computer, are there ladders in the air ducts?" Alice asked.

"Yes."

Henry looked at the vents and realized what was going to happen next. "And there will be one of them at each of the air ducts leading to this room."

"That's why they were in the hallway on the second floor, to distract us from the air ducts leading up to this room. They knew we couldn't see them but we could see the smoke moving around them," Les said.

Les ran over to one removing his automatic from his pocket. "Fire two shots at each vent on the floor and pray their body armor can't stop a nine millimeter bullet."

He knelt down and poked the muzzle of his weapon through one of the holes in the screen on the floor and aimed down and fired two shots into the duct and heard a scream and the sound of a falling body.

Janis, ignoring her dislike of killing, ran to another vent and did as Les did. So did Alice and Judith.

Screams came out of one of the other three ducts with the sound of falling bodies.

A moment later silence filled the room.

Then they heard moans coming from the air ducts and after a few seconds it stopped.

"Is there any way to close these air ducts?" Alice asked.

"Exhaust air ducts have blast covers on them and can be closed," answered the computer.

"Those are on the top, aren't they?" she asked.

"Yes."

"What about those inside the compound?"

The computer didn't respond.

"Why doesn't the damn thing answer me?" she yelled.

"Computer, can the air ducts inside the compound be closed?" Nancy asked.

"No. The air ducts are for the movement of air throughout the compound. The surface air ducts may be closed to prevent harmful air from entering the compound until the cleaners under the air ducts at the top have cleaned the air."

Henry sniffed the air. "Burnt meat. Can you prevent odors from entering this room?"

"Air is now being directed away from this room and out the top through the exhaust vents."

"But we're still getting air from outside?" Janis asked.

"The intake vents are working."

"Relax everyone," Les said as he walked to a chair and sat down. "We've won the first attack."

Alex turned around in his chair and said. "In an hour and forty minutes the satellites will assembled."

"How much time before you can fire upon those space ships?" Nancy asked him as she stepped back against the wall where the air duct was she had fired into and slid to the floor in a sitting position.

"Another two hours," he answered.

Susan leaned back in her chair and said, "Right now they're working on another plan of attack."

"And we've got to work on another plan of defense," Henry said as he just sat down on the floor. He looked at Les. "Got any ideas?"

For a minute Les said nothing. Then he said, "If I were them, I'd make another move for the air ducts. They're the weakest spots in this control room."

"So we've got to figure a way to render those air ducts useless to them," Nancy said.

"Well, we can't close them up, because we need air as well as they do," Alice said.

No one said anything because she was right.

Level turned to Rush with a defeated look on his face and said, "Call your warriors back there is no sense in losing more."

Rush issued the recall. "We have lost six more. Two killed and four seriously wounded. We now have fifteen counting us." He looked at Chester and Rawlings and added, "Seventeen if we can depend upon them."

"You can," Chester quickly assured him.

"Are there exhaust vents on top of this compound?" Level asked Rush.

"And intake vents."

"Where are they?"

"There are two just above the control room and four more in a circle over five hundred feet away. And they all have blast covers on them that can be closed within a second and electric cleaners to clean the air of harmful bacteria and gas."

"Are they open?" Level asked him.

"Yes, they are kept open to bring in fresh air," Rush answered.

"They can't close them because they need air, too," Level said. "But if they can stop the fleet, they will close them and died in this compound with us rather than let us gain control of the control room."

"That would be foolish of them," Rush told him.

"Even without the fleet this compound contains technology that would enable us to control this planet if we got control of the satellites."

"I understand your reasoning," Rush said.

Level thought for a few seconds before he said to Chester and Rawlings, "Help us get into the control room and we will make you honorary Tabor Warriors and give you a million acres of land each with a hundred thousand human slaves to work the land, and to do with as you wish."

"What do you want us to do?" Chester asked.

"Get on top of the control room and prevent those vent blast covers from being closed by jamming rocks into spaces where the vent covers are. And remain up there until you are contacted."

"Is that all?" Chester asked.

"Yes."

"You got a deal, buddy," Rawlings said with a big grin on his face.

"Leave now," Level told them. "Show them how to get up there, Commander."

Rush held up his communicator. "Remember the overhead doors are locked so use the door next to the overhead door on this side of the compound."

Chester and Rawlings studied the way to the outside and left.

"Have body armor brought to me," Level said to Rush. "I will now take an active part in killing those fools in that control room.

Rush issued the order.

CHAPTER 46

"Contact the compound and inform them we are approaching the sixth planet of this system," the Overlord ordered the Captain.

"Yes, Overlord," the Captain said and used the radio on the arm of the captain's chair to call the compound. After a minute of trying he said, "Overlord, they do not answer and there is no interference of any kind to prevent them from replying."

"Commander Rush would not be so foolish as to allow his entire command to go to sleep," the Overlord said.

"The compound could be under attack," the Captain said.

"This is impossible. The last message we received indicated Rush had destroyed all resistance on Earth."

"Then the only explanation for their failure to respond, Overlord, is they have had some sort of equipment failure," replied the Captain.

"Theia and Dram are both accomplished computer operators. They would not allow the equipment to fail. Scan the planet for any indication the Earthlings are interfering with his ability to communicate."

"Roy, scan Earth for any indication of trouble with the Earthlings," the Captain ordered.

Roy began scanning and a minute later he said, "The only thing that is unusual, Captain, is our satellites are being assembled in a group pointing toward the Earth."

"Some of the Earthlings have survived and gotten control of a few of their missiles with their primitive nuclear weapons on them and are preparing to fire them at us," the Captain said.

"How can they see the fleet? They have no one operating their radar," the Overlord asked.

"They are using one of their space telescopes to target their nuclear weapons at us," Roy answered. "Command Rush is also using one to see the fleet."

"The people operating them were supposed to have been disintegrated," the Overlord said.

"Commander Rush would not put them on his priority or secondary list of targets since they have no military or political value," the Captain said.

"What damage could those weapons do to the fleet if the Earthlings managed to fire them at us?" the Overlord asked.

The Captain turned to the computer on the left arm of his command chair and asked the computer if nuclear explosions could damage the fleet.

"Depending upon the distance and number of weapons exploded they could seriously damage the life support systems of the ships in the fleet even if shields were activated."

The Captain told the computer the maximum speed of Earth missiles in space and the number of number of nuclear bombs on each missile and the destructive power of each bomb based upon information the Forerunner had sent them.

"Calculating the speed of five such missiles with five nuclear weapons on each missile they would be able to destroy the fleet at a distance of half a million miles."

"That explains why Commander Rush has assembled the satellites between us and Earth," the Overlord said. "Send a strong message to Commander Rush telling him we know about the assembled satellites."

"Do so immediately, Roy," the Captain said.

Roy did as ordered.

Rush's communicator began to buzz. He pushed the receive button on his communicator and read the message. "They are assembling the satellites between Earth and the fleet, but they are facing Earth."

"What route is the fleet following to Earth?" Level asked him.

"They are coming directly at Earth," Rush said. "The five inner planets of this system are lining up and the fleet will follow that line pass the giant gas planet to Earth."

"That is Jupiter. How close will the fleet come to Jupiter?"

"They will pass it by a million miles," Rush told him.

"We have to get into the control room," Level said. "As soon as the fleet reaches Jupiter they will turn the satellites around to face the fleet and fire the lasers upon it."

"The fleet will maneuver out of the way," Rush said. "They're efforts will be wasted."

"Jupiter's gravitational pull will slow the fleet down even if its ten million miles away, and those satellites can be turned in any direction in less than two seconds. The automatic targeting system on the satellites will target the fleet and that will take only a second, and then they will fire."

Rush's eyes grew wide at the thought of the fleet being destroyed. Only they would be left alive on Earth. "They will tell those on the planet who are still alive about us."

"And we will have no place to run and hide," Level said. "We will be the last of the Warrior Class."

"We cannot allow that to happen, Forerunner," Rush said.

"The air ducts are the only sure way into the control room, and we must do so now while there are seventeen of us left," Level said. "We must pump poison air into the vents to kill them and then enter before the fleet comes close to Jupiter."

"We have no poisons to produce poison air," Rush told him.

"Your medical lab must have chemicals that can render people unconscious. Have the medical officer take them to the ducts on the third floor and burn them. They will produce a smoke that'll knock them out or even kill them giving us time to get into the control room."

Rush called the medical office and told him what he wanted him to do.

"I have chemicals that produce an odorless invisible gas. They will be unconscious ten seconds after breathing the gas produced by the chemicals, and unconscious for five hours," the medical office told him.

"Just think, Chester, a million acres and slaves to do with as we wish," Rawlings said with a big grin on his face as he led the way up the stairs pass the east ramp.

"Yeah, we're going to be real rich," Chester said as he followed him.

Five minutes later they walked out of a door on the side of a hill.

"Sun's coming up," Rawlings said as he looked east.

"That's good, we'll be able to easily see those vents," Chester said as he looked on the ground for a stone he could use. He saw one over a foot long and half as wide two yards away and walked over to it and picked it up. "According to that diagram Rush showed us those vents should be west of here."

"They looked like large rocks," Rawlings said as he looked around. "Over there." He pointed to one and ran toward it.

Chester followed behind him holding the rock by its narrow end in his right hand.

Rawlings dropped down on his knees and began looking over the rock. "There's a little slit here with a -,"

Chester stood a foot behind Rawlings and raised the rock above his head with both hands and smashed it down on the back of Rawlings' head with as much force as he could muster.

Rawlings grunted loudly and fell forward and rolled on his back pain flowing through his brain and blood down the back of his neck. "Why?"

"Because I'm not a fool like you," he answered.

"We, we could be, be rich," Rawlings stammered.

"Don't be an ass," Chester said standing a yard from him and looking at him with contempt on his face. "Level and that Commander aren't going to give us a damn thing. Les and the others are going to win, but they'll die in that control room. And I'll be alive to tell a story that will make me into the greatest hero the world has ever known."

"We are friends," Rawlings said in a slurred voice.

"Like hell we are," Chester said, looking closely at him and seeing blood pouring from the gash in the back of Rawlings' head. "You'll be dead in less than two minutes." He tossed the rock aside and turned around and walked off. "So long, dumb jock."

"If I were them, I'd pump a gas into this room," Susan said.

The others looked at her.

"Better than risking the few warriors they've got left to get into this room. And we don't have gas masks."

"During World War I soldiers who didn't have gas masks used wet towels to stop the gas from getting to them," Les said. "It was crude but it worked for a few minutes."

"What's in those boxes you saw in that arms room, Susan?" Judith asked her.

"I don't know. I didn't check."

"Maybe there's something in there we can use to hold them off," Janis said as she stood up and headed for the store room.

Alice joined her.

The others, except Alex, followed her.

"Remember we have to hold them off for three hours and ten minutes," Alex said in a loud voice as he watched the satellites assembling on the screen.

They tore into the dozen boxes looking for anything that looked like weapons and found mostly dry food.

"Why all this food?" Janis asked.

"Since they've probably got food in the kitchens in this compound, I'd say these are emergency rations," Les said.

"I wonder what type of food HHE is," Henry said looking into a box with a wide red stripe going around the sides of it. 'Fourteen cans' was printed on the sides of the boxes.

Les looked at the other boxes and noticed another had a red stripe on it. "Some rare delicacy I would imagine."

Susan walked over to the box and looked into it. "Notice these two boxes are set aside from the others."

"That may indicate explosives," Nancy said. "Who puts red stripes on boxes of expensive foods?"

"Aliens, my dear," Alice said. "It's a shame we can't use these metal pipes."

"They're barrels for weapons," Henry told her. He opened the box in front of him and removed one of the cans from the box and read what was on top. "These cans contain some sort of explosive."

"How do you know?" Pedro asked him.

"Because cans of food don't have 'do not puncture' written on the tops of them."

"Cans of carbonated beverages do," Alice said. "And if you puncture them that can be dangerous."

"See if you can find something to tie the pipes to these cans," Les said.

"Why?" Alice asked him.

"It these cans do contain an explosive and we tie one of them to one of those barrels when it explodes the barrel will become shrapnel."

Alice walked out of the room and up to the computer and asked, "What is HHE?"

"A high heat producing explosive."

"How can it be set off?"

"By an electrical charge."

She walked back to the store room and asked, "Those cans are a high heat producing explosive, but they need an electrical charge to set them off. Are there any batteries in here?"

"No," Nancy said. "But there is an emergency medical kit."

"So these explosives are useless to us," she said.

"Looks that way," Janis said.

"Maybe not," Les said.

"How do we set off explosives that require an electrical charge without an electrical charge, Les?" Alice asked him.

"Maybe they'll burn?" he said. He turned to Pedro. "Can you control the flow of air into and out of this compound?"

"Yeah, using the main computer," he said. "Why? You think they're really going to use poison gas against us?"

"Yeah," Henry said. "Right now those Tabors are desperate. They must know, or at least, suspect that we've gotten control of those satellites and know how to use them against their fleet. And the best way to smoke us out of here is to use some sort of invisible, odorless poison gas."

"If they could somehow jam those blast covers over the external vents close they could burn something that might produce a poisonous gas to kill us," Pedro said.

"Can we stop smoke from coming into the control from other parts of the compound?" Judith asked him.

"No, the entire air venting systems is connected," he said. "These aliens didn't build this compound with the ability to isolate certain parts of it. The air we're breathing in here they're breathing in other parts of the compound. But we can reverse the blowers."

"They have blowers in this compound?" Alice asked.

"Yeah, just like you have on your furnace and air-conditioning system at home," he told her.

"So let's beat them to the punch and use smoke first," Les said. "If there are towels in the bathroom, let's use them to make crude gas masks or our own clothing if we have to."

"Damn boxes are sticky," Janis said rubbing her hands on her pants. "Now my pants are going to be sticky."

"No they're not," Susan said.

"They are if you touch the inside of these boxes along the edge."

Henry immediately touched the inside edge of the box he'd opened with his left index finger. "We've got what we need to tie the barrels to these cans of explosives."

"The writing on the cans said do not puncture," Alice said. "These cans of HHE could be like aerosol cans." She walked out of the store room and asked, "In what form is HHE in?"

"HHE is a highly volatile gas when exposed to oxygen," replied the computer.

She rushed back in the room and told the others.

"So how do we get these cans to explode without killing ourselves in the process?" Judith asked.

"Very easy," Les said. "We open those vents toss two of these cans down the vents and then drop another down the vent and fire into it."

"You better be real fast," Henry said. "The moment one can explodes the other goes with it."

Nancy picked up one of the cans and looked at it.

"Be careful," Henry warned her.

"The bottom of this can is adjustable," she said.

"What?" Henry asked her.

"The bottom can be turned," she said.

"They're grenades," Susan said.

Les picked up one of the cans and looked it over. "There's no pin to pull."

"Not all grenades have pins to pull, Les," she told him. "Some can be detonated by simply twisting a part of the grenade like these cans."

"Why would they have grenades in a room as important as this control room?" Janis asked.

"Maybe to throw out the top of it," Alice said.

They all looked at her.

"That computer said one of the doors in the control room leads to stairs that lead to an outside door," she said.

"It did, didn't it?" Susan said. "If an accident happened in this compound that made it necessary to evacuate it having a door in the control room would be an easy way for anyone in it to leave."

"That would be a good way for them to come at us," Judith said.

They looked at her with questioning expressions on their faces.

"Well, they've got those tube like laser things," she said. "They could burn their way through whatever door is outside this control and come in here shooting."

"So we ask the computer how to open that outer door. Because if any of those Tabor warriors are left alive nothing we could do will stop them from getting into this control room if they can get pass that outside door," Nancy said.

"Good idea, Nancy," Henry said. "But right now let's start taping these HHE grenades to those barrels and toss them down those air vents, and pray they work."

"We'd better work fast because right now Level and that Commander have come up with a plan to use gas against us I bet," Les said.

CHAPTER

"The chemicals are in place," the medical office said over his communicator.

"What is needed to reduce them to a gas?" Level asked.

"A blast from a blaster is all that is needed," the medical officer replied. "From the moment the Earthlings start to breathe the gas they will begin to lose consciousness. Your warriors should be able to enter the control room ten minutes later. By then the gas will have been detected by the main computer and removed."

"The computer will activate the blowers and blow what's left of the gas out the top of the control room," Rush said. "And this problem will be over."

"I can contact the Overlord and tell them the threat to the fleet has ended," Level said. "All of you who survive will be honored by the Overlord. The dead will be burned with great respect."

They had used the sticky parts of the boxes to tape eight barrels together in twos with two cans of HHE taped to the barrels.

"Now let's get these vent covers open," Les said as he walked to the vents. He looked them over. "There are no screws holding them to the walls."

"Maybe if we pull on them they'll detach from the wall," Judith said as she put her fingers through the openings in the screen covers on the vent covers and pulled back. She pulled with all her strength and stopped. "Pulling won't get them open."

"Computer, how do we remove the metal screens from the air vents," Les asked.

"No information available."

"Great, they built this place without telling the computer everything about it," Nancy said.

Alice, on the other side of the room, pushed against the metal screen. It popped open eight inches. "They're spring operated. Push against them and they pop open."

"Thanks, Alice," Les said. "We open these screens, throw one of the bombs down it, and then turn the bottom of one of these HHE grenades and toss that down."

"Then get the hell away from the vent," Susan said. "We don't know how powerful these grenades are."

"All together now," Henry said.

"Alex, get down on the floor under that desk," Nancy yelled at him.

"I just hope your improvised explosions don't damage the computer," he said as he got out of the chair and under the desk. *Or Earth is theirs.*

They opened all four vents and tossed the taped barrels and grenades down the vents at the same time then turned the bottom of the single HHE grenades they held and tossed them.

The barrels banged against the sides of the vents as they went down while they all ran as far away from the vents as fast as they could and lay on the floor.

"What is that noise?" Rush asked over his communicator.

Zack was standing next to a vent with his weapon out preparing to shoot one of the jars of chemicals the doctor had given them. He looked through the vent screen and saw the barrels and what was taped to them.

"HHE's!" he yelled and ran away from the vent as fast as he could.

The warrior with him ran, too.

The other eight warriors at the vents ran also.

Level and Rush threw themselves to the floor.

The four explosions broke the barrels into jagged pieces and ripped the vents and the ducts into flying slivers of metal. Smoke from the explosions races through the compound. The jars of chemicals next to the vents broke open and spilled out on the floor and burned up from the heat produced by the explosions.

An alarm went off and an announcement was made.

"An explosion has occurred. Harmful gas is being removed from the compound."

Air rushed up from the lowest level of the compound and out it to the outside as fresh air was being sucked in by other blowers.

"Is everyone okay?" Susan yelled as soon as the sound of the explosions died away.

Everyone yelled they were okay.

Alex crawled out from under the desk and stood up and told the main computer, "Report on your operation status."

"Operational status is one hundred percent."

"Do you still have control of the satellites?" he asked as he looked up at the large screen and saw it hadn't been damaged.

"Satellites are still operational and responding to last command."

He dropped back down in the chair and said, "Wonderful."

Les got up and walked over to Alex and said, "Let's see what damage has been done."

"Show all damage done on all levels on the screen," Alex said.

"The cameras are not working on levels three and four," replied the computer.

Pedro was at the computer he'd used checking on the cameras. "Only the cameras on the second level are working, and the explosions were below that."

"Go to the hospital level they may not have shot out the cameras down there," Les told him. "If any of those warriors were killed, they'll take them down there."

Pedro brought up the hospital level. "No wounded or dead warriors so far."

"Those barrels and grenades made noise going down those ducts," Alice said. "They probably heard them and got out of the way before the explosions."

"Maybe not all of them," Susan said. "Those explosions were powerful."

"They now know we know about those grenades," Nancy said.

"Yeah, and they won't be coming up through the ducts anymore," Henry said.

"Those two boxes contained fourteen cans of HHE each, and we've used twenty cans," Nancy said. "That leaves us only eight cans."

"So we've got to be careful with the rest," Alice said.

"They'll get on top and come down at us from the top," Les said.

"They can't do that," Janis said. "We control that outer door."

"Can they open the outer door to this room, computer?" Alice asked her.

"Yes with lasers, I think."

"So let's prepare for an attack from the top," Susan suggested. "Pedro, see if there are any of those warriors outside."

Pedro accessed the cameras outside the compound. "I don't see any of them."

"So let's get ready for an attack from the top," Les said. "Where is that door to the outside?"

Pedro brought up a diagram of the top of the compound. "The top of this compound is a flat top hill ninety-two feet high, and can be easily climbed."

"The damn thing could be Mount Everest and those warriors would still get on top to come in here and kill us," Henry said.

"Show the door to the outside," Les told him.

Pedro brought up the diagram of the doors leading to the outside.

"The inner door is on the other side of this room," Alice said.

"But that outside door is on the side of the hill facing north," Nancy said. "If we go out that door we won't be able to see what's on the other sides of the hill."

"Not true," Pedro said as he brought up shots of the edge of the hill.

"That's just the crest of the hill," she said. "That doesn't show us what's on the sides."

"This place was designed to fight off enemies coming at it from a distance," Alex said. "Not to fight off those that were just outside that control room door."

"Like it or not one of us is going to have to go outside and look around," Les said. "And we've got to do it before they get up there."

"How thick is that outer door?" Susan asked as she looked over Pedro's shoulder.

Pedro looked at the right corner of the screen where detailed information about the door was. "Two feet of steel with another foot of rock attached to the outside of it."

"And a flight of steel stairs led up to it," she said. "About forty steps I'd say."

"That's not important," Alice said.

"Like hell it isn't," Susan replied.

"What do you mean?"

"Whoever is at the bottom of those steps will have a clear shot at whoever is coming down long before they get into a position to see anyone and shoot," Henry said. "But we should get up on top before they do."

"Let's go," Les said.

"I'm coming, too," Nancy said.

"No, just Susan and Henry and me are the only ones who've had military training," he said. "Alice, Judith, and Nancy you stay at the bottom of the steps."

"We can be of use, too," Alice said.

"As our last line of defense," Susan told her as she grabbed two automatics off the desk and gave one to Henry.

"Last line of defense," Judith said.

"If they get pass us, you're on your own, because we'll be dead," Susan said.

"Let's each take one of those HHE cans we might need them," Les said as he headed for the store room.

"You're not a soldier," Alice told him.

"Three years in an armor unit over thirty years ago, and a lot of my training has already come back to me."

"Open the inner door when we tell you," Susan said to Pedro. "And the outer door when we yell back."

"Good luck for all of us," Pedro said.

"How many warriors have we lost?" Level yelled in an angry voice as he got to his feet.

"Report losses," Rush ordered over his communicator.

"Two wounded, Commander, none killed," a warrior answered. "The wounded are being taken to the medical section."

"Are the wounds disabling?" Level demanded.

"Minor wounds to the legs," Dram reported. "We moved away from the vents the moment we heard the noise of metal objects coming down the ducts."

"What the hell could they have used?" Level said.

"HHE's stuck to barrels of weapons," Dram said.

Level turned around and screamed at Rush, "You had HHE's in the control room?"

"That is the most vulnerable part of the compound," Rush yelled back. "I had them put up there for defense if the control room was attacked from the top."

"How many boxes?"

"Two," Rush said. "With fourteen HHE's to a box."

Level calmed down and said, "And now they have them, and that rules out another attack up the air ducts into the control room."

"We should attack them from the top," Rush said. "The cameras on top do not show the sides of the hill."

"How do we get into the control room from on top?"

"We can use the same door to get outside Chester and Rawlings used," Rush said. "The outer door to the control room is six feet wide eight feet high and two feet thick and made of steel with a foot of rock covering it. The one inside the control is only a foot thick and made of wood."

"Do we have anything in the compound that can be used to blow open that outer door of that control room?"

"Yes we have lasers," he said. "But I can open it using my communicator."

"Will they know?"

"No, because only I have the program in my communicator to open it," he answered.

"They will know the door is being opened," Level told him.

"The same program is in the main computer, but it will not alert them unless they ask the computer if the door is being opened," Rush said.

"Then open it and send six of your warriors to the top, and tell them to be prepared, because if we can think of an attack from the top so can they," Level warned him. "Keep the other ten down here with us."

"You speak as if these Earthlings are warriors," Rush said.

"Have they not demonstrated that?"

"It will take ten minutes because they will have to take the long way," Rush told him.

"Tell them to take armored cars with them. Les and his group will be on top and they won't have them."

"That will take time," Rush told him.

Level nodded as he thought aloud, "They've probably got control of the satellites and are preparing to use them against the fleet, but the fleet is still over twelve hours away from Earth. So time is something we still have a lot of. All we have to do is reduce our losses. Send six warriors to the top and tell them to be prepared."

Rush issued the order.

Seven minutes later Les poked his head out the opened outer door and looked around. "Beautiful day but I don't see any Tabors."

"I just thought of something," Henry said and turned around and ran back to the steps to the landing and screamed up, "See if you can stop them from getting armored cars."

Alice, standing next to the door on the inside of the control room, said, "Did you hear that?"

"Yes," Janis said as she said, "Computer, can you lock the rooms where the armored cars are and the overhead doors leading to the outside?"

"Yes."

"Then do it."

"The overhead doors are already locked. The doors to the rooms for armored cars are locked."

"The doors to the garages where the armored cars are has been locked, and the ramps, too," Alice screamed out the door.

Henry ran back up the stairs. "We don't have to worry about armored cars. Where's Les?"

"Outside looking around," Susan said.

Les came running back. "There aren't enough of us to cover the sides of the hills so we've got to think of something else."

Henry and Susan looked at each other and started thinking.

After a few seconds Henry said, "We stay on this side of the hill at the edge. We keep low behind some of those big rocks at the top. One looks forward while the other two look on the sides, and when we see a Tabor we shoot him."

"Sounds good to me," Susan said.

"And if there are a lot of them?" Les asked.

"We shoot as many as we can then run back down onto the steps and go to the bottom and wait for them to come down," Henry said. "Sound like a good plan?"

"It's a plan," Les said. "Let's get into position."

"Remember stay under cover and don't shoot until you can get a kill," Henry said as they moved up to the edge of the hill and got into position.

CHAPTER 48

"Commander, we can't get into the rooms where the armored cars are," Zack said over his communicator.

"They've locked the rooms and the overhead doors, too," Rush said.

"Go outside without them," Level said. "Tell us when you are outside."

"I will," Zack said.

Fifteen minutes later Zack said, "We are outside the compound, Commander,"

"Divide into twos and each group take a side of the hill and one group go over the top," Level told them. "And be prepared."

"Yes, Forerunner," Zack replied.

"Now while they are fighting those who will be coming into the control room from the top have climbing equipment with suction cups for the knees and hands for the remaining eight warriors brought to us in the hall," Level told Rush. "You do have such equipment?"

"Yes, and I understand your plan," Rush said as he issued the order. "While they are fighting our warriors on the surface we will assault the control room using the air ducts."

Level smiled as he said, "Les and his people only wounded two of our warriors, but they also blew large holes in the walls allowing us easy access to the ducts. We will lose a few more but we will have the control room and victory will be ours."

"I've enjoyed watching World War Two movies," Janis said in an idle manner as she relaxed in her chair.

"Why?" Nancy asked her.

"I liked watching how the Allied Forces would attack the Nazis from both sides and -, She turned around in her chair and looked at the open screen on the vent on the wall behind her. "They're going to attack us from outside and inside at the same time."

"We should call the others back," Alice said.

"No, we can't do that," Janis said. "But what we can do is each of us get a HHE and wait next to those vents, if we hear something we turn the bottoms and toss one down."

"I'll get four of those five remaining HHE's," Judith said and ran toward the store room. She came back within a minute and passed them out.

"Hay, what about Alex and me," Pedro asked.

"You and Alex stay on those computers," Janis said. "But be prepared to back us up if we need help."

Susan, Henry, and Les were separated by ten yards with Susan in the middle and each was hiding behind large rocks and desert plants growing around them with their weapons in their hands. Henry and Susan had determined looks on their faces. Les had a worried look on his face as if he was worried he wouldn't remember something from his days in the Army.

"Commander, we are approaching the top of the hill the control room is under," Zack said over his helmet radio. "Start opening the outer door."

"I am doing so now," Rush told him as he worked on his communicator.

"I just got a message to open the outer door to this room," Pedro said. "I'm going to let it go through."

The door is opened appeared on Rush's communicator screen. "The door is open," he said without realizing the response to his command had been very quick.

"Come, let's us attack and killed these inferior Earthlings," Zack said to the five other warriors.

Zack and the warrior with him ran up to the top of the hill from the east side. They ignored Rawlings' body and didn't report it. Two warriors came up to the top from the south side and two came up to the top from the west side. Neither one bothered to look for anyone else on the hill.

The three of them waited until the six warriors were moving closer to each other and were only fifty feet away, and within their sights.

"I see one," one of the warriors yelled and pointed his weapon at Susan.

She aimed at his chest and pulled the trigger on her nine millimeter twice. Les and Henry started firing a second later.

Two bullets from Susan's semiautomatic hit the warrior in the chest and knocked him down on his back. He rolled over on his side and aimed at her just as she fired one bullet into the face plate of his helmet. The bullet shattered the face plate and entered his forehead killing him. She turned her attention to the warrior next to him and fired once for his stomach. The bullet knocked the wind out of him and slowed him down, but didn't penetrate his body armor. She aimed for his face plate and fired once. The bullet passed through the face plate and into his brain and he fell back on his back dead.

"Shoot for the face plates!" Susan yelled. "Their body armor is too thick."

Les shot the one closest to him in the chest once slowing him down then fired for his face plate. The warrior took two steps forward and dropped dead. Les took a chance and aimed at the face plate of the second warrior and fired three rounds at him. The first one missed. The other two smashed through his face plate killing him instantly.

Henry, an excellent shot, shot the warrior farthest from him in the face plate dropping him. The other warrior ran toward him firing his blaster and hitting the ground two feet in front of Henry.

Henry, angry that he'd been shot at, fired two bullets from his nine millimeter directly into the face plate of the warrior's helmet. He dropped his blaster and fell forward sliding to a stop three feet from Henry.

The three of them stayed in position waiting for more, but none came over the crest of the hill.

"They're probably coming up those air ducts into the control room," Henry said. "We'd better get back."

"Guess what we forgot, Henry?" Susan asked him as they started moving back to the open door.

"The electric pistols we've got on our hips," he said.

"The climbing equipment and HHE's are here, Commander," Dram said.

"Put it on and go up those air ducts and be very quiet," he ordered.

Dram on his authority told the eight men at the air ducts to go up the ducts one at a time. "When you reach the screen, if it is not open, pulled it forward and it will open then toss in the HHE you have then drop back down to avoid the explosion."

"The explosion will damage the computer," one warrior told him.

"The computer is surrounded by an unbreakable glass shield and that by an invisible force field. It will not be harmed. Go," Dram said.

Janis, Alice, Judith, and Nancy were standing on the side of each of the four screens covering the air ducts listening for any noise. Everyone was quiet and listening for noise coming from the air ducts.

Five minutes passed before Alice asked, "What's that plop, plop sound?"

"I don't know," Judith said.

"Be quiet, both of you," Nancy said. "I can't hear what they are doing with your talking."

A minute passed before Nancy said, "I hear the same sound. What could possibly make such a sound?"

Alex thought for a few seconds before he said, "Suction cups."

"They're using suction cups on their hands and knees to come up the air ducts, because the ladders were damaged," Nancy said.

"I'm going to toss one of these HHE's down the duct," Janis said as she twisted the bottom of the HHE can and dropped it down the air duct she was next to. She dove to one side and lay flat on the floor.

"HHE!" yelled the warrior in the air duct and pushed the buttons on the suction cups in his hands and dropped back down the air duct to level four. He was too slow.

The warriors in the other three ducts did the same thing and jumped out the openings in the hallway and threw themselves on the floor far from the ducts.

The HHE exploded just as the warrior in duct three was jumping out of it. The explosion blew off both his legs killing him instantly.

"What happened?" Level yelled as the explosion echoed up and down the compound.

"They tossed an HHE down duct number three," Dram said. "We've lost another warrior."

"Zack, are you and your warriors at the door?" Rush asked over his communicator.

There was no response.

"Zack, are you -,"

"Stop asking," Level told him. "They figured out what we were going to do and opened the outer door and sent someone on top to ambush and kill them."

"These Earthlings fight like warriors," Rush complained.

"They are desperate," Level told him. "And now we know overpowering them quickly won't work. How thick are the doors to the garages where the armored cars are?"

"Garages, you mean the rooms where the armored cars are?"

"Whatever," he said. "We're down to only nine of us now. We must now use brute force to get into that room." He thought for a few seconds before he said, "Dram said the computer is protected by a glass shield and a force field, didn't he?"

"It is," Rush told him.

"Then we must have a laser cannon we can fire into the control room."

"All of you take laser cutters that are available and get into the closest room where the armored cars are," Rush said.

"We will obey, Commander," Dram said.

"Then take the laser cannons off four of the armored cars and take them to the air ducts." Rush ordered him

"How much time will that take?" Level asked him

"At least two hours," he said.

"Come let's help them," he said walking to an elevator door. "I wonder where Rawlings and Chester are."

"They have run off," Rush said following him. "You didn't think they would help us once they were out of this compound, did you?"

Level didn't answer him. "Every move we make they'll see because of the cameras in the hallways if they are still working. Have a warrior shoot them out if they haven't already done so."

Rush issued the order.

Susan ran into the control room followed by Henry and Les who was surprised he wasn't breathing hard after what he'd done.

"You alright?" Alice asked him.

"So far so good," he said as he sat down in a chair.

"What was that explosion we heard?" Henry asked as he sat down.

"They tried using suction cups to come up the ducts," Nancy said. "Janis tossed one down the dust and now they've stopped."

"Attack us from two positons at the same time and overwhelm us," Henry said. "That was a smart move on their part."

"But it didn't work," Alice said as she walked over to Les and looked him over.

"I'm fine," he said. "But not the six warriors they sent up to get through that outer door. If you have to shoot at them shoot for the face plates, their body armor can't be penetrated by our bullets."

"They're going for the garages where the armored cars are," Pedro said as he watched them on the screen of the computer in front of him.

"They can't get through them, can they?" Henry asked.

"Yes," Alex said. "Those doors may be made of steel but they can be blown off their hinges using those HHE's, or cut through using those lasers they've got."

"And we aren't going to know unless we hear the sound," Susan said as he looked over Pedro's right shoulder at the screen.

"Why not?" Les asked.

"Because they are shooting out all the cameras," Pedro said. "We can't see them and the only laser beams we've left are those in the cameras on the level below us."

"Stupid of us not to use them earlier," Les complained.

Susan walked to a chair and sat down. "They won't be coming at us for awhile."

"How do you know?" Les asked her.

"Because we've stopped them three times, and cost them maybe half their strength," she answered. "What they are planning to do now is to come at us using those armored cars and those cannon on them if they can get into the garages."

"Those damn things cut through our tanks and armored personal carriers like sharp scissors through paper," Henry said. "We won't be able to stop them a fourth time."

"Maybe not," Alex said. "But in two hours we'll be ready to fire those satellites at their ships."

"What time is it?" Nancy asked.

"Eight o'clock exactly," Pedro said.

"So at ten Alex can fire those satellites and destroy their fleet," Judith said.

"Suppose it takes them less than two hours to break in here?" Les said.

Alex didn't answer he was busy reading the information about the compound on the computer screen in front of him.

"Then they win and Earth loses," Janis said.

"So we try to figure out a way of stopping them again," Les said. He didn't believe they could. *We're out of options.*

CHAPTER 49

May 10, 9 a.m.

It had taken the warriors only a few minutes to get into the garages where the armored cars were. Level told them to place an HHE next to the hinges of the doors and detonate them, blowing the steel doors off their hinges. Four armored cars with one warrior in each were sent to the ramps to go outside. But opening the overhead doors was a problem since the main computer was under Alex's control.

"This plan of yours will not work if we can't get these cars outside," Rush said.

"Dram, is there any way to work around the main computer?" Level asked him.

"No, Forerunner, the main computer controls everything in this compound. We can go out the side doors because they can be opened from the inside, but not the overhead doors because they are electrically operated from the main computer."

Level thought for a few seconds before he asked Dram, "Have you ever heard the expression short circuited?"

"No. What does it mean?"

"It means we create electrical interference in the current that controls the chip that controls the ramps," he explained.

Dram looked at him as he thought then said, "Yes that would work. The microchip that controls the overhead door would interpret the disruption of electrical current as an order to open the doors. But each door is controlled by its own microchip. We'd have to short circuit each one individually. A shot from our blasters would be more than enough to short circuit the chip."

"Where is the microchip that controls the outer door to the control room?" he asked.

"Inside the door at the top attached to the automated door opener."

"What if a laser blast was shot at the door where the automated opener is?"

"If it was powerful enough it would interfere with the current going to the door opener and cause the door to open," Dram said. "But, sir, that outer door has a foot of stone and dirt covering it and the door is steel two feet thick. It would take numerous blasts from a laser cannon to open that door."

"Go and open the overhead doors," Level said.

"Quite intelligent of you to think of such a method for opening the doors," Rush said.

"One of the things I've learned about these Earthlings is they tend to be innovative when a crisis arises."

"What does that mean?" Rush asked him.

"You should have spent time listening to the communication systems of this planet, Commander Rush, while you were supervising the building of this compound," Level told him. "You would have learned a lot about them."

"What is there to learn from these primitive creatures?" he asked in a contemptuous voice.

"Their ability to improvise when a dangerous situation arises such as the one these Earthlings are in now. Let us work with the warriors short circuiting the door openers and think about what else they are planning to do to stop us." He walked off.

"Foolishness," Rush grumbled as he followed him. "Within less than two hours we will prevail."

"So what are they planning?" Les asked as he leaned back in the chair he was sitting in and stretched out his legs and stared at the ceiling.

"They've blinded us to what's happening in the rest of the compound below the second floor so whatever they're planning it's going to be something we don't expect and can't resist," Susan said. She was stretched out on the floor.

"Do we have coffee?" Nancy asked.

Henry, leaning against the wall facing the computer, laughed.

"What's funny about wanting a cup of coffee?"

"Oh, nothing, I just thought of the mess we're in," he said.

"We have coffee," Janis said.

"Water," Les said as he sat up. "Why haven't they cut off our source of water?"

"Because the source of water for this compound is an underground stream," Alex said. "And this computer controls the method of pumping the water throughout the compound. If they could shut that down, they also shut down their source of water."

"Strange they would build this compound without being able to control the source of water," Les said.

"No it isn't, Les," Alex said. "These Tabors didn't expect anyone to detect the presence of this compound. This compound was built to control those satellites and use them against Earth as they have done. According to this computer this compound was built to withstand numerous direct hits by atomic bombs. The top of the roof above us may be only a hundred feet below ground, but the stone ceiling above us has been sealed with a laser in such a manner that makes it impenetrable to our atomic bombs, and its fifty feet thick."

"They sealed the stone?" Alice asked. "How did they do that?"

"According to the computer they simply fused the molecules of the stone together using lasers eliminating the tiny air pockets between the molecules. Even the stone covers for the air vents on top have been fused."

"But they didn't count on us being able to detect that spike they sent out," Les said.

"That spike did what it was supposed to do," Alex said. "It prevented the remaining military installations on Earth from getting control of those satellites if they were detected, and electrically hide this compound."

"Well, it didn't hide the compound because you and Pedro detected it," Judith said.

"We were lucky," he said. "We picked it up as it was being sent out giving up its origin."

"I'm going to make some coffee," Nancy said as she got up from the chair she was sitting in. "Does anyone want a cup?"

"Make enough for all of us," Judith said. "We need something in our stomachs. We haven't eaten in over twenty hours."

"Coffee will be ready in ten minutes," Nancy said.

"So what should we expect next?" Les mumbled more to himself than to the others.

Pedro was studying the electrical diagram of the compound when a message appeared on his screen.

'Doors to the armored car rooms have been opened.'

"They've short circuited the electrical system that controls the doors to those garages," he said.

"They're going to come at us with those armored cars," Susan said.

"It won't do them any good," Alex said. "The outer door to this control room is like the stone cover over this control room. Not even blasts from their laser weapons can penetrate it."

"What if they figure out a way of short circuiting it?" Susan asked.

"Then it's all over for us and Earth," Alice said.

Alex switched the computer to the satellites and put the picture on the big screen. "Within an hour and forty-five minutes that Tabor fleet will be next to Jupiter and I can turn those satellites around and fire their lasers at it."

"When will those satellites be in position?" Judith asked him.

"In another hour and twenty-three minutes," Alex told her.

"Let's hope it takes them more time than that to do what they are planning," Les said.

9:15 a.m.

"We will be ready within less than an hour to attack, Commander," Dram told Rush as he dissembled a laser cannon.

"Very good, Dram," Rush said as he helped carry a laser cannon from one of the armored cars. "We need only one of these laser cannons to fire up one of the air ducts. The heat from it will kill them all."

"But it will not damage the main computer, will it, Dram?" Level asked.

"No it will not, sir," Dram said. "The main computer is shielded against heat and blasts."

"Then let's take this to the third floor and put it in the air duct," he said.

"Then we must reassemble it, sir," Dram said.

"How long will that take?"

"Half an hour, sir, but we must be quiet. If they hear any noise they will toss an HHE down the duct."

"Will it destroy the cannon or the mechanisms that control it?"

"No, Forerunner, it will not."

"Come let's carry this up to the third floor. We'll use the stairs," Level said as he lifted an end of the cannon.

Another warrior took the other end. "Can't we use the elevators?"

"If we do, they'll detect the movement on the computer and shut them down," Rush said. "We must carry it up the stairs. Two more of you warriors help us while one of you get the trigger mechanism that fires this."

9:30 a.m.

"I know what they're going to do," Susan said as she finished her cup of coffee.

"Well, tell us," Janis said.

"They're going to take one of those laser cannons off an armored car and bring it up to the third level and fire it up one of the air ducts," she said.

"That'll kill us," Pedro said.

"Why do you say that?" Alice asked him. "It just may punch a hole in the ceiling."

"No it won't because the ceiling can't be penetrated by a laser blast," Alex said. "But the heat from it will spread throughout this room and kill all of us within a few seconds."

"How much time have we got before you can fire those satellites?" Les asked him.

"An hour and five minutes," he answered.

"So what we do is toss an HHE down each of the four air ducts leading up here," Henry said.

"How many have we got left?" Les asked.

"Seven," Janis said.

"We should talk loud so they can hear us," Alice suggested.

"Why do that?" Judith asked her.

"To drive them away and maybe destroy the laser cannon," she said.

"I doubt if an HHE's will even damage one of those laser cannons," Susan said. She looked at Henry. "You were in the commander's seat in that armored car we had, Henry. Can one of those cannon withstand a blast from one of the HHE's?"

"Yes, I think so," he said. "But Alice is right. If they hear us they'll know what we're going to do and run away, and that will buy us more time."

Janis looked at the clock in the bottom right hand corner of her computer screen. "If we can hold them off till eleven ten we might succeed."

"Alright, one us should get next to each of those air ducts and listen," Henry said. "If we hear anything we start yelling, 'they're coming again' and toss an HHE down the duct."

Les, Henry, Susan, and Alice moved to an air duct with an HHE and waited quietly.

"We must be quiet," Dram said as he and Level and Rush carried the cannon to one of the air ducts.

They carefully sat it on the floor and listened for any sound coming from the control room. They heard nothing.

Level nodded for them to put the barrel into the air duct pointing up.

Within ten seconds they had placed the cannon on its flat base and began assembling the firing mechanism to the base.

Level was smiling because he was sure his plan would work. The Overlord would reward him for his innovation.

Alice heard a soft bumping sound and said in a loud voice, "Hay, do any of you hear anything?"

Level and the others heard what she said and immediately ran away from the opening in the air duct as fast as they could. They threw themselves on the floor a hundred feet away and covered their heads with their hands.

"Toss one down," Susan yelled.

A banging sound of metal against metal was heard and a second later a loud explosion.

Rush raised his head and looked back at the open air duct. "They threw an HHE down one of the other ducts."

Level got to his feet and said, "Send a warrior to each of the other ducts and have him bang on the side of the duct. Tell him to run away from the duct fast after he'd done that."

Dram knew what Level meant. "The sound of the explosion will cover any noise we make."

Rush issued the order over his communicator.

CHAPTER 50

Five minutes later Judith said in a loud voice, "I hear noise." She twisted the bottom of the HHE can she had and tossed it down the duct.

An explosion followed two seconds later.

Nancy at another duct yelled in a loud voice, "There's noise coming from here." She twisted the bottom of the HHE can she held and tossed it down the duct.

An explosion occurred a second later.

"Hold it," Les said. "Don't use any more HHE's. They're playing tricks on us."

"They're running around banging on the ducts to convince us where they are so we can use up the HHE's," Alice said.

He looked at the duct he was at and said, "Maybe, Alice. But what I think they're doing is using the sounds of the blasts to work on setting up one of those laser cannons in a duct. And I'm at the duct the cannon's in."

"Then toss one down the duct," Judith told him.

"It won't work, Level," Les yelled down the duct. "We know what you're doing."

"Get away now," Level said as he jumped up from his kneeling position and ran as far away from the duct as possible.

Dram and Rush jumped up and ran too. When they were a hundred feet away, they threw themselves on the floor and covered their heads with their hands.

There was no explosion.

"Why isn't there an explosion?" Rush asked.

"Because they don't know what duct we're at," Level said.

"They will toss one HHE down each duct every time they hear a sound," Dram said.

"You said there were two boxes of HHE's in the control room, didn't you?" Level asked Rush.

"Yes, twenty-eight of them and they have used up most of them," he answered.

"I think they have only two left. We must work quickly and quietly, and listen for any sound," Rush said. "They will not use any more of those HHE's unless they have to."

"We must come up with a distraction," Level said.

"What sort of distraction?" Rush demanded.

"Noise. We must create as much noise as possible to confuse them," he said. "Have your warriors who aren't working on a cannon turn their communicators to maximum volume and scream as loud as they can."

"But they will toss HHE's down the ducts," Rush said.

"And use up what they have left, no they won't," Level said. "Now do as I say."

Rush issued the order.

A moment later screams began to rise up the ducts into the control room.

"Why are they doing that?" Judith asked.

"They're creating a distraction to force us to use up the two HHE's we got left," Susan said.

"Is there any way to turn off their communicators?" Les asked.

"No, there isn't. Like I said before they're independent of this computer," Alex said. "And they can't contact their fleet because of limited the range of the communicators."

"And we've still got nearly an hour before Alex can fire those satellites at them," Alice said. "So what do we do?"

"Where did that first noise come from?" Henry asked.

"The ducts," Nancy said.

"But which ones?" he asked.

"All of them except the one I'm at," Les said thinking as fast as he could. He turned around and looked at the bathroom. "How many towels are in that bathroom?"

The others looked at him.

"We cut those towels into strips and tie them end to end and tie an HHE to the end and then lower it down the duct and tie the other end of the strips to this vent covering," he said.

"And then toss another HHE down the duct," Nancy said. "They will both explode at the same time doing a lot of damage to the duct and the wall it's in."

"And maybe force them to go to another duct using up time," Susan said.

Janis and Pedro jumped up from their seats and ran to the bathroom. They came out with four bath towels. "Pocket knife, Les."

"On the desk," he said.

Janis grabbed the knife from the desk and started cutting a towel into long strips.

"Hurry," Alice said.

Level got up off the floor and ran back to the duct the laser cannon was in. "Send three of your men to get another laser cannon and put it in one of the other ducts," he told Rush.

"We don't need another laser cannon. One shot from this one will kill all of them in a second," Rush told him as he followed Level to the cannon.

"They know what duct this cannon is in, Rush," he said. "And they are planning something to prevent us from setting this one up. Another one would give us an advantage they wouldn't expect."

"Why are they trying to slow us down?" Dram said as he ran back to the cannon. "There's nothing they can do to stop the fleet from reaching Earth, and they can't stay in the control room indefinitely."

"I don't know what they're doing up there," Level said. "But whatever they are doing its purpose is to stop the fleet from reaching Earth."

Rush ordered all communicators back to normal sound levels then issued Level's order. "We must teach our warriors this tactic of innovation," he said.

"Ready," Pedro said as he brought the strips of tied towels over to Les.

Les tied an HHE to the end of the towel strips and gently lowered it down the duct avoiding hitting the side of the duct with the HHE.

Level leaned forward and looked up the duct. His helmet's face plate provided him with enough light to see up the duct. "Whoever you are what you're doing is damn smart of you." He pulled back and said, "Get as far away from this duct as fast as possible. They're lowering an HHE tied to the end of a rope of towels."

Dram, Rush, and Level ran two hundred feet in the same direction and threw themselves to the floor and covered their heads with their hands and waited for an explosion. There was none.

"Throw the other HHE down the duct," Janis told him.

"I heard running," he said.

"One of them looked up the duct and saw what you were doing, and warned the others to run away," Judith said.

Les pulled the rope of towels back up a yard.

"Why are you doing that?" Alice asked him.

"To make sure they can't reach up the duct and grab the HHE," he said.

Susan smiled and said, "Let's do that to the other ducts. It'll buy us some more time."

Alex turned around in his chair and said, "What's to stop them from shooting an HHE up the duct?"

"I'm surprised they haven't already thought of that," Pedro said.

"Maybe this is the only place where they have HHE's," Alice said. "Why have HHE's deep in the compound if this is the closest part of the compound to the surface?"

"You're right there, Alice," Les said. "They'd want them where they could get to them quick."

"Well, let's all be quiet and listen," Alex said. "We still have over forty minutes to wait."

"We must work very quick and quietly," Rush said.

"Are you sure they can't harm the fleet using something in that control room?" Level asked Dram.

"The main computer up there will respond to their instructions, but to harm the fleet they would have to send false information to the fleet," he said.

"What sort of false information?"

"They could tell the fleet the Earthlings are preparing to fire nuclear missiles at it," he said. "A blast from four of their nuclear bombs wouldn't destroy the fleet, but it could inflict serious damage on it making it impossible for them to launch shuttle craft for two or three days with reinforcement on them after they reach Earth."

"You should have destroyed the underground missiles," Level said to Rush.

"The information you gave us said they would be no threat to us if the political and military leadership of the states on this planet with such weapons were all disintegrated. And that is exactly what I ordered done."

"Yes, I did, didn't I?"

"Yes, you did."

"It wouldn't do them any good, Commander," Dram said. "Once the repairs were made the fleet would send down reinforcements and Earth will be ours. And such repairs would take maybe a day or so."

"There are men in those silos who control those missiles and they know by now their world has been attacked," Level said. "It would be a simple matter for them to retarget those missiles to hit the fleet once it has been detected by a telescope or that International Space Station they have in orbit."

"The satellites would detect them the moment they were launched and notify us and the fleet," Dram said. "The Overlord could wait until those missiles are in space then order the laser cannons on the ships to destroy them millions of miles from the fleet with no damage to the fleet. And there is no one on that space station."

"Earthlings in those silos don't even know about the fleet or where it is. And their telescopes wouldn't allow them to target the fleet," Rush said. "They are no threat to the fleet or us. Only those in the control room are."

"Let us continue with our work," Level said.

CHAPTER 51

Silence filled the control room as they all listened for any sound that indicated the Tabors were preparing to fire a laser bolt up one of the ducts.

Alex spoke softly breaking the silence. "Thirty minutes left before I turn the satellites around and fire on that Tabor fleet."

"How far are they from Jupiter?" Les asked him.

Alex looked at the display on the large screen. "They are approaching Jupiter now. From the looks of this display I'd say they're less than twelve million miles away, and Jupiter's gravitational pull is probably causing them to move a little faster."

"Will the computer tell you when the fleet is in position to shoot at them?" Alice asked.

"I've programed it to do just that, Alice, and I've no doubt it will," he said.

"What do we do after that happens?" Nancy asked.

"Get the hell out of this damn control room," Susan answered.

"How do we do that?" Janis asked.

Henry looked up at the ceiling and said, "Maybe there's an escape hatch above us?"

"No, there isn't," Alex said. "There's nothing above us but solid fused stone. The only way out of this room is the way we came in or by the outside door."

"We came in from the second floor," Susan said. "And they're down there."

"No, they're at the third floor," Pedro said. "The cameras on the second floor are still working and there are only three dead Tabors there."

"Why not use that outer door?" Nancy asked.

"Because that's exactly what they will expect us to do," Les said.

"How are they going to know that?" she asked. "They can't see in here."

"They may have warriors watching that door, Nancy," Susan said.

"So if we save the Earth we die in this room," Alice said.

They became silent again.

"Twenty-nine minutes left," Nancy said as she looked at the clock on the large screen.

"I wonder what they're doing," Judith asked.

"Putting one of those laser cannons together to fire into this room," Janis told her.

"Let's slow them down again," Nancy suggested.

"We've still two HHE's left," Susan said. "Why not toss one of them down the ducts? That should buy us another thirty minutes."

"Throw an HHE down the duct you're next to, Les, and I'll throw one down the duct on the other side of the room," Henry said as he got up and walked toward the duct.

"Remember to jump way back," Les told him as he got ready to toss an HHE down the duct. "Tell me when you're ready."

"I'm at the duct, Les, are you ready?"

"So let's do it," Les said and turned the bottom of the HHE in his hand and tossed it into the duct hitting the side of the duct.

Henry did the same thing.

"Get back!" Rush screamed when he heard the sound of the HHE hitting the side of the duct.

The Tabors at each duct jumped up and ran away as fast as they could and threw themselves to the ground a hundred or more feet away.

The two double explosions and the sound of flying debris and thick black smoke filled the hallway on the third level.

After a minute Dram raised up and looked in the direction of the explosion. "Magnification three," he said and his face plate gave him a clear view of the laser cannon through the smoke. "No damage appears to have been done to the cannon's firing mechanism, Commander Rush."

"They know they will lose and they are becoming desperate," Level said as he stood up.

"Let us return to the cannon," Rush said.

"Let us wait a minute in case they decide to throw another HHE down the duct if we've miss counted," Level suggested. "Time is now with us and against them."

"They probably don't have any more HHE's," Rush told him.

Les sat up from the floor and leaned against the wall behind him. He looked at the clock. "Twenty-five minutes left."

"Let's hope they're waiting for another explosion," Susan said.

Alex was working on the computer. "Pedro, can you get a picture of that corridor we came through to reach the hallway on the second level?"

"A moment, please," he said as he typed on the keyboard. "Got it and it's clear."

"They wouldn't have anyone in that corridor or hallway on the second floor," Alice said. "They're all at the ducts preparing those cannon to kill us."

"And that may be to our advantage," Les said.

"Why do you say that?" Alice asked him.

"Because they wouldn't expect us to leave by the way we got in this control room," he answered.

"Their computers are far more advanced than any we have here on Earth that I know of," Alex said.

"We all know that, Alex," Nancy told him.

"But do you know we may be able to get out of this room by the way we entered if I can rig this computer to convince them we are still in it."

"How are you going to do that?" Les asked him.

"Just another ten minutes and I may have an answer for you," Alex told him. "Pedro, you keep an eye on that hallway on the second level. Janis, you watch the corridor and the ramp."

They both got busy.

"That ramp we came down is empty," Janis said.

"And so is the second floor," Pedro said.

They all sat and waited while another fifteen minutes passed.

"Ten minutes left to firing time," Susan said as she looked up at the screen.

"Toss one of those barrels down those ducts," Alex told them. "But not until I tell you."

"You think they'll assume it's an HHE?" Susan asked him.

"Let's hope they do," he said.

Judith, Henry, and Susan ran got gun barrels and ran to a vent.

"We're ready," Judith said.

"Wait a minute," Alex said as he looked up at the screen.

Les turned around and looked at the screen. "It looks like that fleet is next to Jupiter."

"Now!" Alex told them. "And make some noise."

"You guys ready?" Susan yelled.

"Ready," Judith, Henry, and Susan said at the same time as loud as they could.

"Get back!" Rush yelled to his warriors.

All nine of them ran as far as they could from the ducts and threw themselves to the floor.

Ten seconds passed and there were no explosions.

"They have no more HHE's," Rush said. "They threw down pieces of metal."

Level, lying next to Rush, raised his head and asked him, "Why would they make so much noise? They know we can hear them."

"A diversion for some reason," Rush replied as he got to his feet.

"They are falling apart," Dram said.

"I think there is another reason for that noise," Rush said. "They're trying to distract us."

"From what?" Level asked him. "They are trapped and no diversion is going to help them now, and they certainly know that."

"They're efforts are wasted," Rush said. "We are almost ready to fire one of the cannon."

"Ten minutes," Dram said as he took his communicator out of his pocket and said, "Are all of you ready to fire your cannon?"

"All we need is to start an energy build up and we will be ready," replied a Tabor on the other side of the hallway.

"How much time?" Level asked in a loud voice.

"Ten minutes," the Tabor replied.

"They must be ready to fire that cannon," Susan said.

"I am turning the satellites around to face the Tabor fleet," Alex said as he typed and watched the screen.

CHAPTER 52

"It is good that this planet is here," the Captain said as he looked at Jupiter on the screen in front of the navigational desk. "Its gravitational pull is strong enough to pull any large asteroids away from our new home."

"Captain," Roy said. "The satellites are turning around and pointing in our direction."

"Why are they doing that?" he asked him.

"I do not know, sir," Roy answered.

The Captain pushed a button on the right arm of his command chair and said, "Overlord, the satellites are turning around and pointing at the fleet."

There was no reply but twenty seconds later the Overlord walked out of the elevator onto the control room and to his chair and sat down. "Explain."

"There is no explanation, Overlord," replied Roy. "They are now pointing directly at us and they have been assembled in a circle."

Overlord Brangan looked at the large screen in front of the navigation desk for three seconds then pushed the button for long range communication. "Commander Rush, explain the position of the satellites."

Everyone in the control room was watching the large screen and they heard the Overlord's request.

"They know something is happening down here," Alex said.

"Can those in the compound hear what we've heard?" Les asked.

"No, I'm blocking all communication between them and their fleet, and the fleet is too far away for them to use their communicators."

"How much time before you can shoot?" Judith asked him.

"Another minute and the satellites will be on target," Alex said.

"I thought you said that could be done in seconds?" Susan asked him.

"It can, but the signal takes time to reach them and then they respond."

They all silently watched the large screen and waited. A minute later the words 'on target' appeared on the large screen.

"Thank God these Tabors have such excellent computers," Alex said. "Get ready I'm firing those satellites."

No one said anything.

Alex reached over and pushed the large green button at the top of the keyboard.

The words 'satellites fired' appeared on the screen.

"I didn't see anything that looked like a shot was fired," Les said.

"Because I just fired what is equivalent to sixty trillion volts of pure electrical energy at that fleet of Tabor ships," Alex told him. "And energy is invisible unless you have the right equipment to see it. Display the speed of the ships fired upon."

A still picture of a hundred ships appeared on the screen with the words 'six million miles a minute' underneath the still picture. A second later the words 'zero speed' appeared under the still picture of the fleet.

"They're not moving anymore?" Les asked.

"Yes, they are," Janis said looking at the screen. "Only now they are caught in the gravitational pull of Jupiter."

"Wait a minute," Alice said. "I've seen pictures of Earth satellites moving pass Jupiter at much slower speeds than that fleet was traveling and they weren't caught in Jupiter's gravity."

"Because, Alice, they were using Jupiter's intense gravity to sling shot around Jupiter. Those one hundred Tabor ships were simply passing Jupiter and at six million miles a minute and they could have passed by her without any trouble, but not now," Alex said.

"Without the ability to move they're caught in Jupiter's gravity, right?" Susan asked.

"Exactly," Alex answered.

"Everyone on those ships is doomed," Susan said.

"So they won't be able to attack Earth?" Les asked.

"In a little over an hour they will be a part of Jupiter," Alex said. "Now let's get the hell out of this control room before it's too late for us."

"And how do we do that?" Nancy asked.

"By the same way we came in," Judith said. "But quietly."

"We should fill our canteens with water," Janis said. "We'll have to cross a lot of the desert before we reach water."

"Let's fill them then drink as much water as we can then refill them," Les said. "That way we won't be thirty for a while."

A powerful jolt shook the ship and the lights in the control room blinked off then on again.

"What was that?" Overlord Brangan asked.

No one in the control room answered because they were all busy checking their instruments and computers.

"I have asked a question!" the Overlord announced in an angry voice.

"We were just hit by a powerful discharge of electrical energy- a laser blast, Overlord, from our own satellites," the Captain said as he looked at the computer on his command chair. "And we've lost all power."

"The lights are still on," Brangan said.

"Our speed is now zero," Roy announced.

"We are on emergency power," the Captain said.

"I want to know what is happening and I want to know it now!" Brangan yelled.

The Captain turned toward him and said, "The ship's engines are not working, Overlord."

"Start them up again," he demanded.

"Impossible," Roy said. "That blast of energy has shut down the engines and burned all the electrical components in the engines."

"Use the emergency power to restart the engines," the Overlord told him.

"We have no power capable of restarting the engines the batteries have been drained," the Captain told him.

"Contact the other ships and tell them to take us in tow," the Overlord told him in an angry voice.

"They are as helpless as we are, Overlord," Roy told him.

"What about the life support systems?" the Overlord asked. His voice was filled with fear for the first time in his life.

"They have shut down, too, Overlord," the Captain said. "Their source of power is the engines."

Brangan pushed a button on the arm of his chair and roared, "I want to speak to the senior engineer."

"I am here, Overlord," the senior engineer said a few seconds later.

"Restart the engines," he ordered him.

"I have ordered my crew to replace all the electrical power components in the ship's six engines, Overlord," he said in a voice that had the sound of failure in it. "But -."

"But what?" Brangan roared at him.

"It will take twelve hours to do that. The other ships have the same problem."

Brangan relaxed and said in a calmer voice, "So we will orbit this planet for twelve hours while repairs are made on the engines of all the ships then proceed to Earth to become its masters."

"Overlord, that will not happen," the Captain told him in a frightened voice.

Brangan looked at him with an expression of fear on his face and said nothing.

"This giant gas planet has a tremendous gravitational pull, Overlord. And within a little over an hour the fleet will be a part of it."

"There are small moons closer to this planet than we are and they are orbiting it, Captain," the Overlord told him.

"You are correct, Overlord, but those moons have fixed orbits and are moving at speeds of over forty thousand miles an hour, while we are stationary," he said.

Brangan looked around the control room at the faces of the men and women and saw blank expressions of helplessness. "Why did Commander Rush do this to us? He has always been a loyal and obedient warrior."

Roy leaned back in his chair and put his hands in his lap with an air of resignation. "Commander Rush did not do this to us. We underestimated the Earthling's ability to resist."

"Are you suggesting his command has been taken over by Earthlings?" the Overlord demanded.

"That, Overlord, is the only explanation for what has happened to the fleet," the Captain said.

"There must be something we can do," Brangan cried in a frightened voice.

"The senior engineers on all the ships are working to replace the electrical components, Overlord, but there is not enough time," the Captain said. "Nothing can save this fleet and us."

"We've all had water and our canteens are full. Let's go," Judith said.

"Susan, you and Henry lead, Pedro and I will bring up the rear," Les said. "The rest of you get in the middle of us and make as little noise as possible."

Susan moved toward the stairwell door.

Alex took the communicator off the desk, opened all the blast doors, joined the others, and put the communicator in his pants pocket.

"Why don't we take an elevator?" Nancy said. "We've only got one floor to go down to and we'll make less noise in an elevator."

They all looked at Les.

"If you all think that's the best way out of this control room, then let's go," he said.

Susan walked to the elevator and pushed the call button on the metal plate.

The elevator door opened without a sound and they all got inside. She pushed the button to the next floor and the door closed and the elevator moved down. Two seconds later it stopped at the next level and the door opened. Susan peeked out and saw an empty hallway and walked out of the elevator in the direction of the corridor. The others followed her. No one said a word as they walked as fast and as quietly as they could. They reached the door leading to the corridor and Susan opened the door and looked out. She saw an empty corridor. She walked out the door with the others following closely. As soon as they heard the corridor door close behind them they started jogging. They had gone seventy feet when Judith spoke in a soft voice.

"I just thought of something," she said.

None of them said anything.

"When they find out we're not in that control room, they're going to get two of those armored cars and come out after us as soon as we leave the compound," she said. "We'll be in the open and helpless."

No one said anything.

"Did you people hear me?" she asked.

"Not really," Alex said. "I'll explain when we're outside."

Ten minutes later they were at the southern ramp.

"Now how do we get this overhead door open?" Les asked as they all stood in front of the door.

Alex took the communicator out of his pocket and pushed three buttons.

The overhead door started to open.

"Commander, the southern ramp door is opening," a warrior on the other side of the hallway said over his communicator.

"How do you know that?" Rush asked.

"Because it registered on my communicator," he answered.

"Who opened it?" Rush asked.

There was no reply.

"Medical Officer, did you open the ramp door?" he asked.

"I am on the other side of the hallway working with the warriors here," he said. "The wounded are in the hospital."

"Then who opened that overhead door?"

"They did," Level said with a smile on his face.

"But why, they know there's no way they can escape us once they're out of the compound," Rush said.

"Don't fire the laser cannons," Level said as he turned away from where he'd been working and walked toward an elevator. "They have left the control room because they knew if we fired a laser bolt up a duct the heat would kill all of them. They left by the same way they entered."

"I will order some warriors to get one of the armored cars to run them down and kill all of them," Rush said.

"First we get in the control room and contact the Overlord and tell him what has happened," he said as he pushed a button calling an elevator. "They're on foot and can't go very far. And I know where they are going. All warriors enter the control room by the nearest elevator."

"And where are they going?" Rush asked him as he and Dram and another warrior followed him.

"To the armored car we abandoned four miles from here," he said as he walked into the open elevator. "They can't walk very fast, and we can catch them as soon as we see what damage they've done to the computer."

"The blast doors may still be closed," Dram said.

"No, they're open," Level said with the sound certainty in his voice. "They opened them to get out of the control room."

"How could you possibly know that, Forerunner?" Rush asked him.

"Because I know how Earthlings think," he said. "They opened the blast doors as a way of telling us they no longer need the control room, and that was foolish of them."

Ten seconds later the nine warriors walked out of two of the elevators and into the control room.

Dram walked up to the computer and asked, "Display everything that has occurred in the last five hours."

The computer showed what had happened on the large screen.

"They assembled the satellites and fired a powerful laser blast at the fleet," Rush said in a shocked voice as he looked at the screen.

"They have destroyed the fleet," Dram said in an equally shocked voice.

"How do you know?" Level asked him.

"The display shows the fleet's speed as zero and they are next to that fifth giant gas planet," Dram told him.

"The Overlord will order the engines of the ships started again and they will continue here to Earth," Level said.

"If they can start the engines before they are pulled into the planet," Rush said. "Contact the fleet, Dram."

"Contact the fleet," Dram told the computer.

The contact was made.

"Overlord, is everything alright with the fleet?" Level asked.

"Why have you failed me?" Brangan screamed back in a fanatical voice.

"I have not failed you, Overlord. Earthlings got in control of the control room and we have just regained control. All will be ready when you reach Earth," Level said.

"I am not going to reach Earth," Brangan replied in a calmer voice. "I am going to die in less than an hour and every warrior in this fleet will die with me."

"You can restart the ships' engines," Rush said.

"We don't have enough time to repair the damage done to them," he replied and ended the contact.

"THEY DID THIS!" Dram screamed.

Level nodded his agreement and said, "Yes, and they will pay. We have not failed. We will recreate the Warrior Class as we complete our conquest of this planet. I am now the new Overlord."

Dram, Rush, and the other Tabors turned toward him and came to attention.

"What are your orders, Overlord?" Rush asked him.

"Send two warriors to an armored car and hunt down and kill those Earthlings," he ordered.

Rush issued the order to two warriors who walked to the nearest elevator and pushed the call button. Nothing happened.

After ten seconds one of the warriors said, "The elevator is not answering the call, Overlord."

"Open the door of the elevators," Dram told the computers.

"The right instruction has not been given," replied the computer.

"What is the right instruction?" Dram demanded.

"This unit does not have that information. This unit can only respond to that information."

"They've put a code into the computer the computer can't tell us about until we enter the right code," Level said. "How long will it take you to find that code, Dram?"

"If it is hidden among the information in the computer's storage chip, two hours at the most," he said. "Then I will have complete control of the compound."

"And those fools will still be close enough to be caught and killed," Level said.

"They should die slow and painful," Rush said in a mean vicious voice.

"When you locate them, stun them and bring them back here," Level told the two warriors.

"We will obey," they both replied.

"Let me go first to see if there are any of them out there waiting for us," Susan said.

"There aren't any Tabors outside, Susan," Pedro said. "I scanned the whole area for a mile with those surface cameras before we left."

"Then let's get out of this damn place," Judith said as she walked pass Susan and out the open overhead door.

"Lovely day," Alice said as she walked outside behind Judith.

"And once they get inside that control room they'll be able to see us and what direction we're heading in," Les said as he and Pedro followed the others out.

When they were all clear of the door, Alex pushed a button on the communicator in his hand and the overhead door closed. "We're safe and so is the rest of what's left of civilization on Earth."

"You did something to that computer, didn't you?" Les asked him as he walked over to him.

"Yes, I did," he said as he put the communicator in his pants pocket and looked out in the desert. "What direction should we go to get to that armored car?"

"East," Alice said.

They started walking east. Susan, Henry, Janis, Judith, and Nancy began walking fast.

"Slow down no one's coming after us," Alex told them.

"What did you do to that computer?" Les asked as he walked beside him.

"I programmed it to close up the air intact vents on the top, and to lock all the exits from the compound. The Tabors can go anywhere they want inside that compound, but they can't get out. And the only air they've got is what's in the compound."

"Hell, Alex, they've got hours of air. They may be able to break out of the compound in a few hours, and with their technology and their control of those satellites they could become the new masters of Earth," Henry told him.

"No they will not become the new masters of Earth," Alex said. "We humans are still the superior species on Earth. All we've got to do now is to learn to live together in peace and rebuild what's left of civilization on Earth."

Les looked at him with a thoughtful expression on his face.

"After what the Tabors have done to Earth I think those who have survived have learned living in peace and working together is the only future for the human race," Alice said. "Odd isn't it."

"What's odd?" Nancy asked her.

"Billions had to die for the rest of us to learn the value of living together in peace," Alice said.

"You programmed the computer to remove as much air from that compound as possible, didn't you?" Les asked Alex.

"Right after I fired on that fleet," he said. "I also sent a message to every communication station on Earth that's still working what has happened."

They stopped walking and looked at him.

"You told the world about us?" Henry asked him.

He stopped walking and smiled at them as he said, "No, I've left that up to each of us."

"How much air have they got left?" Judith asked him.

"Considering the size of that compound, about four hours I should say," he said. "Assuming, of course, they all sit down and wait for death."

"That's a lot of air," Susan said. "Enough air for them to figure out how to find your program."

"Less than half that if they start running around trying to get out," Alex said. "And that is going to be quiet impossible for them, because the damn fools built that compound to be impregnable to outside attack."

"Making it impregnable to break out of, too," Les added.

"So we're safe," Janis said.

"That we are," Alex said with a broad smile on his face. "The conquerors have been conquered."

"So let's take our time walking back to the armored car and enjoy the beauty of the desert," Alice said. She walked back to Les and took his left hand. "What are you going to do with the rest of your life?"

"What are you going to do?" he asked as he squeezed her hand.

"Why don't we figure that out together," she suggested.

Les smiled at her and nodded his agreement.

"What should we do, Susan?" Henry asked her.

"Well, considering the condition of the Armed Forces of the country why don't we just take that armored car to the first military base that still operating and give it to them along with all those weapons we took," she told him.

"Go back to where we live," Judith said. "We're all the family any of us has left."

"Does that include Henry and me?" Susan asked.

"It certainly does," Pedro said.

CHAPTER 53

Dram had been working on the computer for over two hours while the other Tabors sat around watching him.

The medical officer raised his head and sniffed the air.

"What is wrong with you, Medical Officer?" Rush asked him.

"Have any of you noticed there is no fresh air current flowing around this room?" he asked. "The air is stuffy and smells of exhaled air."

"The explosions those Earthlings caused have disrupted the flow of air," Level told him.

"The ducts are still intact and the blowers should be working," the medical officer said.

"Computer, are the blowers still working?" Dram asked.

"The blowers have all been shut down," replied the computer.

"Why has that happened?" the medical officer asked.

"The instructions have not been issued to start the blowers."

"What instructions?" Level demanded in a frightened voice.

"This unit is incapable of answering that question."

"Are these instructions in your storage chips?" Rush asked.

"This unit is incapable of answering that question."

Dram leaned back in the chair he was sitting in saying, "Display all instructions in your storage chips."

Thousands of instructions and programs appeared on the large screen.

"Display the program that controls the blowers of the compound," Dram said with a sound of worry in his voice.

"There is no such program."

"Why isn't there a program for controlling the compound's blowers?" he asked.

"The program was deleted."

"When?" Level asked as sweat began to roll down his face.

"Two hours and fifteen minutes and thirty-two seconds ago."

Level stood up and staggered backwards till he backed into the wall and slide down to a sitting position.

Rush looked at him and asked in an angry voice, "What is wrong with you? You act like some frightened civilian."

Level ignored him and asked, "Computer, is there a way to force our way out of this compound using explosives?"

"The compound was built to be indestructible from the inside as well as the outside. Seven hundred tons of HHE explosives would be enough to open the compound to the outside."

"Is there that much HHE in the compound?" he asked.

"Total amount of explosives in the compound is five pounds."

"We can use that to blow open an outer door and escape," Level said.

"No," Dram said. "The only way to open the outer doors is to short circuit the door chips."

"Then we will do that," Rush said.

"Computer, can we short circuit the electric chips on the outer doors?" Level asked.

"Those chips have been deactivated."

"What about the chips that control all the doors?" Level asked the computer.

"All such chips have been deactivated."

"So short circuiting them will not work," Dram said.

"All of us can force the door open," Rush said as he started walking for the door to the outer door.

"That door weights over two tons," Dram said. "We would have to overcome its weight and push it back."

"Then let us do that," Rush said.

"Let's go," Level said as he got up and followed Rush.

The Medical Office shook his head.

Level saw him and asked, "Why are you shaking your head?"

"We can try, but the quality of air we're breathing will not give us enough strength to open that door or any of the other doors to the outside," he said. "And the harder we push the more air we breathe."

"So we will die of suffocation before we can open that door?" Rush asked him.

"Yes, Commander, we will drop from lack of fresh air one by one."

Level turned around and walked to an elevator.

"Where are you going?" Rush asked him.

"To find a place to be comfortable while I suffocate," he said as he pushed a button calling the elevator. When he realized the elevators weren't working, he sat down on the floor next to one of the vents.

Rush turned to Dram and said, "Find the programs that will start the blowers and open the ramps to the compound."

"There are no such programs listed, Commander," he answered as he accepted his death.

Rush took his communicator out of his pocket and said, "Earthlings we will find you and kill all of you and make ourselves masters of this planet."

Alex heard him and took the communicator out of his pocket and answered Rush. "You've got one hour and forty-seven Earth minutes left to do so."

"Medical Officer, is that how long we have before we die?" Rush asked him.

"Within an hour and forty minutes the air will become thick with our carbon dioxide, and we will be helpless to do anything within a few minutes after that," he said. "We will be dead before an hour and forty-seven minutes of Earth time passes."

Rush walked to a chair and sat down and called the Overlord. "I have failed you, Overlord. I deserve whatever punishment you decide for me."

There was no reply.

"Overlord, can you hear me?" Rush asked.

"They have been a part of that giant gas planet for over an hour, Commander," Dram told him.

Chester had made three mistakes after he'd killed Rawlings. He carried no water, he was sixty miles from the nearest source of water, and he was in the desert. Three days later as he lay dying of thirst and watching the morning sun rise in the east, he realized the mistakes he'd made.

. . .

CPSIA information can be obtained
at www.ICGtesting.com
Printed in the USA
BVHW032202120519
548100BV00001B/9/P